All That I Have

All That I Have

Laurent Joffrin

Translated by
Adriana Hunter

W F HOWES LTD

This large print edition published in 2004 by
W F Howes Ltd
Units 6/7, Victoria Mills, Fowke Street
Rothley, Leicester LE7 7PJ

1 3 5 7 9 10 8 6 4 2

First published in the United Kingdom in 2004
by William Heinemann

A CIP catalogue record for this book is available
from the British Library

ISBN 1 84505 718 X

Typeset by Palimpsest Book Production Limited,
Polmont, Stirlingshire
Printed and bound in Great Britain
by Antony Rowe Ltd, Chippenham, Wilts.

The life that I have
Is all that I have
And the life that I have
Is yours

The love that I have
Of the life that I have
Is yours and yours and yours

A sleep I shall have
A rest I shall have
Yet death will be but a pause

For the peace of my years
In the long green grass
Will be yours and yours and yours.

– Anon.

CHAPTER ONE

I first met Princess Noor in a beam of moon-light. It was not under a stone balcony to the strains of a mandolin, or in the languor of a tropical evening with a glass of gin clinking in my hand. It was on 16 June 1943, in the smelly cabin of a Lysander flying low over the sea to occupied France.

For a good hour all I could see of my companion on this mission was a profile, rather like something on a medal, a shadow delineated by the moonlight. As we climbed into the aircraft at Tangmere I had scarcely had time to shake her hand in the darkness. Then we had taken off without a word, deafened by the roar of the engine, gripping the armrests of our leather seats. As we neared the French coast the Lysander banked westwards to avoid the anti-aircraft guns at Cherbourg, and headed for the less fiercely defended coast of Brittany. The light, which had until then been projected to one side of her, suddenly lit her face up fully ... and a Middle Eastern beauty appeared before my eyes. She had smooth dark skin, a graceful mouth, black hair falling over her shoulders, and her huge dark eyes looked at me betraying her fear. A shy smile lit up her face. Her lips quivered. Noor was frightened and she was trying to hide the fact. I was so struck by so much loveliness that I returned her smile but was unable to say a word.

To give an impression of composure, we watched the silvery Brittany countryside scudding past beneath us. Then, overcoming my surprise and rapt admiration, I eventually managed to say something. Any attempt to sparkle was made impossible by my own shyness as much as the noise. A supreme effort of imagination did persuade me to bellow gruffly but politely: 'All right?' She turned to look at me again and her smile widened while her eyes searched desperately for some shred of friendship. She brought her hand out of the folds of her coat and held up her first and second fingers, Winston Churchill style, forming a V for victory. I laughed with her and pursued, still shouting: 'My name is Sutherland,' I said, 'John Sutherland. I'm going to Paris to see Prosper.'

'Nora Wilson.'

And she offered me a fine, dark-skinned hand.

Noor had been given orders never to give her Indian name, Noor Mysore Vijay Khan. Apart from the fact that this elision made things more simple, she was not to let people know her original nationality. She complied willingly: some members of her family were in France, and the Gestapo would have been only too glad to have made use of them.

The pilot had no trouble reaching the Loire, which he kept on his left to avoid the main towns. He was heading east, flying just a thousand feet above the black countryside, turning only occasionally to check that the river was still there.

'I'm going to Paris too,' she said. 'We're taking the same train at Angers. You're in first class and I'm in second. I'm a radio operator, I'm going to be working for Cinema. You must call me Aurora. I'm going to be the "Aurora transmitter".'

Cinema ran one of the networks within the vast fraternity that Prosper had set up the previous year. We were not kept in complete isolation in the SOE. We were allowed to tell each other a certain amount, so long as it would be of no use to the enemy. If we were arrested and one of us spoke, the Germans would glean that there were networks in Paris and the west, Prosper and Cinema. They actually knew this already. They would also learn that a new transmitter/receptor had started operating in Île-de-France, the Aurora transmitter. But they would not have the vital information: the names under which Noor and I were operating, the names that appeared on our identity papers and which we would not disclose to each other.

Noor suddenly looked straight at me and her voice quavered as she asked: 'Do you think we'll come back?'

I found it impossible to speak and my chest felt constricted. There had been a knot in my stomach

3

since the day war broke out. The knot would unravel only on the day the Germans capitulated. It was fear holding me in its grip. Before joining the SOE I had been second-in-command of a commando unit in the Special Boat Service. I had already fought behind enemy lines during the French campaign and in Libya. I had eventually learned to overcome the gnawing feeling which saps morale and drains the joy out of a face. But a girl like Noor . . . I hesitated. What could I say? Everyone in the SOE knew that agents sent to France had a fifty-fifty chance of dying there. In a classic infantry offensive, the attack would be called off if ten per cent of troops had been lost. We were a suicidal infantry unit. We had the worst deal in the war, with the added fear that, if we were arrested, death might come rather too slowly. At night we all dreamt about torture.

So I did the only thing I could think of, what any man would have done in that situation: I put my arm round her shoulder. She huddled against me, shivering with fear. Several minutes later, as the paroxysm passed, she sat back up, biting her lip. I could see her fingernails digging into the palm of her hand. She drew away from me and stared through the steel-rimmed windscreen at the starry sky far above us. 'I'm so sorry . . .' and it was then – romantic English cretin that I was, perfectly impassive in my guise as a secret agent and succumbing to a gush of tuppenny ha'penny sentimentality – that I knew I would love her.

The outline of the château at Angers slid under the wing and a meander in the river glinted ahead of us. The Lysander lost height until it was skimming the trees. Before the arrival of the SOE, no RAF pilot would have wanted to fight in this cumbersome plane. It was so slow that it provided an easy target for the anti-aircraft defence, but the peculiarities of war had turned this fault into a feature. The Lysander had no competition when it came to landing and taking off with all the lights extinguished in a field or on a stretch of moorland, leaving the ground barely 300 yards after it had set off. As far as the Resistance were concerned it was the friendly bird that came on the night of the full moon.

Three lights suddenly appeared on the shadowy ground between the ghostly outlines of bushes. They formed an upside-down L. The Lysander banked round, lined up along the long side and slowed. Facing into the wind, which was standard procedure, the plane landed and bounced on the sloping surface of Vieux-Briollay, one of the SOE's airfields. It carried on to the second light, turned round and taxied back, then turned once more to face into the wind again, ready for take-off. With a gun in his hand, the pilot scoured the darkness opposite the lights. He knew that the agents on the ground were supposed to wait along the right-hand side of the L. His orders were to open fire on anyone who approached from the left.

We were to be met by Henri Blainville. I had

met him in London before he had set off once more without any fuss to risk his life organising transfers for our agents in the Paris region. Blainville was a peerless pilot, enlisted in the RAF, and he carried out his every mission in the elegant and affable style he had adopted. Back in England during a training course some time in 1938 I had watched him hop out of his cockpit after some terrifying aerial acrobatics as if he were coming away from a game of bridge, all smiles and chat, with his chestnut-brown hair neatly combed and his blue eyes perfectly calm. One incident had established his reputation: on a winter's day he had been flying just above the Channel heading for the cliffs of Dover during a demonstration, and the freezing temperatures had created a build-up of ice on the steering cables. The plane was heading straight for the wall of chalk and the controls were not responding. In less than a minute he would be crushed. Instead of frantically shaking the handle, as any other pilot would have done, Blainville stood up – to the astonishment of his co-pilot – and headed for the back of the plane. He opened a hatch and hammered the cables with a spark plug swivel. Then he turned round and gave the thumbs up. The co-pilot pulled on the handle and the plane skimmed over the top of the cliff.

Since the beginning of 1942 Blainville had been acting as travel agent for secret agents. There was not one landing or parachuting within a 200 mile radius of Paris that did not bear his signature: punctual timings and a courteous reception.

Three shadows appeared on the correct side.

'Quick, quick! We need to get out!' cried the pilot.

I heaved myself through the gap, climbed down the steps built into the side of the cabin and jumped down onto the grass. As I turned and held out my hand to Noor I saw two lovely legs thrust forwards and I felt her warm hand grasp mine. Her shoulder brushed past me and for a moment I was wrapped in a cloud of her perfume, ensuring that my poor overgrown schoolboy's heart was completely enflamed.

Blainville waved towards the trees, saying: 'Quickly! Over there!' The smell of the meadows hung in the still-warm air as we ran for cover. We crossed paths with two men who climbed into the rear cockpit we had just vacated. One of them, Blainville told me after the war, would become a well-known politician in France. He would even be appointed as a minister several times. He was known as Morland in the Resistance, and in civilian life as François Mitterrand. Blainville had had cause for hesitation: just a few weeks earlier, Mitterand had still been organising transfers of prisoners on behalf of the Vichy government.

The engines of the Lysander roared and a few moments later the aircraft was just a dot in the sky, quickly swallowed up by the newly silent darkness. Accompanied by the rhythmic singing of crickets, Blainville went round the meadow picking up the three electric torches. Apart from a bit of crushed grass, there was nothing left on this Touraine meadow to show that two terrified SOE agents had just quietly thrown themselves into the lion's den.

There were three bicycles hidden in a thicket and we started pedalling along the fine sandy track which led to the main road. Our wheels kept sinking in and we made slow progress, forced to follow one of the two white furrows separated by a strip of scrubby grass along the middle of the track. Ahead of me I could see Noor standing up on her pedals, her hips swaying rhythmically, her golden calves alternately tensed with effort, her legs lengthened by the wooden-heeled sandals provided by the SOE, in keeping with the canons of fashion in 1943. On the tarmac surface of the main road the pace quickened. The damp pre-dawn air clung to our faces. We rode along the Loire, which gleamed in the moonlight like a long mirror broken up by black islands and white sand banks. It was an exquisite time to be in the silent countryside but our insides were churning with fear.

Blainville led us to the outskirts of Angers. Day was breaking and soon the curfew would be lifted. There were cocks crowing in the distance and lights appeared in the white limestone houses. Blainville forked off into a dark courtyard.

'We'll wait here till it's time for the train. I've got hot coffee in my Thermos.'

He stood next to his bike, took a white enamelled cup out of his haversack and handed it to us in turn. Noor drank hers down in one and thanked him. The coffee was too strong for me, but it was warm and comforting.

'On the journey you mustn't look at the soldiers,' said Blainville. 'The best thing to do is to look as if you're busy. People who take the train during the week need to because of their work. Don't look surprised by anything or stick your nose in the air. France has been occupied for three years. Everyone's used to it.' Then he added more curtly: 'Too used to it maybe.'

If it had not been for this last remark he would have reminded me of the SOE instructors. It was the French touch . . . He went on: 'You will stay in an apartment that Cinema's people have found,' he told Noor. 'It was a good find. No one knows the address, not even me. You can feel quite safe there. Just one thing, don't forget the password. Three weeks ago one agent forgot his and they nearly chucked him out.'

'The train from Le Mans was delayed,' Noor recited, 'they'd run out of coal —'

'You shouldn't tell me what it is,' said Blainville. 'Don't forget it, that's all.'

Noor had to leave first. She was travelling alone under the name Jeanne-Marie Firmin, a children's governess, while I headed for Paris in the first-class compartment with Blainville. I still had a slight English accent so it was safer for me to travel with someone to get through the checkpoints.

'Mademoiselle Firmin,' said Blainville with practised charm, 'it's been a pleasure meeting you, you are quite charming. The station is two hundred yards from here. When you get to the end of the road turn left and you can't miss it. Goodbye and break a leg!'

Noor thanked him, amazed by his last few words. She shook his hand in a restrained English way then she turned to me and smiled, but instead of holding out her hand she leant forward and kissed me on both cheeks. I stood rooted to the spot as her dress disappeared through the gateway to the courtyard, catching a ray of light.

Twenty minutes later Blainville and I were walking along the avenue Hoche whispering to each other while two German soldiers passed talking openly. The station was dark and a sleepy-looking clerk was on guard behind his hygiaphone window in the ticket office. There were three people sitting on a wooden bench, and a large slate board on which someone had written in chalk that the Paris train would leave at 6.53. A sullen ticket inspector punched our tickets, which had been issued in London under the auspices of Maurice Buckmaster, who was in charge of the French section of the SOE. There were several people waiting in silence on the platform in the half-light of dawn. Just thirty yards away, there was Noor turned towards us, watching us steadily and quite openly. Ten minutes later the train puffed and steamed to a halt along the platform. I followed Blainville – impassive in his grey raincoat – and stepped up into the first-class compartment. As I went in I glanced quickly over to the next carriage. Noor had stopped in the same position as me. I thought I caught her eye. She let go of the hand rail for a moment and, just before stepping into the train, I saw her hand hang in the air for a split second. Her first and second fingers were upright, pointing towards the sky. She was making a victory V.

CHAPTER TWO

Although I did not realise it, I had come across Noor before. It was beside the sea in northern Scotland in the grounds of Arisaig, the manor house where the SOE trained their agents in their underhand ways. The February sun lit the heathland that had rusted in the cold, and the sea bore down on frozen beaches and dark coves while the wind flattened the heather which covered the hillside. Along the flanks of the steep valleys there were grim castles with drawbridges. The reefs dotted about the Firth Bay looked like ghosts in the mist. We were like the knights of the Round Table, surrounded by dark forests and crenellated towers, being initiated in the art of combat against the dragon. And just a few miles away, in a granite building by the banks of the river and surrounded by peat bogs, they distilled the best whisky in the world.

I was an instructor. Noor was one of a small group of women who were being trained separately. The SOE did not balk at sending twenty-year-old girls to confront the Gestapo, but shrank at the thought of exposing them to performing gymnastic exercises alongside men! Ah, England . . .

Joan Sanderson had taken them in hand and watched them like a hawk. I am not convinced that their virtue was any the better protected for it. My colleague Joan, an intrepid officer, had very short blonde hair and affected a virile demeanour. She was so affectionate and attentive towards her students that she had been reprimanded by the directing staff. When I saw her after the war – still as blonde, beautiful and masculine – she was working in a modelling agency, doing the casting. She had very clear memories of Noor: she had liked my princess, that was for sure, even though her favourite had been Violette Laszlo, the spitting image of Greta Garbo, with high cheekbones, a regal expression and jet-black hair, the best shot in the SOE, who could put six out of ten shots into a target at 300 yards.

The presence of a little squadron of women had aroused a titillated curiosity in the stylish barrack-room enjoyed by this intake. On the first evening, before their instruction had even begun, clandestine manoeuvres were already in operation. The SOE had agreed for a bar to be opened in the great hall of the manor, which looked out over the impeccably mown cricket pitch. The commando officers like myself disapproved of this peculiar laxity. It transpired that the agents were expected to be able to keep their heads in any circumstances, even under the influence of alcohol. The creation of a pub right in the heart of their training camp was, in fact, an integral part of their military instruction. It all seemed rather strange to me.

I had gone down to have a beer at about nine o'clock and the evening was already well under way. Little groups of young men in uniform had formed round each of the seven female future spies, under Joan Sanderson's steely eye. Of course it was Violette Laszlo who first caught my eye. With a glass of Pimm's in her hand, looking resplendent in her blue RAF uniform (which somehow looked soft and clingy on her), she was holding court in front of four matinee-idol young men who laughed at her least comment and stood gazing with their mouths hanging open the rest of the time. Her long hair and tall, slender frame made her the central focus of the whole room. Pearl Witherington had sat down at the piano and was quietly playing 'As Time Goes By' from the film *Casablanca*. Noor was at the far end of the room. She was shy and self-effacing, talking to Donaldson, one of the instructors, who was leaning towards her with a melting expression. I had not noticed her through the smoke.

At about half past nine Roger de Wesselow – he of the thin moustache and the razor-sharp mind, eldest son of a family of Flemish origin, whose ancestors, brothers and cousins, had fought at Waterloo – started clearing his throat to try and impose silence. He had a white scarf round his neck, he twisted his Lucky Strikes into a cigarette holder and spent most of his time talking about hunting, all characteristics which I found ridiculous. He was the commanding officer of the camp. At the beginning of each course of instruction he would lean against the piano in this way and address the new intake. As the hubbub continued unabated, a tall, dark man with an overshot chin and a twinkle in his eye stood up. He was John Starr, a landscape artist with a modest reputation and a big mouth whom the SOE intended to turn into a virtuoso counterfeiter of identity papers and ration cards. 'Silence, good people and great lords!' he called in a voice that managed to be both solemn and mocking. 'Silence! General Wesselow has a few words to say to you.'

Wesselow shot him an angry look as the conversations died down one by one. He was not a general, but a major. As the last man of the last battalion of the 1940 British Expeditionary Force to climb aboard the last little boat which had come to pick up the defeated army at Dunkirk, in amongst the Wehrmacht's bombs, Stukas and shells, his posting to a training camp had distanced him from active combat and from rapid promotion. Starr's words were, unintentionally, more cruel than they might have appeared.

The major turned to face his audience. 'Ladies and gentlemen, I wanted to welcome you to the Arisaig holiday camp.'

This opening sally was greeted with scattered laughter.

'I am *Major* de Wesselow, and I run this course . . .' He paused for a moment. 'And I will be made a general if I manage to make good soldiers and good spies of all of you . . .' Then, staring furiously at Starr: 'Which, looking at some of your number, means my chances are pretty slim!'

A burst of alcohol-fuelled laughter filled the room right up to its emblazoned ceiling.

'The war that we are going to teach you about here,' he went on, 'is not a nice, lace-edged war, it's not a loyal war, and its rules are a very far cry from the Marquis of Queensberry's.'

In 1950 Joan Sanderson told me that at that point Noor had leant towards her and whispered: 'Who's the Marquis of Queensberry?' She had answered quietly: 'He devised the rules of boxing.' And, seeing that Noor still did not understand, she added: 'The sport of thugs played by gentlemen!' But Wesselow was already continuing.

'Our war, ladies and gentlemen, is a sport of thugs played by thugs! It turns out, in fact and most unfortunately, that our friend Adolf Hitler is not a gentleman.' He stroked his upper lip. 'For a start, his moustache is terribly common.' Laughter. 'It also turns out that our friend Hermann Goering has a bad tailor.' More laughter. 'And that this Mr Himmler looks like an accountant . . . and that during the Blitz they proved their lack of good taste by sparing Saint Paul's Cathedral!'

Slightly stifled laughter: Wren's great dome, which still stood despite the bombings, single-handedly represented London's resilience to every person in the room, however beautiful or hideous they might actually believe it to be.

'But it turns out, ladies and gentlemen, that throughout history there has never been such a concentration of torturers running a big country!'

The room had fallen silent, and an electrifying hostility bristled through the gathering. I realised that Wesselow was consummately skilled when it came to public speaking on the subject of the war. He carried on, his voice now louder: 'Ladies and gentlemen, we cannot let this filth govern Europe. We cannot let them kill everyone. We cannot let them insult us. So we are going to show them that the British Empire can also produce a gang of bastards, bastards just as efficient as theirs, who will beat them on their own territory all the way to Berlin! And that gang of bastards, ladies and gentlemen, is you!'

The major's spirited words were greeted with thunderous applause. Wesselow waited for the clapping to stop, then he added: 'Except for John Starr, who's a bloody coward!'

Amidst the laughter, Starr cried to the company at large: 'Don't shoot, I give up!'

The speech was not over though, and Wesselow continued on a more serious note: 'Some day soon, perhaps sooner than we think, the Allied armies will set foot on the continent. It will be no mean feat. The Canadians –'

Somewhere at the back of the room one of the

rowdier members of the intake pretended to break wind noisily. Wesselow's face changed colour and he raised his voice. 'The Canadians, who are braver than you will ever be, proved that the landing will be no pleasure trip when they got themselves killed at Dieppe.'

No one was thinking about interrupting any longer.

'The whole war will be played out in the space of a day. If the Germans are rested and well trained, in other words if we leave them in peace at all, they'll cut our boys to pieces. Our role, your role, is to make sure they're never left in peace. And to achieve that . . . everything is fair game. You have twelve weeks in which to learn some of the more recognised methods. You will be the first bridgehead of the Allied army in Europe. And never forget it. You won't gain anything from it. Regular soldiers fall in full daylight under their own officers' eyes. You will fall at night, under nobody's eyes. You will be forgotten. You might just get a medal. But it would be awarded post-humously, and your descendants will put it away in a drawer somewhere. But if you survive, when you grow old you will be able to say to yourselves: "I never left those bastards in peace. And for an idiot like me, that's not bad at all."'

A heavy silence weighed on the room. Wesselow took his conclusion from a more famous officer than himself: 'Now, ladies and gentlemen, England is waiting for each of us to do his or her duty!'

He seemed to hesitate for a moment. 'And my particular duty is to get drunk with John Starr.'

Amid the hurrays, he took the young painter by the shoulder and headed for the bar.

It struck me as a good speech but the evening itself seemed ill-fated. How could we turn these whisky-drinkers into élite soldiers in the space of twelve weeks? A normal military training took six months. These reckless civilians had to have all the wile of a commando instilled into them in less than half the time. The SOE was snubbed by the traditional secret service, had been set up by Churchill in a rush of blood to the head, and had an autonomous chain of command (because the Labour party, which had just joined the coalition government, had to be given the reins of one of these offices of information which it so mistrusted, perhaps with good reason). As a result the SOE trailed behind it a reputation of amateurishness. The sight of these Scottish banquets made me fear the worst. I announced to everyone that reveille would be sounded at five o'clock, and I went up to bed.

The following day I did my best to dissuade anyone from holding a repeat of the previous evening. After a gruelling two-hour run across the moors, which left the young recruits on the brink of asphyxia, and an hour of gymnastics amid groans and guttural orders, I gathered the entire troop in a barn which had had a square opening cut out of its very high ceiling. Each recruit was told to climb up the ladder into the roof space and to sit round the opening with their legs dangling down. On my command they were to throw themselves into space and land as best they could twelve feet below. This was the height limit above which fractures were almost inevitable. There were just a couple of minor sprains, which recovered quickly. In the afternoon they started to learn about hand-to-hand combat. I dispatched each recruit to the ground, twisted his arm and laid into his abdomen. At about six o'clock I took them all off for another hour's running with fifty-pound packs on their backs. 'In this sort of work your safety lies in your mobility,' I explained. That evening John Starr was the only one to turn up at the bar, and he was in bed by half past eight.

In an annexe in another corner of the estate Noor was being given not quite such a harsh training. The run was kept down to fifteen minutes, and the gymnastics to half an hour. She had had an opportunity to start some theory classes. Since signing up for the RAF she had learned wireless telegraphy, and she could already transmit Morse at a rate of twenty words a minute, with each letter replaced by the famous collection of dots and dashes. In civilian life operators scarcely managed more than twelve words a minute, but she would have to get up to twenty-four.

The speed of transmission was crucial: in occupied territory both the army's and the Gestapo's permanent bases continuously swept all frequencies. When a new transmitter was detected, the listening-out post would inform the three detection units positioned in a triangle – at Brest, Augsburg and Nuremberg – which covered the whole of France. Once the zone from which the transmission was taking place had been established to within a ten-mile radius, three lorries equipped with goniometers would set off straight away, each travelling slowly as its antenna topped with a spinning steel ring took a bearing for the clandestine radio. With three bearings the Germans could pinpoint the transmitter to within 200 yards. Technicians on foot equipped with hand-held detectors were confident they could find where the transmission was being made. A platoon of soldiers, often from the SS, would follow the lorries. It was an average of thirty minutes before the detection teams burst into the house where the operator was hiding. After the war the SOE confirmed that one in two radio operators had been arrested. Most of them were tortured, deported and executed at Dachau or Buchenwald.

After transmitting for twenty-five minutes an operator would be heading into the danger zone – put another way, after about 500 words, or a text about fifty lines long. With normal operators, the quantity of information transmitted by the Resistance in Europe would have been halved, or the risk doubled for the same number and length of messages. After one week on the course Noor and her fellow recruits had started dreaming in Morse code.

My best trainee was called Derek Darbois. He was a homosexual who had such a precious voice and such an effeminate manner that he could not hope to hide his preferences. He was disarmingly kind and never stinted in his thoughtfulness for the others. On the first day Starr had made a few barbed comments in his direction, and the others had laughed loudly at his clever words. Darbois had gritted his teeth and kept himself to himself. That evening, as the last run came to an end, Darbois, with his pack filled with stones on his back, arrived back a full minute before all the others.

After the initiation in the barn, the apprentice saboteurs had moved on to the winch: I held them up in the air on the end of a rope, a pendulum mechanism would then be set in motion and they would start to swing. Once they reached the horizontal at the end of each oscillation, I let go of the rope: they had to twist in mid-air so that they landed feet first, and then they rolled on the hard, frosty ground. Then I made them climb up into the trees and jump down from ever-higher branches. The civilians who lived around Arisaig called the manor 'Monkey Castle'. A couple of days later I noticed that Darbois had sprained an ankle. He had said nothing, had asked the nurse to bind the joint very tightly and had carried on with his training.

A week later they were climbing three at a time into the willow basket under a great oblong-shaped balloon that the army had let us have. These huge rubber sausages filled with helium were usually used as anti-aircraft defences, positioned above towns and railway junctions, and anchored to the ground with cables. To save on aviation fuel our recruits had to undergo their initiation by throwing themselves out of this flimsy basket instead of an aeroplane. As it gained altitude the basket shuddered and swung in the wind, apparently threatening to come away at any moment. Not one of them climbed into it without the colour draining from his face.

The third group was made up of John Starr, Derek Darbois and Peter Greenwood, a stylish young banker who had spent several years working in Paris before the war. As the swinging basket rose up off the ground I saw the three of them, like the others before them, gripping on to the safety handles. The parkland grew rapidly smaller beneath them and the buildings looked like models dotted about the moor; on the right was the grey water in the bay dotted with great black rocks. Even Starr had stopped making jokes and was staring in silent amazement at the ground. Darbois was ashen.

If they were dropped over France on an operation, the plane would be flying 300 feet up at full speed, so that no change of pattern could catch the eye of a potential witness. It was a dangerous

23

manoeuvre: if the pilot ever made a mistake and dropped his passengers over a hill, the parachutes would not have time to open and they would crash to the ground. But there was no other way to do it. Even at night a parachute could be seen from a long way off. The dropping time had to be kept down to a minimum, and so they jumped at the extreme limit of what would normally be considered safe. After one second of free-fall the parachute opened automatically, then they dropped their packs down on a twelve-foot length of rope. The pack hit the ground first, the drop in gravitational pull on the parachute slowed it down, and the agents rolled onto the grass hoping that no Germans happened to be looking up into the sky at that precise moment.

They did their first jumps from the basket at 360 feet. Just a sixty-foot margin . . . That is the parachutist's fate: the more he trains, the more risks he takes. When the balloon came to a halt at the end of the cable, I checked all the parachutes and I opened the trap door through which we could watch the countryside coming and going as we drifted in the wind. Greenwood was about ready to pass out when I tapped him on the shoulder. 'Go!' The banker bravely threw himself into the void, unable to stop himself crying out in terror. The parachute opened immediately and Greenwood reached the ground a few seconds later laughing very loudly. I tapped on Darbois's shoulder. 'Go!' Nothing happened. Darbois was completely paralysed as he gripped the edges of the opening, his knuckles white and his eyes wide with fear. 'Go!' I said again. Darbois did not move. I was preparing to get hold of his arm and throw him out when Starr came over to him, put his arm round his back and hurled him into the void with a 'Go on, you old poofter, they're waiting for you below!' Once Darbois had landed Starr jumped down before I even had time to shout: 'Go!'

The basket dropped back down as the three novices picked up their parachutes. As we headed for the briefings huts Greenwood strode out jubilantly in the lead, I followed him smiling, and the other two walked behind. 'Thank you for your help,' Darbois was saying to Starr, 'I would never have been able to jump on my own!' I heard a stifled sound and turned round. Starr had fallen over: the right hook Darbois had sent him had knocked him to the ground. Darbois leant forward with his fists still clenched, his elbows pinned to his side and his eyes gleaming; and he rocked from one foot to the other as he added: 'And you probably know that poofters are better at boxing than parachuting.' Starr was back on his feet, rubbing his jaw. I was about to intervene when he said: 'I'm sorry, Derek, I'm a stupid sod.' He held out his hand and Darbois took it. He had tears in his eyes. Starr put his arm round him and said with a twinkle: 'I really am sorry. You're right to stand up for yourself. And, actually, I think you should be entitled to a pink parachute!' Darbois burst out laughing, and I carried on happily towards the huts with Greenwood.

I heard Noor mentioned the following week when an incident brought her into conflict with Timothy Keegan, the sergeant with the permanently furrowed brow and the wild red moustache who taught the recruits to shoot. Keegan (who felt not a little humiliated – after all he had fought with the Indian army and here he was having to teach this odd battalion of women) stood in one of the courtyards by the light of the late winter sun. In front of him was a carved wooden table seconded from the dining room. On it he had laid out the various arms with which the SOE equipped their agents, and he asked the young women to form a circle around him. There were Bulldog and Colt revolvers, like those used in westerns, with their rotating cylinders. There were Ruby, Colt and 'Frenchman' pistols, with the magazine in the butt, rather like the black Brownings that appeared in the hands of gangsters in post-war detective films. Most importantly there was the Sten submachine gun, which had already become the legendary weapon associated with resistance to Nazism.

'Sten,' Keegan explained, 'is an acronym, a set of initials. It's taken from the names of the two engineers who invented it, Shepherd and Turpin, and the name of the town where they're made, Enfield: S-T-E-N.'

Some two million of them were to be made in British factories.

'It tends to go off all on its own,' Keegan added, 'but it will put up with the cold and the wet. And it's the most lightweight of all the killers!'

In a few seconds he dismantled the device, which came apart in four pieces: the short barrel, the firing mechanism, the light metal butt and the rectangular magazine.

'You can carry it in a briefcase or even on you, in your coat,' said Keegan, putting the submachine gun together again. He ran them through the drill empty and then engaged the magazine and let off a few bursts of fire into the grass.

'Fire in short bursts, or you'll empty the magazine too quickly. So long as you hold it firmly, all you have to do is point it from the hip, like this, blind. If the enemy isn't under cover, you'll get them, you can't fail.'

Then he handed the Sten to the first recruit on his right, told her to dismantle it, put it together again and then fire at a wooden mannequin in the middle of the courtyard.

The young women underwent their initiation with all the grace of debutantes. Pearl Witherington asked whether the powder would blacken her hands, then she trembled as she aimed the barrel, but a savage smile spread over her face as she fired. Yvonne Beekman closed her eyes as she pulled the trigger and the bullets disappeared. Cecily Lefort gave a sensuous little cry as she let off her first burst of fire. Violette Laszlo picked up the Sten like an old professional and, without aiming, sent a brief burst of bullets straight into the wooden mannequin's chest.

'My word, miss, that's excellent!' said Keegan.

'I learned to shoot with my husband,' Violette replied.

Mathias Laszlo was a Hungarian industrialist who had taken his wife all over the world big-game hunting, and Violette had taken the sport to heart. With the sheer weight of experience she had become a crack shot. Her husband had joined the Resistance in 1941, but he had been caught and the Germans had shot him. Since then Violette had been preparing herself for the day when she had one of those grey-green uniforms in her sights.

It was Noor's turn. The princess gently raised her hand, palm first, and said very quietly: 'No, not for me. I shan't use it.'

Keegan looked at her and smiled. 'Yes you will, you'll see, it's very easy.'

Noor smiled back and replied: 'I don't want to use it.'

Keegan stared at her, surprised. 'What do mean, you don't want to use it? It's compulsory, it's part of the training.'

'I know, but I can't do it.'

'Everyone can do it! Everyone has to do it! If someone shoots at you, or tracks you down, you must be able to defend yourself.'

'No, I won't shoot anyone. I don't want to kill anyone.'

'In war, miss, you kill your enemies. Otherwise they kill you.'

'I'm sorry, Sergeant, I understand what you're saying, I have the greatest respect for you and for everything that we're doing here, but I couldn't shoot.'

Keegan was speechless, the colour was rising in his cheeks and his moustache had started to quiver. He was about to explode when Violette Laszlo took his arm. 'Sergeant Keegan, she has said she won't do it. I don't think you should insist. She's a radio operator, after all. She doesn't need to shoot everybody.'

'Not everybody, miss. The krauts.'

'Of course, but she can't do it. It's a question of religious conviction.'

Astonished, Keegan turned to Noor. 'Religious conviction?'

Noor nodded, and Violette Laszlo explained that Nora Wilson was of Indian origin. Keegan exploded: 'For heaven's sake, we haven't recruited fakirs into this army, have we? Or a bunch of women in saris? This is war! We can't waste time like this. It's that Gandhi, isn't it, he's put all these ideas in your head. We're not in India now, and you're not fighting His Majesty's nice polite army. You're fighting Adolf Hitler! Do you know who I mean? D'you think he gives presents to anyone who doesn't shoot? You, miss, are going to do me the honour of shooting at this bloody mannequin.'

There were tears rolling down Noor's cheeks. 'I told Mr Jepson,' she whispered, 'he said it was all right –'

'Jepson? Not in this battalion, Jepson! Who is this Jepson? Some big Mogul? A snake charmer? A communist?'

It was Violette who came to Noor's rescue once again. 'Sergeant Keegan, with all due respect, I think you should talk to Major de Wesselow. He will explain –'

'Does Wesselow know about this? I most certainly will talk to him! I'll explain to him that these good ladies have decided to fight the Third Reich with fans and powder puffs!'

He gradually calmed down, grabbed the Sten and thrust it at Diana Rowden. She clamped her thin lips together and, her little chignon jigging with the kick of the weapon, decapitated the mannequin in one burst of fire, which seemed to appease the sergeant.

Selwyn Jepson was the SOE recruiting officer. He was a playwright and the directors of the SOE had chosen him because they felt sure he would have the psychological insight necessary for the job. They had not been wrong: Jepson served them extremely well before returning, with considerable success, to his career as a dramatist. In response to Keegan's complaint, Wesselow immersed himself in Jepson's report on Noor, and he found that her religious convictions were mentioned, but that Jepson felt they were to her credit. As far as he was concerned, the young woman had 'the highest motives imaginable', and his conclusion was peremptory: Noor would make an excellent SOE agent. She was courageous, patient, methodical and an adept radio operator. Wesselow told Keegan to continue with her training as if nothing had happened – Noor would be exempted from shooting. She would cope somehow, after all. Radio operators are not supposed to do a great deal of shooting, quite the opposite: they were given orders to avoid any violent action and to concentrate on the work making transmissions. If Noor did not want to learn to shoot that was her business, and competent radio operators were too few and far between for the SOE to start picking and choosing.

The princess's standing in Keegan's estimation was restored the following week. As well as teaching the young women to shoot, Keegan taught them how to tackle what they called their 'assault course'. In a normal military unit this would entail jumping ditches, climbing a few walls, crawling through mud and getting over various obstacles. The SOE had refined the exercise, taking inspiration from the training methods of the élite forces. You had to jump down from a wall twelve feet high instead of six, to walk up to your neck in ice-cold water for a mile, to crouch hidden in the mud for about twelve hours, to crawl along the ground with machine-gun fire overhead just eighteen inches off the ground, to abseil down a 150 foot cliff, to climb back up the same cliff using prepared footholds but with no safety harness, to learn to attack a sentry from behind and to kill him by burying a dagger in his back or to break his neck with one brutal twist of his head. The women were trained through a toned-down version of these exercises which would still have put off most conscripts in the regular army.

One afternoon Keegan assembled his 'Charm Battalion' in front of a large tree which had a wooden platform built round it about thirty feet off the ground. A rope hung from a branch further up, and fell to the ground beyond the edge of the platform. He asked the trainees to jump from the platform, take hold of the rope in both hands and climb down. In groups of four they climbed up onto the flimsy platform and Keegan called out for them to move forwards and jump.

When Pearl Witherington reached the edge she realised that the rope hung nearly six feet away from it. You had to cover the distance in one leap and catch the rope in mid-air to avoid falling thirty feet to the ground. Granted, you landed on grass, but the parachuting exercises had taught them that a jump of more than twelve feet sends you to hospital – unless, that is, it kills you. The colour drained from Pearl's face as she contemplated the rope and the ground below, and then she called to Keegan to say that it was too dangerous.

'The Gestapo are more dangerous than that,' Keegan replied, 'they're following you, go on, jump!'

Pearl had already stepped back so that Keegan could no longer see her. The sergeant knew that this was a difficult test, so he made a concession.

'All right, Violette, on you go! Show them what you're made of!'

Violette Laszlo stepped forward. She too measured the height and the distance she had to cover to catch the rope, and then paled.

'Go on, jump, for God's sake. Are you frightened too?' bellowed Keegan.

Violette made up her mind. Ashen-faced, she took four steps back and pushed off from the trunk to get into her stride. She took off from her left foot, leapt towards the rope, threw out her arms and tried to catch it. Her left hand missed it. When her right hand closed round it Violette was already falling. Her hold was not strong enough and she continued to fall, slowed only by her hand slipping down the rope. She screamed as the hemp burned her hand. When she was six feet from the ground the rope below was snaking so furiously that it wrapped itself round her bare thigh. This acted as a brake and Violette came to the ground without hurting herself too badly. She got to her feet shakily and looked at her right hand. The palm was red and torn, and blood dripped onto the sleeve of her uniform. She did not even notice that she also had a bright red weal across her thigh. Keegan came over sheepishly.

'Well done, Violette,' he said without much conviction, 'you've shown them how to do it.'

'Stop this exercise, Sergeant Keegan. With all due respect, it's too dangerous,' was all Violette could manage to whisper. 'If they miss the rope, they'll kill themselves.'

Keegan hovered, torn between his duty as an intransigent instructor and common sense, which suggested he ought to keep his recruits alive. He looked at Violette and then up at the tree, and decided to give in. A little voice stopped him. To the astonishment of her friends, Noor had stepped to the edge of the platform.

'Sergeant Keegan!' she cried, 'I think I've thought of a way.'

Keegan hesitated for a moment and then made up his mind. He wanted to see this. 'Good on you, miss! Be careful! You have to grip the rope firmly with both hands. Take a good jump and aim carefully.'

'No, you shouldn't jump, Sergeant. Let me do it.'

Noor was standing at the edge of the platform with the drop just beneath her. The little group watched her, fascinated. Then she put her arms straight down her sides, lifted her chin and closed her eyes. Half a minute passed. Not a sound except for the rustling of the leaves. Noor kept her eyes closed as if she were meditating. Just when Keegan was about to say something Noor opened her eyes, leant forwards slightly and raised her arms until they were horizontal, stretching out towards the rope. Then she fell forward slowly into the air with her whole body in a straight line and her arms stretched out. Diana Rowden let out a little cry. Keegan stood motionless, watching intently, and a droplet of sweat ran down his forehead. Noor's rigid body was now at an angle of about 45 degrees. She was going to fall. But, in that position, her hands just touched the rope. She closed her hands round it, her feet left the platform, and there she was holding on to the rope, firmly attached with her hands and her crossed ankles. She climbed down it quickly. When she reached the ground she turned to Keegan and smiled. There was a split second's silence before Violette whooped: 'Three cheers for Nora Wilson. Hip, hip . . .'

'Hurray!' answered the rest of the group.

Keegan maintained his stern expression amid the applause, but there was a twinkle in his eye. One by one the recruits followed Noor's example and caught hold of the rope without any trouble. On the way back Keegan said loudly: 'Well played, Miss Wilson! I don't know if we'll take you on, but if you don't make it with us, you could always try the circus!'

CHAPTER THREE

Idid come across Noor once more before we left, and once again I did not really notice her. The agents' physical and military training was completed in three months. Wesselow had taken out about ten candidates, who were sent back to their original corps. Joan Sanderson had praised Noor's performance very highly, and had won her case despite Keegan's emphatic reservations; he could not understand why they should send Mahatma Gandhi's followers to fight for the King of England when he knew full well that these cunning characters would not rest until they had broken up the British Empire. Wesselow had found in favour of Noor.

After a period of leave the whole intake met up again in a cottage not far from Beaulieu, in the grounds of the School of Security, directed by Colonel Frank Spooner, an icy redhead with penetrating blue eyes. We were on the banks of a river which snaked through the countryside before throwing itself into the Solent, the strip of sea which separates the Isle of Wight from the coast. The fields were surrounded by hedges buffeted by the winds off the Channel. Along the river there were naval construction sites which smelt of freshly sawn wood, and cosy pubs with frosted glass windows from which sailors' songs drifted in the evenings. The area was famous for its sailing races and the magnificent houses along the waterfront.

The Rothschilds and a number of other very wealthy families had lent their properties to the army. Lord Mountbatten had set up his headquarters a few miles from our cottage to prepare his combined operations for the troop landings. Along the river they tried out the boats which would take the waves of troops onto the Normandy beaches. Like Drake and Nelson before them, a good proportion of the Royal Navy had taken to the water in this sheltered place that had seen the inception of the America's Cup. On orders from Churchill himself, the 'Mulberries' were being built, large floating sections of sea wall which, when the time came, would be towed across the Channel to set up the artificial ports at Arromanches and Colleville. The country house next to us had been taken over by Colonel Passy's BCRA, an organisation as fiercely proud of its independence as it was reliant on the British Army for material support, and a sister organisation to the SOE which was controlled by de Gaulle.

The atmosphere was a far cry from Arisaig. Spooner did not greet his trainees with a stirring speech punctuated by applause, and there was no drinking in the evenings. He explained in a cutting, uncompromising voice that the average survival time for an SOE agent in France was estimated at three months. In the deathly silence that followed he added that the techniques they would be taught at Beaulieu were intended to extend that time limit. This short sharp announcement was worth any number of speeches.

I had already operated behind enemy lines in France in June 1940 and, more importantly, in Cyrenaica in 1942, when we had to destroy the Luftwaffe's aircraft on their airfields in the heart of the Libyan desert, way beyond the front held by the Afrikakorps. But here the aim was quite different: to survive in occupied territory, not in the desert but in amongst the French population, melting seamlessly into them if you were to have any hope of staying alive. I was no longer an instructor but a novice, and that is why I now sat down every morning alongside my former pupils, at an ink-stained desk requisitioned from the local secondary school and set up in the large sitting room of the cottage while a wood fire burned in the hearth.

An expert in secret codes taught us everything about encoding messages using the method of double transposition in columns; a policeman taught us the art of the anonymous letter, which can disrupt the most steadfast administration by propagating rumours, calumnies and misinformation through its ranks; a surly trade unionist, who specialised in picketing amongst striking Yorkshire miners, instilled in us the principles of propaganda and industrial agitation; two engineers explained in detail the weak points in marshalling yards, electrical power stations and car factories so that we would know exactly where to put the explosives that, sooner or later, we would use for sabotaging purposes; a Londoner with a cockney accent, whom the army had plucked out of prison, where he was serving twenty years for various armed robberies, was a great success with his one-week course when we devoted three hours a day to nocturnal break-ins into public establishments.

The most highly prized lessons were those given by Harold 'Kim' Philby. He was a thin man in his thirties with black hair which fell over his tall forehead, hiding his penetrating eyes but not his smile. Philby was sitting pretty. His course was entitled: 'Agent security on the ground, means of detection and appropriate counter-measures'. In other words, he taught us how to save our skins.

Philby was a former journalist who had been recruited by the Intelligence Service and he dispensed his knowledge with great precision, but added a touch of humour, philosophy and even poetry which absolutely delighted us. I had met him at Cambridge and he had become a friend. He was one of those intellectual warriors that every great cause seems to bring to light, with this notable difference: after the war no one would be quite sure who Philby had really been fighting for. Along with Burgess and Maclean, he was to be at the heart of one of the biggest scandals in the history of spying. The three men were recruited into the British Communist Party in Cambridge early in the 1930s, and directed towards Stalin's doctrines. Philby and his two accomplices were idealists, disgusted by English polite society with its caste-like rituals and its contempt for the working class, so they devoted themselves to the Bolshevik revolution.

On orders, they had joined the British secret services in order to infiltrate them on behalf of the USSR. They were brilliant, courageous and cultivated, and they climbed rapidly through the ranks of the Intelligence Service. After Hitler invaded the USSR, they deployed their intelligence and their energies all the more fervently now that their own government's cause and that of the Soviet government coincided. By instructing SOE recruits, Philby knew that he was fighting the mortal enemies of both his parties, the one he was serving and the one he was betraying. For a three-year period he had no inner conflict. Perhaps that was what gave him the discreet air of happiness that hung about him while we were on our course. His service record meant he went on to enjoy a career as a top-flight mole: he was a Soviet agent but in the 1950s he was promoted to the third-highest position in the British Secret Service before he was found out. He fled to the USSR to see out his days in a dacha near Moscow with a prestigious medal from the Soviet Union.

On this particular day Philby was talking once again about the daily life of a secret agent, a life of fear and of waiting.

'The best way to stay alive,' he said, 'is to stay in all day. And all night, too, because of the curfew. To do nothing, to say nothing, to meet no one: that's the only way to be safe. The problem is that, if you follow this prescription, you're no good to us. In other words, sooner or later, an agent has to do something. Even if he's prostrated by his fear, paralysed by it, ashen-faced and dripping with sweat . . . he has to do something. To go out into the street and shout "Down with Hitler!"' for example.'

Smiles all round. Philby smiled too and went on: 'No. Whatever you're there to do, you have to go out, travel, meet other agents, carry out operations and transmit information. That's why we send you into the jaws of hell. Not to hole yourselves up somewhere in the middle of France. Some agents do do that. Others send false activity reports. Which is much worse, obviously.' Then his tone became more serious. 'You have to learn to overcome the fear. Otherwise you're no use for anything. After a while it would be the SOE itself which denounced you, so that it didn't have to go on paying you.'

A doubtful murmur ran round the group.

'No, I'm joking,' he said and there was scattered laughter. 'Still, I don't know . . .' he trailed off before embarking again. 'So, first point, the cover.

A plausible job which justifies travelling and coming and going at irregular hours. Being a ticket collector on the Métro would be a bad cover. You'd be paid to take tickets and to go home every evening at half past six. The SOE wouldn't be getting their money's worth. Bank clerk or shop assistant – same story. But travelling salesman is a good cover. One of the classics, the police keep an eye out for them. Journalist too, only worse. To be avoided. No manual jobs unless your nails are black and your hands calloused. No technical job if you aren't up to speed on the relevant details. Engineer, commercial director, sales inspector, etc. You have to learn every aspect of the profession by heart. You have to be able to talk about it with an expert for hours on end. Same thing with your identity. You have a new life: you have to get to know it as well as the old one. Otherwise you'll be caught out within three days. Train yourself to answer to the new name and, crucially, not to answer to the old one. You could always stumble across someone you knew before the war – you have to be steady as a rock if they speak your name, but try to let them know that they are putting you in a difficult situation. When you travel don't talk to anyone unless you have to. No unnecessary conversations: that would just multiply the risks. You have to walk calmly, not with your head in the air but not staring at people, just busy, content, concentrating. On public transport pretend to go to sleep: it'll put off the bores who can't help themselves talking to you. Or chew tobacco: no one will want to talk to you. But it's a bit obvious. When the ticket inspector comes, or the police, you're asleep. We look harmless when we're asleep. Take all your papers out at the same time: identity card, *Ausweis*, ration card, train ticket. They won't be so tempted to check them thoroughly.'

Next Philby talked at length about passwords. These sentences that two agents who did not know each other had to pronounce before getting down to any kind of business may have seemed slightly ridiculous but they played an important role in personal safety. You had to know them inside out, to say them at the right time in a completely natural tone of voice, otherwise the other party could not be quite sure and might break off the contact or, worse, do something they might later regret. Philby made the class laugh by telling a few stories about forgotten passwords. Then he mentioned an ill-fated rendezvous when the agent totally forgot the agreed words. He was interrogated at great length and then shot on the spot by the over-cautious head of the network.

Each of us listening to him projected ourselves into our new identities as spies.

'You will very often feel as if you're being followed. That's completely normal; secret agents are always paranoid. And they do have a lot of enemies.' A fleeting smile played on his lips. 'First of all check whether or not you really are being followed. Usually, a few changes of direction through some quieter streets will prove that there's no one behind you. It's the effect that the fear has on you. But sometimes of course you are right: someone is following you. In that case, you mustn't panic. You still have one thing in your favour: if you had been found out you would have been arrested straight away. The enemy isn't sure, that's why he's following you. With a good plan, you can get away from him.'

He stopped, then pointed to Violette Laszlo, who was watching him with a slightly dreamy expression from the back of the class. 'Miss Laszlo, how would you go about it?'

Violette flushed suddenly, raised her eyes to the heavens and looked around. Several of the others winked at each other. Violette could not disguise her inclination for Philby. She put her make-up on most carefully before his lessons, gave him long, searching looks and smiled at his every word. The instructor found the pupil to his taste. They had been seen walking together by the river.

'I don't know . . .' she said. 'I . . . I . . . I might turn round and walk past the person following me. If he turns round, too, then I've been pinpointed.'

Philby smiled again. 'Oh no, my dear Violette. If you do that the policeman will know you've spotted him. He will have confirmation of what was only a supposition: you really are an agent, or a Resistance worker, or someone who's got something to hide, anyway. No you have to throw off the tail without them guessing. If you undertake any sort of obvious manoeuvre to get away from them, you point yourself out.'

Violette, slightly put out, replied: 'But how can you possibly do that? If you get away, the enemy will realise.'

'Not necessarily,' Philby retorted smoothly. 'If, for example, you spot a bus or a taxi coming towards you from the end of the road, you start looking at your watch and looking agitated, like someone suddenly realising they're running late for an appointment. When the bus, or taxi, reaches you, you hop on as it passes. He won't be able to follow you, but he won't be absolutely sure that you spotted him. In other words, you have to escape in the most natural way you can.'

'Any more examples?' Starr called from his bench seat.

'The shop with two doors is a possibility. You go in from one street and go straight out onto another. The policeman won't be able to follow you immediately so by the time he's inside the shop you'll already be outside again. On condition that the second door is a big, proper one. If it's a staff door he'll realise that you've deliberately lost him. You will have been clocked as an agent. In other words, as soon as you arrive in France one of your first tasks is to identify escape routes near your headquarters that allow for you to throw off a tail naturally. It's tough work and it takes a long time. But it's worth doing.'

Greenwood raised his hand. 'Shouldn't we have a weapon on us at all times? At worst, I suppose you could get away by shooting . . .'

Philby's face darkened. 'You'll never have a weapon on you, you poor devil! How would you explain the fact that a travelling salesman was walking about with a cylinder Colt on him? You have to behave simply, naturally, to be completely consistent with your official activity. The first thing the enemy will look for is any inconsistencies in your behaviour. Everything depends on how solid your cover is.'

A crystal-clear voice rose from the first row. It was Noor's, but all I could see of her was her long, dark hair. 'What about the radio?'

'What do you mean, what about the radio?' asked Philby.

'We have to keep changing our point of trans-mission,' she said. 'That's our first instruction. So we have to walk about with the radio, don't we?'

Philby smiled. 'You're right, Miss Wilson. That's why being a radio operator is the most dangerous job. You do have to move your set regularly. It weighs thirty pounds. If you're stopped with it, it's all over. You should always try to maintain that it's electrical or photographic equipment. You never know . . .'

'And if we're captured?' the same crystalline voice went on.

There was absolute silence in the room.

'If you follow my instructions well, there's a good chance you won't be caught.'

'Mr Spooner told us our life expectancy was three months,' Noor continued, unabashed. 'So there must be a good chance we will be caught. I'm not being defeatist, I'm just repeating what Mr Spooner said.'

Philby hesitated. Violette Laszlo upheld Noor's point: 'There must be some procedure in case we are arrested, for goodness' sake!'

'There is one, yes,' Philby said, now looking serious and attentive. 'I was going to talk to you about that next week –'

'No, straight away,' called Starr from the back of the room. 'It's the best bit!'

Philby smiled. 'If you're caught, stick obstinately to your cover.'

Starr was not satisfied. 'No, give us more details. How do they go about it?'

Philby threw him a black look. 'Right, as you please. Often the enemy will suspect you without actually being sure. You may have been denounced by a neighbour or a colleague. But then there are lots of false denunciations. Or your name has been given by a brother agent who has talked under torture. But the Gestapo can't trust what he's said: an agent under torture can lie and fabricate. In that case, I say again: your only hope lies in your cover.'

Starr was still not satisfied, and Greenwood and Darbois supported him. 'Tell us more. What do they do?'

'First of all they'll see if there's a file on you,'

47

said Philby. 'They'll study everything that could be of use to them. They're very professional. They're often enlisted men who worked as policemen in Germany before the war. Then they'll take you into a bare room. If there's a mirror then you're being watched from outside through a two-way mirror. There are always two officers. The first one sits at a table interrogating you and taking notes, the other holds back, sitting by the door. The second one is very visibly armed to discourage any attempt at violence. The first is brutal, arrogant, threatening. The second is silent. When the first one goes out the second one might talk to you and seem quite friendly, as if he disapproved of the first one's methods. It's the most classic trap: the second one will try and worm information out of you in confidence. Or they might take you to see their superior who'll pretend to disapprove of the way they've treated you to win your trust. Or it could be the cleaning woman, the nurse or the porter who leads you to believe that they don't like the Nazis to get into a friendly conversation. At the beginning of the interrogation they'll start off with questions about your work. They might also ask you obscure questions about France, daily life, your childhood, politics or your itinerary when you were arrested. They're looking for those telling, minor gaps in your knowledge: you may not know the name of the last president of the Conseil even though you live in France. You don't know the price of bread. You do addition or division the

English way and not the French way. You don't know the name of the last person to win the Coupe de France, etc. Or they might suddenly give you a false piece of information about a town you're meant to have been to or people you're meant to have met. Something like: "Do you remember the Café Glacier at Antibes?" If you don't put them right, if you go along with them, they will have cornered you: there isn't a Café Glacier in Antibes. Will you remember that, Miss Laszlo?'

Violette nodded.

'Except that there is a Café Glacier in Antibes. It's the most famous café on the main square.' He smiled again. 'They can keep coming back to the same question or the same episode twenty times. They'll stop from time to time to offer you a cigarette or a sandwich and to get into a more casual, informal conversation. Another trap. Or they'll stick a declaration – which may be false – under your nose, claiming it's been made by another agent who's fingered you. They'll describe the SOE, saying they know every last detail about the organisation and about your activities. And this is what's probably hardest: you will feel as if they know everything, that there are traitors in our midst, etc. In fact they use a mixture of fact and fabrication. They do know a lot. But a lot less than they will say. If you pay attention and stay calm and coherent they won't be able to do anything to you. They won't move on to torturing you. Not out of humanity, but because they don't like wasting time. If they're still in any doubt, they'll let you go with their apologies and they'll keep you under tight surveillance. The best thing to do in this instance is to disappear and get back to England. The SOE does not employ agents who've been arrested, because we cannot know whether or not you've talked. The best thing to do is to lie low. Make no contact with the SOE and travel home via Switzerland or Spain. Unless you move to a different region and change your cover. But that's very complicated . . . The best thing is to ask for instructions from London by radio.'

Then I raised my hand. 'And if they know who we are?'

We could sense that Philby had been expecting and dreading this question.

'In that case, they will try to get you to betray . . . to give the names of other agents, the sites of parachute drops, the procedures, the letter boxes, the arms caches, etc. If you resist they will use beatings and then worse –'

'The advice,' Starr interrupted, 'is to say nothing, whatever happens, I suppose.'

Philby replied slowly and solemnly: 'We ask just one thing of you: hold out for forty-eight hours. That's how long the other members of the network need to get to safety, on the understanding that they know you've been arrested. But, as you work in teams, they'll know. Just forty-eight hours. Afterwards you're freed from your word. No one has any guarantee of standing up to the treatment they can inflict. Even the bravest amongst us. All we ask of you is forty-eight hours. I know that's a long time. But they have a limit: if they're too brutal, they risk killing you and losing the information. You have to hang on for forty-eight hours. After that, you can tell them everything. Do you see why you have to know as little as possible about the organisation, and why we use this whole paraphernalia of false names, nicknames and covers.'

Noor spoke up again: 'And what about the radio operators? If we're taken, we're caught red-handed. After the forty-eight hours can we say everything, the codes, the frequencies, the security messages?'

Philby turned towards her. 'There is a special procedure. Obviously ideally you don't tell them anything. As soon as the Germans have the codes and the recognition messages they carry out transmissions trying to pass themselves off as the operator they've caught. If they succeed in tricking us they can request parachute drops that they then intercept, have agents sent out that they then arrest, transmit false information, etc. They are very good at it. They know that each radio operator has their own style, an involuntary signature in the way they send the Morse. So as soon as their listening posts have picked up a set, they don't just send out their detection lorries, they also assign it an agent of their own to listen to it day and night, and train to imitate the operator's style. And if they get hold of the set they can put it straight back into service, copying the style of the operator who's been arrested.'

'But we have recognition signs,' Noor objected. 'One to indicate the beginning, then a deliberate mistake which has been agreed with London, so that we can be recognised. If that mistake isn't there, London knows that someone else is transmitting instead of us.'

Philby nodded. 'That would be what they wanted from the interrogation. They'd try to get your codes. You will be given a little silk handkerchief with the letters inscribed on it and you will learn the coding key by heart. They'll ask for them. What they want above all is the little recognition signals Miss Wilson has mentioned. If you talk after forty-eight hours give them the first safety code, but not the second. We'll know that the set is in German hands. We'll go on as if nothing had happened in order to protect you, then after a few weeks, we'll break off the contact for some spurious reason. And that will be the end of that.'

'And if we feel we're not going to last forty-eight hours?' Violette Laszlo asked blankly.

'You have to last,' Philby said, as if to close the subject. 'That is the organisation's rule. You are soldiers. This isn't a pleasure trip, Violette. You have to respect your responsibilities. When our army lands in France, the front-line soldiers will be killed too. Your honour is at stake. Speaking too early means sacrificing your fellow agents. You'll have their deaths on your conscience.'

He let the room stand silent for a moment.

'If their brutality is too much for you, you have two options: escape or suicide. Escape is rare. But you must try at the least opportunity. As for suicide, you will have little pills. If you're at the end of your tether, use them! If they were taken when you were searched, there's the window, the wall, electric wires, etc.'

A firm little voice spoke out. It was Noor again: 'Yes, Mr Philby, we have to hold out. There is no other solution. But what will they do to us? Beat us?'

Philby looked her right in the eye. 'My instructions forbid me to give you details of their methods. In any event, anything is possible. They've gone right back to the Middle Ages, Miss Wilson, and that's the truth. That's one of the reasons we're fighting. They're fascists. They don't care about human life or any of our values. To them the worst atrocities are just a duty if they are useful to their cause. They have no scruples, no restraint, no moment's hesitation. I'd like to refer you back to the formula used in our manual: "The Nazis combine sadism with science." That's pretty clear, isn't it?'

It had grown dark outside. No one had thought to put the light on. Each of us sat in tense silence looking at the ghostly half-light that had descended on the room.

CHAPTER FOUR

The great detective Sherlock Holmes lived at 221b Baker Street. The master spy Maurice Buckmaster lived at number 64. Arthur Conan Doyle gave his fictional hero this address, and it became a legendary one; by an amusing quirk of fate, Winston Churchill assigned the SOE to a building in the same street. The Prime Minister's secret army were working a hundred yards from the world's most famous detective: a proximity that must have delighted Churchill's colourful sense of strategy.

At nine o'clock in the morning on 15 June 1943 I climbed out of a black car parked in front of the imposing building with its tall, small-paned windows which housed the SOE's headquarters. An army chauffeur, who appeared to be almost mute, had driven me straight from Beaulieu to London through the magnificent English countryside and the dilapidated suburbs. 'Buck' wanted to see me. The head of the SOE's 'Section F' (French section) did not like to be kept waiting; I had to break off my course as a secret agent to travel to London.

I was happy to be back in this great city which I had been deprived of by the war. My childhood in Cowes on the Isle of Wight, surrounded by dairy herds and sailing boats on the Solent, had kept me far away. It was during my weekends as a student at Cambridge that I had discovered the polluted air, the wet pavements and the burning passions of this city where everything happened and everything glittered. As a budding journalist in charge of the News in Brief column, I threw myself wholeheartedly into the urban underbelly where every kind of vice bared its face. I spent my days in the lower depths of current events, and my nights in the warmth of pubs and gentrified soirées. Dickens was my guide and London was the chosen prey of the ambitious reporter I became, flitting from the working girls in Whitechapel to the intellectuals in Bloomsbury. I knew the idealistic academics at the London School of Economics as well as the disillusioned policemen down on the docks: what more could you ask for when you have a passion for human passions, that special drive that makes a good journalist?

The war made me love London all the more. Torn apart by the Blitz, carved up into sections by the Home Guard, and lit up at night by the anti-aircraft searchlights, the great, dark city had found its true grandeur in the depths of its despair. As Churchill said, it was the 'finest hour' for London as well as the whole Empire. Surviving impassive under fire, decimated by the Luftwaffe and holed up in the underground stations, Londoners remained as steadfast as their monarch, who had refused to leave the perfect target that was Buckingham Palace. From arrogant aristocrats to resigned labourers, from polo players to punters at the dogs, from widows with their neat little buns to beer-swilling workmen, all of them emaciated and united by this trial, they battled on in the same way, surviving by their humour and their indifference amid the explosions and the wailing sirens, knowing they owed their survival to a handful of whippety young pilots, and that any weakness on their part would be a blessing for Goebbels. After the war every one of us, low-lifes and gentlemen alike, would feel nostalgic for those times. Churchill was at his best. His homage to the heroes in the RAF was on everybody's lips: 'Never, in the field of human conflict, was so much owed by so many to so few.' He would go out from time to time to look at a bomb crater, walk through a smoking ruin or share a joke with a gasping casualty, and the cheering crowd would always broaden his smile, that special smile which somehow looked powerful and carnivorous as it wrapped itself round a huge cigar.

Then the Blitz abated. The German planes had better things to do in Russia. As operations developed and the Americans became involved in the war, a jumble of different uniforms invaded the streets of London at the same time as the echo of saxophones playing. The undernourished but still sexy Englishwomen smiled at these well-fed 'boys' as they landed in their hundreds of thousands from the 'Liberty-ships' from the New World. The pubs were filled with smoke from their mild cigarettes, and parties swung to Glenn Miller's intoxicating riffs as the auxiliaries' skirts spun round and round. At the BBC, news from the front jostled with the sounds of swing. The Germans were retreating to a jazz rhythm.

After each operation and after each training course I would come back to London as quickly as possible as if retreating to my lair. And on those evenings when I mingled with its exhausted but confident population, drinking in the atmosphere of sinister crisis and absurd hope, I would not have wanted to be anywhere else in the world. That was where you had to be, that was where you had to fight. During those years that were so decisive for humanity, we were at the epicentre of history: London was the capital of freedom.

I was taken into a soulless office by a 'female auxiliary' with her forage cap pinned to her blonde hair. Buckmaster sat in an armchair behind a large table with a green-leather top. He was not alone: his assistant, Nick Bodington, sat on a stark, upright chair to his left. Was it because we were so close to Baker Street (I could hear its hubbub rumbling through the window)? The pair of them could not help but remind me of their mythical neighbours, Sherlock Holmes and Doctor Watson. Buckmaster was tall and thin with a sharp eye and disdainful set to his jaw. He spoke evenly, precisely, carefully. Bodington was bouncy and enthusiastic.

Buckmaster spoke first, indicating the chair opposite him. 'Sutherland, we're delighted to see you. How are the recruits?'

'It's a good intake, sir. Wesselow has whittled out the lame ducks, and Spooner will finish off the selection process. Those that come out of Beaulieu will make very good agents.'

'Yes. I've read the files. They'll be very welcome – they're needed. Our networks in France are now operational. We're going into a phase of full activity. They need strong connections, arms – a lot of them – radios, couriers . . . We think that, by imposing this compulsory work scheme, Pétain has given us a unique opportunity. The French are a wait-and-see nation, but they don't want to go to Germany. They'd rather use more clandestine methods. We can now have a massive recruiting drive. The Gaullists and the Communists have already started, but they need logistical support, and the role will fall to your trainees. In fact, I can now tell you that the landings are already being planned. You'd probably guessed that, I'm not revealing a state secret. But it could happen rather sooner than you thought. Perhaps in the autumn.'

'I understand, sir. We're moving up a gear.'

'Precisely. The squabble with the Intelligence Service has calmed down. They have accepted that we are useful. They have given up on trying to deprive us of the means: we have the planes, the arms, the radio sets. The ball is in our court.'

'Will MI5 take us seriously?'

Bodington spoke up: 'When we gave them the first plans for defending the Channel, they had to recognise the fact that we had our uses. C even said so at an inter-service meeting!'

C, I was to discover after the war, meant Stewart Menzies, head of MI5 and MI6, the two big departments of the Intelligence Service, the one dedicated to espionage, the other to counter-espionage. Menzies had taken the inception of the SOE in 1940 as a personal snub, and had gone to great lengths to prevent the creation of this army of amateurs. Faced with the results of their work, he slowly admitted his mistake.

'You will leave for France at the next full moon,' Buckmaster went on. 'We need professionals on the ground. Soon we will have to start taking action. Everything we've done over these last three years has been geared towards that.'

'Do you mean that we will be starting to take military action very soon, even before D-day?'

'It's a possibility. Nothing has been decided for certain. Once you are in France you will receive instructions by radio. But that's not what this meeting is about.'

Buckmaster took his time, joined his hands and fixed me with a penetrating stare. I realised that we were getting to the nuts and bolts. 'At present our networks cover the whole of France. And not badly. We are particularly pleased with the Île-de-France network. It's directed by a tremendous chap, Francis Suttill, whom we call Prosper. In the last two years Prosper has got together over a thousand patriots in the Paris region. He has several radio operators, a lot of couriers and agents in all the major towns round Paris. He has set up hiding places, landing strips and parachuting sites, and he has trained his local recruits. He has provided us with a wealth of information and, more importantly, he has started a programme of sabotage around the capital in factories, in stations and on railway lines. He runs the principal Resistance organisation in Paris. The Gaullists have less manpower than him and the Communists fewer trained fighters.'

I could not really see why Buckmaster wanted to describe the successes of Prosper's network to me in such detail. Once I got to France, if I were arrested, I would know too much, but Buckmaster had anticipated this: 'You're wondering why I'm telling you all this. You're quite right. There is a good reason.'

He turned towards Bodington, who was fidgeting in his chair.

'We are worried about Prosper,' Bodington started. 'First of all there are the stories that have come from a number of agents returning to England for instructions. To put it bluntly, Prosper is not very careful. He is incredibly brave, but we think he's taking too many risks. And, more significantly, we have had some incidents which have drawn this to our attention. We've parachuted arms, explosives and radio sets round Vendôme several times. We had a safe landing site along the Loire, near a château owned by a member of the network. We now know that all the containers were seized by the Germans. The owner of the château had to go into hiding – the Gestapo nearly caught him. We also know that several of our dead-letter boxes in Paris have been identified. Norman, Prosper's radio operator, has nearly been caught red-handed twice, but he'd only been transmitting for five minutes.'

'These things happen,' I said. 'Bad luck. It doesn't necessarily mean that Prosper's cover's been blown or that his network can't stay the course.'

'Of course,' Bodington rejoined. 'But we have reason to be seriously worried. The radio operator from the Tailor network, an organisation that Prosper ran around Chartres, suddenly stopped transmissions without any warning. Five days later he started up again. The problem is that he then omitted the second recognition signal. We carried on as if nothing had happened and corresponded normally without saying anything in particular. After a week he requested a parachute drop of arms at Vendôme. So as not to put him on his guard, we arranged the parachute drop but we warned off another agent without going through Prosper. The agent quietly made his way there, and he saw the Germans picking up the containers.'

'What this means', said Buckmaster, 'is that Tailor's radio operator has been taken and the Germans are using his radio to manipulate us. If the Germans manage to use our radios to their ends we are facing the most enormous catastrophe. We have to be absolutely clear about this. Our theory is that Prosper's network has been infiltrated. There is a traitor – or several even – working alongside Prosper. If we warn Prosper by radio we run the risk of having him killed. If the traitor is close to him he will know about the message and he will have him arrested. We need someone we trust to investigate in situ.'

I understood what he wanted before he had formulated his conclusion. Baker Street clearly was a source of inspiration: I was going to have to turn detective to flush out the traitor who was threatening the main network in Section F. Sherlock Holmes would have had no obligation to accept. I did.

'Are you sure of Prosper?'

My question was as good as an acceptance. I had missed the ceremonial acquiescence and gone straight to the next stage. It was Bodington who replied. 'Yes, one hundred per cent. He is a mystic, a crusader. He would gladly choose to die for the cause. We are in no doubt about that.'

'So, is there someone else you suspect?'

'No. We're completely in the dark. He has a courier called Andrée Borrel, a very beautiful woman . . . and his mistress. We have absolutely no reason to suspect her. You can depend on her. Norman, his radio operator, seems more . . . flimsy. He could have given in under pressure. You'll have to see when you're there. It's a start. There's also Blainville, who organises all the transport. You can trust him. Utterly and completely. I knew him before the war. He's an accomplished pilot and he chooses our landing sites, and he's never got it wrong. He took all kinds of risks to get to London and he has been of tremendous service to us since we sent him back to France. You can confide in him, he'll help you. But he and Prosper are the only two you can talk to. We can't be absolutely sure about the others.'

'Do you have a full description of the network?'

'Yes,' said Bodington. 'You'll find a copy of it at your hotel.'

This answer made me laugh. Holmes and Watson had thought of everything. I could not say no. Theoretically, the SOE relied on volunteers, but Buckmaster and Bodington knew who they were dealing with: my service record spoke for me. A commando officer never turns down an assignment. I had to find the traitor who was threatening the Prosper network, otherwise the whole landing could fail. When all was said and done it was very simple.

'So, when do I leave?' I asked stiffly.

'Tomorrow evening, from Tangmere.'

CHAPTER FIVE

Meanwhile, alone and anxious, Noor was setting out in her career as a spy. The SOE had established a tradition: the test of God. Each agent was given an assignment in England. They had to take up residence in a town somewhere or other in the country and make radio transmissions for three days. Or report back with as accurate a ground plan as possible of an arms factory or a power station. Or even plot the schedule and habits of a prominent politician for the purposes of assassination. Obviously, the authorities were perfectly unaware of these more or less whimsical treasure hunts. The apprentice spy had to outplay the frighteningly efficient surveillance of not only the police and the army, but also Churchill's Home Guard with its thousands of members – the elderly, adolescents, invalids and veterans – who patrolled fully armed, vigilant and on their toes, through every neighbourhood, town and village in the country. There were also the counter-espionage facilities of MI5, which were concentrated around strategic targets. In the space of a few months this surveillance system had dismantled the networks that the Germans had set up in Britain. The Abwehr and the Gestapo tried to infiltrate with other agents: they were all discovered and summarily shot within a few days. MI5 even succeeded in turning around several of them, who went on to work for the Intelligence Service. In other words, Spooner and Philby's pupils had to succeed where professional German spies regularly failed.

If SOE agents were arrested, they were ordered to stick to their covers. They were authorised to give a telephone number for the SOE if there was a direct threat to their physical safety. It goes without saying that the careers of these imprudent or unlucky agents ended there.

Noor had been sent to Portsmouth on a simple assignment: to count the warships in the harbour, to describe what type they were and how they were armed, and to send this information by radio to listening station 53A in Grendon. The exercise was under real conditions: Grendon was one of the communications centres used by agents disseminated throughout Europe. The operators there were permanently on the alert, working as they did under a menacing inscription: 'Remember, the enemy is listening'. Each switchboard operator was assigned a certain number of clandestine radio transmitters – they were the invisible fairy godmothers of the European Resistance.

Noor took the train from Victoria Station to Portsmouth. She had been told to set off from

London in order to set the scene. She already had her cover: in England she was Nora Wilson, a nanny for smart families, who was heading south to look for work in the seaside resorts along the coast, just as, when she got to France, she would be the governess Jeanne-Marie Firmin, who was living in Paris while she looked for work. The only thing that might draw attention to her was her heavy suitcase containing her Mark II radio. She was frequently relieved of this burden by considerate men. As they handed the suitcase back to her, they invariably asked: 'What on earth have you got in there?' To which she replied with a smile: 'My books. I work as a translator.' The case was locked shut; only the police would be able to check its contents. But all her papers were in order: she got through all the checks without any trouble.

When she arrived in Portsmouth she took a room in a bed and breakfast near the big beach on the Solent. Noor was cutting her teeth as a spy in the place where I grew up, in the great naval and merchant harbour town huddled round the docks with its black cranes and rusted pontoons, and where the smell of the sea seeped up every street. A sign of fate . . . Portsmouth was one of the Royal Navy's most important bases. There were already vessels of every tonnage piling into the port in preparation for D-day. The big warships were waiting in the harbour to the east of Cowes between the Isle of Wight and the coast, where

Nelson's and Collingwood's ships once crept for respite between two campaigns against the French navy. The military port was out of bounds to the public. But there was no security system which could stop a young woman who was out of work from strolling along a sunny beach with a folding chair and some watercolours in amongst the first bathers of the season.

Noor had left her suitcase in her room and had slipped on a summer dress. With a chair under one arm and her box of watercolours in a wicker basket, she had set off along the street, passing clothes shops that were still closed and hotels with columned façades. She sat facing the sea and wrote out her report in the back of her sketching pad. Thanks to the literature she had been given at Beaulieu she had been able to study the outlines of the major vessels, and using a code she had devised for herself she wrote: 'Two rum babas with cherries and pineapple slices, three apple tarts, five chocolate eclairs and twelve cheesecakes.' Any suspicious policeman who took it into his head to stop her on her way home and check her sketch pad would not readily work out that this list actually meant: 'Two battleships with 360 degree pivoting cannons and anti-aircraft guns, three cruisers, five destroyers and twelve motor torpedo boats.'

Things became more complicated when it came to transmitting these results to Grendon. Noor had spotted a large deserted warehouse behind her hotel where sailing equipment was stored; but as the season had not yet started no one ever seemed to go there. As she ate her supper that evening Noor chatted with the manageress about the consequences of war on the tourist trade, then she went up to her room. At about midnight she slipped out through the back door with her heavy suitcase. It had taken her two hours to encode the message even though it was not long, because she had to be absolutely meticulous with the ciphering: one little mistake would have thrown the recipients into confusion and she would have had to send the entire message again another day.

The warehouse was just off the little courtyard at the back of the hotel. Noor was hampered by the suitcase and had trouble scaling the fence before making her way to the building. The door was locked but she had learned how to pick a simple lock with a piece of wire from her lessons with the rather colourful 'Professor of Breaking and Entering' at Beaulieu. It was dark inside but the moonlight sifted in through a series of fanlights. She made her way round the masts and sails, and climbed a few steps up into the workshop area, which smelt of wood and glue and was cluttered with ropes and spars. There was a window which looked out onto the street, and by the light of the moon Noor opened the suitcase and strung the ten feet of fine wire which constituted the antenna round the room. When she switched the Mark II on, the tiny red bulbs seemed to throw a terrifying amount of light onto the walls, so she covered them with her handkerchief. The light still filtered through but not with such brilliance. Noor could already feel great drops of sweat running down her forehead and falling onto the black Bakelite surface of the radio.

The first SOE radios introduced in 1941 operated on mains electricity. A crucial mistake: once the Germans had identified which area the transmission was coming from they had simply to cut the power supply to one building at a time for a few seconds. When the transmission suddenly stopped and then started again just moments later, they had located the building. Hence the addition of batteries to the new transmitters like the Mark II. Noor took out the two pieces of quartz which would determine the frequency of the transmission. She used the lid of the open case as a book rest for her notebook, put the handset with its built-in key to one side of the transmitter, and sent out her call sign. The high-pitched ditty of the Morse code echoed through the hangar and sounded louder to her than a blaring alarm bell. She switched to listening mode and glanced outside. The road was deserted; all she could see in front of her was a long windowless wall interrupted by a gateway sealed with a pair of massive iron doors.

Grendon replied with the prearranged code: she could begin her transmission. Noor looked up at her notebook, where she had written the encoded message, but she had to take her handkerchief off the bulbs and bring the book closer in order to read it. The white walls reflected the eerie reddish light; anyone walking past in the street who happened to look up would see the glow and raise the alarm. But Noor had no choice. Even though her mind was paralysed with fear and the infernal racket of the Morse seemed to carve right into her, she launched into transmitting her coded message. The Bakelite was splattered with droplets of sweat. She had assessed that it would take about ten minutes to send all the information – the list of vessels, the arms on board, their positions in the harbour and a few details about how they were guarded – and this was comfortably within the usual security limit of twenty-five minutes.

Five minutes later she heard a long mechanical grinding sound in the street outside. Noor glanced out of the window and shuddered: the double-doors had been opened, and she watched as three lorries sped out through them under a harsh over-head light. Two of them turned left, the other right. A metal loop started to rotate on the roof of each lorry, somewhere just above the driver – these were the detector antennae she had heard so much about.

She immediately broke off her transmission and worried at her bottom lip with her teeth as she thought what to do. The terrible and ridiculous truth dawned on her: she had taken a room too close to the harbour. The featureless wall on the other side of the street was the security wall round the naval compound, and, as in all military bases, they had listening-out posts and detector lorries. The sudden appearance of radio communication on British territory that could not be accounted for had raised the alarm. In the space of two minutes the various listening posts had used a system of triangulation to track the point of transmission to Portsmouth, and had warned the mobile detection unit, which had gone straight to work under the very eyes of the terrified culprit. The three lorries were now taking up positions so that they could plot her location. They did not know exactly where the transmitter was, but if the transmission continued the whole area would be cordoned off by the military police within ten minutes.

Noor leapt to her feet and, with her heart pounding uncomfortably, took down the antenna, packed it away, put the handset back into its compartment and closed the case. But she had not wound the antenna up properly and it spilled out on the right-hand side so that she could not shut the case. Noor swore under her breath, and coiled it up again. With the case shut tight she hurried down the little staircase, opened the door and listened. She could no longer hear the lorries, but the lights were still on on the other side of the wall. Noor closed the door again and headed towards the back of the hangar and the wire fence. By half past one she was back in bed with her eyes locked onto the window and her ears bristling at the least sound as she shook convulsively. She expected to hear the military police arriving in their cars at any moment, to hear shouting and hammering on her door. Then she tried to reason with herself: she had transmitted for only a few minutes and had stopped transmitting as soon as she saw the lorries. They must have driven out and parked on the outskirts of the town, waiting for the transmission to start again so that they could establish where it was coming from. All she had to do was lie low, the danger would pass.

At four o'clock there was still nothing, but Noor was too agitated to sleep. She had to sleep, though, and she decided to use one of the pills she had been given by the doctors at Beaulieu. She took out her sponge bag but, fumbling in the dark, she spilled its contents on the floor. She had to switch on the light and pick up the pills, which she then laid out on the bedside table. For a moment she panicked: the sleeping pills were mixed in amongst powerful, Benzedrine-based stimulants and a cyanide pill. It would be just as well not to get it wrong. Noor went back over the mnemonic designed to avoid any confusion: blue for bed, red for action, black for death. Not complicated. She swallowed half a blue pill and switched the light off. The sleeping pill was too strong: she was woken at four o'clock in the afternoon by the landlady drumming on the door, worried that she had been taken ill. She reassured the woman, got up and went out, ravenously hungry. Still bleary from the pill, she sat in front of a big cup of hot coffee in a fish and chip shop where retired fishermen sat playing cards and regaling each other in their booming voices, and she thought about what she should do next. She would have to move to another town to throw them off her trail.

She went back to the hotel and paid for her room, and then took the train to Southampton, which was just twenty minutes away. She took a room in a little bed and breakfast on the outskirts of the town, a long way from the harbour. The next day she wanted to hire a bicycle but none of the hire companies was open because it was not the summer season. In the end she bought an old one from a garage, and she scoured the town with its red-brick walls and its tired-looking window displays. It was a long search: empty warehouses were few and far between. She ventured onto a couple of construction sites but each time a watchman appeared from nowhere and chivvied her away. The town's parks were no less deserted. She wondered whether it would be easiest to make her transmission from the bed and breakfast, but then she remembered the appalling noise the Morse code made in the quiet of the night.

The following day she went further afield, outside Southampton, with her case attached to the back of her bicycle. The first field she saw was full of cows, who came over and sniffed at her within minutes of her hopping over the fence. The second was too close to a farm. The third was perfect, but a farm worker suddenly materialised just as she was about to unravel the antenna. She only just had time to shut the suitcase and jump back on her bike. She was furious and decided that England was an over-populated country where it was impossible to spend more than ten minutes on your own. At about five o'clock in the evening she made a decision. She was pedalling up a hill which culminated in a thick wooded area, and she found a path which disappeared into the under-growth. A hundred yards further on she came across two forestry workers, who stopped and stared at her, but she carried on round two more bends and came to a stop. She was surrounded by the rustling of the woods. She hid her bike behind a bush and waited, motionless, listening attentively. It was nearly six o'clock, and she thought it would be better to wait until night-time. It was not a very big wood and she had hardly been spared from bad luck so far. Someone out for a walk or a wood cutter could arrive at any moment, and she did not want them hearing the high-pitched Morse code. At nine o'clock in the evening, when it was dark, she felt that no one would come out to the woods now, and she determined to make her transmission. This time everything went well: the message was expedited in under ten minutes.

Noor got back on her bike and headed for Southampton feeling light-headed with relief. As the lights of the town came into view along the coast below her, the gates of a level crossing came down in front of her. She stopped but when no train had appeared a good minute later, she leant on the barrier and looked to left and right. No sign of a train. She lifted her bike over the barrier, leapt over it herself and crossed the rails. A shrill whistle stopped her dead in her tracks and she looked round in terror. A policeman she had not spotted until then was staring at her from his sentry box.

'So, going through level crossings when the barriers are down, are we? That's dangerous, you know. You're breaking the law.'

Noor felt herself falter and sway. 'I . . . I didn't see you . . . I'm so sorry,' she said, cursing herself the moment she had spoken.

'Oh, so there has to be a policeman present for you to observe the law, does there?'

'No, no, but I couldn't see a train.'

'That's no excuse. The train's on its way. If you do this too often, you'll be run over. Where have you come from, anyway?'

'I . . . um . . . I've been trying to find work.'

Noor had not looked at a map, and was feeling increasingly uncomfortable. The train hurtled past with a metallic clatter. She started talking again, loudly, pointing vaguely behind her. The policeman thought she was saying something and once the train had passed he went on: 'Have you come from Bingham? That's quite a step!'

'Yes, I'm a nanny but I'm out of work. I'd heard

that there was a family in Bingham looking for someone.'

'All right, all right . . . You've got your papers on you, I hope.'

The policeman looked her up and down with a discreetly admiring eye. Her summer dress clung to her, and her long, bare legs glowed golden in the torch-light. She took her handbag from under the straps holding it to the suitcase, opened it and handed him all her papers. The policeman glanced over them and handed them back.

'All right then . . . but next time I'll book you. Be careful, for goodness' sake!'

Noor counted her mistakes as she made her way back to the hotel – it was a catastrophic list. And that was exactly what Joan Sanderson thought when she made her describe every detail of her mission when Noor returned to Beaulieu. Noor had succeeded: she would not be dropped but she had been very lucky. Of the forty agents sent 'on missions', three had failed. They had come back with a bobby on either side of them and down-cast eyes, to the absolute fury of Spooner, who lost no time in telling them they were dismissed. Noor had escaped this humiliating fate – it was a miracle. The novice spy slunk off to bed sheepishly.

At three o'clock in the morning the door was flung open, the light came on and a voice bellowed: 'Get out of bed, Nora, you're under arrest!' Befuddled with sleep, Noor saw two men in grey raincoats and three armed soldiers from the military police crowding round her bed. Behind them Spooner and Joan Sanderson watched the scene in horrified silence. One of the men threw back the bedclothes, revealing Noor's body, which was scantily covered by her short night-shirt. The other yanked her arm, pulled her to her feet, pushed her through the door and made her walk barefoot through the darkened corridors of the manor house. When Noor struggled and protested one of the police officers grabbed her violently by her hair and pushed her forwards, yelling: 'Silence!' She looked over to Spooner, who shrugged impotently and said: 'I can't do anything, they're quite within their rights . . .' Once they were outside Noor had to walk over the gravel, which dug agonisingly into her feet. She was put into a police car and driven somewhere about half an hour away. The car stopped in a deserted street and Noor shuddered: she recognised the windowless wall in Portsmouth that she had seen from the workshop when she had tried to make her transmission four days earlier. The car went through the heavy pair of doors. Moments later the little group was inside a concrete blockhouse, heading down into its basement. Noor ended up sitting in a bare room on a cold metal chair, with a big lamp bearing down on her and with her hands held together by painful handcuffs. The first policeman stood facing her across a little kitchen table, while the other leant against a wall to one side and watched her.

'Nora Wilson, you are accused of spying for the Germans. You have used your training mission as an opportunity to spy on the Royal Navy and to transmit your findings by radio. If you co-operate with us, you will not be in any danger. If not, you will be shot at dawn tomorrow.'

Noor was petrified. She tried to look at the policeman through the beam of light from the lamp. Her dark eyes were screwed up in pain and brimming with tears. She shook from head to foot, and her fingers tensed and contorted as she tried to speak.

No words came out.

'Speak clearly, Nora Wilson.'

'It's a mistake,' she whispered, looking at the ground, 'I'm not a spy, I'm a British citizen –'

'First and foremost you're a member of a family of Indian rebels,' said the policeman. 'You have infiltrated our Army to serve your cause and the cause of the Germans. Admit it.'

'I have nothing to admit. I'm in the RAF. I signed up so that I could fight for you.'

When he heard this, the second officer came over to her, stood in front of her and slapped her with full force.

'Liar!' he barked. 'We know everything. You went to Portsmouth by train from Victoria. You took a room in Winifred Small's bed and breakfast. You tried to make your first transmission – which we were unable to intercept – from Portsmouth three days ago. You tried again in the Southampton area the day before yesterday in the evening. The transmission came from an area somewhere between Southampton and Bingham. We have decoded everything – the information was of crucial importance to our country's defence. You are a spy, Nora Wilson.'

'I'm not!' she retorted. 'I was on leave,' she went on flatly, 'I was looking for nannying work, looking ahead for when I have longer periods of leave. I need money to help my family. They came to England to fight. My brother has signed up too.'

She was gradually gathering her wits, and Philby's lessons were coming back to her. Her cover. She must stick to her cover.

'This little performance is going to cost you dear, Nora Wilson. A policeman caught you at the level crossing at Saltwood Junction. You gave him a completely incoherent explanation. You had a big heavy suitcase on your luggage rack. Can't you see you're trapped? You have only one means of escape: you confess, then you will be reintegrated and all of this will be hushed up. If not, you will be shot tomorrow morning. We will inform your family and they will always remember you as a spy. Come on, Nora! you haven't any choice.'

'I am a nanny. I went to look for work in Bingham.'

'In Bingham? Oh, I see, in Bingham!'

As he talked, Noor looked round. To her left, in the shadowy side of the room there was a huge mirror built into the wall. The police officer was talking again: 'And who did you go to? Which family in Bingham was it, please?'

'The Starkeys. But they didn't have any work for me. Then I came back because my leave was over. I can assure you there's been a mistake.'

The officer hesitated. 'The Starkeys? I'm warning you that if this is a lie we will be able to prove it. You will be shot tomorrow morning!' And he turned to his acolyte. 'Check it,' he said.

'What, now?'

'Check it!'

They were left alone. Noor had sat back up. There was a long pause, then the man looked at her. 'Why are you laughing?'

Noor composed herself instantly, then she turned to the mirror and stuck out her tongue. The other police officer came back. 'It's true. They did interview a girl answering her description. They wanted to take on a nanny, but for the summer. They gave her a cup of tea and she left on her bicycle.'

The other man looked astonished, and Noor started to speak again. 'Philby was right,' she told them to their amazement. 'You have to stick to your cover. In fact, you haven't got proof of anything. I went to paint on the beach. I looked for work. I came back. That's it. You don't have anything. Everything you do know you were told by Joan Sanderson. She must be there, behind that mirror.'

The two officers burst out laughing, and the door then opened, and Spooner and Joan

Sanderson came in. Spooner was smiling quietly to himself, but Sanderson was beaming. She came over to Noor, took her by the shoulder and gave her a hug. 'Pure witchcraft!' she said. 'You told me you didn't have an alibi, you said you didn't even know where Bingham was!'

'Yes, but I was mortified. And I was worried about the policeman on the level crossing. I went back to Bingham before catching the train. I went and talked to people in the pubs and eventually someone mentioned the Starkeys. I went over. They were very nice. It was the day after the incident with the policeman on the level crossing. But I thought no one would think much about a day's difference. At least I was in with a chance.'

'Right,' said Spooner, 'it's late. The session's over. We're going back to Beaulieu.'

Noor turned to the two police officers. She shook the first one by the hand and said: 'Thank you, gentlemen!' Then she went over to the second and, putting all her weight behind her, slapped him.

A committee met at Baker Street to decide the fate of the recruits. Reports had already been put together by the instructors and directors at the various training centres. Acting on this advice, Buckmaster then made the decisions alone in the presence of all those who had followed the candidates during their training. Bodington had given Noor a eulogistic report.

'I have taken into account the objections that

have been raised,' he concluded. 'But this young woman has demonstrated a great deal of determination. She is a very good radio operator, and she passed the final test despite a few blunders. We would like her to join the Prosper network, which is well organised. I give her a favourable vote.'

'As you will have seen from my report,' Spooner retorted, 'I am dead against her. Miss Khan refused to learn to shoot, which really is going a bit far. She spent her whole time asking astonishingly naive questions. She's terribly emotional. She's just a mystic who has only the vaguest idea of the realities of war. I'd even say of reality in general. On top of that she's built like a Chanel model, or a ballet dancer! She'll be snapped up within a week, I'll wager my next leave on it! And as if that wasn't enough,' he added with a commiserating smirk, 'she writes poetry.'

'Her name is Vijay Khan,' Joan Sanderson corrected testily. 'Khan is a noble title in India. I'd like to remind you that Julius Caesar and Alexander the Great also wrote poetry, Mr Spooner, that's not a criterion. And what if she is beautiful, it puts the men on the checkpoints in a fluster. It's an asset not a handicap!'

'But she comes from a background of people fighting for Indian independence. How can we trust her for a second?'

'She risked her life to get to England,' Sanderson replied. 'Her brother has enlisted in the Navy.'

'Well, let's talk about him! He's refused to carry arms too.'

'He has religious convictions like her. It happens. To compensate for that he's asked to be placed in a particularly dangerous unit which doesn't actually use arms directly. He's on a minesweeper. It's extremely dangerous. There's nothing cowardly about the people who do that.'

'That's not what I'm saying,' Spooner retorted. 'I'm saying she'll be stopped, caught. She's naive.'

'But when we set up our simulated interrogation, she saw through it within ten minutes. That's not bad.'

'I'm not suggesting that she's stupid. Quite the contrary, she's an intellectual. She got out of that one because she quickly realised that it was a mockup interrogation. But, Mrs Sanderson, that's not going to be possible with the Germans. They really do interrogate people, you know. Did you see her at the beginning of the session? She was so frightened I couldn't even hear what she was saying! You're sending her to her death. And you're putting the organisation in danger –'

'These are powerful arguments,' Buckmaster intervened. 'Wesselow, you haven't spoken a word . . .'

'She's brave. She followed the courses perfectly well apart from the incident with the shooting instructor. Jepson has assured us that we can trust her motives –'

Selwyn Jepson interrupted him a little emphatically: 'She has the highest and purest motives that

I have ever come across. She would fight for us without a moment's hesitation.'

'And without an ounce of competence,' Spooner added. 'This is madness. Or murder, depending on how you look at it!'

'It seems to me Philby wasn't displeased with her,' said Bodington to defend Noor. 'And we all know that bravery comes out on the ground.'

'In that case,' retorted Spooner, 'why bother getting a committee together? Let's draw lots!'

'No, no,' Bodington went on patiently. 'It's clear that this young woman wants to fight. She has volunteered three times. We have people from all over the Empire in our army. It's not because they love us, it's because they hate the Nazis even more. And we should make the most of the fact.'

'I don't think that was the point Spooner was making,' Buckmaster interrupted. 'He thinks she is incompetent. Which is more serious.'

'We've sent other agents who were not necessarily more competent to France.'

'Here we go again,' said Spooner. 'Why bother having a meeting?'

'It so happens,' Bodington said, raising his voice a little, 'that we don't have enough radio operators on the ground any more. We are preparing for major events. Communications are going to be absolutely crucial. This Miss Vijay is –'

'Vijay Khan,' Joan Sanderson corrected.

'Vijay whatever you like, Sanderson! What I'm saying is that this Khan is a very good radio operator. Is she running any risks? Are we running any risks? This is war! Prosper needs her. She must go. And that's final.'

Buckmaster had lifted his hand. He leant forward, clasped his hands round his face and stared at the varnished top of the desk behind which he was presiding. Thirty seconds passed. 'Bodington is right. We need radio operators on the ground. She'll leave at the next full moon.'

'You're the boss,' said Spooner. He stood up and went out but before he shut the door he turned and added: 'May she rest in peace!'

CHAPTER SIX

Noor was weak by the time she arrived at Montparnasse station. She was so frightened she had been unable to eat or sleep. Exhausted, she stopped in the buffet for a while before heading for the Métro, but when she sat down in the noisy room with all its comings and goings, she was gripped by panic. She could not remember how to use her ration tickets. Did you give them before ordering? Or was it afterwards? Did you tear off the coupons? She had forgotten. Philby had told her again and again: there are informers everywhere. One mistake would give her away. The customer sitting on the red moleskin behind her could be a policeman, the patron behind the counter an informer, and even the fat woman who was exasperatedly calling the waiter could be. Noor looked at her watch and pretended to change her mind, then got up swiftly and made her way to the entrance to the Métro on the other side of the boulevard Montparnasse, her tummy still empty and her heart pounding.

An hour later she was climbing the succession of staircases at number 72, rue de la Pompe, where the Garrys lived and provided a safe haven for the Cinema network, even though – peculiarly – the building was directly opposite a police station, where an officer sweated in the sunlight as he stood guard. That was where the great French philosopher Henri Bergson had died. Early on in the war the Jews from the La Muette region of Paris had had to come and queue outside this police station to be listed. The authorities had let Bergson know that he would be spared this formality, but he was so enraged by the Vichy government's decree that he refused to accept his dispensation, and took his place in the long queue the very same day, demonstrating his solidarity with those whose religion he shared, even though he never went near a synagogue. It was a very cold day and Bergson was not warmly dressed. After a couple of hours the old philosopher was taken ill. He was dead a few days later.

Noor knew nothing of this little scene, just as most Parisians knew nothing of this suffering that they themselves did not have to undergo. Feeling more confident because she had arrived safe and sound, she climbed the stairs of the imposing, bourgeois building with a bunch of carnations in her hand. She had been told the Garrys were a respectable couple. She pictured Madame Garry as a capable woman, rather starchily patriotic, running the Cinema network with her husband. She had thought that flowers would break the ice nicely. The Garrys lived on the third floor, and she had to go up on foot: in order to make economies, Parisian lifts served only the upper floors during the war. Noor arrived slightly out of breath, and she put her suitcase down on the dark red and green patterns of the carpet. She rang the bell. The door opened and she stood speechless: a very young girl with blonde hair and wearing a light summer dress smiled out at her. Noor felt confused.

'He– hello. This is the Garrys' apartment, isn't it?'

The girl hesitated for a few seconds before saying: 'Well, yes! Come in!', eyeing Noor a little suspiciously.

'Are you Madame Garry?' Noor asked.

'No, I'm her sister-in-law, Émile's sister, Renée!'

'I see . . . Is Madame Garry not here?'

'No, she's gone out. She'll be back in a couple of hours.'

'Oh, in that case, I'll come back later.'

'No, no,' said the girl with an increasingly dubious expression. 'Come in, sit down.'

Noor went into a sitting room with a beautifully waxed parquet floor covered with an oriental carpet. The Empire-style furniture and the seascapes in gold frames gave the room a rather serious ambience. On the right there was a desk with carved feet, and taking pride of place on the desk was a lamp held up by a silver eagle. On the left there was a black-lacquered upright piano set between two tall windows with fine muslin curtains.

There was a musical score open on the music rest. The young woman was watching her, she seemed to be waiting for something. Noor sat on the edge of the sofa, put her suitcase down at her feet and crossed her hands over her knees.

'What a lovely apartment . . .'

'Thank you. It's rather conventional, but it's comfortable.'

'No, it's really lovely.'

An awkward silence settled. Noor looked at her feet, the ceiling, the walls. 'It's hot,' she said.

'Yes, we're having a very hot June this year. But I'd rather that than the cold of winter . . .'

'Oh yes!'

Another silence. After about a minute the girl got up. 'Right. . . well . . . would you like some coffee?'

'Yes, please,' said Noor, exhaling with relief, 'I'd love some . . .'

The young girl went out and Noor could hear her footsteps on the creaking floorboards. The kitchen was some way away. She heard a door close. Why was Madame Garry out when London had warned her that a young woman was on her way to join the network as a radio operator? Had she been arrested in the meantime? Had Noor walked straight into a trap? Noor got up and glanced out into the street. There were now two policemen outside the station. She was convinced they were staring up at number 72. The silence felt uncomfortably heavy. Noor headed towards the door. It would be better just to get out! She would come back. Perhaps . . .

She slunk across the hall, turned the door handle and tried to open the door. Locked. Noor started to tremble. She looked right, left, behind her, trying to find a way out. Then she nearly jumped out of her skin: standing squarely in the entrance to the corridor, with her hands on her hips, the young girl was watching her reproachfully. 'It's locked.'

'I see . . . I wanted to come back later . . .'

'Without saying goodbye? No, now that's a bad idea. Everything will become clear, you'll see. I hope so, at least. Come into the sitting room, please. Sit down.'

Noor thought. There were two policemen standing guard outside. Nothing for it. She headed slowly back to the sitting room, her head held low. Her lips were quivering. Then Renée Garry put on a slightly mocking voice and, talking loudly and clearly, said: 'Was the train from Le Mans late? Had they run out of coal?'

Noor's expression changed completely. This was precisely the sentence that she was supposed to have spoken. It was the password! She had forgotten it. She had thought to buy flowers but she had forgotten her password. That was why the young girl had been looking at her so oddly. She had been waiting for the agreed sentence – hence the whole ridiculous scene! Noor looked at the girl apologetically, then she thought of a solution and said: 'It's true, all the coal's been taken for the Reichsbahn.'

This was the other half of the password, the bit that Renée was supposed to say in reply. The two young women burst out laughing. 'It is you! Thank goodness! But how could you forget your password? I can't believe it!'

'I'm so sorry. I was expecting to find an older woman. I was surprised.'

A door opened and a fair-haired young man came into the sitting room. He had a roguish lock which lolled over his forehead, and he wore a white suit with wide lapels. If it had not been for an air of authority that hung about him, he could have passed for a pupil at the nearby *lycée*, one of those well-to-do young men without a care in the world who was just waiting for the end of the war without foregoing any of life's pleasures. He held out his hand to Noor and spread his other arm in a welcoming gesture. He was laughing as much as the two women. 'Hello, I'm Émile Garry. I spied you through the doorway. You didn't say the password. I was beginning to wonder who you were.'

'I'm so sorry. It's certainly taught me a lesson.'

'It doesn't matter. Would you like something to eat? You must be hungry and Renée never made that coffee.'

The young girl leapt to her feet. 'Come to the kitchen with me and we can talk.'

She smiled at Noor and put her arm round her waist, and the three of them headed out of the room laughing and chatting like three school-children.

'I hope the journey wasn't too gruelling?'

'No, not at all. The sky was clear and the landing ground was good and flat.' Noor preferred not to reveal the exact landing spot.

Renée opened a pot and delved around in it, picking out the black beans. 'They mix real coffee with grilled malt. You have to sift through it! I do think you deserve real coffee.'

'There isn't any left in England. Not for civilians, anyway,' said Noor.

'Will your radio be parachuted in?'

'Yes, not far from Viroflay.'

'We'll go to Viroflay on Sunday. The Adamowskis are having a party, and we'll be there. You'll stay there after that. What would be good for us would be if you made your transmissions from the School of Horticulture. The Adamowskis are used to it. We'll go and pick up your radio then we'll set it up in the greenhouse. Renée or my wife will get the messages to you. I ferry the network organisers backwards and forwards. Cinema covers a large area of Normandy, including the Atlantic Wall. There's quite a lot of traffic! The last radio operator was flushed out. We managed to get him home but we haven't had anyone since. We're glad you're here.'

Renée had finished fishing for coffee beans. She threw them into the wooden grinder and started turning the handle.

'You should give her something to eat straight away,' said Émile. 'The coffee can wait.'

Renée took out a blackish loaf of bread and a grey substance with a consistency vaguely reminiscent of butter.

'I'm sorry if this seems tactless,' said Émile, 'but I can't not ask you this. What are the English doing sending a young Israelite girl to France? That's tempting fate a bit, isn't it!'

'Oh,' said Noor, embarrassed and surprised, 'I'm not a Jew, I'm –' Then she thought better of it. 'Well, I'm not of English extraction, it's true. But I'm not a Jew. Far from it! And all my papers are in order. I even tried them out on the British police.'

Renée was spreading two slabs of bread with the rationed margarine. When she heard what Noor was saying, she stopped and listened to her in amazement. This test with the British police clearly seemed inadequate to someone who had to cope with German police checks every day. Then she went back to her work, adding a layer of grape jelly and handing the slices to her guest. Noor took them and wolfed them down.

'You haven't eaten for a while.'

'No, I haven't. I also forgot how to use the ration tickets. I felt happier waiting till I got here.'

This time Émile and Renée looked at each other surreptitiously and cast their eyes to the heavens. 'But didn't they explain it all to you in England?' he asked with an edge of irritation in his voice. 'I thought you went through rigorous training programmes.'

'Oh, yes! They explained everything to me.'

'You just didn't remember it all . . .' said Renée.

'We had to learn the most incredible amount. Secret codes, how to operate the radio, firing a machine gun, carrying out a burglary and so on. It would take years to remember it all!'

'Of course,' said Garry, not attempting to hide his irony.

Seeing their incredulous expressions, Noor added: 'But don't worry: I passed my exams. It's just, you know what it's like, once you've passed them you forget it all.'

Noor concentrated on trying to lick the dribbles of grape jelly from her fingers. After a couple of minutes, probably suddenly aware of the silence around her, she looked up. Renée and Émile had forgotten all their manners and were standing staring at her open-mouthed, like two statues depicting utter consternation.

CHAPTER SEVEN

Silence. That is what really struck me about Paris: the silence. The Occupation had handed the city back to pedestrians. Cars were few and far between, depleted by the lack of fuel. People travelled by bicycle and sometimes in horse-drawn vehicles. And they walked. They walked endlessly through those streets where there was no longer the hubbub of pre-war traffic or jostling crowds or rush-hour bottlenecks. They walked to the sounds of birdsong in the trees, to the discreet hum of conversation between passers-by, to the gentle whirring of bicycle wheels and the tinkle of bells on handlebars. And, as soon as they left the wide avenues, they walked in silence.

Blainville did not like the Métro. 'Secret agents can afford to use taxis,' he said as we came out of Montparnasse station. We tried to take one of those strange vehicles with gas generators which had flourished because of the shortages. The only way of distinguishing them from the others was a black metal box attached to the nearside wing and a little chimney spewing smoke rising above the roof of the car. There were too many other people with the same idea and we had to make do with a *vélo-taxi*, a little carriage pulled by a cyclist in white trousers and a navy blue sweater, with a red kerchief tied round his neck.

The city sat serenely in the June sunshine. The streets lay wide open for their quiet pedestrian traffic, bathed in calm sunlight. Shadows fell cleanly across the façades of buildings making them look like a stage-set of the eighteenth century. Leaves rustled on the trees, and young women bicycled past with their dresses rippling in the wind. Looking down the rue de Rennes from the station, the bell-tower of Saint-Germain at the far end looked like a lighthouse against the blue of the sky. The lights turned red outside the café Les Deux Magots and a girl on a bicycle came to a stop lightly and neatly next to us. Sitting in the back of the taxi, all we could see of her was her waist cinched into a flounced skirt, and her slim calf as she put her foot to the ground.

Then suddenly everything changed: it was not her stockings which gave her pretty leg its silky, golden glow. It was a thin layer of paint. The strap on her wooden shoe had rubbed against her and revealed a strip of white skin on her ankle. I knew why this made me feel so uncomfortable. The town looked magnificent but it was all artificial, like the young girl's stockings. A cloak had fallen over the city, and her people lived in a vice, down-trodden, fearful and spineless. The silence in Paris was the silence of shame.

The passers-by on the boulevard seemed somehow diminished. They walked along huddled into their worn clothes, carrying empty shopping bags. The grey-green uniforms lounged on the terrace of the Café Flore. There were officers with their red collars and their upturned caps taking photographs of each other on the place Saint-Germain-des-Prés. At the end of the rue Bonaparte there was a bookshop I used to go to before the war to look for old history books. As we passed it I read an inscription which had been daubed across the window in white paint: *Judische Gesellschaft* – Jewish business. Once we were over the Seine and had turned right in front of the Louvre onto the rue de Rivoli, we saw the huge red, black and white banners hanging from the Hôtel Meurice and the requisitioned Naval Ministry. So big, and obvious, and insulting. The W. H. Smith's bookshop where I used to buy English books had become 'The German bookshop of the front'. At every crossroads the roadsigns with their heavy gothic letters drowned the French inscriptions in their shadows. As we waited for a green light on the place de l'Opéra I read a poster on a billboard advertising a show at the Lido, *Asian Dream*. It had been translated into German.

In fact the showbusiness world had not suffered too much from the Nazis' arrival. The theatres were full, the music halls were busier than they had been before the war and the cinemas had it better than ever. Paris had rolled out the red carpet under the Nazis' boots. The rations could barely guarantee survival for France's population of 40 million, but – thanks to a crippling rate of exchange – France was like a leisure park for German soldiers on leave. As our cyclist-chauffeur bore us along, I succumbed to humiliation. My mood darkened at each new discovery. Blainville was watching me.

'Feels strange, doesn't it?'

'Yes . . . Of course, I've imagined it, but when you're here it's different. Last time I was in Paris was in 1939. I remember Reynaud telling the Chamber of Deputies: "We will defeat them because we are stronger than them!"'

'He'll be proved right in the end. The Germans aren't the strongest any longer. The Russians and the Americans are going to crush them. It's just a question of time.'

'And it could be a long time.'

'Maybe not. Even the French have had enough. Ever since Stalingrad they've stopped believing in the Germans. They remember Napoleon in Russia. They like the old Maréchal because they believe he's protecting them. But the scales are dropping from their eyes. They're beginning to realise that the old bugger's a traitor. If it weren't for him our legal government would be in London, and France would be on the right side. De Gaulle is coming to the fore. And, anyway, what they did to the Jews has not gone down well at all. Even anti-Semites can't understand why they're deporting whole families. The compulsory work law is playing into the hands of the Resistance. Our young men don't want to go to Germany. They prefer the Maquis.'

'Will they get up and fight if the Allies make their landing?'

'Yes. No doubt about it. They'll be on the winning side.'

'Well, we've still got to win.'

'It's do-able. The German troops here aren't of a very high standard. The best are in Russia. But we mustn't let them all bunch together at the landing sites. If that happens, there isn't a hope. That's what we're here for. To worry away at them, to sabotage, guerrilla warfare . . . and flying.'

He left the word hanging in the air, his eyes slightly hazy.

'Do you miss the RAF?'

He turned to me and smiled. I knew that Blainville was an accomplished pilot, and he was grateful to me for mentioning his real job.

'Sometimes, yes. It's a cleaner kind of war, when all's said and done. One plane against another and the whole sky for the pair of them. Really, warfare should be an art. The bravest and the most intelligent would win. Like in Alexandre Dumas's books!'

'But we're spies, that's like something out of a book.'

'No. It's a bloody awful life. You'll see, Arthur. We're not soldiers. We're killers. Mind you, we use every kind of ruse, subterfuge, intrigue, the whole apparatus of deceit. Deceit could be a form of art . . . like chess. Or poker. But in Dumas's books the spies aren't sympathetic characters. Look at Milady or Mordred! No child wants to be Milady or Mordred. Everyone wants to be d'Artagnan. I'd rather be at the controls of a Spitfire. Now, that's a proper game!'

'When you go back to England you'll be able to fly again.'

'When I go back? Your bosses want me here. They prefer spies to pilots. That's probably why we're going to win the war!'

After going up the rue de Montpensier, along the front of the Palais-Royal, the *vélo-taxi* stopped outside a porch in the rue Vivienne. As I stepped under the archway with my suitcase in my hand, I read the words 'Jazz Club de France' on a golden plaque. In the courtyard beyond I could hear the warm mellow notes of a saxophone oozing from a long, low building.

'Prosper often has meetings here,' Blainville explained, 'it's a good cover. All sorts of young people come here to perform.'

As I turned to listen to him on our way into the club, I bumped into a young man coming out. 'I'm so sorry,' I said.

'Watch where you're going, for goodness' sake. You're not a German, are you!'

The boy had a peculiar haircut; it was long down the back of his neck and wavy over his temples. He had a very high white collar, his jacket looked too long and his trousers too short, and he was carrying an umbrella which reminded me of the little-mourned Neville Chamberlain's.

'Don't worry,' said Blainville, pulling me into a lobby where there was a large poster graced by Django Reinhardt's brilliantined hair and thin moustache. 'He's a *zazou*!'

'A what?'

'A *zazou*. They're the young half-wits who pretend they don't give a damn about anything, especially the war. They listen to jazz, wear clothes that are too short or too long, and spend their lives in cafés.'

'Aren't they even anti-German?'

'No, they say they're a-political. Which probably means they're for Pétain. There are lots of them here, they come for the swing, as they say.'

'But swing's American.'

'Yes, it's the only good thing about them!'

We had come to the end of a corridor and were standing in front of a door with a red light shining over it. The Jazz Club de France was a Mecca for French jazz, and it had a hall for performances as well as recording studios. Someone turned a key and opened the door. An impish face appeared. It was Derek Darbois, my student from Arisaig. He beamed at us and shook my hand at length.

'John, it's so good to see you!'

'Derek, what are you doing here? I knew you were on assignment, but I didn't know it was for Prosper!'

A voice hailed us from behind Darbois: 'Hello, Arthur, what good timing! We were just talking about you!'

A young man stood up; he was tall, thin and pale with short spiky hair, shaved over his ears, a long face and feverish sky blue eyes. He smiled broadly and held out a slender, slightly shaky hand. Prosper was true to his reputation: he looked like a knight straight out of Walter Scott, so impassioned and romantic. By using my pseudonym he brought us back within the confines of security. Darbois looked at him sheepishly. He had taken the name Oscar in homage to his beloved Oscar Wilde. And ever since then he has only ever been Oscar to me, my brave parachutist.

There were two other men standing round the table in the studio. At the far end of the padded room there were microphones perched on their silvery stands in front of a window through which we could see the recording console. But instead of saxophones on the table in front of Prosper's friends there were three revolvers, two Sten submachine guns and a strange pistol which consisted of a wide metal tube with a small grip built into it, and a primitive trigger made from an ordinary hook.

'This is Vienet and Kerleven,' said Prosper, indicating the two men.

Vienet leant over the table to shake my hand. He was about forty, slightly tanned with a neat parting in his greased hair. He could have stepped straight out of Renoir's film *La Règle du jeu* with his silk scarf round his neck and different-coloured handkerchief peeping from the breast pocket of his linen jacket. He dragged rather affectedly on the long, yellow-filtered cigarettes which he took from an engraved metal case. Kerleven, a ruddy-faced man with a moustache, a crumpled blue suit and a dubious shirt, nodded to me. 'Can we get back to our conversation?' he said impatiently.

'If you like,' said Vienet. 'I want to make it clear that I don't approve of this mission.'

'But Iago's a traitor, for God's sake!' Kerleven retorted. 'It would be quite right to execute him, and you all know it! His interventions on Radio-Paris are pure poison. His speeches are costing us several divisions. He's the most famous collabo-rator in France after Laval! If we kill him the Resistance will prove its own strength and Vichy will take a terrible blow!'

I realised that they were not using the real name of the man they were calling 'Iago' for security reasons.

'If we execute him, they'll kill dozens of hostages,' Vienet cut in. 'Vichy won't take it lying down, nor will the *Milice* or even the Germans. They'll kill at least fifty innocent people.'

He turned to Prosper and added: 'When your people assassinated Heydrich they wiped out entire villages.'

In Prague, the year before, an SOE commando had lobbed two grenades into Reinhard Heydrich's open-topped car. He was second-in-command of the SS, Himmler's right-hand man, and he had been killed, but the Nazis had made massive reprisals. A village that they suspected had harboured the British parachutists was surrounded and burned to the ground with all its inhabitants. To date several thousands of civilians had been eradicated.

Prosper did not rise to the bait, and Kerleven went on: 'This is war, Vienet! We're not the ones killing hostages, it's the Nazis. They're trying to stop us taking action. If we let the fates of a few civilians stop us we'd be paralysed. And, let's be honest, the Germans' crimes are useful to us. They alienate them from the population and help our recruiting.'

'Well, that's a good communist line of argument!' Vienet cried furiously. 'You'll do anything, won't you. But I'm sticking to the instructions issued by Free France. They've asked me to prepare for the landings, and that's what I'm doing – spying, sabotaging and organising! That's what we're meant to be doing. Blindly killing people – that's not for us. The truth of the matter is that the Party wants to take power within the Resistance! And you're just trying to outdo them.'

'We're not talking about killing people blindly, we're talking about execution,' retorted Kerleven. 'As for the Party, it's fighting the Germans in every available way. That's what's upsetting the Gaullists. You want to sit back and wait, Vienet, and that's the truth of it!'

Their voices were rising with each interjection, and Prosper raised his hand. 'Gentlemen! We've been working together for long enough, we shouldn't come to this! Anyone divisive in the Resistance is working for the Nazis. Let me say it again: I don't give a damn for your political ideas. Whoever kills Germans – that's my man. That's England's man. And that's all there is to it. Anyway, I'm the one with the arms and ammunition. And this is what I think: for once I think Kerleven is right. It's time we upped the ante. Arthur's just arrived from London, he can confirm that it won't be long to the landings. We can't waste time polishing our machine guns for D-day. We've got to act now. That's what London thinks and that's what the Allies think.'

He turned to me and I nodded my agreement. Buckmaster and Bodington's words were fresh in my memory. They had clearly passed on their instructions.

'I suggest we mount Operation Iago,' Prosper went on. 'He's symbolic and he's a bastard. You're not going to weep for him, surely, Vienet?'

Vienet was struggling to control himself. 'Of course not! Stop it, Prosper! This is a strategic debate, and I've given you my point of view. But if you're acting on orders, do what you like. I'm convinced that it's our job to prepare for a revolt. That's the line the Algerian government are taking, and so's General de Gaulle. So that's the line I'm taking.'

'You can stand on the periphery, René,' Prosper said as if he were talking to a friend now. 'We need you . . . your contacts, your people. I'm providing you with two professionals, here. I'm providing you with arms, here. But you must do your share of the work.'

'I won't go,' Vienet replied curtly.

'We'll take care of it!' said Kerleven. 'Don't you worry about it! We don't need anything to do with your crooks from Pigalle! We've got plenty of activists.'

'Absolutely out of the question,' replied Vienet. 'The Party won't get all the glory. I'll let you use my people. They may be crooks, but they know what they're doing. That's the advantage! I personally won't go, I don't approve of it. But I won't give you the pleasure of handling it all on your own –'

'Very well,' Prosper interrupted, 'so we're all in agreement. I'll recap. Vienet gives us the information via his contact. He lends us six men – three for the commando force who'll get in, three for the cover – and two drivers. Added to that we'll have Kerleven's activists and our two friends, Arthur and Oscar. But one thing has changed. We're not going to kill Iago, we're going to abduct him so he can stand trial.'

'You must be mad!' Kerleven erupted after a moment's surprised silence. 'You're complicating the operation. It's far too difficult to take him away. He'll put up a struggle. You're putting everyone in danger.'

'Hey, hey!' Vienet laughed. 'All hail the return of the Party line. A murder or nothing! Assassinate! Assassinate! Take it as gospel!'

'If he resists,' Prosper went on, ignoring Vienet's sarcasm, 'then you kill him. Safety must come first. But if we can kidnap him, think of the publicity the operation will get! We'll find a way to get him to London. Can't you see the effect it'll have on the Vichy people! And it would avoid the problem of hostages. We've got to give it a try.'

I was impressed by Prosper's authority. His reasoning was flawless, even if he was adding to the risks. The other two argued on for a while, and then came round.

'One last thing,' Prosper added, 'what you see on this table are the weapons we'll use. You know about Stens and revolvers, they're available at the usual cache. But this pistol is a bit different. It's a Welrod. There's no brand name for it, it's been made specially for our department. This is what it does!'

He took the chunky tube with its rudimentary grip, stood up and aimed at a pile of sheet music on top of a little cupboard on the left-hand side of the studio. I saw Oscar and Vienet who were opposite me tensing slightly as they waited for the explosion. Prosper squeezed the trigger. The pistol jerked but there was only a hollow sound rather like a hammer knocking on a pipe.

'It's got a silencer!' he said, laughing. 'Not bad is it?'

We all started to smile as Prosper stepped forward, leaned over the pile of scores and picked the bullet out from the torn pages. "7.65 calibre, nine possible shots if you adjust the breech like this each time. Ideal for our more discreet operations!'

He handed the gun to Vienet. 'It's a present from the British army. You can't refuse us anything now, René!'

CHAPTER EIGHT

I spotted him almost straight away. He took a vélo-taxi just behind me on the place de la Comédie Française, and I automatically registered the coincidence. Now he was following about a hundred yards behind me. All the way to the rue de Rivoli everything seemed quite normal: two vélos-taxis heading for the place de la Concorde, one behind the other – nothing exceptional about that. But when I asked the cyclist to go over the Louis-Philippe bridge, along the quai Voltaire and then to go back onto the *rive droite* over the Concorde bridge – an itinerary that would be completely absurd for anyone but a tourist – the other one followed us. I paid off my vélo-taxi at the bottom of the Champs-Élysées, and I walked along a tree-lined side-path with my little suitcase in my hand. He stopped a hundred yards in front of me, paid his cyclist and then went and sat down on a bench. How could this be happening? A tail on my first day?

I had infringed Philby's law of behaving completely normally. But I felt that my peculiar choice of route could in fact have been in keeping with my cover. The SOE had provided me with a wealth of Belgian identity papers to explain my slight accent. I was a typewriter salesman from Anvers, a job that sat well with the fact that I had been a journalist: I knew how to handle and repair typewriters, I could discuss different models and comment on new techniques. And a Belgian rep like myself could very well wander aimlessly round Paris to make the most of a long summer's evening as the sun went down slowly over the city.

After the meeting at the Jazz Club, we had gone to have supper at the Jardin du Palais-Royal at the bottom of the rue Vivienne. We had walked two by two: Darbois and myself, Vienet and Blainville, and Prosper had been joined by Andrée Borrel, a vivacious brunette with a bobbing pony tail and a candid eye, who was both his courier and his girlfriend. We reached the restaurant from the corner of the colonnade built by the Duke of Orléans, which ran round the garden and in front of which Camille Desmoulins had harangued the crowd one fourteenth of July. Each of us looked carefully along the rue Vivienne; it was deserted and would have been easy to monitor, but I was sure no one was watching us.

A seventh man was waiting for us at the restaurant. He was Gilbert Norman, a radio operator with an even more feverish glint in his eye than Prosper, and white lips under a little black moustache. This man is frightened, I thought to myself, quite clearly he is drained by his fear. A subtle feeling of anxiety swept over me but it was soon forgotten. We were welcomed in by a jovial *patron* who obviously knew Prosper. 'Here you are, the Maréchal's club!' he said out loud, smiling from ear to ear. He found us a table under the foliage out on the terrace, as far as possible from a noisy table where six German officers were drinking champagne. He brought us a bottle of a Burgundy that Prosper liked and quipped: 'Another one the English won't get!' I was confused and dismayed. Prosper's professionalism was dazzling, so how could he have been so unwise? Not only had he become a regular at an inevitably louche black-market restaurant but he had also allowed the *patron* to guess his own activities? Halfway through the meal the latter really surpassed himself; as he served us a plump duck *à l'orange*, he said loudly: 'And now the *plat de résistance*!' I was the only one who failed to laugh, and Prosper leant over to me.

'You know, we've been in Paris for nearly two years. You do have to relax from time to time. Otherwise, none of us would stay the course. We spend a lot of money, but that's quite normal. Agents can't live like everyone else. If they relied on ration cards they'd always be hungry. They take all the risks – they need some compensations. We live in luxury but tomorrow we might end up in a torture room on the avenue Foch. That's fair. And, anyway, these expensive restaurants are safer than you'd think. The Gestapo would never guess that we go to places full of Germans. That's not where they're looking for us.'

'But if one of us is caught, we all are!'

'You have to learn to trust. Otherwise we wouldn't do anything.'

Just then a paunchy, greying SS officer came in with a girl on his arm who had been poured into a clinging blue silk dress. To my astonishment, Vienet got up, crossed the terrace and greeted them ceremoniously. The officer replied with a pinched smile.

'That's Kieffer,' Vienet said as he came back to sit down. 'About the most unpleasant man I've ever seen.'

He was right. Kieffer was one of the directors of the Gestapo's operations in Paris. He oversaw the bloodied interrogations in the avenue Foch and on the rue Lauriston. Seeing Kieffer, Blainville turned to Vienet and said: 'I've heard the Germans have arrested some important people high up in the Resistance in Lyon,' and Vienet promised to find out. He was the deputy-director of the Compagnie Radio-electric, one of the biggest French manufacturers of electrical equipment, which made all sorts of sensitive devices from machine tools to radio-telegraphy sets. He saw the Germans every day and worked for the Gaullist Resistance. For reasons I did not really under-stand, he had set up his network with a couple of powerful pimps from Pigalle with whom he had connections. These low-lifes provided him with a

112

colourful collection of 'foot soldiers', most of them from Corsica and Italy, and all of them exceptionally proficient. A minority middle-ground party had rallied round the collaboration with Bonny and Lafont, the two heads of the French Gestapo. But the majority, either to preserve their own interests or out of patriotism, had chosen to fight with the Resistance. The bottom line was that the grass roots were less likely to be collaborators than higher circles.

We finished supper at eight o'clock, and I left them and walked along the rue de Valois to find a *vélo-taxi*. It was two hours until black-out time, but I felt like getting back to my hotel in the seventeenth arrondissement. A sleepless night and a tense journey, swiftly followed by a briefing for the first operation – I needed to sleep.

That was, up until the time that I realised I was being followed. I was now heading towards the Étoile with a knot of fear in my stomach. There was still over an hour until the black-out. I had to lose this tail without raising his suspicions, and to think about the implications of the incident. Granted, the headquarters at the Jazz Club still seemed safe: it was after leaving the restaurant that I had been picked up. But to have been spotted the very day I arrived – well played! There was definitely a rotten apple in Prosper's barrel.

After crossing the roundabout at the bottom of the Champs-Élysées I stopped in front of the Confiserie Martial with its display of sugared almonds lorded over by a cardboard marquis in a red coat and a plumed hat. From there I could watch my stalker's reflection in the window. He was standing about ten yards from me, quite unperturbed. He was a very young man with his hair swept back off his forehead, wearing a light suit with wide lapels and patent shoes which implied wealth. The deluxe model state policeman! He stopped at a newspaper kiosk and bought a copy of *Je suis partout*. What a good pun, I thought – not just 'I am everywhere' but 'I follow everywhere' as well. I carried on up towards the Arc de Triomphe doing all sorts of mental gymnastics. How could I get away when I had had no opportunity to find escape routes in advance, no buildings with two entrances, no little back streets? What about the Métro? I did not know it well enough. A museum? A shop? They were closed. A cinema? He would have wasted no time in calling for reinforcements and having all the exits manned. A park? I could lose myself in a thicket of trees or a maze of little pathways. Risky: he would see what I was trying to do straight away.

On my right I saw the entrance to the Galerie du Lido, and I went in, looking for inspiration. At the far end of the arcade lined with luxury boutiques there was another entrance. I could have run through and disappeared in the street at the far end. But my state policeman would then know that I had spotted him. I stuck to what Philby had taught me. I started wandering past the darkened windows as I concentrated my mind. The policeman appeared in the entrance to the arcade, leant against a shop window and buried himself in his newspaper. On the right-hand side of the passage I saw a queue of people, which included a good many Germans. They were waiting at the entrance to the Lido. The officers in mess dress and their girlfriends in evening dress mingled with businessmen in dark suits taking their wives to see the show. There were also several groups of men talking loudly and sniggering.

A little further along on the right, almost at the end of the arcade, a black door suddenly opened. Two young women came out and headed towards me. They wore light, floaty dresses and they tottered on their high platform shoes; they were not especially pretty but they were tall and well put together. When they reached me they stood head and shoulders taller than me, and I realised that they were dancers leaving the music hall. I cut to the head of the queue and asked whether there were any seats left. A quarter of an hour later a uniformed usher was taking me into the hall with its plaster columns and crystal chandeliers, and sitting me down at a table for eight, between two German officers accompanied by a couple of uninspiring girls. I had managed to keep my suitcase, explaining that it had 'all my samples in it', and a good tip had seen to the rest. I headed back into the foyer just before curtain-up. My guardian angel in the shiny shoes was still standing in the arcade, confidently waiting for the end of the show and quite sure that the audience would come out of the same doorway. He must have checked. I went to speak to the theatre manager.

'Is it possible to meet the dancers after the show?' I asked cheerfully.

'Oh no, sir, that's out of the question!'

'Is that where they are?' I asked, winking and nodding in the direction of a side-door I had spotted on my way past. And I handed him another banknote.

'Yes, that's where they are,' he said, putting it in his pocket. 'But I can't let you in there. There's someone on that door after the performance.'

He hesitated, then whispered: 'If you like, you can wait for them outside at the end of the arcade. There's an unmarked black door. That's where they come out. Good luck!'

The band was beginning to play, I went back into the auditorium and sat down at my table. The room was in near darkness and we had been served with champagne. On the stage there were a dozen or so girls dancing a Pekinese-style ballet to the strains of Chinese-sounding music and against a backdrop of pagodas and a peculiarly pink sky. They wore Oriental make-up and black wigs in tall, complicated hairstyles. But their silk tunics were only thigh length, opening and closing to reveal the full length of their legs, and every time they leant towards the audience their breasts appeared where the tunics crossed over.

I waited until the beginning of the next number – a team of jugglers round a woman of Amazonian proportions in a black panther suit and black tights. I leant towards my German neighbour and said: '*Entschuldigung*' as I stood up.

He paid no attention and, crouching in the dark with my suitcase in my hand, I headed for the back of the auditorium. A quick check: none of the waiters who had started twirling between the tables serving *foie gras* had noticed me. I went back up the stairs. Deserted. The staff door on the landing was not yet under guard. I went through it and walked past the doors to the dressing rooms, which gave off a blend of sweat and perfume. At the end of the corridor there was a narrow staircase with a 'Fire exit' sign over it. I went down it four stairs at a time. On the ground floor I came to a metal door with one of those safety locks which you can open from the inside by pushing down on the horizontal metal bar, but which closes again automatically. I pressed down on the bar carefully and opened the door slightly so that I could look through the gap between the hinges without being seen. I peeped out. The young man was still there. He had brazenly sat himself down on the little step at the entrance to the arcade and was reading his newspaper by the light of a sign. He had his back to me. I gently slipped through the door and held it so that it did not slam. Just three strides and I was at the entrance to the arcade on the opposite side to the Champs-Élysées.

I disappeared round the corner and walked quickly to the end of the street. Saved! My tail would try to find me when the show ended, but there would be quite a crush. I could assume that he would attribute his failure to the crowds.

Half an hour later, a few minutes before black-out time, I was climbing the steps to the well-to-do building that the SOE had assigned as my safety refuge in Paris. I had decided it would be better not to go to the hotel that had been booked for me near the place Wagram. The fact that I had been followed did not bode well, and I had to be doubly careful. There were two possible explanations. Either Prosper's network had already completely blown its cover, having fallen victim to the sort of indiscretions I had glimpsed at the Jardin du Palais-Royal. (Perhaps the *patron* was an informer, and had warned the police. In which case, I had been followed because they wanted to find out about the new boy. They would want to watch me, identify me and then decide my fate: leave me and watch me so that I could help them trace the whole network . . . or arrest me). Or there was a traitor in the group of us who met at the restaurant. One of them had tipped off the Gestapo before I left. In that case, the list of suspects was short: Prosper, his girlfriend Andrée Borrel, Norman the radio operator, Vienet, Blainville and Darbois.

Prosper, Blainville and Darbois struck me as very improbable culprits. Buckmaster and Bodington trusted them implicitly. And if one of them were betraying the network why was it still active? If any one of the three were a traitor he would have been able to dismantle it quite easily months ago. Vienet, on the other hand, with his German acquaintances, seemed highly suspect.

Should we go ahead and kidnap the man they called Iago? I went back over the meeting at the Jazz Club. We had discussed only the principle of the operation, but had not established any practical details apart from the strange alliance between communist activists and petty criminals. We were meant to have another meeting with Prosper, Kerleven and Vienet to discuss the plan of attack. I made my decision: the best solution would be to see Blainville. He was totally safe. I would tell him I had been followed and we could decide where we stood.

As I reached the third floor, completely lost in my thoughts, I heard the sound of piano-playing. I rang the bell. The piano stopped. The door opened and a young blonde girl appeared. 'Good evening,' she said, eyeing me suspiciously, 'can I help you?'

'Good evening,' I said, looking at her inanely. I was supposed to say my password but, after all the complications of the day, I had forgotten it.

'Umm . . . oh, yes! The, um, taxi broke down . . .'

'Look, you see,' came a crystal-clear voice, tinged with laughter, 'he's forgotten his password too!'

It was Noor, standing watching me ironically from the doorway to the sitting room. She was wearing a narrow skirt which hugged her waist, and a slightly puffy white top which showed off the golden glow of her arms and throat.

'No, I haven't forgotten it. The taxi broke down outside the Hôtel Lutétia. There you are!'

'And the Germans helped you,' replied the young blonde girl, giving the other half of the password. 'Hello, I'm Renée Garry.'

'Arthur.'

'Come in. You know Aurora, and this is my brother Émile and my sister-in-law Claire Nadaud. We were just listening to Aurora playing Ravel. She's very good!'

Noor smiled and looked down. She was lovelier than ever, slim and golden in her white top, with her straight black hair falling over her shoulders. I looked right at her and she looked back at me with a slight smile.

'Would you like something to eat?' Renée asked.

'No, I've had supper, thank you. But I'm so sorry I've interrupted your concert. Please carry on. I'd love to hear Aurora play.'

'No,' she said, 'you must have all sorts of things to tell us.'

'I hope you haven't had any trouble,' said Émile.

'I have,' I said frankly. 'I was followed.'

He was amazed, and he asked anxiously: 'All the way here?'

'No, no. Don't worry. I shook him off on the Champs-Élysées by pretending to go to the Lido. I wouldn't have come here otherwise.'

'Are you sure?' Renée asked.

'Yes, absolutely, you don't need to worry at all.'

'I hope so,' said Émile. 'This apartment is very well protected. We are the only three people who know about it. It belongs to a cousin who's moved down to the Côte d'Azur. I haven't made it available to the network. London knows about it, and now you two. That's all. But how can you have been spotted on your very first day?'

'A group of us were at a restaurant with Prosper. At the Palais-Royal. The man picked me up as soon as I came out. He was a young man with patent leather shoes.'

'Are you sure he was following you?'

'Yes, I made a bit of detour. He stuck behind me. There's no doubt at all.'

'Prosper is something of a hero,' said Émile, 'but he often takes absurd risks. I've been to that restaurant once. I didn't like the *patron* at all, and I checked carefully that I wasn't being followed when I left. They're too well known there, it's absolute madness. I never went back.'

'Aren't you worried that the network's cover may have been blown?' I asked.

'I don't think so. They would have arrested us all a long time ago. No, they must know that Prosper goes to that restaurant. But they haven't actually dared follow him: they would have been noticed. They tailed you because they thought, being a new boy, it would be easier . . . well, probably!'

Garry's deductions seemed tenuous. I would go over it all with Blainville.

'Did Prosper send you anywhere?' Garry went on. 'Have you been given an assignment?'

'Yes, for Saturday. We're going to settle the details tomorrow.'

'Good. You can live here. But be very careful! We're going to the Adamowskis on Sunday. Aurora needs to pick her radio up. We've only got Norman at the moment and he can't cope with all the work.'

'Yes. And, to be honest, he looked . . . tired to me.'

Garry gave me a quick, knowing look. 'Yes. As you say . . . Cowburn will be there, I think you know him.'

Cowburn was legendary in the SOE. He had built a formidable sabotage network in Normandy.

'I've heard about him. Are we going to work with him?'

'Yes. His network often works with ours in Normandy. We've got a major operation in the pipeline. And you're going to be much needed!'

As he talked I looked over towards Noor, who was watching us in silence, drinking our words with her great, dark eyes. She was sitting on the edge of the sofa and her skirt had eased up over her knees. Then she saw what I was up to and, shyly – almost awkwardly – she sneaked a smile at me as I listened to Garry and gazed at her.

'But you must be exhausted,' Garry was saying.

'We'll talk about all this in the morning.' He looked at his watch. 'Eleven o'clock! I bet you haven't slept a wink since yesterday.'

Ten minutes later I was coming out of the bathroom and heading for my bedroom when Noor came out of her room. She was in a night-shirt, barefoot and holding a wash-bag.

'Good night,' she said when she reached me.

I held my hand out to her. She took it, hesitated for a moment and then leant forwards and looked up at me cheekily. I kissed her cheek, taking a fraction of a second too long. Then I put my arm round her shoulder and she escaped with a giggle. I was left standing in the middle of the corridor as she opened the door to the bathroom. Before she went in she turned and smiled at me and kept her eyes on mine as her beaming face disappeared behind the door.

CHAPTER NINE

Prosper was right: the Welrod silencer worked well. Culioli had made his way slowly over towards the first guard posted by the porch. He had taken out his gun and fired from ten paces away. The guard had slumped to the ground with a sigh. I was posted on look-out twenty yards away on the corner of the rue de l'Université, clutching my Sten in my sweaty hand, and I had hardly heard the hollow crump of the silenced detonation. The other guard was pacing up and down a little further on. When he saw his colleague in a heap on the ground he ran over. Too late. Beauchamp appeared from the boulevard and silently put a bullet in his back. Moments later we were dragging the two bodies into the courtyard. No one had seen anything in the dark street. The Department of Information was silent in the heat of the June night. Everything was quiet. Two more of Vienet's men, wearing Vichy police uniforms, had taken up the dead men's posts. Three FTP activists led by Darbois burst into the guardroom, immobilising four more policemen who were playing cards, and they had cut the telephone lines to the switchboard. Culioli was in charge of the first team.

'Up we go!' he hissed.

Before confirming the operation I had talked at length to Blainville in a bistro on the rue Gît-le-Coeur. He had listened intently to my story with his lock of chestnut hair falling over his forehead and his dazzling blue eyes burrowing into me. He thought for a moment. The tail started at the restaurant: that fact was to be our starting point. The stalker was not very clever: the second clue.

'He's a regular policeman,' he said. 'Otherwise you wouldn't have spotted him so quickly. We'll have to stop going to that place. We've taken too many risks. The Jazz Club isn't under suspicion or they would have searched it already. I'll warn Prosper. They haven't sniffed out the network or we'd all be in cells in the avenue Foch. It's the restaurant, it must be!'

We saw Prosper the following day. He responded forcefully. 'Right, no one goes back to the Jardin. And I'm going to move to another apartment, they could have followed me. Andrée and Gilbert will do the same. But Vienet is strong enough. I'll warn him and he'll sort himself out. Is your friend Oscar safe?'

'Yes,' I replied, thinking of Darbois's boundless enthusiasm and zeal. 'I don't even know where he is. London found him his bolt hole. No problems there. But can we keep Operation Iago going under these conditions?'

Prosper hesitated for a long time. 'The network was set up to act,' he said eventually. 'Obviously there are risks, but we've been living like this for two years. We know that. No, we mustn't let this affect us. Let's do it, whatever they're up to!'

We took up our positions on the rue de Solferino close to the Seine at ten past midnight the following Saturday, outside the Department where Iago – whose real name was Philippe Foligny – worked. Vienet's reconnaissance work was very dependable. Foligny lived there with his family. He went out only at the weekend or to go to the rue Cognacq-Jay to record his editorials for Radio-Paris. He also went to the Hôtel Matignon to confer with Brinon, the Vichy representative in Paris, or to rue de Lille to meet Abetz, who monitored all things journalistic and intellectual in France on behalf of the Germans.

There was no one on the white stone staircase, where our hurrying footsteps were muffled by a brown carpet. There was a doorman asleep at his table on the first floor. I grabbed him by the collar and drove my revolver into his mouth. 'Quiet!' I said as he convulsively showed us he would not move a muscle. The activists tied him up while he swore his patriotism. The way was clear.

At the end of the corridor there was a pair of carved wooden doors. Culioli opened them and I was the first person to go into the office. Sitting at a leather-topped desk at the far end of the room was Foligny, whom I recognised, having studied his face in press photographs. He was bent over a signature book, signing letters. When he saw me with my revolver pointing directly at him, his face changed.

'But . . . but . . . what is this? Are you mad?'

I ran over to him and buried my gun in his belly.

'Not one move! You are a prisoner of the Resistance. You are going to follow us and we won't hurt you. You will have a fair trial.'

Foligny did not move, but I could tell from his expression that he would not agree to anything. He was a man of about fifty in a black suit, with sparse, gleaming hair, and big tortoiseshell glasses, which hid his eyes. His large, hooked nose gave him a solemn dignity, but it was erased by the sneer of his downturned lips. Vienet's men had swarmed into the office, pointing their sub-machine guns at him.

'Stop, murderers!' someone suddenly screamed. 'Stop! We'll have you shot! Help, help!'

It was Foligny's wife. She had been lying reading on a green sofa at the back of the room where we could not see her when we burst into the room. Now she stood trembling with fear and shrieking at us. Her dress floated behind her as she fumbled for a pullcord, which I could see hanging from the ceiling. Culioli threw himself at her. But Foligny had escaped from me and had walked round his desk towards Beauchamp, who was backing towards the door with the barrel of his gun pointing forwards.

'Come on,' said Foligny, 'this is absurd! You've no idea what you're doing. Hand me the gun. You can leave . . .'

'Stay where you are,' said Beauchamp, 'or I'll shoot. Careful, now.'

As if oblivious to the danger of his situation, Foligny carried on walking determinedly while his wife screamed.

'Stop, stop!' Beauchamp cried. 'I'll shoot.'

Foligny seemed not to hear him. He looked at him openly, held out his hand and almost seemed to smile. 'Come on! This is ridiculous. The building's under guard. Give me your gun. You can leave . . .'

'Stop!' Beauchamp yelled.

The shots rang out. Foligny's suit was splattered with red. He crumpled slowly with his arms reaching out in front of him. His head smacked to the ground. His glasses bounced to one side and his wife screamed hysterically. Culioli went over to Foligny and put a bullet through his neck. The body twitched.

'Let's go, now. Quickly!'

'Bastards!' Mme Foligny called after us. 'Bastards! Murderers!'

Culioli rammed her with the butt of his gun and she fell silent. I waited until everyone was out before leaving the body and the woman. She was screaming again. Just as I was about to leave I saw that there was a door open behind Foligny's desk. Standing stock still in the doorway there were two children, a little boy and a slightly older girl, in their pyjamas, their eyes wide with horror.

Foligny's murder caused a tremendous uproar. We managed to get away without any trouble, some in cars, others on foot along the Seine. I ran along the embankment with Culioli and waited under the Alexandre III bridge till the end of the blackout, hiding under the metal girders until dawn. At five o'clock, with our Stens dismantled and hidden in our coats, we left separately and headed for the Métro station by the Grenelle bridge. Prosper's team had certainly demonstrated how efficient they were. The information gathered by Vienet had been excellent, and the whole team had acted with perfect cool. Or nearly. Foligny had been too brave. The collaborating newspapers highlighted Foligny's resistance (the word was used deliberately) and the cruelty of the commandos who had killed him in front of his wife and children. These 'terrorists' and England's hand in their operation were slated everywhere. And the accusations were in fact justified. Vienet could not be faulted for the objections he had raised. By killing Foligny, a mere commentator who had not killed anyone, the Resistance had demonstrated their determination, but they could hardly claim the moral high ground. Right up to the end of the war that murder was to be a key theme in Vichy propaganda. The Germans did not retaliate (they took revenge only when one of their own was killed); they left that to the *Milice*, the unofficial police force set up by the furiously committed collaborator Darnand. Brutes in uniform and Basque berets were unleashed all over France. In Paris and Lyon dozens of prisoners – political or otherwise – were taken from their cells, with the blessing of the occupying forces, and shot.

But Kerleven, who had been in favour of the execution, was triumphant. Politically speaking, the savage response of the *Milice* more than compensated for the negative effects of the nocturnal assassination. Foligny was given an elaborate funeral, attended by Laval and the entire government. A message from Pétain was read out. Vichy usually disapproved of taking hostages, especially if the Germans were the captors. On this occasion the government left it to the *Milice* to use means they condemned in the hands of the Nazis. Vichy was suddenly forced to display its hatred. Pétain was no longer a shield for the French, he was a protagonist in a vindictive civil war. Churchill talked about 'setting Europe ablaze', and Foligny's assassination was in line with that instruction. The SOE was doing its job. I had no scruples about it.

One thing worried me. Security in Prosper's network seemed to be intact. The tail that I had had to deal with had changed nothing: we were able to liquidate a notorious collaborator right in the middle of Paris without suffering any losses. But, before we had decided to operate in the rue de Solferino, we had thought we would take Foligny at home, at Vésinet, in his weekend house on the banks of the Seine. A quick bit of research had persuaded us against it: the house was guarded by a relay of three police cars and there were probably just as many guards on the inside; the door was blocked by spiked barriers; and the walls were topped with thick barbed wire. Culioli and I had had a look round the neighbouring area. The planned kidnapping would have been impossible. We were about to leave when I acted on intuition: I went into the baker's at the end of the street in which Foligny lived. I handed him my ration tickets and bought a loaf of black bread. As he gave it to me I said in an offhand way: 'Plenty of police around here, aren't there!'

'Yes, it's some man from Radio-Paris. You know, *"Radio-Paris ment"*,' he added with a wink. Every day, 'the BBC broadcast a pastiche of 'La Cucaracha', which punningly said *'Radio-Paris ment, Radio-Paris ment, Radio-Paris est allemand!'* – 'Radio-Paris tells lies, Radio-Paris tells lies, Radio-Paris is German.'

'Has he been under guard like this for long?'

'Yes, ever since he's been on the radio. Mind you, the barbed wire's only been there since yesterday.'

I had gone back to Paris deep in thought. A coincidence? Or did the police know that Foligny was a target? In that case why did they not increase the security on the rue de Solferino as well? Perhaps they had not envisaged an attack at the Department, which was a stone's throw from the German embassy in a part of Paris bristling with policemen on sentry duty and German soldiers. They had reinforced the surveillance at Vésinet. That changed everything . . .

CHAPTER TEN

Noor had an anthology of poems in her hand and there was a thick school notebook beside her. On the cover of the book, with its pastel-coloured engraved design, I could see the words: 'Arthur Rimbaud. Complete Works'.

'You see,' she said, seeing me reading it, 'I'm surrounded by men called Arthur . . .'

She smiled at me, her face dark against the sunlit countryside speeding past behind her through the window of our compartment.

'Yes, but I'm not a poet. I'm a killer.'

'You're a soldier, not a killer. You're too kind for that.'

'I'm not kind, Aurora.'

'Of course you are.'

Her dark eyes lit up as she laughed. From time to time the sun peeped out from behind a building or the railway embankment and lit her face. Her delicate features would emerge from the shadows. Through her fine blouse I could see her white bra and her flat, golden tummy.

We were alone in the compartment in the Versailles train, sitting side by side facing in the direction we were travelling. Like a young married couple visiting their parents, we were going to see the Adamowskis for Sunday lunch. Professor Adamowski taught at the School of Horticulture in Viroflay, which harboured various activities of Prosper's network. He made a habit of receiving friends on Sundays, with a good Burgundy and a rabbit stew – the rabbits came from the school's breeding hutches, which had multiplied astonishingly since the beginning of the war. I had voiced my doubts to the Garrys once again. But, as they drove us to the Gare Saint-Lazare (they were travelling to Viroflay by car because it was best to avoid travelling in groups), Émile had reassured me, using all the same lines of argument as Prosper. 'There's a lot of tension around us. We need to meet up from time to time just for the sake of it, when it's got nothing to do with the network. We keep each other warm. Otherwise it would be too difficult.' I pointed out to him that a quick sweep at Viroflay would break down the SOE's most important network in France in one fell swoop. 'If we thought like that, we wouldn't do anything.' Always the same reasoning. There must be some truth in it. I promised myself I would talk to Philby about it if I made it back to England.

We were passing through the station of Conflans. I pointed to Noor's book.

'Do you like Rimbaud?'

'Yes, very much. But that's not why I've brought it with me. The keys to my code are taken from his poems, especially from *A Season in Hell*. A good find for this mission, don't you think? The Adamowskis have picked up my radio, and I'm going to make my transmissions from their house. I've brought my notebook,' she added, pointing to it.

To adhere to the minimum security requirements, the system of double transposition meant that the encrypting keys had to be changed frequently. Rimbaud's verses dictated the order in which operations would be carried out. Somewhere in England there was a radio operator with the same volume of poems as Noor, and she would follow a prearranged system, using the same verses to decode the messages.

Noor was smiling as she went on deliberately provocatively: 'And, to be frank, the Indian poets are better than Rimbaud.'

'What? But Rimbaud's the best. No one has ever been as inventive, as graceful. Just think, he'd never even seen the sea when he wrote "The Drunken Boat". He'd only seen the seascapes in the library at Charleville, but he still managed to depict it better than Byron.'

'Have you read any Indian poetry?'

'No.'

'Real poets don't actually express themselves – God speaks through them.'

'God?'

'Yes, God. Poetry is one of the paths to wisdom. It allows us to reach God.'

She spoke with calm confidence. My unbeliever's

eyes saw red. 'But Rimbaud didn't believe in God. He sympathised with the Commune, and the Commune shot bishops with firing squads. You've got off on the wrong foot with your pious theories. Rimbaud was a genius, full stop. His art came from within him, not from heaven!'

'It's not a theory. Rimbaud was a visionary. He didn't realise it but he was a visionary. If he had realised it he would have been an even greater poet. Just like the Indian poets that you don't know. They write by divine dictation. It leaps off the page at you when you read them.'

'Do you write too, then?'

She turned towards me, wide-eyed. 'How did you know?' she asked, furious.

'I'm very sorry, Aurora. But I ought to admit something to you. I've read your file. They gave it to me at Arisaig.'

'Oh, yes, you're an instructor,' she mumbled, biting her bottom lip and adding quietly: 'They promised to protect my family.'

'They're in England.'

'Yes, but my younger brother and my sister stayed in France. If the Gestapo find them I would never forgive myself.'

I was mortified. 'Don't worry, Noor,' I said, taking her arm gently, 'they won't find a thing. If they get me they won't ask me about that. Anyway, I'll make sure I don't talk.'

'You can never tell in advance. That's what Philby said, didn't he? And you know my name.'

'It's a pretty name. Light of day . . .'

She looked at me and her eyes softened. 'Don't try and dig your way out of it now!'

She sounded happier and was beginning to smile through her anger. I melted on the spot. I could no longer stop myself putting my arm around her shoulders as my heart beat faster. She looked towards me with a kindly expression which I instantly disliked. She pecked me on the cheek and said gently: 'No, we mustn't. I'll explain.'

The School of Horticulture in Viroflay was a mill-stone building with a red roof, set in parkland which was dotted with trees and surrounded by an irregular wall that protected the various forms of cultivation. The windows had red-brick surrounds, and a large greenhouse stood reflecting the midday sunlight in the middle of a lawn. We went in through a forged metal gate which stood open, and walked up the twists and turns of a white gravel drive which left dust on our shoes. We had taken our bicycles on the train, and had bicycled from Versailles to Viroflay between the suburban houses nestling in the foliage. Now we pushed our bicycles up the driveway, crunching the gravel. There were all sorts of trees and shrubs, whose names I did not know, planted on either side of us.

'Did you see the cypress trees?' Noor asked.

'Yes, yes,' I said almost convincingly.

'There,' she said, pointing at them.

I was incapable of distinguishing a cypress from a lime tree, an infirmity I put down to my love of the sea, which distanced me from all things land-locked. This made Noor laugh. 'You're too rational, John. That's your flaw. It's either one thing or the other. Black or white. The sea or the land. Life's not like that. It's more complicated!'

We had reached the front door, but before we had even rung the bell, a stout woman in a fuchsia-coloured jacket appeared on the doorstep. She spoke with a sort of determination, clearly enunciating every word.

'Hello! I'm Hélène Adamowski. Come in! You must be Aurora and Arthur.'

She led us along a corridor with slightly peeling wallpaper, and various sets of shelves filled with faded leather-covered books. The corridor led to the sitting room, which opened out onto a huge veranda. On three sides of the room the walls were completely masked by tall bookcases, with yellowed paper inscriptions stuck to each shelf. Given pride of place in one corner of the room were a globe on a mahogany frame and an astronomer's telescope on a copper stand. On the far side of the room there was a baby grand piano behind a screen. A cello in its tattered leather case had been propped up next to a painted wooden harp. Professor Adamowski rose to his feet as we came in, bursting out of his over-tight suit and with sweat stains on his shirt collar; he seemed a busy, awkward figure, but behind his thick glasses his eyes twinkled mischievously.

'I'm delighted to see you. You've come such a long way! Come and sit down. I think you know nearly everyone.'

As they sat on seats dotted around the veranda, sinking into the cushions and each with glass in hand, I recognised Prosper, Norman, Andrée Borrel, Blainville, Vienet, Émile Garry, his wife and his sister. The men stood up when Noor came over. She went round, shaking their hands. I caught each of them looking her up and down admiringly, and I saw a ripple of jealousy run through Andrée Borrel . . . A tall man I did not know stood up at the end of the seat. He had an aquiline nose, and very low eyebrows, which made him look rather melancholy, although this impression was quickly erased by the warmth of his smile. His long face was framed by a great mane of curly hair, and he had an exuberant, slightly affected voice.

'Good day to you, mademoiselle. Cocteau.'

Astounded, I stared at the stranger. It was indeed the poet, Cocteau. I was absolutely amazed, but before I had recovered from the surprise Adamowski was picking up the conversation that our arrival had interrupted: 'No, my dear Prosper, the Resistance was wrong to kill Foligny. You've seen the results! They've executed dozens of people. And who can approve of killing a father in front of his children? It's such a gift for the Vichy propaganda machine.'

I wondered for a moment whether the

Adamowskis knew that Foligny's assassins were making up their table for Sunday lunch. I soon realised they did not. Despite the sheer madness that this friendly gathering constituted, Prosper had respected a minimal need to keep departments separate.

'This is war, Professor,' he replied. 'If the collaborators want the Resistance to leave them alone, they just have to stop collaborating with the enemy. And if the Germans don't want to be killed, they just have to go back to Germany!'

'Yes, I know. But you can choose your weapons, all the same. These FTPs are too hard, they'll discredit the Resistance.'

'The Communists aren't resisting,' Vienet cut in. 'They're preparing to take power. Our friend Prosper doesn't want to face that fact. He's an idealist.'

'There are Communists in lots of networks,' said Blainville. 'They're always very heroic.'

'They've been heroic since June 1941,' Vienet retorted. 'That's what worries me about them.'

I was still wallowing in the surprise of meeting Cocteau in person, and I watched him as he followed the conversation attentively; then, when he saw it flag, he rekindled it with an impulsive sally: 'But what is a collaborator really, when it comes down to it?'

There was an awkward silence. The false naivety of the question made us feel uncomfortable. Some dragged on their cigarettes, others sipped their glasses of port. Hélène, the perfect hostess, intervened: 'What do you mean, Jean? You must know, they're people we have no respect for who work for the Germans.'

'But I see Germans the whole time. Abetz is always inviting me to the embassy. Does that make me a collaborator?'

'My dear Jean,' Vienet replied a little tartly, 'you could always say no. It wouldn't cost you anything.'

'The first couple of times I claimed I had flu. But I can't have flu every week! Life can't suddenly stop. Abetz is charming and, anyway, Paris can't keep any secrets from him. He can recite Mallarmé just as beautifully as he can Goethe. I'm getting to know them, these Germans. A lot of them condemn Hitler's excesses, you know. The German army isn't necessarily Nazi. The other day Choltitz even implied that the generals could overthrow Hitler and make peace with the Americans. And Choltitz is the governor of Paris . . . and that's not to be sniffed at!'

'Forgive me, my dear Jean,' said Vienet, clearly annoyed, 'I have the greatest respect for literature, but you're talking nonsense! The Nazis are barbarians. They bomb towns, they kill civilians, they deport Jews, they –'

'Your American friends also bomb towns. More than the Germans, I seem to think.'

'You can't make comparisons. They're at war. There comes a time when you have to know which side you're on.'

'So there's a good way of bombing civilians is there?' Cocteau asked. 'I'll make a note of it! To be honest, I don't understand anything about politics. I'm better off doing something I know about, writing plays and poems.' He stopped for a moment, as if searching for a point. 'You have to live,' he went on, 'that's the only rule. The baker makes bread, the wine grower makes wine, the poet writes poems. I don't like ideas, my dear Vienet, I prefer people!'

Seeing that he was being too serious and that he was embarrassing our hosts with his paradoxes, Cocteau changed his tone and added: 'Especially young men.'

Everyone laughed. Cocteau was known for his flamboyant homosexuality, which enraged the bourgeoisie and was an important part of the mythology that had grown up around him. But, despite his humour, he had gone down in my estimation: I was disappointed by his petty, passive attitude. A little voice piped up at the far end of the veranda: 'You can't talk like that if you like poetry, monsieur.'

It was Noor. She had not understood the allusion nor why we had all laughed. She was pursuing the discussion. 'The Nazis don't only want to kill people,' she said gently. 'They burn books, they want to annihilate our minds and spirit.'

Cocteau looked amazed and he scrutinised Noor silently. It seemed for a moment as if he were admiring her. With just one sentence she had

142

reduced his wafflings to nothing. The poet wanted to maintain that poetry was above the mêlée, but we all knew that Nazism crushed every form of culture. Hitler posed a threat to poets too, and to all kinds of artists. This neutrality from someone in Cocteau's position emerged for what it really was: a bad excuse. I looked over to Noor with a mixture of affection and pride.

'Mademoiselle,' said Cocteau, 'I lay down my arms. You're right . . .' His voice trailed away and he gazed out of the window before adding slowly: 'I'm really a social butterfly of a poet. Wilde said socialism didn't work because it took up too many precious evenings and parties. The Resistance does too. I wouldn't be able to fight. And I wouldn't survive without my society life. There it is!'

We watched him, moved by his confession. He turned towards Hélène Adamowski, who was looking at him with a kindly smile, her head slightly cocked on one side.

'My dear Hélène,' he said, 'when your American friends arrive, I hope you'll plead my case!'

'I'll plead your case if you draw my portrait, Jean!'

Cocteau was also famous for his drawings, which he usually signed with a little star. He could get right to the soul of his model with a few bold pencil lines.

'My dear Hélène, if it means I'll be forgiven, I'll do it as soon as we've had coffee!'

★   ★   ★

The conversation over lunch was witty and spirited. Cocteau gave a sparkling account of Parisian society life, the latest plays and the new films. He heaped praise on Clouzot's film *Le Corbeau – The Raven –* in which life in a little French village is turned upside down by a series of anonymous letters. The film reflected the denunciations and the atmosphere of mistrust which were poisoning day-to-day life all over France.

'Now, there's a true act of resistance!' said Cocteau.

'You're right,' Vienet replied, 'it doesn't take much to blow up a train.'

But Blainville disagreed with the poet: 'It's full of people betraying each other,' he said. 'The heroes are pretty degenerate, too, and that's exactly the image the Germans want the French to have of themselves.'

Cocteau retorted that depicting reality did not necessarily imply approval of it. The film was shocking, almost heretical, and that was what made it an act of resistance: its refusal to be conventional and its rejection of accepted attitudes.

'I know,' said Blainville. 'Some people think there's something original and non-conformist about collaborating. I don't mean you, my dear Cocteau, I mean Drieu or Brasillach. They think they're preserving their freedom. They think they're breaking with convention. But they're just traitors and, at heart, they're just base and selfish. They'll be shot when the Liberation comes.'

'But surely you're not going to shoot writers!' Cocteau exclaimed.

'Why not?' asked Blainville. 'The war's for everyone, and that means writers too. They should even be setting an example. There's a sort of beauty in combat. Look at Malraux, he's a writer, he joined up in Spain. He knows how to fly a plane, obviously . . .'

'You're all being too serious today,' Hélène Adamowski said. 'You're talking about politics again!'

The conversation set off in another direction. When the rabbit stew arrived amid exclamations of delight, I started feeling a sort of frustrated impatience. Noor was seated between Vienet and Blainville, and the pair of them were vying for her attentions. They both had the facility of men who know how to please, and Noor was laughing uninhibitedly and gratifying each of them in turn by looking them right in the eye. When Vienet leant towards her he casually put his hand over her wrist. Blainville put his arm along the back of her chair and whispered something in her ear. I found the whole performance profoundly irritating! Luckily, we moved back to the veranda for coffee, and I sat down next to Noor.

'You were having fun,' I said slightly irritably.

'Yes, great fun,' she said, laughing.

She leapt to her feet when she saw that Renée Garry was serving out the coffee. She took the tray of cups and handed them out to everyone, swishing her dress as she twirled between us. Renée went to get more cups and Noor turned to Cocteau and asked: 'Would you like sugar?'

'Yes, two, please,' said the poet with a broad smile.

Noor took the two lumps of sugar, dropped them into the bottom of the cup and then started pouring the coffee, holding the lid of the cafetière. Hélène Adamoswki, who was watching her, suddenly took hold of Noor's arm and I heard her whisper reproachfully: 'Be careful, Aurora! You're serving the coffee the way the English do. In France we put the sugar in after the coffee. Didn't they teach you that?'

'Yes, yes, you're right. I'll be more careful.'

Five minutes later Cocteau stood up, took Hélène Adamowski to one side and asked her to pose for him, sitting on a Louis XIII chair in front of the French windows. Adamowski then turned to Noor and said: 'Come with me, Noor, I must show you the conservatory.'

She went out with him and Norman followed them. They were going to set up the radio set, which had been parachuted in the day before on a spot Blainville had located not far away. The 'Aurora radio' was coming into service. As the group began to disperse, Prosper and Blainville came over to me. 'Arthur,' said Prosper, 'let's go for a walk in the grounds.'

Émile Garry came with us, and we walked along a white pebble path in the sunshine. 'Right,' said

146

Prosper, 'I've seen Cowburn. It's an important operation. Our boys are having a lot of trouble hitting the station in Dreux from the air. It's very well defended and they've really reinforced their anti-aircraft defences; the bombs are falling either on the industrial area or on the town itself, never on the tracks. It would be easier to attack it from the ground. Cowburn has all the equipment we need for the sabotage. He needs men he can trust to make up a cover team. Sabotage using plastic explosives takes about twenty minutes, and they need protecting for those twenty minutes. I've arranged a meeting for you the day after tomorrow in Dreux at Cowburn's house. Well, his operations base, to be more precise. He's very well organised, you'll see.'

'I've been thinking about what you said about the barbed wire at Vésinet,' Blainville intervened. 'It's clear they'd stepped up protection around Foligny. They didn't think we would dare go into the Department offices right in the middle of all the embassies and ministerial buildings. Still, they knew something. But it's not as if there were many of us who were in on the Foligny job. Having said that, there could have been leaks from the likes of Kerleven or Vienet. We didn't know about it . . . This time we must really tighten up the cover team.'

'We're not going to stop our operations because there have been a few leaks,' said Prosper. 'Far from it, we've been given orders to step up our activities. We just have to be more careful. You'll see Cowburn's plans. And just do everything Blainville says absolutely to the word.'

Noor and I went back to Versailles on our bicycles. She pedalled along slowly in the light of the setting sun, and I followed her lazily with my head in the air. She had strapped her radio to her luggage rack. The SOE had parachuted in two radio sets for her, and she had left the other one in the Adamowskis' conservatory. This luxury was not a waste of resources: if they had only one radio each the operators would constantly have to carry it around with them. They reduced their risks by changing the site of transmissions but they would increase them just as much by travelling with the radio. With two radios their comings and goings were not so dangerous.

As we turned a corner on the side of a hill we caught sight of the forest of Versailles in the valley below us with the warm light pouring over the foliage, and we could just make out the outline of Paris in the misty background. Noor stopped, put down her bicycle and walked over to the edge of the hillside. She was silhouetted against the blazing sky and I went over towards her. She shivered. I looked over towards the horizon with her as I put my arms round her waist, and she rested her head against my shoulder.

'You're going off on an operation,' she said.

'Yes, I'll be away from Paris for two or three days.'

We stood in silence for a moment.

'I know you're a killer,' she went on. 'But look after yourself, all the same.'

'We're professionals, you know,' I said in a deliberately solemn voice.

'Yes. But come back. We can talk about poetry.'

I held her a little closer and leant over her. I saw a tear running down her cheek.

'Noor . . .' I started to say. But she pulled away, strode back over to her bicycle and set off without a backward glance. I followed her in a state of complete confusion. That evening, as I went to sleep in my little room in the Garrys' apartment, I realised that, standing looking down on that forest, I had lived a moment of true happiness.

CHAPTER ELEVEN

They clipped the chain round the gates with the metal cutters, and it slipped to the ground with a dull clink. I could only just hear it from my observation post on the first floor of the Hôtel du Bocage. Dreux station stood silent in the darkness before me; I could just make out the rails gleaming in the moonlight. Over to the left where the countryside was bathed in the pale white light, I could hear a cricket calling. Further away to my right I could make out the dark outline of the depot. From time to time the slender, fleeting beams of the commandos' torchlight flitted across the darkness. To my left the avenue Mangin ran from the passengers' entrance with its glass canopy towards the town centre, where it disappeared into the night. I brought up my Winchester to take aim, then rested it back down on the window ledge, next to a long cylindrical torch in a green rubber sheath. My heart was not beating too quickly. My palms were just a bit clammy, as they were before every operation. I had chosen the room on the corner between the station forecourt and the avenue. I had taken it two days earlier with Darbois, who was now out on the landing with his Sten in his hand and his bag of grenades slung across his shoulder. He was watching the staircase through a half-open door. Not a sound. The other three hotel guests were asleep. The owners had shut the entrance gate at one o'clock, and had gone off to bed. They were going to be woken with a start in twenty minutes' time.

Three days earlier we had set off with Émile Garry on the train from Paris to Dreux, and we had walked to Cowburn's house. He ran the Tinker network, which frequently worked closely with Émile and the Cinema network. With money from the SOE he had bought a little house on the northern outskirts of Dreux. It had a garden full of apple trees surrounded by a tall white wall, and it was set a little way away from the other houses. The ground floor and first floor were furnished as if someone were living there, but the basement – which was as extensive as the other two floors – was an arsenal. Cowburn was a short, thickset, rather cantankerous man with straw-coloured hair and permanently knitted brows. He gathered us round a trestle table on which he had laid out all the equipment: rows of hand grenades with their metal safety catches, the inevitable Stens, Brownings and two Winchester rifles with their short magazines protruding over the trigger. One of them had been fitted with long-distance sights. On the apple racks behind Cowburn there were rows of yellow bricks: the blocks of plastic explosive, which gave off a strong smell of almonds. Cylindrical containers that had been picked up on successive parachute drops had been propped against the walls in the corners of the basement.

Cowburn bent down to one of the metal barrels and took out a tapering steel tube with a pin through its widest point, and a metal tag on the pin. 'They're set at forty minutes. You sink them into the plastic like this, then you pull out the pin by pulling the tag. Exactly forty minutes later, bang!'

He had driven the detonator into the yellow plastic but had left the pin in.

'I want to remind you that you must mould the explosive round the axles and under the cylinder. Always the right-hand cylinder. That way the krauts can't use parts from one locomotive to repair another. According to my calculations, it'll take you about ten minutes per engine, at the outside. As there are six of you in the unit and there are twelve engines, that makes a total of twenty minutes. If you hear shooting, carry on. You only leave if you're given the order. By me! I'll be at the entrance, on the gate. Arthur will keep watch from the Hôtel du Bocage. If there's any danger he'll send the signal with his torch and we'll pull back.'

There was a site plan spread out on the table. Cowburn indicated the places as he mentioned them. There were fifteen of us round him, some sitting on either side of the trestles, others standing behind them.

'The cover team is split into two. One half will be in front of the guardroom, there, to the right of the depot. The others will be on the station forecourt, facing the avenue Mangin. Marguerite . . .' He looked up and scoured the room. 'Where is she?'

'She should be coming, there shouldn't be any problem,' said a tall, thin man in a woollen cardigan. 'Something must have held her up.'

Cowburn frowned even more deeply. 'Right. One last thing.' He leant underneath the trestle table, and when he stood back up the group recoiled slightly. He was holding a dead rat in each hand. He smiled. 'You'll be taking our friends with you. You're familiar with them, I imagine . . . Whatever you do, don't pull their tails!'

As he said this we heard a sound overhead and then footsteps on the stairs. The basement door was opened and a young woman came in. She was wearing a beige coat and her face was partly hidden by a scarf. 'I'm sorry,' she said, coming over towards us as she put her hands behind her head to undo the knot, 'I was with a friend.'

She shook her black hair loose rather beguilingly, and her face appeared in the lamplight. I experienced the strange shock that her beauty had on people: it was Violette Laszlo. I knew she had landed in France on the full moon before I arrived, but I did not know where. She glanced round the room, greeting people with a tilt of her chin. When she saw me her face lit up into a broad smile. She was about to say something to me when Cowburn cut in: 'Your private life is your own business, Marguerite, but please respect our timings, for God's sake! You wear a watch, don't you? Now I'm going to have to explain everything to you. That's a waste of time. You know that these big meetings are dangerous.'

She lowered her head sheepishly, but flashed me a conspiratorial look when Cowburn went on. 'Marguerite will be posted here,' he said, pointing to a place on the map.

He took the Winchester with the long-distance sights and handed it to Violette. 'That's for you.'

While I stood watch at the Hôtel du Bocage, Cowburn's men had made their way into the depot. The engines were kept in a vast, circular hangar, which looked strangely disturbing in the darkness, each one on a set of rails arranged in a star formation around the central turning plate. The six saboteurs spread out with their heavy bags over their shoulders and started to crawl under the massive machines to put the explosive round the axles and the cylinders. There was one man standing guard by the entrance, and thin shafts of light filtered from a blacked-out window overlooking the depot. Everything seemed to be quiet. The commando unit were wearing dark clothes and rubber-soled shoes, and they had come into the depot at the far end from the guardroom, through the gate the engines themselves used. The

154

Germans were showing no signs of life. A train went past with all its lights out, filling the station with its deafening rhythm. It hurtled off into the distance and the gentle murmurings of the countryside settled again. I looked at my watch. Eighteen minutes past three. It was ten minutes since the chain on the gate had been cut. Another ten minutes or so and the unit would be able to slip away through the back entrance to the depot, on the far side of the rails, where one of the men should already have cut a hole in the mesh fence with his wire cutters.

That was when I heard the motors. A distant thrum at first, then growing louder and louder, coming from the far end of the avenue Mangin. I strained my eyes, trying to see something. A moonbeam passing between two buildings picked out the convoy. It was travelling fast, without headlights. I saw the commanding officer's car, it was open-topped and there were two people in it. The driver was wearing a crash hat, the other man's head was unprotected. Just behind them, towering over the first car, was an armoured car with its barrel pointing dead ahead, and behind that there were several covered trucks. I counted five before turning to look for Darbois. There were more behind them. 'A convoy!'

Darbois hurried over to the window, leant out and then shrank back quickly for fear of being spotted. 'We'll have to call it off!' he said. 'There must be at least a hundred of them! They've got an armoured car!'

I picked up the torch in my right hand, keeping my other hand on the Winchester. Then I hesitated. Cowburn had not wanted us to withdraw if a patrol came along. We had to hold it up, and only give the signal to retreat if the ploy failed. The avenue Mangin was the only direct route from the station to the town, where the German barracks were. Our reconnaissance work had shown that all reinforcements and supplies had to use it. We had the avenue in our sights. Cowburn was taking quite a risk, but it was a calculated one. The problem was that the Germans had not sent a patrol – they had sent a whole regiment. They were creeping up with their lights off to catch the commando unit; they must have been tipped off by the guardroom, who probably let Cowburn's men get into the depot before calling for reinforcements.

All these thoughts streamed through my head and paralysed any form of decision. A few more seconds and it would be too late: the convoy was about to arrive in front of the station. It would then be free to spread out and trap our men. I aimed my torch at the depot gates where I knew that Cowburn would be watching me anxiously, having heard the engines. I did not have time to touch the switch to make a signal. A gunshot echoed round the square. At the same time I saw a little blue flame coming from the main entrance to the station, just opposite me. I turned back to look at the avenue. Ten yards from me I could see the driver of the first car slumped over his steering wheel with a big patch of dark brown where his nose should have been. On the second gunshot a piece of skull flew in the air and the officer was thrown backwards in his seat. The car slowed and ground to a halt diagonally across the road, blocked by the pavement.

Violette Laszlo had not hesitated for a moment. She had been hiding in the station concourse since two o'clock and she had located a position from which she could take aim down the avenue. When she saw the Germans she had opened fire without stopping to ask herself any questions. Granted, from where she was in the station, she could not appreciate – as we could from our vantage point – how big the convoy was. She was more than a hundred yards from the soldiers, who had not heard the gunshots through the sound of the engines. Once they were in her sights, the two men had not stood a chance.

A silhouette popped up out of the top of the armoured car, and I heard an anguished cry: '*Was? Was ist denn los? Obersturmführer!*'

Recovering my senses, I aimed at him and fired three times. The silhouette fell to one side. The body stayed sprawled over the top of the vehicle, half out of the little trap door.

With my Winchester still poised, I yelled at Darbois: 'The armoured car! Quick!'

He launched himself down the stairs. The convoy was now blocked by the first car and had come to a halt. We could hear men calling from further down the line. They wanted to get out of the lorries. Two men, bent double and clutching their machine guns, slunk up the line to the first car. This time I had not even had time to adjust my rifle when I heard two gunshots from the station. The first soldier fell flat on his face and, seeing this, the other one tried to hide. He was not quick enough. The second shot went straight through his thigh as he threw himself to the ground between two lorries. He started to scream, writhing and quivering on the ground. Violette was shooting a large-bore. I heard bursts of machine-gun fire from the back of the convoy. The second cover team was also attacking it. I could hear cries from the other lorries, then orders shouted to the head of the column. The armoured car started to manoeuvre itself free so that it could move on towards the station.

It was not fast enough. Darbois and I had spent a lot of time reconnoitring the area. Beyond the hotel on the corner, the avenue Mangin was lined with tight-knit rows of red brick workmen's bunga-lows with little gardens at the back. There were just narrow passages between them providing access from the street to the gardens, which were separated by low hedges. Darbois raced out of the hotel (having bumped into the bleary, pyjama-clad owner as he emerged from his room), leapt over three of these hedges and went along one of the passageways towards the street, just behind where the armoured car was. He jumped out, aiming his Sten straight in front of him at shoulder height. He ran towards the lorry behind the armoured car and fired two bursts, one at the driver who collapsed, and the other at the tarpaulin over the back. There were screams from inside the lorry.

I could imagine the soldiers who would have been sitting on the benches facing each other, now floundering on the floor of the lorry amongst the wounded. Darbois dropped his Sten so that it hung down his side on a strap, and he buried his hand in his bag. A German helmet appeared from behind the lorry. I fired three times. The soldier backed away. Covered by my fire, Darbois took a grenade, walked right up to the armoured car, coolly counted up to four and, as if he were tossing an apple into a basket, he plopped the grenade through the trap door which was still half filled with the body of the soldier I had killed. Darbois threw himself to the ground. The explosion was instantaneous. Flames sprang out of the vehicle's narrow windows, and its gun barrel was launched forward by the force of the explosion. A plume of smoke billowed from the trap door as Darbois scuttled back into the passageway.

Another two gunshots rang out from the station, which was still completely dark. A lorry suddenly slewed to a halt. Unable to make out human targets, Violette was aiming at the tyres. There were soldiers lying under the lorries trying to return the fire as best they could, but they were also being shot at by the second team commanded by Garry. I could hear their gunfire over to my right. I realised that Cowburn had given the order to fire at the depot's guardroom to stop the soldiers getting out. The Germans had thought this through well. They had let the commando unit into the depot and had reckoned they would be able to catch them in a pincer movement between the convoy and the soldiers on guard. Which meant that they were expecting us. But I had followed Blainville's warning: we had reinforced our cover teams.

The burning armoured vehicle now blocked the front of the convoy. I could hear the fire roaring, injured men crying out and orders still flying. I looked at my watch. Twenty-four minutes past three. Another five minutes, according to Cowburn's estimations, and the work in the depot would be done.

'Violette,' I called from my window, 'you carry on blocking their way! We'll go to the back of the convoy!'

I ran out to the staircase, then I too came across the hotel owner with his wife in her dressing-gown clinging to him at the foot of the stairs. 'Take cover,' I yelled, 'go down to the cellar!'

I went out into the courtyard and followed Darbois's example, jumping along the hedges. 'To the back of the convoy! They're going to try and come round!' I called.

Protected by the bungalows, which lay between us and the road, we made our way to the back of the convoy through the gardens. I heard Violette fire three times. The soldiers were trying to leave the lorries. A risky exercise. Garry's men had them in their sights. As soon as they were in Violette's line of fire, they were hit. We stopped twice and both threw grenades up and over the roof of one of the bungalows. The soldiers responded to each explosion by firing at the fronts of the houses. I imagined the inhabitants had taken refuge in their cellars. The convoy was paying a high price for the operation. Fifty yards further on we went back onto the road along one of the passageways, and I saw that the last lorry had pulled back. It was turning round to find another route to the station – a manoeuvre which would be disastrous to us. We could contain the soldiers cornered in the stationary vehicles, but if they spread out we would be outnumbered in no time. Garry and his group had fanned out along the other side of the avenue. 'The lorry!' I cried, pointing at it.

Three men lined up across the road and fired their Stens at the same time. The two rear tyres collapsed. The lorry carried on on its bare wheels and then ground to a halt with a terrible screech.

The success of the three marksmen proved fatal to them. Standing with their backs to the convoy, they had become perfect targets. A burst of gunfire sounded from behind them. One of them crumpled to the ground with a cry and lay lifeless. I returned the fire immediately and the other two ran for cover. Darbois threw a grenade. It exploded under the lorry which caught fire. The soldiers leapt to the ground one by one, falling under our fire. All along the column there were soldiers jumping to the ground and firing towards us. We could not hold out much longer. Taking cover under a garden wall, I looked at my watch. Thirty-two minutes past three. I pulled a red plastic tube from my inside pocket and broke off the end. A rocket flare flew sixty feet into the air and a red light sailed down across the sky, slowed by a little parachute. It was the emergency signal to order a general retreat. After firing a few more shots at the soldiers lying between the lorries, we disappeared into the dark streets, each following his own itinerary for withdrawal. After running through the streets for five minutes I climbed into the back of a blue Citroën parked 200 yards behind the avenue Mangin, and I cried: 'Go! Go!' The driver smiled and set off. I could make out a dark, quivering silhouette next to me on the rear seat. As we left the town, the moon cast its light over us and I suddenly saw Violette Laszlo's perfect face looking at me. I took her arm and squeezed it in an act of complicity. She laughed nervously, and her lips trembled. There was a savage glint in her eyes.

There was almost as much fuss about the operation in Dreux as there had been about Philippe Foligny's assassination. Since the beginning of 1943 there had been more and more attacks on railway lines, but this one had taken a disastrous turn for the occupying forces. About thirty soldiers had been killed by a commando unit of just seventeen resistance workers, only three of whom had fallen: a humiliating figure. On top of that, the sabotage itself had gone on to have tragically farcical repercussions. After we fled, more than a hundred soldiers took up positions round the depot. The second-in-command had given the order to go in and attack, to no avail, since Cowburn had withdrawn many a long minute earlier. Then, with the lorries' headlights trained on the locomotives parked round the turning plate, the Germans set about trying to find the explosives as the officers barked orders into the night. One man's thin beam of torchlight picked out a detonator buried in a dark lump of something under the axle of the first engine. Cowburn's men had smothered the explosive in black grease to camouflage it, although they could not completely conceal the detonators. A lieutenant familiar with explosives came over to defuse the bomb. Just as he lay down under the engine, in exactly the same position the saboteur had used before him, he spotted a black rat lying behind the wheel, between him and the axle concerned, and he picked the animal up by the tail to move it aside. Moments later, blinded and disfigured, he was screaming and waving the stump of his right wrist which spurted blood. When they saw that the lieutenant's hand had been blown off by one of Cowburn's traps, the other soldiers shuffled back in horror. 'They've put traps every-where!' they said. One of the soldiers had seen another rat under one of the other engines. Shocked as they already were by the fate of the reinforcements convoy, they were hardly in a hurry to get under the engines.

The second-in-command rang his headquarters from the guardroom. There was a lot of arguing, to-ing and fro-ing, and shouting before the officer finally came back furious, having been accused of cowardice by the fortress commander. He himself lay down under the first engine to remove the detonator from the explosive, under the anxious eyes of his soldiers, some of whom were sure that his attempt would blow the whole place up. He was just about to succeed when the sixth engine, some twenty yards away, blew up in an explosion that could be heard within a five-mile radius, leaping a prodigious six feet into the air. A soldier who had been leaning against it was pulverised. The others, who had been some way away, were thrown to the ground. The officer stood back up and immediately gave the order to evacuate the depot.

Five minutes later the fortress commander, von Litroff, arrived in an armoured car, wearing a long black-leather coat and with his crookedly buttoned shirt collar peeping above his green and red uniform. He launched into a furious diatribe and ordered the soldiers back into the depot. Seeing the men's faces, he stopped in front of the first engine and stood with his legs apart, rapping his boots with his whip. 'Come on!' he thundered. 'Get to work!' At that precise moment the third locomotive exploded just fifteen yards from him. He left the depot carried by two soldiers, grazed by falling debris, his uniform ripped and burned, and his eardrums burst by the explosion. The Germans stood furious but powerless in the smoke and the shafts of the lorries' headlights, and watched the successive explosions of the remaining ten locomotives. Despite the barrages that had been set up, the town's inhabitants had gathered round the station, a crowd of people in pyjamas and dressing-gowns, watching the show. There was a chain of German soldiers holding back the crowd on the place de la Gare, but with every explosion the workmen behind the chain cried: 'Olé!' The soldiers threatened to shoot them to keep them quiet. The following day the Germans shot fifty hostages.

CHAPTER TWELVE

I was looking at Darbois. His fine face, his slight figure, the rather precious way he had about him, his languid expression – there was nothing to suggest the aggression he had demonstrated at Dreux. I could picture him again lunging forward with his machine gun poised as he ran towards the lorry. It took a rare dose of courage to run out from between those bungalows under the noses of a hundred or so German soldiers. And even more to count before throwing the grenade. I thought about the prejudices that dogged all the Darboises on this earth. Homosexuals were thought to be timorous, to panic at any sign of danger and to be congenital cowards. I felt the beginnings of a sense of pride. I had been this boy's instructor, this boy whom every last adjutant in the regular army would have excluded from any difficult action. I smiled to myself as I thought that commando officers – along with priests, doctors and policemen – were probably amongst the best judges of human nature. They saw men as they really were. They assessed them without blinkers.

We were in the train from Rouen to Paris; it had

166

started to rain and the Seine valley sped past us through a veil of water. As we had spent so much time round the station at Dreux for two days, it was better not to leave from there. We had left our weapons in Cowburn's arsenal and, after six hours' sleep in the little house with the apple trees, had been taken to Rouen in the blue Citroën. I had spoken briefly to the head of the Tinker network, and he had told me his thoughts about Prosper: heroic but hardly serious. The fact that the Germans had arrived halfway through the operation was a clear indication of where the network stood, he said. Some people would have to be sent back to England, probably including Prosper, who had run his course; the less trustworthy elements had to go, at least, to flush out the system or the traitors, etc.

As I looked, without really seeing, through the haze of rain at the countryside, I juggled these bitter thoughts with Blainville's warning. Two operations, two betrayals. I swiftly told myself that the two events were different, and even separate. Operation Iago had been run by networks in the capital, the sabotage in Dreux by another organisation, run by Cowburn and completely unrelated to Vienet or Kerleven. This blindingly obvious fact set me thinking. I took out my notebook as Darbois fell asleep, lulled by the rocking of the train. I wrote a list of names of the people who knew in advance about the plan to assassinate Foligny, and, opposite it, those who knew about Dreux.

There could, of course, have been some quite independent indiscretion or betrayal on each occasion. Other people I did not know could have caught wind of the plans. At the bottom of each list I added an X and a Y to represent these uncertain elements. Then I compared the two lists, striking out the names that appeared only once. The result stared me in the face, terrifyingly.

I did not want to believe it. My methods were crude; they took no account of the uncertainties of this clandestine way of life and the grey areas that hung around the networks, especially for someone like me who had only just arrived from England. And yet there was immutable logic in the reasoning. If there were one informer and one alone, he would appear on both sides, by definition. And he was well placed: Prosper had kept the purpose of his plans as secret as possible. One minor player, sent back by the Germans? Perhaps . . . But there had to be two, very distinct from each other, one in Paris, the other in Dreux, both betraying at the same time . . . Coincidence.

I looked at Darbois again. His name appeared in both lists: he had come with me twice. I felt I could eliminate him straight away. I trusted him completely. Then my sense of reason came to the fore again. I had been sent to find the traitor, as a detective tracks down an assassin. I could not make do with just logical deductions. I would have to double-check them. Buckmaster would not be satisfied with suspicion, intuition and supposition.

He needed to be sure. The security of the main SOE network in France depended on my abilities as a sleuth. I looked through my lists again. They effectively gave me a handful of possible leads. I remembered the scraps of news I used to cover before the war. That is how the police proceed too: they mark out a field of possibilities. Then they close off the doors one by one. The last one left open is the one.

Darbois. A thousand objections raised themselves at the very idea that he might have gone over to the enemy. Why would he have started betraying the moment he arrived? Unthinkable. Nor could he have set up links with the Germans in England. If he were to be an enemy agent, he would have had to be arrested, sent back, reintegrated into the network . . . All that in the space of a few days. And how would that explain his total commitment in both operations? Impossible. Then I thought of Buckmaster again. Whatever happened, I was going to have to report back on this mission. He would ask for proof. He would make me tell him everything, down to the last detail. If I missed a single lead, however unlikely it might be, I would be open to criticism. He would say my report was insubstantial and my methods random. And, anyway, the other names on my list were scarcely any more plausible than Darbois. Why should I ignore him? I might as well start with him. Just to put my mind at rest.

★　★　★

He was walking along the rue d'Amsterdam, quite openly. At Saint-Lazare, at my instigation, we had checked that no one was following us. Three return trips through the station concourse. Not one person had changed direction. Not one had doubled back on themselves. I had joined a queue for *vélos-taxis* and Darbois had set off on foot to head up towards the place Clichy. A minute later I had run along to the corner of the place du Havre. He was walking quite quickly.

I had left a good hundred yards between us before following him, my eyes locked onto his back, ready to slip into a doorway if he showed any sign of turning round. He did not look back all the way to the rue Joseph-de-Maistre, which went off to the left behind the Clichy bridge after the Gaumont Palace, and there he went into a dilapidated building opposite the Bretonneau Hospital. I had his address, that was a start.

Having nothing specific to do, I stayed at the end of the rue Joseph-de-Maistre where it crossed the rue Lamarck in the square Carpeaux, which took up one side of the crossroads. I was hidden by a bush but, if I leant forwards, I could see Darbois's building. The rain had stopped. The clouds were breaking up and the June sunlight was bouncing on the wet leaves on the trees in the square. A young woman wearing a hat with a feather, reminiscent of Robin Hood, was watching over two children playing in the sand. She had thick-soled, lace-up shoes. I wondered whether her legs were painted.

Darbois came out at seven o'clock. He went back up the rue Joseph-de-Maistre, turned into the rue Tholozé and then started to climb up the Montmartre hill towards the place du Tertre. He had changed and I could see his dark-brown hair gleaming as if he had just washed it. I saw him from behind but something told me he had put on a tie. When he reached the square he did not even glance at the painters daubing their canvases in the evening light, watched by little crowds of tourists in which I could make out a number of grey-green uniforms. He went over to a restaurant with frosted-glass windows, which cast a warm light out onto the street. A red-canvas sign hung above the façade with the name Les Canons de la Butte. I stood in the middle of the square, hidden in the crowd, in front of an easel displaying a large painting of the Eiffel Tower in bright, garish colours.

The restaurant was set below street level, on the slope towards the Butte. Darbois went down two steps before opening the door. I saw his silhouette inside as he sat down to the right of the door with his profile still clear through the slightly frosted glass. There was a man sitting opposite him, who stood up to greet him. I walked round the square and arrived on the left-hand side of the pavement above the restaurant. Darbois would not be able to see me, or perhaps just from behind as I passed the window. But I was higher up than him and he would not think to look up. So I moved on towards the Canons de la Butte to have a look through the window. What I saw chilled me to the bone. Sitting opposite Darbois, with a glass of red wine in his hand, and with his cap resting on the table beside him, was a German officer.

The place du Tertre was emptying. The painters were putting away their brushes, and the shops were closing up. The only places still open were the three restaurants with their commanding views over Paris. It was nine o'clock. An hour to black-out time. If I waited there I would run the risk of being picked up by a patrol. I could go into a restaurant, but there was not one which afforded the sight lines I needed over the Canons de la Butte. I went back to the rue Joseph-de-Maistre. Darbois would have to go home sooner or later. In the hallway of his building there was a bald carpet leading to a staircase with worn treads. The ceiling lamp threw out a dirty, yellowish light. I did not know which floor Darbois lived on, but in the shadows under the staircase there was a little storage area with a child's push-chair, a broom and a floor mop. Hiding in there I could lean out and see the big metal and glass door with the little buzzer above it. I sat down on the floor with my legs bent behind me, leaning against the wall so that I could not be seen from the door. The building was silent. I could just hear a radio in the distance playing a mournful song about being 'alone tonight'. After about half an hour I fell asleep.

I was woken by the tinny rattling of the door

mechanism. I looked at my watch. It was ten past midnight. I leant forward cautiously. Darbois had half opened the door and was leaning back against it, facing the street. I could make out the dark outline of the German officer in front of him; they were talking quietly. I could not hear what they were saying, but the conversation went on for a couple of minutes before Darbois opened the door by backing against it. Then suddenly, to my amazement, the German stepped forward, took Darbois by the waist and kissed him on the mouth.

The young man broke away, crying: 'No, not now!' Then he shut the door, pushing it with both hands. Through the window I could see the German's silhouette as he hesitated, then turned on his heels and disappeared. I was shocked. Darbois came across the hall and set off up the stairs. I leapt to my feet, stood across the bottom of the stairs and cried: 'Darbois!'

He turned round. His eyes wide with horror, he stood stock still and stared at me.

'I think you owe me an explanation,' I said, 'let's go up!'

He looked like someone whose world was falling apart.

'Come on! Up you go, I'm following!'

I was very wary. Obviously we had travelled from Rouen to Paris unarmed, but I had instinctively adopted a pose in preparation for close combat, with my legs apart, my fists clenched and my arms held a little way away from my body. He was staring at me. 'It's not what you think!' he said. 'I didn't tell him anything! He's . . . he's . . . a friend!'

I took one step on the staircase.

He turned slowly towards the top of the stairs and started to climb them with heavy shoulders as if crushed by what was happening to him. On the third floor he put his hand into his pocket, explaining: 'I'm getting my keys.'

He opened a door covered in peeling brown paint. He lived in a little three-room apartment which looked out onto a dark courtyard. The walls were dirty, the carpets stained and the furniture sparse. He turned round, waved me towards a chair covered in red leatherette with wooden arm-rests.

'I know what you must think,' he said heavily, 'I'll explain.'

I sat down but my face did not soften. I indicated that he too should sit down and I said curtly: 'Go on then!'

As he gradually unfolded his story, hesitating and stumbling on his words, it began to seem credible. He was all alone in Paris; his only contacts were a few clandestine dead-letter boxes and episodic conversations with Andrée Borrel, although he had to take all sorts of precautions before he could meet her. His days were empty and his evenings painfully boring. On his third evening he had walked to Pigalle, which was not far from where he lived. He soon found a bar with blacked-out windows and a pastel-coloured sign, where those who shared his preferences met.

'How did you find it so quickly?' I asked rather naively.

'I'm used to it, I've done it before, do you understand?'

I more or less understood. In every nocturnal establishment the Germans made up a substantial proportion of the clientele. He had met a young officer who had bought him several drinks before asking whether he could see him again.

'But didn't it bother you that he was German?'

'Yes. But he seemed nice. He works in the propaganda department. He's in charge of the newspapers. And, can you believe, he doesn't like the Nazis!'

'A real fairy story,' I said.

He did not pick up on the sarcasm.

'I can assure you he doesn't know anything about me. He thinks I'm studying History of Art at the Sorbonne. That's my cover. And I am actually a student of History of Art. At Oxford.'

Then he looked me right in the eye. 'I like him. And that's it.'

'And if I gave you the order to kill him?'

'You wouldn't. What would be the point of that?'

He was gradually regaining confidence. My voice softened. I was beginning to believe his story. I was looking for a flaw, a weakness. 'How can you prove you haven't talked to him?'

He thought. 'I can't. Except that you're still walking free. But the Gestapo could have decided to wait, not to arrest you straight away.'

'But what do you talk to him about?'

'About everything, nothing, the war, life, the future . . . love.'

He stared at me again with a note of defiance. I realised that I had no means of checking what he was telling me. But what I knew of him made his story plausible. Almost endearing. And if this officer were also an agent who was manipulating him, it would be an extraordinary coincidence. Generally someone 'handling' a suspected spy does not kiss them on the mouth . . . The baroque aspect of the whole affair pleaded in Darbois's favour. We sat in silence.

'John,' he said suddenly, 'would you like a glass of cognac? My apartment is pathetic but I have bought some alcohol . . .' He waited for a moment, and then added: 'Could I ask you something?'

'Yes. I'll try to answer. But first of all, where's that cognac.'

He talked as he got up and opened the badly hung door on a cupboard. He took out two glasses and a bottle of Martell. 'Why did you follow me? Do you not trust homosexuals?'

'No. I want to know why the Germans knew about the two operations we've taken part in.'

'I wondered that yesterday. It's a miracle we succeeded. Cowburn had put his job together well. What a funny man! But they didn't know anything about the rue de Solferino.'

'They did. They'd reinforced the protection round Foligny at his home in Vésinet. I suppose they didn't think we had it in us to attack him in the heart of Paris, near the German embassy. That's why they hadn't reinforced defences at the Department. But they knew.'

He looked at me thoughtfully. 'So there's a traitor, then. And you suspected me. I understand.'

'Yes, there's a traitor. That much is clear.'

'You have no idea?'

'No. Theories. But I can't check them. Prosper is above suspicion, and so is Blainville. Vienet didn't know anything about the operation in Dreux, and neither did Kerleven. Cowburn knew nothing about Foligny. It doesn't hang together. They've been organising operations for months. If one of them were the traitor, everyone would have been arrested a long time ago.'

'The theory that it was me was the only realistic one, then.'

'No. It's the same thing. I could check it. I've decided to believe your story. That's all. In fact, I've been wondering ever since that dinner with Prosper at the Jardin du Palais-Royal. Do you remember it?'

'Yes, we were very careless. I was horrified by the *patron*.'

'No, it's not that. Or not just that. I was followed as soon as I left.'

'Really? And what did you do?'

'I shook him off. But he can't have known me before that. I'd only just arrived. So they'd been informed. Or they were watching the restaurant.

Or someone had tipped them off. Probably from the restaurant, by telephone.'

Darbois sat bolt upright, his expression had changed. 'Something's coming back to me. Do you remember Vienet going to talk to a German?'

'Yes, he told us it was Kieffer.'

'I got up to go to the gents at the same time, and someone followed me. When I came out he was in the telephone kiosk. It was an open one in the corner behind the swing doors, you know, like in saloons in the Wild West. He broke off what he was saying, put his hand over the mouthpiece and whispered: "It's my mother, I like to call her regularly." As I went back to sit down I wondered why he'd told me that. As if he needed to give me an explanation. Then I didn't think any more about it. You reminded me when you said the informer must have rung from the restaurant.'

'But who was it?'

'Prosper.'

CHAPTER THIRTEEN

Noor took my hand. 'Wait! There's something strange.'

'What? I can't see anything . . .'

She had forced me to stop. She dragged me away from the alley, into the trees and shrubs around the house. She was straining her neck as she peered through the foliage, as if trying to make something out. Then she closed her eyes and tipped her head backwards, her nostrils quivering.

'I'm sure of it, there's something wrong.'

'But what?'

We were instinctively whispering to each other, standing still holding on to our bicycles. We laid them down on the grass and moved silently towards the house, going from one tree to another.

We had to send the results of the Dreux operation to London. Noor had already made the transmission once, not from the rue de la Pompe but from a little apartment in the rue de la Tour nearby; the Garrys owned it and they had offered the use of it to the network. The safety regulations meant that the site of transmissions had to be changed as frequently as possible. We were going to the

Adamowskis' house to take advantage of their hospitality and of the conservatory, where the green wire of Noor's radio antenna was set up permanently, hidden among the plants. We were getting close to the cypress trees that Noor had pointed out to me the previous Sunday. I spread the dark-green branches to risk having a look, but I jumped back. Just twenty yards away, all round the house and along the walls of the school, there was a tightly bunched line of German soldiers. They were peering into the buildings while the officers rang the doorbell. There was a grey car and two covered lorries parked outside the house. The officers were becoming impatient, tapping their feet on the doorstep.

Now it was my turn to take Noor by the arm and back away. I put my finger to my lips and pointed towards the entrance gate. Bent double, we slunk back to our bicycles. We lifted them up as quietly as possible and pushed them through the grass to the side of the white gravel path. Once through the gates, we leapt onto the saddles. We started pedalling furiously, and then everything went wrong. The wall was uneven and falling down in places, but we had to ride along it to escape down the little road which led to the main road. We had been bicycling for less than a minute when a German cap appeared through a gap in the wall thirty yards ahead of us – an officer walking along on the other side. He must have been sent to look round the grounds for other buildings. He saw us and shouted: *'Halt! Halt!'*

I accelerated and called to Noor: 'Faster, faster!'

He put his hands on top of the crumbling wall and jumped over to our side. I accelerated even more, but Noor was not following me. The man fell into a ditch, picked himself back up and stood in front of us to block our way, still shouting furiously. He raised one hand towards us and with the other he opened the holster on his belt. If we passed him he would shoot us in the back before we were ten yards away, so I instinctively headed straight for him and knocked into him. He was thrown backwards and his pistol flew out of his hand. He was about to stand up to get his gun when Noor arrived. She skidded to a halt, threw down her bicycle, picked up the gun and trained it on him. The man froze. He hesitated, swaying from one foot to the other while Noor kept aim at him with her arms held out at eye level. Then he started shouting, even louder than before: *'Hier! Hier! Sie fliegen! Zu mir! Zu mir!'*

I was still on the ground. 'Shoot!' I begged Noor. 'Shoot!'

She shook as she pointed the pistol at the man, keeping him in her sights. But she did not shoot. She bit her lip, staring at the man almost helplessly.

'D-d-don't move!' she said.

As I stood up I said: 'Shoot, for God's sake, shoot! The others are coming! Shoot, damn you!'

Seeing her hesitation, the German lunged towards her.

'Shoot, Noor, I beg you. You'll have us arrested. Shoot, for God's sake!'

She suddenly made up her mind. She squeezed the trigger but the gun remained silent: the safety catch was still on. Then the German leapt at her, his arm outstretched to grab the gun. Fifty yards behind us, on a level with the gates, I saw several soldiers coming out of the grounds. We had had it. But instead of backing away, Noor suddenly ducked to the left and thrust her right foot forwards. The wooden heel of her shoe hit the officer violently between the legs. As he doubled over in pain, she brought her arms together above her head, holding the gun with both hands, and brought it down on his bared neck with all her strength. The German collapsed and lay motionless. His cap rolled a little way away from him and I could see blood on the back of his head.

Noor threw me the pistol. I took the safety catch off, held it at arm's length and fired three shots at the soldiers. One of them was hit in the shoulder, the others took cover behind the wall and called for help. We picked our bicycles back up, and by the time a German started firing at us we were already turning the corner.

Two minutes later I heard an engine starting up. We were pedalling frantically but they would catch up with us in no time. Two hundred yards away to our left I saw the edge of the forest, on the far side of a hedge. 'There!' I cried.

I forked off towards the shadowy undergrowth

with Noor following twenty yards behind. We lay our bicycles down behind the hedge and in just a few strides we were into the trees. I turned round and took Noor's hand, and we knelt behind an outcrop of bracken, watching the road. The grey car appeared, followed by a lorry. We could see the driver concentrating on the road and the officer with his closely shaved temples leaning forwards, hoping to catch sight of us round the corner. They had not seen us slip away and, as they accelerated towards the main road, we could make out their profiles scouring the road ahead of them intently.

'They'll be back in three minutes,' I said.

I dragged Noor further into the woods. I was furious.

'When I say shoot, you have to shoot, Noor. It was an order! You nearly had us killed.'

'I made a vow that I would not kill anyone,' she said. 'I thought you knew that.'

We were walking quickly, pushing through the undergrowth with brambles snagging on our clothes. I kept listening out in case the Germans came back. Nothing for now. The further we got into the woods the better our chances would be.

'Listen, your philosophical rubbish is all very well, but it doesn't stand up in times of war.'

'It's not rubbish. It's a set of rules.'

'What rules? It's all nonsense! Anyway, you did shoot. You didn't think about the safety catch but you did shoot!'

'That was to protect you,' she said plaintively.

'If you'd learned to shoot, we wouldn't have come so close to being caught.'

She grabbed my hand and squeezed it. 'I don't like it when you're angry. Try to understand. I'm not like you, I'm not rational and straightforward.'

She smiled.

'Anyway,' she added, 'Sergeant Keegan didn't teach me to shoot. He taught me close combat.'

Émile Garry and his sister were just going into the building on the rue de la Tour when the concierge came out of his little *loge* and raised his eyes to the ceiling, pointing up towards the floors above. They turned on their heels, frustrating the two policemen posted at the door of their apartment. They walked quickly towards the rue de la Pompe a hundred yards further on. At twenty past six they came into the apartment that Noor and I had reached an hour earlier.

'Ah! You're here!' said Émile Garry. 'They didn't catch you! The Gestapo are in our building on the rue de la Tour.'

'They were at Viroflay too. They nearly caught us.'

'At Viroflay? Well, they must have picked up a fair few from the network. It all happened at the same time. Now they'll follow up their leads. What a disaster!'

'Who knows about this apartment?' I asked.

'No one. Except for you two, my wife, my sister and myself. That's all. The woman it belongs to

184

is in the south. She's a pretty distant relation. They won't be able to trace it back to her. And even if they did they wouldn't find her. She's hiding in the country. And the apartment's not in her name.'

'So we can stay here for now.'

'Yes, you stay here. But we won't. I need to be able to move freely for Cinema to work. If I stay here I won't be able to go out at all. They'll be looking for us everywhere. We'll have to leave straight away, before they've had time to send out descriptions. Otherwise, we'll be stopped at the station.'

'Do you have a good hiding place in Normandy?'

'Yes. I've never used it. And no one in the network knows it. No problem. And, um . . . we're going to get married, Claire and I.'

'Really? I thought . . .'

He smiled. 'No, we're engaged. The wedding's been planned for a long time. It's a pity I can't invite you. The service will have to be a bit more discreet now – very discreet even!' He disappeared into the apartment to pack his suitcase.

'Can't we go out at all?' asked Noor.

'No,' I said, 'except to buy food. They saw us at Viroflay. They must have taken several of Prosper's people. Some of them knew us. We'll have to wait. A week or two. Then, we try an outing.'

'There are provisions here that'll last at least three weeks,' Renée explained.

'But how are we going to make transmissions?' Noor asked.

I thought for a moment. We absolutely had to warn London. Not so much about the operation in Dreux but about the current dismantling of the Prosper network. Otherwise any further drops and the arrival of any more agents could have disastrous consequences. 'Have you ever made a transmission from here?'

'No. I did from the rue de la Tour once. We were going to Viroflay. You knew about it.'

'Never mind. It's a case of needs must. We'll do the transmission this evening, at the radio contact time. Ten minutes, not a second more. I'll write the message now.'

'I'll get my notebook,' said Noor. 'We've got two hours, I'll encode it as we go along.'

Garry and his sister came into the salon, carrying big suitcases. 'Aurora, Arthur,' said Garry, 'it's been a pleasure knowing you.' He was smiling, but the fear in his eyes belied his apparent serenity.

'Before you leave,' I said, raising my hand, 'tell me, who do you think gave us away?'

'I don't know. Funny things have been going on for two or three weeks. The Germans had been warned at Dreux. There were arrests in Sologne ten days ago. The Prosper network wasn't watertight, that much is sure.'

'I've got an idea about that,' I said.

He put down his suitcase and sat on the sofa, listening intently as I explained my theory. I omitted the detail about Prosper that Darbois had given me.

'You have three names in your list of suspects. If they've all been taken this time, it'll all be over. We'll lose the Prosper network. A catastrophe, but a limited one. But if whoever is guilty is still at large and we still don't know who it is, the situation would be really critical. Several networks would be in danger. And no operations with London would be safe. We'd have to find a way of identifying them that was absolutely unequivocal.'

'I'll think about it, but I can't go out.'

'No. For now you can't move. It's too dangerous. They're going to work their way back up the line in the Prosper network. It'll take them ten days, a fortnight. Then they'll take the pressure off and we'll be able to move again.'

He took his notebook out, wrote a few words in it and tore out the sheet of paper. 'That's a *poste restante* address in Dreux. When you're ready send me a postcard with some bland piece of news. I've got an agent in the office there. When I get the card I'll come to Paris. I'll be by the pond in the Jardin du Luxembourg at midday two days later and on the following two days. Will you remember? Learn that address by heart and burn the paper. I also have a dead-letter box through which I can communicate with Blainville without having to telephone him or go to his house. If he hasn't been taken too, that is . . . It's one of the little second-hand booksellers, the last one on the quai de Montebello if you're heading towards the Sainte-

Geneviève bridge. Look in the last box, the one nearest the bridge, and look for a copy of *Madame Bovary*. If there's a message for you, it will have been slipped into the book. If you want to get a message to him, leave it in the book. He'll find it. To minimise the risk, come along the boulevard Saint-Germain and go into the café near the rue des Bernardins. Then you won't be seen from the embankment. The bookseller's with us. If the letter box isn't safe, he puts a poster of Aristide Bruant on the side of the box of books, so that you can see it from the café. If the poster isn't there, then you're all right.'

I took in everything he said, and he went on: 'Finally, you can always ring Vienet. This is his real name and his work number. But watch out, he had close links with the Prosper network. Several people who knew him have probably been arrested.' He handed me a piece of paper. 'Say you're calling on behalf of a M. Joumard. Only talk to him himself, obviously. If the Germans have got him, someone will try to pass themselves off as him on the telephone. Be careful! Look at all the details, learn them by heart and then destroy the pieces of paper.'

He spoke firmly, in a dogmatic way that was completely at odds with his harmless, schoolboy looks. While he spoke his sister had gathered up their luggage. He stood up and I followed him to the door, with Noor just behind me. He turned round and, instead of shaking my hand, he put his arm round me. Then he hugged Noor too. 'Good luck,' he said, 'break a leg. I think that, as soon as they're tipped off, the powers that be in London will tell you two to go back to England. If the Germans have found the whole network, which is perfectly possible, we'll have to start all over again. London will want to have everything under control.'

'I can't go back straight away,' I said. 'I need to be able to answer the question they're going to ask me first . . .'

CHAPTER FOURTEEN

The radio was making a terrifying amount of noise. The high-pitched sound of the Morse echoed through the whole apartment and, it seemed to us, all round the stairwell too. The neighbours must have been able to hear it. We even felt that the policeman standing guard on the other side of the street would be onto us before the end of the first word. Such are the torments of clandestine radio transmissions.

We had hung the antenna round the back courtyard through Noor's bedroom. It was an internal shaft of space, closed on three sides and with metal rungs up one of the walls for roofers and chimney sweeps. On the fourth side there was a garden down below us and a big patch of sky in front of us. The radio waves would pass easily in that direction. By leaning out, I had managed to hook the steel wire over a catch holding back a shutter. Then, moving to another window, I caught hold of the free end of the wire and completed the job by repeating the process on the shutter at the second window, not far from the rungs that went all the way down to ground level. Noor was sitting at a dressing-table, probably Renée's, which she was using as a desk. Above the tilting oval mirror there were pictures of American actors – Clark Gable, Spencer Tracy and Alan Ladd – next to a postcard of Pius XI and a stylised religious picture of Father de Foucauld in his white tunic embossed with a red heart and a cross. On the bookshelves in the sitting room I had noticed Daniel-Rops's *History of the Church* bound in dark-red leather, back copies of the Roman Catholic newspaper *La Croix* and, most notably, the complete works of Father Lacordaire, Montalembert and Albert de Mun, which had very visibly been read. Everyone had his or her own reasons for joining the Resistance. With the Garrys the commitment derived from their Catholic faith.

Noor had put the headphones on and had started transmitting her call-sign with her left hand on the little steel hammer which created the signals when it came into contact with the metal base, and her right hand holding open the notebook where she kept her passwords and her coding keys. The halting melody of the Morse was mesmerising. Noor had suggested that I play some chords on the piano while she worked her way through the message, but I could not play three notes. The sound of the martyred piano might have raised suspicions in itself. In short, we had to suffer this test of nerve, filling the whole apartment with the sound of the Morse and praying that no one would hear it.

I had made the message as succinct as possible: 'Prosper network partly destroyed by enemy. Cinema still active. Aurora radio too. Arthur and Aurora without news Prosper and Blainville. Interrupting activities one or two weeks. Mole hunt ongoing and now essential. Awaiting instructions.' Noor was quick. Her transmission took less than ten minutes, but as I hid behind the sitting room curtains with my eyes trained on the street, watching the policeman pacing up and down the pavement opposite, it seemed to go on for ever. The noise stopped.

'Have you finished?' I cried.

'Yes,' she said, 'I'll have to wait for an acknowledgement.'

Then I heard the click as she closed the suitcase after packing away the headphones, the set itself and the two quartz crystals which she put in a special compartment. 'I'll have a reply in two hours. I think they'll want to reply.'

As she said this I spotted a lorry crawling along the street with a circular antenna turning slowly above the cab. 'Noor,' I said, 'they picked up the transmission.'

'The English?'

'No, the Germans!'

The lorry moved away. The transmission had finished: they could not find us now. But, my God, they were quick!

'I don't think we can make any more transmissions,' I said. 'The Germans must have a detection centre very nearby. They now know there's an English radio in Passy and it's going to drive them mad.'

'We'll go somewhere else next time,' said Noor.

She had come back into the sitting room. I looked at her. The culottes she had been wearing to bicycle to Viroflay hugged her waist, and the wooden-soled shoes lengthened her legs. Her calves were scratched by the brambles and the undergrowth which had saved us from our pursuers.

'Those need looking at,' I said.

'Yes. There's no hurry. I'm more hungry than anything else. Let's have a look in the kitchen.'

As I followed her down the long corridor with its noisy parquet floor, I could smell her perfume, as I had at Vieux-Briollay, the night we landed. I suddenly understood the situation that had been created by the misfortunes of the Prosper network: I was to be a prisoner for a long time, night and day, with the woman I loved . . .

Supper was amicable but tense. We were waiting for the nightly radio contact from London and, even though we did not talk about it, we were thinking how precarious our situation was: two agents cut off from any contact with the Resistance, confined to an apartment surrounded by hostile forces with no means of communication except for a fragile, intangible thread of dots and dashes. Noor busied herself around the kitchen, seeing where the provisions were kept, how the cupboards were organised, how the cooker worked. She cooked some rice with a sauce from a bottle calling itself Viandox, which was very salty. She took an indeterminate piece of cheese from a cloth and found a crate of wizened but delicious apples on the bottom of the dresser. There was a stock of cider in the larder. We were not in gastronomic mood, the meal was merely expedient. I got up to do the washing-up. She watched me with amusement.

'It's nice of you to help me,' she said, 'given that you're such a man of action.'

'We're both agents out in the field. You're not here to serve me.'

She smiled at me, took a pot of coffee from the larder and tried to fish out the coffee beans as she had seen Renée Garry doing. 'There's not much real coffee! I don't know if I should carry on picking it out. In a couple of days we'll have nothing but the ersatz left.'

'Never mind,' I said. 'We need to keep a look-out this evening. Real coffee would be a help.'

She poured the coffee in the sitting room, putting the sugar in first in the way that Hélène Adamowski had criticised.

'Noor, make a bit of an effort. Do it the French way!'

She corrected herself, biting her lip.

There was still more than an hour before the radio contact. The apartment was wrapped in a nocturnal silence. From time to time we heard the sound of a car, very probably a German one, in

194

the distance. We had one light on in the sitting room, it filled the room with a shadowy half-light. The only sound was the curtain rustling as the evening breeze lifted it from time to time. I wanted to go back over the day's events. I had learnt this while working on special operations: every manoeuvre requires a 'debriefing' to release the tension and to give the men an assessment of their courage and competence. They needed it.

'You didn't get him by shooting, but you did with the close combat,' I told Noor. 'I wouldn't be surprised if he was dead.'

'I hope not. I might have hit him a bit hard, but you were pestering me,' she said with a smile.

'If I hadn't we'd be locked up in the avenue Foch. The Adamowskis must be. They're probably being interrogated as we speak . . .'

I left the sentence hanging in the air. A sinister silence descended. Noor realised that it would be better to avoid the subject. 'I have to say Keegan was a very good instructor, even if he did come down a bit hard on me. He was a bit old-fashioned, that's all. When he was telling us how to get a man between the legs he used so many euphemisms we didn't understand a thing. That is until Violette Laszlo said: 'Oh, you mean in the balls, Sergeant!' He went bright red! But he taught us devilishly well. I'm not afraid to go out alone at night now.'

'Noor, can you explain why you made a vow that you wouldn't kill anyone when we're fighting the Nazis?'

'No, not now,' she said after thinking for a while. 'It would take too long. They're going to call in three quarters of an hour. But I promise I will. If you'd be interested.'

'I'm interested in everything about you.'

I said this both gently and solemnly. She sat thinking with a smile playing on her lips, then she seemed to reach a decision. She looked at her shoes and said: 'John, there's something I should admit to you. I like you very much, you know that. I must be open with you.'

She spoke rather quietly, separating out each word.

'Well . . . I'm engaged. He's in the same organisation as us. You may know him. He's called Donaldson. I met him at Arisaig. He's very strong. Like you. And he's good-looking. Like you. I saw him again when we were on leave in London. He was parachuted into France two months ago. He runs the Scientist network with two other agents, a radio operator and a courier. Like Prosper. From what he told me, the two networks were meant to be working together. The day he left we promised each other we would get married after the war, if we ever got out of all this. There . . .'

Every word she had spoken seemed to pierce through me. Seeing my devastation, she came and sat next to me. She took my hand and looked at me imploringly. 'Don't hate me. If we had met earlier.'

Hearing these words, a glimmer of hope awakened in me.

'But we met in the plane,' she went on. 'It was fate. I love him and I want to keep my word. It only seems fair.'

I could not see what fairness had to do with it, but I could feel the resignation spreading through me. It was a question of loyalty – I did not stand a chance.

At eleven o'clock Noor put her headphones back on. This time we could relax: they could not detect us receiving radio messages. I saw Noor's hand moving swiftly across the white page of her notebook. She was jotting down sets of completely meaningless five-letter words. The exercise took twenty minutes. Then she put the set away again. Now she had to do the transcribing. 'Stop looking at me like that,' she said, 'it'll upset me.'

'I'm the one who's upset.'

She smiled and concentrated on her work. She put the words one underneath the other, forming squares with five letters on each side. She wrote the key above them. It was from Rimbaud's 'The Drunken Boat': *'je ne me sentis plus guidé par les haleurs'*. She made the transposition by using the order dictated by the key, then she started the operation. This time the message appeared clearly, one letter at a time. I could imagine Buckmaster or Bodington, contacted at home with the news, leaping into a cab to get to the office in Baker Street, conferring briefly with others to put together a reply, then calling an auxiliary to make the transmission. 'Happy to know you're safe and sound,' they said. 'Archambault tipped us off.'

Archambault was a pseudonym for Gilbert Norman, Prosper's radio operator, whom I had seen several times. I immediately thought it strange that he should still be at large when Viroflay and the Garrys' apartment had been discovered. Whoever gave them away should have given away the radio operator too, he was such a key player in Prosper's organisation. The message went on: 'Prosper apparently free. But network badly hit. Other networks linked to Prosper also threatened. Stay hidden. Mole hunt useful. Traitor at large. Keep going. *Bon courage.*' Despite the clipped telegram-style wording, I recognised Buckmaster's style; he always endowed his relationships with agents with all the humanity and compassion of which he was capable – which was considerable.

'That's all very good, but it doesn't help us much,' I said.

'It's absolutely vital that we don't do anything!' said Noor. 'Let's get some sleep.'

An hour later, lying in the dark watching the rays of feeble light filtering between the louvers of the shutters, I thought of the two messages of the day: London encouraging me to carry on with my mission, and Noor asking me to stop making overtures to her. Two instructions that would be equally difficult to follow.

CHAPTER FIFTEEN

There in the heart of Paris it was as if we were on a desert island: cut off from the world and thrown together. On the first day we paced round the apartment not knowing what to do, reading, writing and cooking. At ten o'clock in the evening Noor put on her headphones and deciphered the message from London. Nothing major came out of it: encouragement and warnings to be careful. Not a word about the fate of the Prosper network. Once we had decoded it, we went back to the sitting room.

'This can't go on,' I said. 'I must contact Blainville and Vienet to see where we stand.'

'Wait a few days, at least. The agents who've been taken have to hold out for forty-eight hours and then they can talk. This isn't a good time to go out. They must have sent descriptions of us to all their police stations. There's one just over the road. You could be arrested as soon as you step out onto the pavement!'

'You're right. But if we stay shut up here we're no good to anyone. It's ridiculous and I can't stand it.'

'You have to learn to accept your fate,' Noor said sententiously, her eyes twinkling maliciously. 'Calm down, I've found some port in the bookcase. The English like port, don't they?'

'We're more keen on sherry.'

'There isn't any,' she replied. 'We're in France, my dear, you should be able to remember that!'

I was starting to relax a little. Noor opened a horizontal flap built into the bookcase to reveal a well-stocked bar dominated by a jeroboam of Gwalynlivet whisky.

'I'd rather have some whisky.'

'A glass of whisky for the gentleman! I'm so sorry, sir, we don't have any ice.'

'You drink it without ice,' I told her reprovingly.

Noor poured my whisky in a straight-sided glass and poured herself some port in a smoked-glass goblet. She raised her glass and said: 'Here's to England! And to Prosper, in spite of everything!'

She sipped her drink, put down her glass and went over to the piano. 'The French say music has a soothing effect.'

She sat down on the velvet stool, with her back arched and her head held high. She opened the piano and started to play. It was a Beethoven sonata, a nostalgic piece. 'The only thing I like about the Germans is their music,' she said over the tune.

She concentrated on her playing, accompanying the tempo with little movements of her head and upper body, and changing her expression as the music gained momentum or slowed. I was hardly a music-lover, but it seemed to me that her technique was good, that she mastered the score so well that she went right to the heart of what the composer had created.

When she finished I clapped and took her glass over to her. She thanked me with a slow blink of her eyes.

'That was beautiful, Noor. It was a bit sad, of course.'

Piqued, she turned to me, put her glass down on the piano and said: 'Too sad? Why should that matter!'

She launched into a piece where the notes bulldozed into each other and the chords shifted in peculiar, unsettling harmonies.

'Who's that by?'

'Erik Satie. You don't know him in England. You're too conformist! I've worked with him.'

'You've worked with the composer? But . . . are you a professional musician?'

'No. I thought about it, like the rest of my family. But then, I prefer literature. But I really liked studying under him. More than with Ravel.'

'Ravel? How did you meet him?'

'He was a friend of my father's.'

'Noor, it's time you told me about yourself. Do you remember, you promised me yesterday. We've got all this time ahead of us, you said so yourself. I want to know who you really are. I keep finding out extraordinary things. You've said too much or not enough. Now the time has come to sit yourself down, Nora Wilson. I have ways of making you talk.'

I stood up, poured her a big glass of port and I held it out to her. 'Go on, tell me.'

She laughed. She stood up, kissed me on the cheek and went to sit in the depths of a brown-leather club chair with her legs stretched out in front of her and her head tilted back slightly. She spoke for more than two hours without stopping and only occasionally interrupted by my questions. I sat ensconced in the sofa, listening to her as I sipped my whisky. By the time we went to bed, long after midnight, I was looking at her in a different light.

'My story,' she said, 'starts in a palace with a hundred minarets and a thousand windows. It was built on an island in the middle of a river in the south-west of India. It's a beautiful, silvery river which snakes through the tropical forest and flows into the ocean.'

'The palace of your ancestors?'

'The palace of my ancestors. It was destroyed.'

'Who by?'

'By you, the English.'

'Really? But who did it belong to?' I asked, shifting the subject.

'A tiger.'

'A tiger?' I asked with a smile. 'One of your ancestors was a tiger, then?'

'Yes. He was called the Tiger of Mysore.'

'Never heard of him!'

'Well obviously, you English have forgotten him. But he managed to ruin your lives. My ancestor was called Tipoo Sahib. Doesn't the name mean anything to you?'

'No . . .' I said slowly.

'Ignoramus.'

'But does anyone know who he is?'

'What do you mean does anyone know? Such ignorance! He played an important part in history. He was an ally to the French against you, the horrible English colonialists. Mysore was a vast Muslim kingdom in Southern India. My ancestor had to find allies in order to fight you. He found them in France. First of all Louis XVI, then the Republic, then Napoleon. He was the Sultan of Mysore. He had a tiger on his flag. The Westerners knew him by the name of Tipoo Sahib. He was a very important sultan, you know, very powerful and very cultured. He had thousands of books in his library and tens of thousands of soldiers in his army. He was a religious leader, too, a Sufi. He was in direct contact with God. Every moment of his life, he was carrying out a spiritual exercise, like Saint Ignatius of Loyola. It all sounds incomprehensible to you, doesn't it?'

'No, no. We have mystics in the West, too,' I said defensively.

'Hmm . . . I'm not so sure. You with your rational thinking, you think mystics are people who float a foot off the ground all day and who sleep on a bed of nails at night.'

'I imagine the Tiger of Mysore didn't sleep on a bed of nails.'

'My ancestor slept on a feather bed with two or three of his thirty wives. He was fanned by slaves, but he had a highly developed sense of religion. In his day there was true respect. Thieves had their hands cut off and women who committed adultery were stoned. Anyone who did not share the sultan's theological views was impaled.'

Noor was smiling at me with an ironic glint in her eye.

'It was a time,' she went on, laughing as she spoke, 'when people stuck to their principles.'

'Do you share their principles?'

'No. We put a bit of water in our wine. Our contact with the West has diluted us.'

'Why was he at war with us?'

'But it was you who were at war with him. It was you who conquered India. The sultan is a hero of national independence. For years he fought off all the expeditionary forces that the English sent into the jungle. The soldiers died run through with lances or bitten by rattlesnakes or eaten by tigers. He was a strategist and he had allied himself with France. He knew they'd been wanting revenge on England since the Seven Years War. For a while he gave backing to the great sailor – who you won't have heard of – whom the French called the Bailiff de Suffren. Suffren was an eminent captain who never lost a battle against the Royal Navy! Not bad, hey? Then the Sultan suggested the French should come to join him by land. That's why Napoleon went to Egypt. But he got it wrong.'

'There must have come a time when our government had had enough, surely?'

'Yes. The imperialists won. The redcoats arrived with a stronger expeditionary force and everything they needed for a siege. They were commanded by a Richard Wellesley, the brother of the future Duke of Wellington. They surrounded the palace at Mysore in the middle of the river. They breached the wall so that they could get into the palace. The sultan held out for four months. During the night he had the part of the wall that had been destroyed during the day rebuilt. But the food supplies ran out and towards the end they were being served grilled rat on gold plates in his court.'

'That's what happens if you try to defy England.'

'Oh, you can laugh, Mr Imperialist. After the war, India will get its independence and you won't find it so funny.'

'But I'm not in favour of the Empire, personally. I don't like colonialism.'

'Well then, listen to my ancestor's heroic end. With respect! The English launched their assault. The ministers had arranged for the sultan's family to leave through underground passageways. Tipoo Sahib was in his library. He was reading his vellum copy of Dante's *Inferno*. They came and begged him to leave. But he said: "No, my place is with my soldiers who have defended me so valiantly." An hour later he came out of his private apartments in full ceremonial dress with a curved sabre in his hand. His ministers followed behind him, they had had to renounce the opportunity to use the underground passageways themselves, and they were pitifully afraid. They would probably have preferred a little less heroism . . . He stood on the walls and went right to the front of his troops. But the English were stronger. Once they had broken through the wall they streamed into the palace courtyard in battle formation, in three ranks, firing rounds at regular intervals. Each time dozens of soldiers fell. Then they mounted their bayonets and buried them into the last row of defending soldiers. My ancestor's soldiers fought to the very last man. They were all massacred by the English, who represented civilisation, as everyone knows. The following morning, Tipoo Sahib's body was found mutilated and covered in blood in a heap of other bodies. They recognised him from the diamonds in his ears, at his neck, and on his wrists and ankles. He was my most famous forefather.'

'So you are a real princess?'

'What do you mean, a real princess? Of course I am. My dynasty is as old as the Windsors. What insolence! I should have you impaled.'

Noor had taken off her shoes and tucked her legs underneath her. She spoke animatedly and her eyes sparkled or darkened depending on the mood of the particular episode. I got up and poured her some more port, which she accepted.

'Are you really interested in this story, you the rational, left-wing journalist?'

'Noor, your story is of interest to me by definition. You know that.'

'Don't start chatting me up again. I'm here to teach you something.'

'So,' I said, more helpfully, 'your family escaped along underground passages . . .'

'Yes. They were driven out of Mysore and found themselves outlawed in a continent that was dominated by their English enemies and their Maharajan allies. Tipoo Sahib's family led a miserable, nomadic existence. They were taken in by friendly families but always forced to move on to escape the English. Many years later they reached Baroda in northern India, where they were able to settle. My family upheld their traditions. In every generation the eldest boy was initiated in the mysteries of politics and religion, with a view to being a leader and a sage. In Baroda, my grandfather, who was the sultan's great-grandson, became a master Sufi. He was recognised within his own community as a great musician (he played the sitar exquisitely, you know, it's that big Indian mandolin) and as a sage, a *wali*. Disciples came from all over the country to follow his teachings. He spent most of his time on the roof.'

'On the roof?'

'Yes, on the roof. He lived in a big house built of

red stone. He sat cross-legged overlooking the town, and meditated. He thought about the metaphysics of Sufi and about sacred Islamic texts. You should think about it a bit more, you Westerners. There'd be less hardship and unhappiness in the world.'

'But we do think!'

'About how to kill off your neighbour, most of the time.'

'Well, you do have a point.'

'You see! Anyway, my grandfather studied the texts. They have several meanings. The most important ones are hidden under the most obvious, first meaning. You're not going to follow this . . .'

I laughed and indicated for her to go on.

'My grandfather hardly ate at all. He was contemptuous of earthly pleasures. He preferred carrying out spiritual exercises. He said that was the best way to give God all the space he needs in our souls. This is the great Sufi idea: you come to know God through personal discipline, through meditation and by renouncing earthly temptations. You have to be able to reject the *naf* completely.'

'The *naf*?'

'The *naf* is our egotistical instincts, everything in us that is lowly, mediocre and evil. My grandfather's only earthly passion was music. He'd been playing the sitar since he was two. He was a gifted composer, and he'd become a great master of traditional music. He said that music was one pathway towards God. Sufi chanting melodies express the essence of divinity. Those who compose them are actually writing down what Allah dictates. Do you know the melodies?'

'No.'

'Obviously. People came from all over India to hear him. During the dry season a string of musicians would come to the house. They brought gifts and they were allowed to stay for a week, living on a bowl of rice a day. They had lessons with the master, and he perfected his knowledge of subcontinental music.'

'Did you live with him?'

'No. I wasn't born in India.'

'Really? Why not?'

'You're always in such a hurry. The *wali* had a son called Ajit. He'd been raised like all his forefathers, learning about philosophy and music.'

'Was he your father?'

'Wait! One day, when he was ten, Ajit ran down onto the terrace. He'd been watching the last light of day and had seen the stars coming out. He said: "Father, how can we talk to God when he is so far away, beyond the stars?" His father was meditating, sitting on the floor in his bedroom. He made him sit down in front of him and said: "My son, God is not in the sky. That is the most important truth. God is everywhere, in each of us, in things, in nature, in the beauty of nature and in the suffering of men." For Ajit this precept had important implications: we should see God not only in things that are superior to man, as you do in the West.'

'I don't believe in God,' I told her.

'What?'

'I don't believe in him.'

'I'm going to have you impaled,' she teased.

'It's not my fault! You can't get it to order.'

'Yes you can! But let's move on. That's not the question. I'll carry on. Western religions put God up in heaven, in the sky.'

'That much I understand.'

'Or maybe in the thunder and lightning. Or even on some fabled mountain where no one can see him, like Mount Olympus or Mount Sinai. But we should also see God in inferior things. God is in children, in animals, slaves and beggars. He's in the untouchables and the poor just as much as in a maharajah's palace. That's what my grandfather thought. Everyone, therefore, has a right to the same degree of respect. One day Ajit, along with some other schoolboys, was making fun of a simpleton who was jabbering away to himself. They threw stones at him. The *wali* flew into a terrifying rage. He scolded his son, saying: "This man is a *mahdjub*. The Law of the Prophet tells us to protect him. Because God may speak through his mouth one day. We don't understand what he's saying. But his madness may lead us to the truth. God doesn't always choose the wise and the strong to be his disciples. He often prefers the madmen. They have kept their innocence."'

'Your grandfather was a wise man.'

'Of course. One day he called Ajit into his room

210

and said: "I'm old. Soon I will be called to God. You must continue my teaching, Ajit. I have a new mission for you, a different one. Your brothers can run the community in Baroda. I've been meditating over this for more than a year, and I'm sure that I have found the right way. Our Sufi wisdom is spread throughout the East, in Islamic countries, and in Hindu and Buddhist countries. But it is unknown in the West. You must go far away from here and find new disciples in the countries of the West. They are powerful nations. Thanks to their books and their guns, they dominate the world. If we want our message to be heard, it must be propagated over there. Then it will spread throughout the world. When Saint Paul wanted to spread Christ's message he went to Rome. Nowadays Rome is London, Paris and New York."'

'What an undertaking!'

'My dear, my family expect a lot. We're ambitious. What point is there in being on this earth otherwise?'

'And did your father obey him?'

'Yes. When the *wali* died his family respected his wishes. They took over the running of Baroda and Ajit travelled. Firstly in India, to get to know it. He brought his own wisdom into contact with other masters of religion and music. Then one day, with a little suitcase in his hand, he set off for the station. He felt heavy-hearted but full of hope. His mother, his uncles, and brothers and sisters assembled on the porch of the big, red house and watched him with tears in their eyes. And he left.'

I was wedged deeply into the sofa, sinking into a soft torpor, while Noor – with a faraway look in her eyes – relived the story of what she had left behind in order to sign up to the army that had defeated Tipoo Sahib. She started speaking again: 'It's two o'clock already. Let's get some sleep. If this is of any interest to you, we'll have all the time in the world tomorrow.'

'But how did your father think he was going to spread the Sufi faith in the West on his own, with no money and no contacts? He wasn't exactly Saint Patrick, and it wasn't a rather backward Ireland that he was trying to evangelise. But America and Europe!'

'Mr Westerner, you should remember that it took Sheherazade a thousand and one nights to tell a story. You people in the West are in too much of a hurry.'

As we passed each other in the corridor, each heading for our bedrooms, I could see the nostalgia in her face. Later, when I passed her door, I heard her crying. Moved and upset, I opened the door gently. She was lying down facing the wall. In the shadows I could see her back shuddering as she sobbed. I went over, sat down on the bed and put my hand on her shoulder. She did not move but she took her hand out from the sheets and held mine. I lay down next to her, on top of the blanket, and put my arms round her. She nestled against me without turning round. I felt a rush of tender affection for her. For a long time she lay there motionless and silent. Her crying quietened gradually. Then she sighed deeply and said: 'I should be stronger. I'll tell you the rest tomorrow, I promise. I mustn't let myself go like this.'

'But I don't want to upset you, Noor. Don't talk about it any more. I'll tell you about my life!'

'No, no. I've got to overcome my memories or I won't be able to do anything. But I do want to hear about your life. You've lived through so much.'

She turned round so that she was facing me in the darkness. There was a moment of suspense, then she kissed me on the cheek. In a turmoil, I kissed her too, on her forehead as I would a child, and I left the room. When I listened carefully at her door ten minutes later I heard the regular whisper of her breathing.

CHAPTER SIXTEEN

The doorbell echoed round the apartment. We looked at each other in silence. Who was looking for us? The police? Other members of the network?

We were having lunch, Jerusalem artichokes seasoned with margarine and a few onions that Noor had found – with a little cry of joy – in the bottom of the larder. I had spent the whole morning by the window, sitting on a chair with a notebook in my hand. Hidden behind the muslin curtain, I had made a note of all the comings and goings at the door of the police station. By lunchtime I was reassured to have established that the police changed shifts every two hours; there was a gap between stints, probably because they were having a quick drink and a chat. This pause lasted at least five minutes, sometimes ten. And it was even longer at lunchtime. I would therefore be able to leave the building without their seeing me: I just had to wait for the end of one guard duty at eight o'clock, ten o'clock or noon. So I was not a complete prisoner. I could sneak to the Métro station without risking arrest. After that it was up to the grace of God.

As I ate my artichokes I announced to Noor that I intended to set out on an expedition the following day.

'Wait another day,' she said imploringly. 'The Germans must be on red alert.'

'If you like. But I must do something. This is too stupid.'

'An agent's first duty really is to stay alive. So don't try to be too clever. Wait a bit! Tomorrow –'

The doorbell interrupted her.

I put my hand up to tell her not to move. We did not officially exist: we should not answer the door. We strained our ears in consternation. All we could hear was the silence in the building and the faint hubbub in the street. After about a minute we heard a very distinct rustling sound. Then it sounded as if someone were going down the stairs, and the red carpet was deadening the sound of their footsteps. Without breathing a word I tiptoed towards the front door with Noor close behind me. I saw a piece of white paper. It was a letter which had been slipped under the door. I picked it up. It was from the Calvados region and it was addressed to Renée Garry; there was no sender's address. I opened it and saw the opening words: 'Dear Arthur and Aurora'.

The news was not good. According to Garry, the Prosper network had been decimated. There had been dozens if not hundreds of arrests. He had no news of Prosper himself, but his girlfriend, Andrée Borrel, had been injured and arrested in the middle of the street right under the nose of another agent who had given the word straight away. Gilbert Norman, the radio operator, had been taken on the terrace of the Brasserie La Lorraine. He had arranged to meet a contact, who managed to slip away when he saw him surrounded by policemen. Many, many others whom I did not know were in the Gestapo's hands. With Norman captured, the Prosper and Cinema networks were without a radio operator. There was only Noor left. Garry was asking us to relay the information to London. But he begged us to be very cautious and to wait eight days before looking for somewhere to make a transmission. He also told us that he would be married the following day in a little church in Normandy, with just a curate and the child choristers.

The afternoon was gloomy. We sat reading in the sitting room and avoided commenting on Garry's letter. We waited for the evening radio transmission. At nine o'clock we settled ourselves next to the dressing-table in Noor's room, facing the picture of Father de Foucauld, which was half hidden by the radio set. This time the message was substantial and it took Noor a good half-hour to decipher it. She went wrong in one transposition and cursed as she started again. London confirmed the Prosper network's difficulties, and the number of arrests. We also learned that Cinema was intact, as was Tinker and the network run by Cowburn in Dreux. On the other hand, Scientist, the network to which Noor's fiancé, Donaldson, belonged, was in danger: it had close links with Prosper, who had been very involved in its inception. Many of Prosper's agents had worked with Scientist. Now they were prisoners, which posed a threat for their comrades. They also congratulated us warmly for the success of the operation at the station depot in Dreux.

I leapt with surprise at the next part of the message: London was advising us to wait a few days and then to contact Gilbert Norman, who, the message said, had escaped the round-up along with Prosper. These two and Blainville, it went on, would be able to rebuild the network once the danger had passed. Then there was a telephone number for us to ring. I looked at Noor.

'Are you sure about the transcription?' I asked.

'Yes, I think so.'

She looked at her notes, checked a few things and nodded.

'Yes,' she said. 'We've read it correctly.'

'How can it be possible? Garry's written to tell us Norman was taken, and London's telling us to get in touch with him. Somebody must be wrong.'

'Or somebody's lying.'

'Why would they lie? I can't understand it. There's a mistake in the communications. London must have misinterpreted a message.'

'I don't think that London could get the wrong end of the stick. That's impossible if you follow our procedures. The messages are very clear once

217

they've been decoded. You can't get a name wrong or mistake one sentence for another. Not with Morse and double transcription. Either it's clear or it's illegible. There's no halfway house or ambiguity.'

I looked at Noor and thought. She knew what she was talking about. That was why she had been sent to France. And I suddenly thought of Buckmaster and Bodington. When they explained my mission to me, they had warned me: one radio set had been put back into use by the Germans. They had realised this and had cut off the contact after continuing communications for a short time. That would explain the incompatibility of the messages: Norman's radio set had crossed over to the other side, I thought. Gilbert cracked under torture, or he was a traitor. The Germans had taken over from him, and they were the ones telling London about the dramas in the Prosper network. And London is passing it on to its agents! I felt quite giddy when I glimpsed the mortal danger we faced. If we had not received Garry's letter, we would have rung the number given to us by London. Why would we have questioned information sent to us by our immediate bosses? That number would have led to a meeting with Norman, and we would have walked straight into a trap.

We argued animatedly for a good hour. I was all for immediate action: writing to Garry to warn him, and contacting Vienet and Blainville. Noor kept emphasising the risk involved in any over-hasty action. And what had happened to Prosper? Was Norman the traitor? Was it Prosper? Or someone else? We had to investigate, to warn London about the Norman radio, find Prosper and find out the truth about him, and God alone knew what else. We had to get on and do something.

'Let's wait until tomorrow,' said Noor. 'We're all worked up because of our theories. First of all, let's think of a way of checking these intuitions. It's late, soldier!'

She took my hand and led me to the sitting room. As if it were a ritual, she opened the door to the little cupboard in the bookcase, took out the bottle of whisky, the port, a straight-sided glass and a goblet. She poured the Gwalynlivet into the one and the port into the other, handed me my whisky, then took off her shoes and buried herself in the club chair, bringing her knees up under her chin. The second night of my Sheherazade was beginning.

'Ajit, my father,' she said, 'set sail from Bombay in a rusty steamer. He was wending his way slowly westwards. The sea was dead calm, flattened by the suffocating heat, and the hold was full of noisy families and painfully thin labourers going to try their chances in America.'

'Did your father have any money?'

'No, very little. He slept on the bridge. He leant

against his little leather suitcase and kept his sitar by his side at all times. I've seen photographs of him at that time. He was an elegant young man, very gentle but with a feverish expression. And one day he saw the statue holding up her torch right there in front of the boat. They went into a wide bay where the horizon was blotted out by tower blocks. He waited in the corridors on Ellis Island until a man in a blue cap stamped a piece of paper. He was entitled to stay in the United States for five years.'

'But he didn't know anyone.'

'He did. He had the address of a cousin who'd moved there six years earlier. He lived in the depths of the Bronx, the far end from Manhattan. Travelling on foot, he found the street three hours later. He told me about it. He could easily have mistaken it for Baroda! The only difference was the height of the buildings. They were black with smoke and there were fire escapes zig-zagging backwards and forwards up the walls. Apart from that, all he could see was women in saris, little brown-faced children playing round the fire hydrants, brahmans in their white caps and little shops dotted with Indian inscriptions. His cousin greeted him respectfully. He offered him tea in a little earthenware cup. He found him work, sewing on shirt sleeves twelve hours a day in an underground workshop that saw only a glimmer of daylight.'

'And what about his Sufi teachings?'

'Wait! With his first week's pay he had some

posters printed to say that a young *wali* had come from his country to talk about the "Mysteries of God".'

'Did anyone come?'

'Not many. He'd put the notices in shop windows and on workshop doors in the Indian quarter. The owners had checked that this wasn't any sort of socialist propaganda. Four days later he stood up to speak in front of sixteen very religious Indians. They were exhausted by their day's work and two or three of them fell asleep while he was preaching. But he was pleased.'

'Did he have any better success?'

'A bit, yes. He stayed in the Indian community in New York for three months, getting quite a reputation as an orator and a sage, and he was able to stop working because he lived on offerings made by his first disciples.'

'That was a start.'

'Yes, but he soon realised that he'd reached a dead end. It wasn't enough just spreading the Sufi message in the immigrant population. His father had talked of "evangelising the New World".'

'He had to convince the Americans!'

'Precisely. So he thought of using music. He had the address of a musician who had come to live in Baroda ten years previously to learn to play the sitar and to compose traditional melodies. He ran a music school in southern Manhattan, quite a fashionable conservatoire, in fact. He went to see him in his dog-collar like a clergyman, with his darned old white tunic and his turban. The man was courteous, asking about Baroda and his father, etc. After about half an hour Ajit asked whether he might ever be able to teach in his conservatoire.'

'Quite a bold request.'

'Yes. The conservatoire employed professional musicians who had studied in the United States. But the director asked him to play the piano, which was nice of him. And he took him on on the spot! My father had played a Liszt sonata which was technically very difficult. The following day he was appointed as the conservatoire's substitute teacher.'

'That's incredible!'

'No. My father was very special. Anyway, the man had a brilliant idea: he told him he should also teach his Indian music. He was interested in it because it was fashionable in the West. My father didn't know it, but there was a wave of interest in all things Eastern gathering momentum. The following year the conservatoire started running a class in traditional Sufi music as well as a series of conferences. I've seen the poster for it, he showed it to me once. It said: "Under the instruction of 'the Master of Indian wisdom Pir-O-Murshid Ajit Vijay Khan'".'

'Pir-O-Murshid?' I asked.

'It means: "Master of wisdom",' she explained.

'So the poster said: "the Master of wisdom master of wisdom"?'

'Yes, exotic words always sound so impressive!

He was immediately very successful. He was both erudite and simple. He was often funny too and he was polite in a peculiarly British way. Because there is such a thing.'

'It's the one good thing about the imperialists,' I teased.

'He became the man everyone wanted to know in cultured circles in south Manhattan. I think he appealed to the bored women who ran New York's society life. He talked of a tolerant brand of spirituality, taught meditation exercises and the slow movements of yoga. He was frequently invited to dinner or to private conferences over a cup of tea in the imposing residences on Fifth Avenue. He'd grown a beard and he only ever wore a long white tunic and a brightly coloured silk waistcoat. He was very attractive!'

'A society figure?'

'If you like. The following year one of his rich admirers persuaded her husband to set aside some of his income and create a foundation to be run by Pir-O-Murshid. He was able to rent a house near Eighth Avenue and he used it to continue spreading the word of his faith and teaching sacred music. He took his conferences further afield to other cities on the east coast and even to San Francisco and Los Angeles. When he went back to cities on later visits he noticed that there was always a nucleus of faithful followers who came to every conference, and he suggested that they should set up a centre for Sufi faith and music in their own city. Then members of these communities would come to stay with him in New York so that he could teach them, and they could go back and find disciples of their own.'

'But what about you?' I asked impatiently.

'I'm getting to that! One evening, when he'd been speaking to a philanthropic society in Boston, a thin, rather sad-looking young woman with beautiful chestnut hair asked to speak to him. She wanted to achieve mystic wisdom by having private lessons. She was the daughter of a rich Boston family who were prepared to pay a good price. After three lessons, Ajit refused any more money and asked for her hand in marriage. The girl's name was Ora Wilson and his proposal made her very happy. She was my mother!'

'Odd for a girl from Boston to marry a guru,' I said a little dryly.

'A guru? Well, if you like. She was very religious, fascinated by the Sufi faith and by my father as well. She became a begum.'

'What's a begum?'

'It means princess. The Princess Ajit Vijay Khan. It's better than Miss Wilson, isn't it?' Noor asked playfully.

'Definitely, yes! And you took Wilson as your pseudonym because of her . . .'

'Yes, I really love my mother. And the RAF thought my name was a bit complicated. They asked me for an Anglo-Saxon name, so I chose Nora Wilson.'

'So you were born in the States?'

'No, I was born in the Kremlin, in Moscow.'

'In Moscow?' I asked incredulously.

'Ajit never forgot his father's message. America wasn't enough. He also had to find a foothold in Europe. In the summer of 1912 he set off on a steamer again, but this time he was with his wife and travelling first class. His reputation went before him. His address book was well stocked with musical and society figures. In two years of preaching and concerts he managed to extend his Sufi centres into Geneva, Amsterdam, London, Berlin and Paris. He arranged for his brothers and sisters to come over from Baroda to form an orchestra of sacred music. The donations kept pouring in. He was hosted by royalty, a friend to the powerful and a necessary accessory to high society. Institutes of theology and university philosophy departments fought over him. His interpretation of Islam was discussed in seminaries and amphitheatres throughout Europe.'

'Did he forge his own doctrine, then?'

'Yes. His ideas evolved as a result of his contact with Western societies. The more he learned the more he understood the European and American state of mind, and the more he adapted his own thinking. He kept Sufi thinking as his springboard – their mysticism, their constant struggle with the *naf* and the exercises that lead to a direct knowledge of God. But he created what theologians call a syncretism. A synthesis.'

'So he was a prophet really?' I ventured.

'Well, he wasn't as successful as Jesus or Mohammed,' she said with a smile, 'but he did create a religion. He took the elements he felt were best established in the other religions and integrated them into his talks, he brought in disciples from all over Europe. He gave his conferences in four languages, you know. It was incredible. He would speak first in the local language, then he would translate his own words successively into French and English and German, according to the audience. He looked for examples and supportive arguments in new scientific and mathematical discoveries. He spoke in parables and symbols, but he always expressed himself with tremendous clarity. He wrote several books which have become classics of modern Sufism.'

'Did the other Sufis accept him?'

'More or less. It's a fairly tolerant religion and, traditionally, there was a constant succession of great masters. There was nothing exceptional about him in that. There had been a lot of them before him. But there was something original about him. Traditional Sufis are attached to the Eastern origins of Sufi thought and its Islamic sources. They felt that this attempted synthesis between Christianity, Buddhism and Islam was bordering on heresy. But, well, they couldn't burn him or stone him.'

'Or impale him.'

'Or impale him, because he was in the West. It

has to be said that in your decadent, faithless society people are a bit safer.'

'You see, without a god, men are freer,' I said, half seriously.

'Yes, but they have no hope,' she retorted quickly.

'Possibly. At least they're not put in prison to give them any hope.'

'Touché, Mr Rational!'

'But why Moscow?' I asked, keen to get to her part of the story.

'Because Rasputin asked my father to come.'

'Rasputin?'

'Yes, the monk who became a close confident of the Tzarina.'

'Now, I've heard of him!' I said triumphantly.

'At last!'

'But he was mad!' I added.

'No he wasn't. He was a mystic.'

'He was a crook,' I said defiantly. 'He was corrupt, he spent all his time fondling the ladies-in-waiting and going to see prostitutes.'

'Perhaps. I was too young to notice. My father always said that he was an interesting mystic. My mother was pregnant. Rasputin advised her to have her baby in the Kremlin. She wanted to pay homage to the clarity you experience with knowledge, the clarity that dispels darkness, so she called me "Light of day" – Noor.'

'Did you stay in Russia?'

'No. We were driven away by the war. We left for London, where there was an active Sufi community.

Then the government made our lives very difficult because we spent a lot of time with friends of a man called Gandhi, who was closely involved in the independence movement.'

'I've heard of him.'

'Well done, congratulations! We had to run away, driven out by the English imperialists once again.'

'You set off again.'

'Yes, to France this time. There were four of us by then. My brother Vilayat was the eldest. He could play several instruments, he spoke four languages, he could ride and he was making daily progress in his knowledge of mysticism. I also had a theological and musical education. I learned to play the harp and the piano, and I learned about Sufi literature and poetry. My father decided to set up a centre for his European community near Paris. He bought a huge house near Suresnes; it was set in parkland on the side of a hill overlooking the whole town. He created a terrace on the roof, with a stone balustrade. He would go up onto the terrace several times a day, and he would sit cross-legged on a little fringed carpet, facing towards the sun and meditating. He baptised the house Fazal Manzil. That's where I grew up. Every year he would gather his disciples from all over the world in the meadow in front of the house and he would hold an annual seminar, welcoming representatives of the world's major religions. Fazal Manzil became the main Sufi base in Europe.'

'Did he hold any form of service?'

'Of course! In the evenings my family would gather with a few disciples in the second sitting room on the ground floor. He would take a big book from an Indian sideboard, he would go over to the lectern and read a few verses taken from the great religious texts of the world. He took them from the Koran, the Bible, the Torah or from Buddhist teachings. He put them in groups in keeping with his own thinking, creating a coherent collection of doctrines.'

'Did you go to school?' I asked.

'Of course! Do you think we just lived by ourselves like a sect?'

'Well, no . . . I wondered . . .' I said vaguely.

'I went to school in Suresnes, then at the *lycée* in Boulogne. The rest of the time I wrote poetry, played the harp or chatted with my mother. I'd have friends over and I would tell them stories. I was quite popular.'

'That doesn't surprise me. Is your father still alive?'

'No. He's dead. One evening in 1935 he asked Vilayat and me to go and see him in the little office he'd had built on the terrace. He looked very drawn and he seemed out of breath. I can see it so clearly. It was a beautiful evening with the sun setting over Paris. He said: "My children, I shall soon be called back to God. Tomorrow I shall leave for Baroda and you will see me no more. That is as it is. We must accept the trials of this life. As soon as he is ready to, Vilayat will take over my teaching. Noor will help him as best she can. You will marry to perpetuate our lineage, and you will apply yourselves to communicating my discoveries to the world. You will also look after the begum, who will need you." We stood there speechless. He took us in his arms and hugged us to him. Then he added: "Goodbye, my children. I have loved you very much. We will see each other again later, with God. Don't be sad. My fate is an enviable one. I am moving closer to the light." We were in tears, and he ended by giving us a sort of political legacy: "A great test lies ahead of you. There will be a war. This Hitler is a madman, an evil tyrant who wants to conquer all of Europe. Whatever their current leaders believe, England and France will have to confront him." For the last four years we had heard the rantings of the Nazi rallies from the varnished wooden wireless in the sitting room, and each time my father's eyes would turn to stone and he would nod his head, saying: "These Nazi doctrines are precisely the opposite of my teachings. These men want to be masters of all humanity. They feel only loathing and contempt for the humble and the poor. Our faith is based on respect and freedom. I must warn you that you cannot remain neutral. In the path that you have chosen, you must commit yourself alongside these two countries – France and England – which have welcomed us, which have protected our house and our faith, even if they did not understand it. That is my wish."'

★   ★   ★

There was a glimmer of defiance in Noor's eyes as she spoke these words of her father's. She stopped speaking and I looked at my watch: ten past three. She stared at me as if emerging from a dream, and she smiled. 'You're going to have to go through the same exercise, don't forget,' she said.

'Oh, mine won't take half an evening!'

CHAPTER SEVENTEEN

At twelve o'clock the following day, just as he had at the same time the day before, the policeman on duty outside went into the station. I leapt down the stairs straight away and turned left out of the front door towards the café on the corner of the rue de la Tour. It was called Aux Espagnols and it was near the Spanish church in Paris. I had cut short Noor's objurgations by proving that our inactivity was putting other agents in danger. I went in, ordered a cup of coffee at the counter and asked to use the telephone. The patron took it from the shelves behind him, pulled on the lead and put it on the counter in front of me.

'Wait a minute,' he said, 'I'll just put the timer on.'

He went over to the corner where they sold cigarettes and tobacco – where there was precious little to sell apart from a few postage stamps and lottery tickets – and turned a black handle. I heard the line clear through the earpiece. I dialled Vienet's number and waited. There was a poster in front of me promoting an aperitif called La Mère Picon, and another one above it praising the 'Legion of French volunteers against Bolshevism'. A woman's voice answered.

'Good morning. Could I speak to M. Millet, please.' This was Vienet's name. 'It's M. Joumard.'

'M. Joumard?' she asked, clearly separating out the syllables as she repeated the name. I thought I could hear a quiver of excitement in her voice.

'Yes, M. Jou-mard.'

'I'll get him for you, just a moment please.' And Vienet was on the line in an instant.

'Hello, M. Joumard?' he said anxiously. 'Is that Alfred Joumard?'

'No, Arthur.'

'Ah yes . . . Arthur! But remind me where we last met?'

I could see Vienet was feigning ignorance. He wanted to be quite sure it really was me he was talking to and not a Gestapo agent who had got hold of his number during an interrogation. The current round-up called for caution.

'We saw each other at the school, didn't we, on Sunday ten days ago,' I replied. 'Do you remember? The professor was there, and the poet.'

'The poet . . .' he said, 'do you mean Brasillach?'

'No, Cocteau.'

'Oh yes! And you were with that charming young woman, weren't you? I've forgotten her name . . .'

'Aurora.'

'Aurora, that's right. Very good, very good.'

'Would you like any more details,' I said with a smile in my voice.

'No, there's no need. But you understand I can't take any risks. How are you, Arthur, and how's Aurora?'

'We're fine, but I need to see you. It's urgent.'

'Yes, of course. And I imagine you don't want to have to go far.'

'You understand perfectly.'

'Tell me when and where, and I'll be there.'

I thought for a moment. I was going to give him the address of the apartment, but there was a slim chance that Vienet had been arrested too and had been sent back out by the Germans. The Gestapo could be standing right next to him, listening in on us. I should not give him my address. Neither could I envisage using anywhere very far from the rue de la Pompe: I would run too many risks just getting there. I glanced round; on the other side of the crossroads, opposite the café, there was a bakery. The junction between three roads formed a little square outside it.

'Come to the junction between the rue de la Tour and the rue de la Pompe in twenty minutes. It's near the Pompe Métro station. There's a bakery at the crossroads. Go in and I'll be inside.'

'All right,' he said.

He had not asked for more time: that was a good sign. I knew that his offices were on the Champs-Élysées, about quarter of an hour away on foot, or three minutes in a car. If he had asked for longer I could have suspected that he or the police needed the time to set a trap. All the same, I decided to remain cautious. I paid the *patron* and set off looking round the square as if trying to find an address. As I reached each building I tried to have a quick glance inside if the door was open or if there was a bay window. At the third building I found what I was looking for: an empty corridor with no *loge* for the concierge. I went in, closed the door and stayed inside. I could look out at the bakery through a little pink-tinted window behind a metal crossbar, but I could not be seen from the road. If there was a trap all I had to do was wait there. And if they searched round all the buildings, I could always escape over the roof-tops.

A quarter of an hour later a car passed in front of the café. I recognised Vienet; he did not stop but kept looking to left and right to see the lie of the land. Three minutes later the car came past again without stopping. The third time it stopped in front of the café, Vienet stepped out, walked straight over to the bakery and went in. I waited. There were no cars following him. Apart from one customer coming out of the café with a dog on the lead, the crossroads was deserted. I opened the door to the building a fraction. Glancing sideways, I could make out the policeman kicking his heels outside the station. Everything seemed quiet.

A customer came out of the bakery. Still nothing. Two minutes later, Vienet came back out onto the pavement with a loaf of black bread in his hand

and a rather surprised expression on his face. He stopped and looked round, peering down each of the three roads that met there. Still, I waited. Vienet stood motionless. He looked at his watch, then started pacing up and down outside the bakery. Four minutes later he crossed the street and opened his car door to leave. Just then I stepped out onto the pavement and cried: 'Vienet!' He saw me and spread his arms by way of asking me what to do next. I pointed towards the café and he headed towards it. Then I looked in every direction: no sign of any commotion, no cars speeding towards me, no men in raincoats closing in on me. I too crossed the road and went into the café.

I stayed with Vienet for two hours and this time I understood why I never quite took him seriously: with his made-to-measure suit, his handkerchief in his breast pocket, his greased-back hair, thin black moustache and wheedling smile, Vienet was the spitting image of Jean Sablon, a French singer I had seen perform before the war, who had brought to France the whole 'crooner' style of some of America's more endearing jazz singers. He offered me a cheese omelette, a piece of brie and a *paris-brest* pastry. The omelette was tiny, the brie tasted of nothing and the *paris-brest* was made of coarse flour and saccharine. I paid scant attention to the food: I was knocked sideways by the news from Vienet.

He told me that Norman had been taken first on the terrace of the Brasserie La Lorraine. Two

Gestapo officers had collared him, pinning him with their guns as he drank his beer, and a third one was waiting for him in a black car. They took him straight to 84, avenue Foch. This was one of the headquarters of Section IV of the Paris Gestapo, the Nazi police run by Himmler and by Heydrich until he was assassinated by the SOE. In 1940 responsibility for them in France had been handed to Helmut Knochen, a fiercely intelligent doctor of philosophy and Nazi fanatic. It was he who had recommended to Hitler and the higher-ranking officers that they should set up the Vichy government and limit their repressive operations in France so that the whole country could be transformed into a vast haven of rest and recuperation for the German army. The activities of the Resistance, armed by the SOE, hindered this policy. He was prepared to do anything to re-establish the security of the base he had set up for the Wehrmacht.

Section IV was dedicated to the 'anti-terrorist' campaign, and to detecting clandestine radio sets. It was run by two cunning and brutal military men, Boemelburg and Kieffer.

'They don't always use force,' Vienet explained. 'They have years of experience, and they know that psychological pressure can be just as effective. But they won't shy away from anything if these techniques don't work. They were the ones who tortured Moulin when he was transferred from Lyon.'

'Who's Moulin?'

'He's Max, the one de Gaulle sent to France to sort out the Resistance. He was taken, along with several others, at Caluire near Lyon about ten days ago. When he arrived at the avenue Foch, Kieffer complained about how brutal the local Gestapo had been because they had beaten Moulin so much. But when Moulin refused to speak – just as he had in Lyon – the people from the avenue Foch tore him to pieces. He didn't speak a word. Then Boemelburg arrested him at home in Neuilly to "work on him". He didn't get anything. Not a thing!'

His unconditional admiration for Moulin's courage came across quite clearly in his voice.

'When he came to the end of his tether he threw himself against the walls of the cell. He died when they were transferring him to Germany by train. That's one solution Norman didn't choose.'

'Did they torture him too?' I asked.

'They didn't have to. Norman was spent. He cracked straight away.'

'What do you mean straight away?'

'Boemelburg and Kieffer have a terrifying assistant called Ernst Goetz. He used to teach French and German; now he's in charge of radios. He organises operations for sending radios back out there in German hands; they call it the "*Funkspiel*", the radio game. He knows your organisation very well.'

'I must have seen one of his lorries. It came past our apartment the day before yesterday.'

'Did you make a transmission from your hideout? You mustn't ever do that. They're very well equipped in this part of Paris and they work very quickly.'

'Don't worry. We won't do it again. We were too frightened.'

'This Goetz put a complete diagram of the structure of the SOE under Norman's nose, with all the addresses in London, the training camps, the names of the major players and the geographical layout of the networks in France. Everything they had learned from interrogating other agents. They also told him almost everything they knew about the Prosper network, which is a lot. Norman resisted for a while. But Goetz had a recording of a particularly nasty torture session. They played the tape loudly in the next room. Norman collapsed after quarter of an hour. He admitted who he was, what he did, who he reported to, etc.'

Gilbert Norman's surrender had had catastrophic repercussions for the Prosper network. The first result was the battalion of German soldiers invading the school in Viroflay. The gardener who worked on the greenhouses, several instructors and a handful of students were taken away in a lorry. Professor Adamowski had not been at Viroflay; he was waiting for one of Prosper's couriers in his apartment in Paris in the square Alboni. When two men from the Gestapo rang the doorbell, he opened the door and said: 'Ah, there are two of you. I've been expecting you!' Rather amazed, they went into the sitting room and waited for him to come back with some coffee before taking out their cards to show that they were the German police. It took him a full minute to understand. He was taken to Fresnes and the policemen stayed in his apartment. At six o'clock that evening they greeted Hélène Adamowski, who protested indignantly, saying she did not understand anything they were saying. The professor was so persuasive he managed to convince the Gestapo that his wife knew nothing of his activities. She was released, but he underwent a particularly cruel interrogation.

Prosper's friend Andrée Borrel was meeting someone at the Naval Museum at the Palais de Chaillot. Seeing an unusual concentration of single men waiting at the entrance on the place du Trocadéro, she ran towards the rue Franklin. A lieutenant in the French Gestapo shot her, the bullet went through her lung and she was taken, dying, to the Hôpital du Val-de-Grâce, where her life was saved by army surgeons. When her condition improved she was transferred to the infirmary at Fresnes.

The restaurant owner at the Jardin du Palais-Royal was also arrested. He was to be punished for failing to let the police know that there were members of the Resistance among his regular clients and that his restaurant acted as a dead-letter box for Prosper. He was shot.

Prosper himself had taken refuge in an old hotel

on the rue de Mazagran near République. He was out when the Gestapo arrived. The *concierge* could not disguise the fact that a M. Desprée had taken up residence the day before. Prosper came into the hall at ten o'clock and saw two men in rain-coats reading their papers on the sofa. He fled, but the street was full of police officers. He was tackled, thrown to the ground, handcuffed and taken straight to the avenue Foch.'

'Did he talk?' I asked when Vienet told me this.

'No. But they made him read Norman's state-ment. It said everything. Including the names of Prosper's parents. Luckily, they both live in England. So Prosper came up with an agreement for the Gestapo.'

'An agreement with the Gestapo!' I said incred-ulously.

'Yes, an exchange, a compromise.'

'Compromising what?'

'He offered a list of the arms caches and landing sites, and the names of several members of the network, in exchange for the safety of all his agents.'

'But how can you negotiate with the Nazis? They won't keep their word!'

'I don't know. Anyway, that's what he did,' he sighed.

'Did they agree to it?'

'Yes. Kieffer and Boemelburg signed a piece of paper. Knochen gave it his approval and Prosper gave them what he had bartered.'

'Everyone?' I said, still finding it hard to believe.

'No, not everyone. Not you, or Aurora or some agents that the Germans will find it difficult to identify. Prosper had to choose those he thought had already lost their cover or were about to.'

'And did they take them?'

'Some of them. Very few, in fact. Thanks to Norman's confessions they had followed up leads and had already arrested more than a hundred people in the Paris area. On the other hand, they did confiscate all the weapons. Quantities of them.'

'It's incredible!' was all I could manage.

'Prosper was something of a mystic, you know. When he was taken, his whole world collapsed. He was very aware of what he represented. Too aware. And too convinced of his own importance. He once said to me: "You know if I want to, I can start the landings. If I give the order for an insurrection, Paris would be torn apart by this war. The Allies would be forced to follow suit." That's what he said, without a glimmer of humour. In the end he thought he could negotiate on equal terms with the Germans. He lived like a madman. He's been here with us for three years, hiding himself, running incredibly risky operations, and keeping the whole organisation at arm's length. It gets to you in the end.'

As I listened to Vienet, a whole different world opened up to my shocked mind, a world in which heroes were caught in traps, in which the best clandestine fighters became the most naive, in which a secret agent thought he was on a par with ministers and generals. Madness is inherent in this sort of secret army. I could see the ravages it caused as I listened to this Gaullist leader describing the downfall of a great crusader, Francis Suttill known as Prosper, one of the best soldiers the British army had known.

Something made me feel unsure. 'How come you know so much about it? I know you know Kieffer, but he's not exactly going to tell you what he does.'

Vienet smiled. 'I thought you would ask me that earlier. You've still got a lot to learn. I have two sources. The Germans set Norman free for a couple of days, and he tried to trap one of my boys, one of the ones who was on Operation Iago with you. When Norman told him that he and Prosper had made an agreement with the Gestapo, the hair nearly stood up on his head. He tipped over the table and fled. The café was bristling with policemen, but he took them by surprise. They chased after him because they didn't know that before the war – and before turning to petty crime – my chap had been Junior French champion in the 10,000 yards. He'd lost them within ten minutes. The cretins didn't have any cars nearby.'

'And the other source?' I asked, still sceptical.

'I've got someone at the avenue Foch. And it's not Kieffer.'

Vienet was wearing his crooner's smile. I wondered whether I should believe him or put him on my list of suspects. I told myself that if he

243

were a traitor he would already have given me away. Or he would have tried to find out where I lived so that he could also take Noor and her radio. During the trials after the war I learned that Vienet's agent at the avenue Foch was called Marie-Rose Holveldts, a pretty girl who cleaned the offices for Section IV. She was the mistress of a Gestapo officer called Karl Haug, but at the same time she passed information to the Gaullist network. Thanks to her, Vienet had already outwitted several traps set by Goetz and Kieffer. The crowds had almost shorn all her hair when they invaded the Gestapo offices in August 1944 at the Liberation, but several representatives from the Forces Françaises de l'Intérieur had backed her up, and network heads testified for her at her trial. She was acquitted.

'But who gave Norman away?' I asked Vienet.

'I don't know. Maybe he was careless? Or part of the network was already exposed.'

I decided to tell him about the suspicions they had in Baker Street, the beginnings of my enquiry, the two operations that the Germans had known about in advance, and the theory I had come up with on the subject.

'You could be right. Your reasoning is logical, anyway. If the hypothesis is true, we're in an even more dangerous situation than I thought.'

'But if the traitor is Prosper?'

'Everything is always possible,' Vienet said resignedly. Then he added: 'But I don't believe it.

I don't feel it. He and Norman cracked after they were arrested. Not before.'

'Well, that doesn't leave many people.'

'That's why the situation is even more dangerous. If there's a traitor at large, he'll carry on sending false information to London and helping the Germans. No one is safe.'

'Especially as London thinks Norman is still free and active. They radioed that to me last night.'

'How could they –' He stopped himself suddenly, as if a precise memory had just come to him. 'But, Christ almighty! I've just remembered something. It seemed extraordinary at the time and then I forgot all about it. When Norman spoke to my boy he tried to convince him by saying that London had dropped them. That's what agents who break under pressure often try to say. That justifies their surrender. But Norman was more precise. Radio operators have two security checks. You know this better than I do: if they're taken they give the first one to the Germans but they don't mention the second. The message arrives without the second password, and London knows that it's being transmitted by the Germans. When Goetz forced him to make transmissions for him, Norman followed the procedure. But London came back with this unexpected reply: "Repeat your message, you have forgotten the second security check." Can you believe it! I thought Norman was lying to catch out my boy, when actually it's perfectly clear: London was so bloody negligent that they alerted

Goetz to the fact that one of the security checks was missing, and when Norman sent the message again with the second password, they imagined he was working in perfect freedom. They, therefore, think Norman is free. You must warn them as soon as possible. They'll believe you.'

'I've got a letter for Garry,' I told him. 'He's free to move about in Normandy. He'll be able to let London know through his network.'

'Yes, that's a good idea. But you must carry on with your enquiry as well. I can help you. I'm going to try to find out whether Prosper had any contact with the avenue Foch before he was arrested. Which would explain everything.'

CHAPTER EIGHTEEN

He took me by the shoulder just as I was going into the building. But after leaving Vienet I had only had to cover thirty yards between the café and the doorway. It was exactly two o'clock. I had waited for the change of shift outside the police station to venture back.

'Police!' he said.

His hand was strong. He forced me to turn round and he brandished a red, white and blue card in my face.

'Don't move! There are twenty policemen in that station and I've got a whistle. You don't have a hope!'

I thought about breaking free and trying to run. He would have shot me straight away. If I got away I would have every policeman in the sixteenth arrondissement on my heels. With a sinking heart, I decided to fall back on my cover and I obeyed him, saying: 'But . . . what does all this mean? I haven't done anything! By what right?'

'We will explain.'

I crossed the street with him and went into the police station. The blood had drained from my

247

face and there was a stabbing pain in my chest. The policeman at the reception greeted him by pointing two fingers towards his képi. He was drinking a cup of coffee with the man taking over his shift.

'This way,' the superintendent said.

We went up to the first floor together and I sat down in a room with wood-panelled walls painted a dirty yellow. There was a big portrait of Maréchal Pétain on the wall, two narrow cupboards with slatted wooden doors held on runners at the bottom, a big green-metal desk laden with rubber stamps, files and paper clips, with a black Bakelite telephone to one side. Through the bars at the window I could see the lower half of the building where Noor was waiting for me in the silence of the apartment. He walked round the desk and sat down in a swivel chair covered in green leatherette. He had closed the door. He was a fat man with a bristly moustache, a ruddy complexion and astonishingly mobile eyes under his salt-and-pepper eyebrows. He had been wearing a grey canvas hat which he had hung on a coat-hook as he came in. He asked me for my papers and started looking through them carefully. 'You're a salesman?'

'Yes. For typewriters.'

'You're Belgian?'

'Yes, from Anvers.'

'Are you working at the moment?'

'Yes. I was trying to find new customers.'

'Were you going to see a customer?'

'Umm . . . yes.'

'What's their name? Which floor?'

'Umm . . . the Abeille insurance company on the second floor.' This was improvisation. I was paying for a professional mistake: I had gone out without a credible story to tell, and I was starting to tie myself in knots.

'You haven't got any samples with you.'

'No. I was just making an initial contact.'

'You've got a funny accent for a Belgian.'

'Really? I . . . umm . . . I wouldn't know. It's just my accent.'

'When did you arrive from England?' he suddenly asked in English. The trap might have worked if he spoke English well, but he had a strong French accent which reminded me of Maurice Chevalier in American musicals.

'Why are you speaking to me in English?'

'There isn't a company called Abeille at 72, rue de la Pompe, and you have an English accent. That's why.'

He took out a file and handed me a thin sheet of typed paper. Halfway through the long text there were reproductions of two pencil-drawn portraits. On the right-hand side there was a young woman with dark hair, a dark complexion and regular features. On the left, a young man with wayward hair that looked fair, sunken cheeks and a slightly upturned nose. The text was a summary description of two terrorists, members of a British network who had escaped arrest in Versailles.

'I was at the Café Aux Espagnols. I was just behind you. Because you looked like the police picture, I listened in. I caught snatches. There it is. Don't bother denying it.'

I could not utter a word. I was overwhelmed by my accumulation of mistakes. I should have realised that in a bistro so close to a police station there could easily be policemen eating around lunchtime. I thought of Vienet, who had probably also been followed and would be arrested shortly. He would think I was a traitor. *The* traitor.

'It says here that you took part in the attack at Dreux.'

I could give no reply.

'If you did, my congratulations. It was a very good operation.'

I looked him in the eye. He had said it so naturally that I was tempted to believe him. At the same time I thought that this trap was as obvious as his attempt to make me speak English.

'Yes, I know,' he went on. 'You won't say anything. It would be too easy to make English agents speak like that. But you'll soon see that it wasn't a trap. So remember this: not everyone in the French police is a collaborator. Old Pétain is a good man. And he's going gaga. Laval's leading him by the nose. Lots of the French have realised. Including those in the police. They've made us do some appalling things. To the Jews, amongst others. We warned those we could. But what do you expect? Anyway, please make it clear to your bosses that not all the French police are bastards. You'll come to see that when you make your landings. There'll be some surprises. Vichy is going to fall from a great height. I was with La Rocque, against the commies. But marching alongside the Germans, no thanks! You can turn your back on something. No one thinks the less of you for it. Well, I can tell you're not going to say anything. That's to be expected.'

He stood up suddenly and said: 'This way!' showing me the door.

I stood up. He opened the door and stood aside for me to pass. Amazed and still believing this was a trap, I did as he said.

'And really, that business in Dreux was spot on! I laughed like a drain when I read the reports. All my men laughed!'

Guided by a courteous gesture from him – which I could only interpret as heavily ironic – I went back down the way I had come. The policeman on reception was reading a book by Gyp. He glanced at us lazily and carried on reading when he saw the superintendent. The other man had taken up his shift outside. On the doorstep the superintendent held out his hand to me. 'Go on then, a good day to you!' he said with a wink. 'And if you have time, make an effort to come up with a more credible story. And practise your French! If you have any problems you can come and see me. Superintendent Trochu. Discreetly, *of course*!' he added with another wink, saying these last two words in his accented English so that they came out as 'erv korss'.

Thoroughly disconcerted, I stood silent and motionless on the pavement. With his eyes sparkling under his thick eyebrows, he waved at me impatiently to make me move on. 'Go on then. *Bon courage!*'

I crossed the street as if in a dream. As I went into the building where Noor was waiting for me, I turned back. The superintendent was talking to the sentry. The latter turned to look at me as I pushed the door. He looked me right in the eye. And, as if saluting a senior officer, he brought two fingers up to his képi.

Noor fell into my arms. I must have rung the bell four times, shouting through the door to tell her there was nothing to worry about, before she made her mind up. She watched me through the spy-hole, wondering whether there was a squad of policemen on the floor below waiting for her to open the door so that they could throw themselves on us.

'Oh!' she moaned, pressing herself against me. 'I was so frightened!'

'It's all right, it's all right, it's over!' I said gently.

'I saw you following that fat man into the police station. I thought we'd had it. I was going to escape through the courtyard if he came over. I got my radio ready. Then I saw you coming back out again. I didn't understand a thing. What on earth happened?'

She was still in my arms and I was beginning to find my misadventure extremely pleasant, even if my legs were still quaking.

'You won't believe it. When he stopped me, I could see myself being imprisoned, tortured, shot. I've never been so terrified. I could hardly speak.'

'But what did he want?'

'I don't know. He saw right through me straight away. I didn't have a shred of a convincing cover to give him. I was a salesman without samples going to see a client who doesn't exist. Philby was right, Noor. Never go out without a good story. Otherwise, you don't last five minutes.'

'But didn't he do anything? Or say anything?'

'No, nothing. He explained that not all the French police are bastards.'

'Is he in the Resistance?'

'No. I don't think so. But he's on the right side. He'd received a circular about us. That's how he recognised me in the café at the end of the street. He showed me the drawings of us. Not bad. There's no question of us going outside together. We must do something to change the way we look.'

'Oh, I'm so happy! You can't imagine! I was distraught. I want to kiss the man!'

We both laughed.

'He congratulated me for the operation in Dreux,' I told her.

'I hope you thanked him.'

'Well, no. I thought it was some horrible trap.

Earlier he'd tried to speak English. But he sounded like Maurice Chevalier.'

We were enjoying this more and more. She had stepped back slightly but was still leaning on my arm which was round her waist. When she laughed she leant towards me and her forehead rested on my chest. I could feel her body pressed against mine. The sudden relaxing of tension, my happiness to be free, and her affection so nearly like a lover's sent an exultant thrill through me. I took Noor by the shoulders and gently turned her so that I could look her in the eye.

'Noor,' I said, 'we don't have much time. We're going to have to leave Paris, make contact and send transmissions. We could be taken. I keep thinking about it. You must do too. These could be our last days before they kill us.'

She looked at me searchingly as if she had been expecting and dreading what I was going to say.

'Noor, you know that I love you. Tomorrow or the day after I may have to face another policeman who won't be on our side. I would never forgive myself for not having the courage to do this. I love you, Noor. You are the bravest, most beautiful woman I've ever known. You're the woman of my dreams.'

'Oh, don't say that! It's too much . . . I can't help thinking about the danger either, about time passing, about how much time there is left.'

I pulled her gently towards me to kiss her. She let me. But at the last moment she turned her head and buried herself against my chest. She too was holding me very tightly now.

'But I can't. I've given my word, do you understand? I love you very much, John, you know that. But I can't!'

She was biting her lip. We stayed in each other's arms for a long time, standing in the middle of the hall, without saying a word. She cried softly. Then I took her by the shoulder and led her into the sitting room.

'We must prepare a message for London. Vienet explained everything to me. We must tell them. Vienet thinks Prosper isn't the traitor, but I'm not sure. He did do the most extraordinary thing; he made an agreement with the Gestapo.'

I told her briefly about my conversation with Vienet and his confirmation of my most important mission: to find out who was talking to the Germans.

'But how are we going to carry on with the enquiry?' she asked when I had finished.

'I've got an idea.'

That evening my life turned upside down.

At ten past nine, Noor set up her radio on Renée Garry's dressing-table, took out the quartz and started listening. She sat upright on her chair and the headphones formed a hairband for her long black hair. As usual, I was sitting on a chair to her right to help her and to read the messages as soon as she transcribed them. The transmission started at a quarter past nine. In the silence of the apartment I could hear the dots and dashes of the Morse through the dampening haze of the head-phones. Noor's hand sped over her notebook, putting down the groups of letters as they came. She darkened a whole page with the incomprehensible words. Then she put the headphones down, switched the radio off and started to decode the message. It took a good thirty seconds to decode each letter, so the message emerged one letter at a time during its slow gestation. London sent news of various networks. Nothing new on Prosper. Tinker and Cowburn had escaped the raids, as had Cinema, run by our friends the Garrys. It was suggested that we should make contact with them as soon as was practical to analyse the ways in which the SOE's activities in and around Paris could be set in motion again. London also instructed us to maintain contact with the Resistance and to help them, as far as it was possible, to send their messages to England. Baker Street emphasised the need to resume military operations as soon as possible. The organisation was ready to arrange for arms and other materials to be parachuted in at our request.

Noor gave a little scream. I leant forward to see what she had written: 'SCIENTIST NETWORK DIS'. I looked at her. She was terribly pale. I glanced at the notebook. There on the table, in amongst all those letters which held the rest of the message, hidden by the code, a terrible piece of news was about to emerge. It was like a mortal threat lurking on the innocent paper of that little school book.

'It's . . . it's not possible,' Noor said numbly. 'Yesterday and the day before they said that everything was fine with Scientist. . . It can't be possible!' Donaldson, her fiancé, was in that network.

I took her hand. She looked at me and her eyes were full of anguish. The cruel irony of the situation weighed my heart down. There were tears rolling down her cheeks. 'Oh, well,' she said. 'I have to know!'

She leant over the notebook again and total silence descended on the room. I just waited for her pencil scratching across the paper. I read the last word.

'SCIENTIST NETWORK DISMANTLED'.

'No, no,' she said. 'It's not possible!'

But, with her mouth twisted with tension and her body trembling, she carried on: 'SCIENTIST, COURIER AND RADIO OP'.

She paused for a moment, terrified by what she might decode. I felt a glimmer of hope. It was possible, after all, that Donaldson and his colleagues had survived the demise of the network. There could still be a miracle. I took her shoulder. She transcribed the first letter: 'K'.

'No!' she cried, stifled by sobs. 'No!'

She transcribed the next few letters. Then she gave a terrible scream and threw herself backwards. I read the word with its misshapen letters: 'KILLED'. She put her head in her hands. 'It's so unfair. The bastards! They got him. In a month. How? He was so confident. So calm.' She stopped, and then started again almost immediately: 'It's this man, the one we're looking for, who gave him away! The bastard,' she said, staring straight ahead with her fists tightly clenched in her lap. 'It's not possible! Not him!' she whispered and she fell against my shoulder, racked with sobs. A muffled scream rose from her throat. She leant forwards as if she were going to be sick, with her arms crossed over her stomach. A long very quiet wail escaped from her as she sat doubled over. I could not speak or move. A quarter of an hour passed. It was as if she were in a trance, and I had no idea what to do. I waited, helplessly, until the shock dissipated.

She suddenly sat back up and started transcribing again, stony-faced. 'SCIENTIST, COURIER AND RADIO OP KILLED IN SHOOT-OUT'. 'Ah!' she said, tight-lipped, 'they put up a fight. I hope they killed lots of them.'

The message went on: 'AVOID ALL CONTACT WITH MEMBERS OF SCIENTIST. ONLY NORMAN AND PROSPER STILL RELIABLE.'

'But they're still feeding us that nonsense about Prosper and Norman!' I said.

'Until we've radioed them,' she said, 'they'll stay in the dark. We'll have to find a way to get out.' Her reddened eyes were no longer crying. Her face now looked pained but full of determination.

'We'll see about that tomorrow,' I said. 'I'll meet Blainville, using the methods Garry told me about along the embankment with the bookseller. And I'll call Vienet.'

'You mustn't be the one to take all the risks. I can go out too.'

'No, not straight away. You're more recognisable than I am.'

'What we really need,' she said, 'is some dye. You're very fair and I'm very dark. If we changed that they'd have a lot more trouble.'

'I'll look for a hairdresser tomorrow.'

This practical conversation soothed her. She took my hand and we went into the sitting room.

'I won't tell you any more about my life tonight,' she said with a sad smile. 'But let's have a drink. I need it.'

I gave her a big glass of port and poured myself some whisky. She relaxed into the big club chair and undid her shoes. She sighed from her very depths. 'He was a wonderful man,' she said. 'He died fighting – that doesn't surprise me.' A tear welled in the corner of her eye. She went on slowly in the quiet of the evening: 'He loved life. We were going to get married, but after the war. He didn't want to leave a widow behind, he said. He could look his own death in the face. He told me that if he was killed I should live my life. I should remember him but live my life. The bastards got him. When it comes down to it, they got the best of us.'

'There'll be many more who die. We can't win without that. But the country will remember him. He did what was right. He confronted the beast. We have to confront it too.'

'And what if the beast wins?'

'No. If men like Donaldson are ready to die, we'll win.'

She poured herself another glass of port. She moved slowly as if weighed down. Her face looked serious and sad in the half-light. She sat back down, frowning, her expression suddenly fierce and sharp. 'We've got to do something,' she said in a louder voice. 'We can't stay here. We've got to act. Whatever happens. I remember what Wesselow said at Arisaig. Do you remember? "We won't have left those bastards in peace. And for idiots like us, that's not bad at all!"' She smiled bitterly and added: 'At least we will have made something of our lives. We mustn't let the bastards choose for us. If we have a few days left the choices will be ours, not theirs.'

'We'll go out tomorrow.'

As I heard her overcoming her pain with what struck me as an extraordinary effort of will, my admiration for her rose to new heights. If that was possible.

'I've got an idea about how to track down the traitor,' I said, and I explained my plan to her. She listened, concentrating on every word. At one point she raised a technical objection. I gave her the reasoning behind the move, and she thought of a solution. Then she stood up. 'Let's go to bed. We've got a hard day ahead of us tomorrow . . .' Her voice tailed off and then she added: 'And today was hard enough.'

I stood up with her and she leant against me. I took her to her bedroom door and was about to kiss her when she burst into tears again. Our plans had taken her mind off her pain, but the night that lay ahead was bringing it all back. I held her by her shoulders again. 'You have to be strong,' I said. 'Think about what we're going to do. It's the only solution.'

Her whole body shook as she sobbed. I opened the door and took her over to her bed. She turned to face me and put her arms round my neck, with her head on my chest. Her tears made little damp circles on my shirt. Then she suddenly collapsed as if her legs could no longer hold her, and the next moment we were both on the bed, locked motionless in each other's arms. She was crying quietly, saying: 'I'm so sorry, please forgive me.' And she gradually calmed down. After about a quarter of an hour she turned towards the wall, hunched over with her knees drawn up to her chest. I could feel her rounded back against me, and I felt I ought to leave her now. I withdrew my arms from around her, but she said: 'Stay!' and put out her arm to switch off the bedside light. I pressed the switch for her and we stayed there in silence, like two children giving each other a bit of reassurance in the dark. She shuddered with sobs from time to time, and sighed more and more quietly. Then she went to sleep.

Snuggled against her, overwhelmed by my love for her, I listened as her regular breathing filled the silence in the room. I could hear a gentle breeze in the garden below and, in the distance, the muffled sound of a car passing. The moonlight filtered through the shutters, making her black hair gleam and cutting up the silhouette of her shoulder in front of me. I gradually succumbed to sleep. As I sank deeper, I could see her smile in my mind's eye, and my sleepy imagination pictured her graceful movements. A feeling of hope washed over me, but it was mixed with a sense of shame.

Something on the bed had moved. In one glimpse I saw both my watch glowing where my arm was bent back – it was four o'clock – and Noor's silhouette sitting on the bed. She was unbuttoning her top roughly, jerkily, making her hair swish backwards and forwards across her shoulders. In my sleepy state, I wondered what was going on. She bent her arms round behind her back: she was undoing her bra. Then she took off her dress. I opened my eyes wide and the blood beat in my temples. She turned towards me, put one arm round my shoulders and drew me to her. I put my arms round her. I could feel her warm, bare skin. My heart beat so hard that it hurt. 'Noor . . . what is it?' I said stupidly.

'Shh, don't talk. Don't try to understand. I've thought about things. We don't have time. I don't want them to steal my life.'

And she kissed me with a sweetness and a passion I could never have imagined. I held her in my arms, stroking her naked back. She let out a little cry which changed into a gentle moan. When I lowered myself onto her thigh, she bent her leg and put it round mine, and kissed me all the more fervently. I felt her supple torso against me. She pulled back and undid the buttons of my shirt. Her fingers became forceful, imperious. She bent over me, as if concentrating on some delicate task. As she revealed each part of my body she kissed it slowly and stroked it lightly with her hand.

At dawn I fell asleep again, feeling perfectly replete.

CHAPTER NINETEEN

At midday Noor shook my shoulder. She was washed and dressed, in a sleeveless blouse and a pair of culottes. She had put a tray on the bedside table with a steaming teapot and slices of toasted black bread.

'Come on, up you get, soldier!' she said, laughing.

'Noor . . .' I started to say.

There must have been God knows what sort of solemn expression on my face because she put her finger to her lips and smiled. 'No. Don't let's talk about it. It was a moment of happiness. There's nothing to add . . . We should forget . . .'

'What do you mean forget?' I asked.

'Yes. Forget. It was fantastic, John, but it never happened. We were like two children in the night.'

I was stupefied, mortified. 'Children?' I asked a little angrily. 'Quite grown-up children, I would say.'

'Perhaps,' she said with a laugh. 'But we must forget it. I have to.' Her eyes were somehow veiled and would not look right at me.

'Well, I'm not going to be able to forget.'

'John,' she begged, 'we are friends, aren't we?'

'Friends! No we're not, we're not friends. Friends . . . that's a terrible word!'

'But it's the most wonderful word.'

'Noor, please don't make fun of me.' It was my turn to beg.

'I'm not making fun of you. It was the worst night of my life and the best. That's all.' Then her voice softened as she added: 'I need time . . . Do you understand?'

I understood only too well.

'Let's talk,' she said. 'I'm going to go and get some hair dye this morning.'

'No, it's dangerous. You're too easy to recognise.'

'But if you go to a hairdresser and ask for dye, they'll be suspicious straight away.'

'I'll find something to tell them. I'll have to manage.'

She sat down on the bed with her cup of tea in one hand. With the other she handed me the toast.

'There weren't any croissants,' she said.

'It will still be the best breakfast I've ever had, my love,' I said, looking her in the eye.

'Don't call me that.'

'Oh? All right! If you like . . . my love.'

She laughed as she tried to look angry. I put my arm round her neck and she kissed me on the cheek.

'No! No more kisses on the cheek. I can't bear it, please!'

'John, don't let's have an argument.'

'Oh, let's! Why not, don't you think?'

'Right. Lieutenant, we're at the front. We must restore discipline!'

'No. The war starts at two o'clock. It's not time yet.'

She laughed and kissed me lightly on the lips. 'Oh, what a grumpy face!' she said.

I finished my tea and disappeared into the bathroom. I saw myself in the mirror: the happiest of men and the unhappiest. In the bottom of my heart, even though it was masked by anger, I could recognise my fear. The fear of losing her having only just won her. I was being chased out of the Garden of Eden.

The hairdresser on the rue de Passy looked at me oddly, but she sold me the two bottles of dye. The story of my bed-ridden mother had clearly not convinced her. But the sight of the banknotes had dispersed her suspicions. I had taken two notes of large denominations from the false bottom of my suitcase. The SOE's delicate missions did have that advantage: you were never short of money. It was forged money but it was made by the technicians at the Bank of England, under the vigilance of the Minister for Economic Affairs, who worked with the SOE. I imagined the little thrill these illicit activities would give to the civil servants who, in peacetime, were responsible for the security of the currency.

Then I met up with Vienet again at Aux Espagnols, checking this time that there were no clients who might overhear our conversation. I avoided mentioning Superintendent Trochu, but

I explained my plan to him. He approved, suggesting one minor modification. 'I'll come myself. It'll be safer,' he said. 'But dye your hair first. Otherwise we're taking a lot of risks!'

I went back up to the apartment four stairs at a time. Noor took the bottles and carried a chair into the bathroom. She sat me down with a big towel knotted round my neck. The bitter smell of the dye spread throughout the apartment. Noor had rifled through the medicine cupboard and found one of those wooden spatulas used to press down a child's tongue to look at their throat. 'My mother sometimes dyed her hair,' she said.

She had diluted the black dye in a bowl, and was painting it on, a lock at a time. I watched her in the mirror as she worked attentively, bent over me, her supple back arched and her thighs pressing against the fabric of her culottes. She caught me looking at her and shook her head with a smile, which managed to put me in a bad mood. I turned to talk to her, and the contents of the bowl spilt over my head, streaming over my face like a brown waterfall. She burst out laughing. 'That's what comes of thinking bad thoughts.'

I tried hard not to smile, keeping a steely eye and a hard line to my mouth as I wiped myself with the towel. She finished her work and we then had to wait for the dye to take. I sat down on the sofa in the sitting room and Noor sat at the piano. She played a Mozart concerto, which gradually soothed me. When it was time to go out, she went

267

to the door of the apartment with me, closely studying my appearance. I had put on my other, more formal suit, with a tie and well-buffed shoes.

'I think that'll do,' she said. 'I can hardly recognise you.'

'Yes,' I said. 'I'd noticed.'

There was no poster of Aristide Bruant on the side of the bookseller's box. The way was clear. Hardly daring to sit down, I had made my way there on the Métro, searching the faces of all the other passengers. I had changed trains at Michel-Ange-Auteuil and got out at Maubert. Then, looking behind me every thirty seconds, I had walked along the rue des Bernardins towards the Seine. I had calculated that the last bookstall on the quai de Montebello would be on a level with the end of the little road that ran past the church of Saint-Nicolas-du-Chardonnet with narrow, decrepit-looking buildings on either side of it. As the road opened out onto the embankment I saw the café that Garry had mentioned. There was a terrace under a removable awning, and a small interior area with four tables. I sat down at the back of the room: I would be in shadow to anyone passing outside but I myself could see the embankment clearly in the sunlight. On the pavement opposite, all along the parapet above the Seine, enthusiasts fingered through the stalls of old books. The poster warning of danger was not there. The bookseller was sitting on a folding chair to the left of his stall, reading a book covered in translucent rice paper. I waited a few minutes while I drank a synthetic fruit juice, which was a peculiar brown colour. Over to the left on the far side of the river I could see through the trees swaying in the gentle summer wind to the buttresses of Notre-Dame cathedral, holding up its grey tiled roof above the nave. Everything seemed normal. No sentries looking for something to do near the stall. The customers who had been looking through the boxes of books were moving away. None of them retraced his steps. No cars parked nearby. There were just young women on bicycles, a few *vélo-taxis* and occasionally a German car with its little red and black flag. On the Île de la Cité there were soldiers in uniform walking by with their heads in the air, and others sitting at terraces looking at the Seine as it shone under the blue sky.

I stood up, crossed the street and stopped in front of the bookstall. The long box of books was open with engravings pinned to the raised lid. I ran my finger along the dusty spines of the books. The copy of *Madame Bovary* was the third book in the back row. A furtive glance to left and right. I took out the note I had written and slipped it into the thick volume where the pages had been cut apart by hand. I looked through the other rows, then carried on steadily along the embankment towards the Saint-Michel bridge.

When I reached the corner of the rue Dante, on a level with the square in front of Notre-Dame, someone tapped me on the shoulder. Terrified, I leapt sideways. It was Blainville. His blue eyes watched me with an amused twinkle and his wayward lock of hair lolled in the breeze.

'I was worried about you,' he told me. 'Thank goodness, you're here! I've been coming here at five o'clock every evening. Today I saw you arriving just as I was leaving. I followed you to make sure you really were alone.'

'I'm so pleased to see you,' I said, shaking his hand.

'Let's go and have a drink. My café's not far from here.'

Blainville owned a bistro on the corner of the rue Gît-le-Coeur and the rue Saint-André-des-Arts. He had bought it with money from the SOE, having persuaded London that it would be an excellent way of arranging rendezvous without fear of unwanted company. He had in fact been so forceful with his arguments that Baker Street had felt obliged to give in, if only to avoid upsetting such a valued member of the organisation. It was an expensive-looking café with a copper counter, leather armchairs and gleaming coffee percolator. The terrace spilled over slightly onto the narrow road, which was lined with stalls on the pavements outside the university bookshops. He introduced me to his wife, who was behind the till, a small, plump woman in a brightly coloured dress. I was struck by the contrast between them; I would have expected him to have a tall, slender, sophisticated wife.

He spoke to her abruptly to order a beer and a pastis. She brought the drinks and closed up the café (any more customers would have been a hindrance to us); then she went straight back behind the counter. 'So how did you manage it?' he asked me. 'Our friends are in a sorry situation.'

I told him about our narrow escape at Viroflay: Noor's intuition, the struggle with the officer and our flight through the woods.

'That young woman's extraordinary,' he said. 'I'm only half surprised. She's got no experience but all the nerve.'

'Yes, she's extraordinary.'

'And what a figure!' he added with a connoisseur's enthusiasm.

I threw him a black look. He changed the subject. 'I've been in touch with Prosper's people two or three times. A lot of them have been rounded up. The Adamowskis have been taken, and poor Andrée Borrel was very nearly had. They're holding her at Fresnes. She was injured as she tried to escape. They've arrested about a hundred people, at least. I thought of hiding, but I'm too vulnerable anyway. If anyone talks they'll arrest my wife and I'd have to give myself up. It looks as if no one's talked.'

I imagined that Prosper and Norman had given away the caches and the landing sites without mentioning that there was someone who organised the trips. After all, the Germans need not know that there was an agent who specialised in finding new landing sites and supervising the landings.

271

'But who gave us away?' I asked suddenly.

'I don't know,' he said, 'but I think poor Prosper was exhausted. They might well have caught him before this round-up and come to some sort of agreement with him. He may have made a fool's bargain with them. He's brave, but his agents mean a lot to him. These people in the Gestapo know what they're doing and they're clever. They must have offered to spare his men, or something like that. So he gave in and everyone was taken, or almost . . .'

'Do you think it was him who told them about the operations in the rue de Solferino and at the station in Dreux?'

'Maybe. He probably gave them snippets in keeping with his agreement without actually causing the operations to fail. That way, the Germans knew part of what was going on, but not enough to stop everything.'

'Are you sure of that?'

'No, I'm guessing, assuming. But when you put everything that's happened in the last two weeks together, it's the most coherent hypothesis. Prosper paid heavily himself. He was incredibly sure of himself. When he saw the Germans getting close to him he must have decided he'd rather nego-tiate. As if he were one leader talking to another . . . This sort of lifestyle sends people a bit mad, you know. You lose any sense of what's normal.'

Blainville was using the same reasoning as Vienet, but reaching diametrically opposite conclusions.

'For now,' he went on, 'it's not easy for Aurora to make transmissions. But you might be able to get in touch with Norman. He's still active.'

'But Vien –' I started to say, but stopped myself straight away, and just said: 'but . . . but I thought Norman had been arrested!'

'No,' he said, looking at me wonderingly, surprised by my response. 'No, that's not what I've been told. Norman's still free.'

'But I know from Garry that he was arrested on the terrace of the Brasserie La Lorraine!'

'Really? But they assured me –'

'Who assured you, London?'

'Oh no! I haven't had any contact with London since the round-up. It's one of the survivors, someone you don't know, who's in touch with both Norman and myself. He told me that we could use his radio!'

I made a conscious effort to hide my disquiet. Blainville was telling me exactly the opposite of what Vienet and Garry had said! Why the discrepancy? Had Blainville been fed a line?

'Can you trust this contact?'

'Yes. One thousand per cent!'

'Right, we'll have to see. Either way, I think Norman's in their hands.'

'I'll check that as soon as possible.'

'Henri,' I said, looking him in the eye, 'we need your help. Without Prosper we don't have any kind of weapon. London has ordered us to carry on with military activities. We need materials. Could you

273

arrange a parachute drop in the next few days? I'll come to get the stuff. We have two safe apartments. We could store Stens, revolvers and plastic explosive in them. At least we could do something then.'

He thought for a moment and then said: 'Yes. Near Bourgueil, in Indre-et-Loire, I know a site that hasn't been used yet. I've got a cache in an isolated property. It could work.'

'Good. Give me the grid references for the site, I'll tell London and I'll get back to you to confirm it. They're ready, they'll work quickly.'

He stood up and walked to the back of the deserted café. Five minutes later he came back with a Michelin map and opened it on the table. He pointed to a wooded area a little to the north of the Loire, not far from Saumur. It was bordered by two villages, Gizeux and Courléon. In the middle of the green shape which depicted the woodland someone had written 'Chaumont'.

'It's there,' he said. 'It's some people who joined the Resistance in 1940.'

He opened the map right out and counted the folds to the left and the right. He reached the site and said: 'Fourth one on the second row!' Then he took a ruler to measure the site's abscissa and ordinate along the rectangle formed by the folds. He took a paper napkin and wrote the word 'Indigestion' on it in tiny letters with his propelling pencil. Then he put the Michelin map number for the Indre-et-Loire area, 37, the number of folds and the figures he had calculated with the ruler.

They intersected on the exact site. London had an identical set of Michelin maps: the pilot would have no trouble locating the place. Blainville had a peculiar habit of giving his landing sites the names of illnesses. There was 'Cancer', 'Influenza', 'Pneumonia', 'Tuberculosis', etc. And now the site at Chaumont was called 'Indigestion'. I crumpled the paper napkin and put it in the bottom of my trouser pocket. If I were searched, there was always a chance that the police would mistake this rag for a handkerchief and would not notice the tiny pencil-written figures.

'If you want,' he said, 'I could give the details to Norman. He might find it easier to radio them than you.'

'I can assure you, Henri, Norman's been arrested,' I said.

'All right. I'll be clear in my own mind about that soon enough. Send the transmission yourself if you want to. Will you come with Aurora?'

'Don't worry. We'll be there. I'll give you the details as soon as London answers. And we can agree on how we distribute the material. Shall I get hold of you through the bookstall?'

'Yes. On the embankment, I can check how safe it is. If you're followed, I'll know.'

I must have made a thousand detours, tied my shoelace four times and watched the street reflected in a dozen shop windows to catch anyone following me. Nothing. My conversation with Blainville had confused me. His accusations against Prosper made sense. Prosper's betrayal, however well intentioned it might have been, explained everything. But something worried me. Prosper, Norman, Blainville, Vienet and one other . . . All these different hypotheses jostling in my head. I told myself I would know everything in a few days' time. When I was sure I was not being followed, I decided to go down into the Métro. At Trocadéro I went along the avenue Paul-Doumer, an indirect way of getting back to my safe haven. I turned right along the narrow and deserted rue de la Tour, where I would easily be able to spot a tail. No one. At twenty-five past eight I rang the bell in the apartment, where Noor was waiting for me. She opened the door. I could see straight away that she had been crying. Her eyes were red and her face was pale. She did not avoid my kiss.

She had made a little cold supper. We ate quickly so that we would be ready to listen to the news from London at nine o'clock. Nothing new, just a repeat of the previous day's news, including the fate of the Scientist network. Noor cried again, but quickly recovered herself. Baker Street was very keen for contact with us although they reiterated the need for caution.

'I'll ask Vienet,' I said. 'We need to transmit our request for a parachute drop. Then we'll know.'

'I'm going to dye my hair tomorrow,' she said. 'You won't be the only one who goes out.'

'We'll see.'

In the half-darkness of the room I felt a surge of desire for her. I held her tightly to me. Again, she did not resist, and let me stroke her gently. Then she said: 'You're forgetting our rendezvous!'

Five minutes later she was sitting in front of me, her legs and feet bare on the leather of the armchair, and a glass of port in her hand. 'Today, it's your turn to talk.'

'But there's nothing interesting about my life.'

'There is for me,' she said softly. 'It couldn't be more interesting. Where were you born?'

I decided not to put up any resistance. After all, it is quite nice talking about yourself. Particularly to the woman you love.

'In Cowes, on the Isle of Wight in the South of England. Where they organise lots of yacht races.'

'I know it very well!' she said, laughing. 'How funny. Well, I really know Portsmouth and Southampton.'

'My father worked in Portsmouth, at the naval shipyard. He took a boat across the Solent every day.'

'Was he an engineer?'

'No, a mechanic. We lived in a little flat on the high street in Cowes, it was above a fishing shop. He had to get up really early to catch the ferry, but it was cheaper than Portsmouth. My father assembled the hull and the heavy parts of the bridge to build ships. I was really impressed by him as a little boy. He had big dark goggles to protect his eyes and he used a blowtorch, which sent sparks everywhere. I thought it was the most difficult job in the world.'

'Perhaps it was.'

'Perhaps. It was certainly one of the hardest. When I was a boy he worked ten hours a day, including Saturdays. Then everything changed. Luckily. But my father paid dearly for it.'

'Why?'

'He was in the union. He was even one of the leaders. During the big miners' strike in 1926, he brought the naval shipyard out on strike.'

There must have been an edge of pride in my voice because she said: 'He was a fighter, too.'

'Yes. The strike lasted three months. Longer than the miners'. After six weeks there was nothing left to eat in the house. My mother was in despair. My father went to fish in the river at Cowes when he wasn't on duty on the picket lines. There were four of us, four children. I remember begging door-to-door round our area. I had a white tin-plate begging bowl with the word "Solidarity!" on one side and "Death to the scabs!" on the other. If they wouldn't give me any money, I turned the begging bowl round so they could see the second slogan! Then I'd run away. Hardly anyone gave me anything. There were a lot of scabs.'

'Scabs?' she asked, bewildered.

'People who weren't on strike. The directors had done a lock-out. People were starving. They'd plundered all their savings to survive, in some cases they'd used money they'd been saving to buy a little house. There would often be women fighting in the street outside my house. The ones whose husbands weren't striking insulted the others and vice versa. One evening my father came home with an even more gloomy expression on his face. He spoke to my mother for a long time. I was hungry, I couldn't sleep. I could hear what they were saying. The directors had got together a militia. One man had defected and warned the workmen. They were planning to attack the following day. My mother was terrified. She said we wouldn't be able to resist a militia. They were thugs and they wouldn't pull their punches. They were armed. They had dogs. And everyone knew the police would turn a blind eye. But my old man said we had to fight, or everything they'd done so far would mean nothing. My mother was in tears and he tried to comfort her. He explained that it was a question of honour, that his life wouldn't have any meaning if he stood down. Then he suddenly caught sight of me. I had peeped my head round the door of the bedroom that I shared with the others. I'll always remember it. I was twelve. He said: "Aren't you asleep? Come on, then," and he sat me down at the kitchen table. Which was also the dining room table. Still watching my mother out of the corner of his eye, he talked to me. His voice sounded strange. He must have been very moved. She was crying. "Well, son, the bosses are going to attack us tomorrow. If I don't go I won't be able to look at myself in the mirror ever again. The way I'm bringing you up, my boy, is to teach you to stay on your feet. You mustn't give in, you have to face up to things, even if they seem much stronger than you. If you don't, you're nothing. Force is the only way with these bosses. They'll always try to get us. We've got to stand up to them. Otherwise, the workers will never have their say. They'll always crush us. Maybe some people will be wounded. Maybe some'll die. Maybe I won't come back. But you'll be able to tell everyone that your old man stood up to them. And that's it!" The following morning the militia charged the picket lines with iron rods, cudgels and truncheons. They had three guns. But the workmen were ready for them. They'd set up an ambush in amongst the ships under construction. They had steel bolts, heavy-buckled belts and clubs. They caught them by surprise, trapped between two groups. The thugs panicked. The men with guns fired. Two men died, two workmen. The police didn't move a muscle. But the militia was completely crushed. They almost all ended up in hospital. My father came home with a great gash on his head and a split in his top lip. He had bandages all round his face. But I'd never seen that look on his face! The whole town went to the funeral for the two workmen. And we sang the "Internationale" by the graveside.'

'Was your father a communist?'

'No. Not at all. He didn't like the Bolsheviks. He said they were dictators. There were very few communists in England, anyway. My father was with the Labour Party, like most workmen. But most of all he was with the union. The bosses lodged a complaint, accusing the strikers of attacking their regulating forces. They had the law on their side. Picketing was illegal. But this was all under MacDonald's government. He was a Labour Party man too. He asked for a report from the Minister of Employment. The report concluded that the bosses had provoked the workmen, and that caused a hell of a scandal. The Conservatives went wild. For once MacDonald held good. So the managers of the naval shipyard decided to negotiate. Because of the deaths the whole town was against them. They conceded almost every-thing: a forty-eight hour week instead of fifty-four hours, better pension, health insurance, unem-ployment fund – and even a week's paid holiday. This was ten years before the Popular Front! The whole lot! When we knew what was in the agree-ment my father got all the union leaders together at our flat. They sang and cheered all through the night. Even I did. We had to carry them home at dawn. The next day my old man said: "You see, my son, you must never give in!" But the bosses at the yard got him in the end. They watched him every minute of every day. A year later they managed to lay the blame for some mistake on him. He was fired. He appealed, and won, but they paid the fine and refused to take him back on. They put the word around all the other bosses and he stayed out of work for six months with the pathetic little indemnity they got at the end of the strike. The union helped him, but he was going to have to move house to find work. He didn't want to move away. That's when my mother left. She couldn't take any more. She was French, from Granville in the Channel. He'd married her when he was travelling, on a trip to France by the Cherbourg ferry. She went back home, and I've never seen her since. She's at Granville. I've got an address, but I haven't had the courage to go there. She never sent any news and my father never got over it. He eventually found some sort of work in a small yard in Cowes, building yachts. He was on much less pay, but he liked the work. There was something noble about yachts. Not as noble as cargo boats and liners, but noble all the same. On Sundays he would take me round the Isle of Wight in a boat from the yard. He taught me to sail. He was at peace on the water. The rest of the time he worked like an ox to support us children. He never travelled anywhere or went anywhere.'

'Did he remarry?'

'No. He said he was too old. Actually, he was still in love with my mother. She was too pretty . . . . He suffered terribly. But he never complained, never in front of us. Just every now and then he would come home a bit late, a bit unsteady on his feet. That's all. He saved everything he could. He sent me to college then to university. I worked hard. We often talked about politics at home. He read the paper every evening and we'd always discuss the news. He talked about the English middle classes, capitalism, fascism. During the Spanish Civil War he organised some fund-raising and in 1938 he told me: "This Chamberlain man is weak and stupid. He's given in to the fascists. There's going to be a war!" He went to the demonstrations, but not that often: he was busy looking after us. The union arranged evening classes for workmen's children who wanted to do well in their studies. We had free books and advanced classes. When I came down from Cambridge he came to the ceremony by train. He put on his only suit, and starched his shirt himself. He stood bolt upright in the front row, next to all those gentrified families, as proud as a lord. When he saw me in my black robes he burst into tears. When we got back to Portsmouth, his friends from the union had brought a brass band to the station. We cried like babies. We didn't know what to do with ourselves! He was happy at last. I think. Then he died. In the summer of 1939. He'd inhaled too much steel dust. He died in six weeks, in no pain. On the last day he called me to him and said: "You've got a good job in London. I read your articles. They're good. So look after your brothers and your sister!" Then he added: "Now you're flying high, but never forget where you came from! Never!" and he squeezed my hand. That was all. It was enough.'

'You're right. It was enough. Now I know why you're here.'

CHAPTER TWENTY

Noor, too, had respected her father's wishes. We were still talking long after midnight, caught up in our alternating confessions. The levels were going down in both bottles and the alcohol kept us going. Noor continued with her story: after Ajit's death their lives continued peacefully, and only the begum brought any unhappiness into Noor's life. After her husband's death she had withdrawn to her bedroom on the first floor of the house and drawn the curtains. She never left that room. She had her meals brought up to her and she lived most of her life sitting cross-legged in the half-light, meditating. She never smiled, hardly read and rarely spoke. Only Noor could have long conversations with her. Her skin became paler and paler and her voice weaker and weaker. She was withering like a plant starved of sunlight.

Noor became increasingly charming, knowledgeable and talented. She took various children who lived on the hill under her wing and told them stories about her country, the India of impenetrable jungles and fabulous animals. She learned to play the harp with Mme Bardeaux, who made her play Lili Laskine (who went on to become an eminent French harpist). Ravel came to her lessons from time to time and spoke about Indian music with Noor and her brothers, who were learning to play the violin and the cello. One day Noor decided to write down the stories she made up for the children from Suresnes. She found a small publishing company and published her first book, *Tales from Jakarta*, a collection of stories full of generous princes and speaking serpents. A friend suggested that she should show them to a radio programmer, and every week throughout 1939 Noor would go to the Radio-Paris studios to record one of the tales, reading them in her gentle voice to a background of Sufi music. The people at Radio-Paris said she had quite a following. She carried on through 1940, despite the strange war that had broken out, while continuing with her literature course at the Sorbonne and her harp lessons. In June everything was turned upside down. The family listened in horror to the radio reports that the French army had suddenly been defeated, and no military propaganda could hide the fact any longer. They pored over their old leather-bound atlas and studied the maps of the eastern *départements* of France to work out the positions of the various armies as reported in the reassuring official communiqués. There was no doubt: the theatre of operations was making daily progress westwards and coming closer and closer to Paris. Noor's younger brother and sister decided to leave for the south to avoid capture if and when the Germans arrived. Noor and Vilayat stayed with the begum, who followed the events from her darkened room. They remembered Ajit's warnings about the Nazis. Hitler's racist obsessions seemed like a mortal threat to them. And, on 12 June 1940, Noor and Vilayat heard a cannon thundering far away to the north-east. Some French detachments had passed by Suresnes in the last few days, pathetic, disbanded units making their way along the Seine. So the two young people settled themselves in the sitting room, Vilayat on a leather chair and Noor on the sofa with her legs folded under her. Through the window they could see the whole of Paris in a heat haze. The birds were singing in the garden below them, and rays of sunlight made pools of yellow on the sculpted bookcase filled with rows of books on theology. There was a sitar lying upside down on the pedestal table next to Noor, and the harp stood behind Vilayat, wrapped in its case.

'We can't stay,' Vilayat said. 'We must go south. Mother won't survive here, in her bedroom. The French won't hold out. Hitler's won in France. We must go.'

'But the French are going to carry on fighting.'

'No. They won't be able to. It's like in Poland six months ago. They've got tanks and aeroplanes, the French aren't ready. They're beaten, for sure. We can hear the cannon. The Germans are near Paris.

It'll only take a month! But the English aren't going to give up. The king has summoned Churchill. We know all about him, Noor. He's the one who gave our father so much trouble. He's an arrogant Englishman, but he's hard. He's fanatical about the Empire. He's been speaking out about the Nazis for years. He'll stand up to them, that's for sure. It's easier for the English, they've got the sea.'

'So, we'll have to go to England then. The English will protect us.'

'Yes. But we must do more than protect ourselves. We have to fight, our father told us so. We must fight these Nazis. They want to kill religion and freedom and everything that makes life worth living. Let's fight with the English and the French. Well, with the English, anyway.'

'But we can't fight. We've made an oath. No violence, no murder, no assassination. This isn't our world, Vilayat. And, anyway, we can't do anything that's of any use. Do you really want to fight with your cello, Vilayat?'

'We'll learn. When a country's at war, they make millions of soldiers out of civilians. We're just civilians, that's all.'

'But I don't want to kill. Never!'

'I've been thinking. There is a solution. We'll ask to be assigned to non-combatant units. We'll be useful. We won't have guns but we'll be useful.'

'The English will laugh at us! When they see this pair of savages from some weird sect asking to sign up on condition that they don't have to kill.

We're going to look ridiculous, Vilayat. No, either we're in the army or we're not.'

'But, for goodness' sake, they need everyone! We can help them. Anyway, we don't have any choice. If we stay in France we'll be sure to do nothing. The war's going to spread, Noor. We've got to be part of it!'

'But what are we going to tell the English when we get out of the boat? Goodness only knows where they'll send us. It's the army who assigns people. Well, I imagine it is. If everyone turned up with their own special requests, they wouldn't be able to make it work. Fighting a war without fighting! They're going to think we're cowards.'

'There is a solution,' said Vilayat. 'We will tell them: our religious convictions forbid us to kill but we want to fight. Send us to dangerous units, but ones where you don't have to shoot anyone. Even very dangerous units.'

'But what does that mean, a dangerous unit? If it's dangerous then you must be figh–'

'No, not necessarily. Scouts and people who do reconnaissance behind enemy lines don't fight. But they run a lot of risks. Big risks. The people who navigate ships aren't armed. But when a shell explodes it doesn't choose between the armed men and the others. There are lots of jobs like that. They could accept that, couldn't they?'

Two years later, one October day in 1942, Noor went into the Northumberland, a hotel not far from the war office which had been requisitioned by the army, where the SOE recruiter held his interviews. Selwyn Jepson received her in a bare room. Looking very seductive in her navy blue RAF uniform, despite the flat shoes and the severe skirt, Noor sat down gracefully before him on a wicker chair in front of the kitchen table serving as a desk on which he had her military file.

Noor had left Paris on 16 June 1940 with her older brother and her mother, in the old car with running boards which had been put away in the garage at Fazal Manzil years before. Claire and Idayat, the younger two, had taken the more modern Citroën to take refuge on the Côte d'Azur, where they were to stay for the length of the war. The elder two with their mother had headed towards Bordeaux, where the government had taken refuge, amongst the terrified crowds walking along the sides of the road, and the eclectic collection of vehicles, laden with passengers, trunks and suitcases. Sleeping outside, eating as they drove along, quickly hiding under a tree or in the shadow of a wall when they heard an aeroplane engine, it had taken them three days to reach the port, which was still allowing occasional boats to leave for England. A Stuka had machine-gunned down some refugees right in front of them, and they had had to move the bodies off the road to carry on. The two women had taken refuge in Bordeaux station while Vilayat went to the port to find places for them on a cargo ship, and while they were there, the roof of the building was hit by a bomb. The glass canopy had exploded, showering the crowds of refugees with broken glass. Vilayat had eventually managed to secure two places on the last boat. Noor and her mother had leant against the ship's rusty rails, watching the coastline of their adopted country disappearing in the twilight. The following day they had replied as best they could to the immigration officer's questions, and he had granted them – as citizens of the British Empire – a provisional pass. Vilayat had gone all the way back up to Nantes to find a passage. Three days later the family had been reunited in a dark little flat in central London, which had been rented with the help of a family they had known the last time they were there. The begum had bravely withstood the trials of the journey, but her depression was overwhelming her again. Alone in a foreign city and with no resources, she could not see that she had anything to look forward to. Noor, ever cheerful, had talked about enrolling at London University and going to concerts at the Albert Hall. Vilayat had gone to the RAF recruitment offices the very next day and had nearly been thrown straight out. He wanted to train to be a reconnaissance pilot, but he refused to fight. He would risk his life on every mission, but he would not shoot anyone. After a whole week of interminable discussions in countless offices, thanks to his intelligence and his acuity, he had eventually achieved what he wanted. After a first phase of examinations, it was discovered that his eyesight was poor, so he asked to be transferred to the Navy and, if possible, to a minesweeper. There too the job seemed to be sufficiently peaceful but still dangerous. The Navy had had the wisdom to take him on. At the end of the war he was to be awarded the Victoria Cross.

Instead of heading to university and to concerts, Noor had imitated her brother. They had both felt as if their father's shadow were looming over them. The RAF had taken her on as a secretary, then she had applied to train as a radio operator and she had started her training on 28 August 1942. Some time later she had seen an advertisement on the walls of the room where she had her lessons. It called for bilingual volunteers to carry out an important mission, without actually specifying the nature of the mission. She had written off to the address, and now there she was, sitting opposite Jepson, an officer with a pleasant face and a touch of premature baldness.

In civilian life Jepson was a playwright and film scriptwriter. After the war he would go on to enjoy considerable success. He was already very familiar with the showbusiness world and, after writing so many dialogues and intrigues, had acquired an intuitive understanding of human character. He usually interviewed applicants at length, without revealing his intentions, then he would see them a couple more times to make a more detailed assessment, before deciding with Gubbins and Buckmaster (the two men in charge of the SOE) how to proceed with the candidature. With Noor, things happened a little differently.

As usual, Jepson spoke in English before abruptly switching to French, which he spoke fluently. If the candidate hesitated, Jepson would bring the interview to an end. Noor passed this first test without any difficulty.

'You've joined the RAF. But why have you come forward as a volunteer? You're not English.'

'I was born in Moscow but I spent part of my childhood in London. Then I lived in France. Both those countries welcomed me and now they're allies. It seems only right that I should fight for them.'

'You're Indian, like your father. The Indians have nothing to do with this war.'

'The Indians can't possibly hope that Hitler will win. He represents the exact opposite of everything they believe.'

'The Indians are asking for independence, and it's England who's refusing to grant it to them. Not the Germans. How can we be sure of your loyalty?'

'India will have its independence one day. It is written. But at the moment we have a common enemy – Nazism.'

'Does your father share your opinion?'

'My father is dead. My mother is in London, and my brother Vilayat is too. We left France in June 1940, to come to England.'

'Is your brother in the RAF?'

'He was in the RAF. His eyesight isn't good enough so they sent him to join the Navy.'

'Before the war you wrote children's stories?'

'Yes. I studied literature and music in Paris.'

'Do you play an instrument?'

'The piano, the harp and Indian instruments. We're a musical family.'

'I see from your file that you and your brother have been given a dispensation. You don't want to be assigned to a fighting unit, is that right?'

'Our religion is very strict on this. We are not allowed to use violence.'

'But, in war it's everyone's duty to be violent!'

'Not always. Winston Churchill doesn't kill anyone.'

'I don't imagine you're planning on joining the government.'

Noor laughed politely and shook her head. 'You have to understand us. I know that it's a little hypocritical, but all religions are a bit hypocritical aren't they? We are not allowed to kill anyone. But we're not stupid. This is war. We want to do our bit. The Nazis are monsters, and we must fight them. In exchange, we're prepared to accept dangerous missions.'

Jepson contemplated her in silent astonishment. 'But if you were threatened you would have to defend yourself, wouldn't you?'

'Perhaps. We'll see. For now, that's not the question.'

They fell silent while Jepson thought. He seemed

to reach a decision. 'It might become the question,' he said.

Silence again.

'I asked you to come here because we need volunteers for a dangerous mission,' he eventually continued.

'I thought that.'

'Very dangerous. We're looking for bilingual soldiers to send to France. They're English agents but they don't wear uniforms. If they're taken they don't have the benefit of any form of protection. They may be interrogated, perhaps brutally.'

'What do they have to do?'

'You're on a radio transmission course with the RAF. We need radio operators. If you accept this you would follow an intensive course, not only for radio operating but also for every kind of clandestine method of warfare.'

'I don't want to kill.'

'That's not the question. You undergo your training and then you're sent to France as a radio operator so that we can communicate with the Resistance networks. You have a one-in-two chance of coming back. There is no financial reward, and it won't afford you any promotion. Your pay will be put to one side while you're in France, and you will be given the money on your return. If you don't come back it will be sent to your family . . .'

He left his sentence hanging in the air. They were silent for a long time. Noor looked him right in the eye with a calm smile on her face.

'Do you think you would be able to accept?' he asked.

'Yes.'

Jepson was usually wary of over-hasty acceptances, but this time he cut short any hesitation. The young woman seemed to him to be an idealist, even over and above what he could have imagined, but she was by no means impulsive or reckless.

'Why?' he asked, just to set his mind at rest.

'Because that's what I came here for.'

It was four o'clock in the morning. We were befuddled by alcohol and lack of sleep. When Noor stood up she swayed, then she saw what the time was. 'We're mad!' she said.

'No, I'm the one who's mad,' I said, going over to her. I took her by the waist. She seemed tired, but there was a gleam in her eye. Surrendering, she moved closer to me with a smile playing on her lips. I kissed her full on the mouth, it was a long kiss. She moaned. She put one leg round me to press herself closer to me. I undid her skirt and then her top, and soon she was naked in my arms, slowly unbuttoning my shirt. When I had no clothes on, I fell backwards onto the sofa. An hour later we fell asleep with the sitting-room light still on.

I woke at eleven o'clock, blinking in the daylight filtering through the closed curtains. I switched off the light, then I took her languid body in my arms and carried her to her bedroom. She woke up and kissed me. Once in bed, she held me to her, shuddering. At four o'clock in the afternoon we were hungry. She cooked, wearing my shirt over her bare legs. Having eaten, she went and sat at the piano and started playing a Beethoven sonata. The tails of my shirt revealed her golden thighs right up to her hips. When she got to the third sonata I went over to caress her under the shirt. She carried on playing, with her eyes closed. She faltered with every movement of my fingers, then she stopped playing and slipped down onto the carpet.

We woke for the radio transmission at quarter past nine. London reiterated its suggestion of a parachute drop. We had to go out.

'I must see Vienet tomorrow,' I said. 'Let's get to bed. We haven't got such a nice day ahead of us.'

'There's just one problem,' she said.

'What's that?'

'I don't feel like sleeping.'

CHAPTER TWENTY-ONE

With my Colt in my belt and my jacket buttoned up, I leant against the windows of the Cinéma Les Acacias, where the photographs from *Les Enfants du Paradis* – Arletty, Pierre Brasseur and Jean-Louis Barrault – had been pinned onto a red-velvet background. I was watching the avenue Mac-Mahon, which ran down from the Étoile and crossed the rue des Acacias a little further on to my left. I was part of an ambush along with some men Kerleven had introduced me to, men from a very special section of the maverick, partisan force, made up of Jews, Armenians, Spaniards and Portuguese, known as the FTP-MOI. It was run by an Armenian called Manouchian, and it specialised in sabotage and assassinations. Manouchian's men had known glory: the German propaganda machine had had red posters put up all over France, featuring portraits of all of them with their unpronounceable names mingled in with photographs of derailings and weapons seized in raids. The Germans wanted to show that these so-called patriots were in fact foreign communists, who were both killers and 'bloody wops'. Having been relegated to public loathing by the occupying forces, they struck me as being eminently likeable. Their French was not good and they spoke little, but they did a great deal and the German army was afraid of them.

Noor and I had made contact with Vienet at the Espagnols. He had sent us by car to a forest in Picardie, where Noor had been able to make her transmission without any trouble. We had finalised the details of the planned parachute drop in Touraine with London. Blainville had been informed by means of the letter box on the quai Montebello. He had confirmed everything. The weapons would be dropped over Chaumont on 11 July towards one o'clock in the morning. Blainville would take them to a house that stood on a mound in the middle of a clearing, three miles from the closest village. It remained for us only to get to Touraine to take delivery of them. It was a dangerous operation. When we wandered about Paris we took acceptable risks, but getting through checks at stations was quite another matter.

Vienet had thought of Kerleven, and, when asked, the communist had agreed to transfer us to Touraine. He had a dependable route, thanks to the rail network of the Resistance: we would travel in the cab of a locomotive. The Germans very rarely checked up on train drivers, and, if they did, it was always possible to hide in the tender where the coal was kept. You came back out black with soot, but safe and alive.

'My dear Arthur,' Kerleven had said, 'I'm helping you out, and I'd like you to return the favour. I've seen you at work with your friend Darbois. You're very good. Our friends from Manouchian's group have set up an operation near the Étoile for the day after tomorrow. They need two marksmen. You do the job, and we'll take you to Saumur, there'll be two of them, and we'll bring you back. That's fair, isn't it?'

It was difficult to refuse. After all, the SOE had sent me to France to help the Resistance . . . every element of the Resistance. Manouchian was a small, swarthy, nervy man with a piercing expression, a black moustache and a neck so thin that there was a gap round the inside of his shirt collar. He had explained the operation to me. He had come up with an original system of covers which required a great deal of composure and good marksman-ship. He told me I was the perfect candidate. And so, two days later, I found myself leaning against the Acacias' window, automatically checking the reassuring shape of my Colt under my jacket.

At eleven thirty-two, the two men waiting in the avenue Mac-Mahon – one on a bench, the other leaning against a tree – set off after giving us a little nod. Thirty seconds later, I saw a German lorry coming down the avenue with a driver and an officer in the cab. The back was open, with no tarpaulin, so that the two rows of soldiers could travel in the fresh air. I saw each of the two FTP men coolly take out a grenade and count to four as they watched the lorry's progress. The driver had not noticed them. The lorry drew level with them, they stepped out into the road and threw their grenades simultaneously. They exploded immediately. A torn-off hand flew up and landed in the road along with a helmet and some pieces of tunic. The soldiers' legs were reduced to a seething mass of blood and bones. One of them bent double to hold in his entrails, which were spreading onto the floor. The dead lay slumped on top of each other. The survivors screamed in pain, sprawling on the benches and in the blood on the floor of the truck. The lorry stopped. The officer stepped out, pistol in hand, dazed.

There was another lorry behind it. It braked abruptly. The soldiers jumped down onto the road to run after Manouchian's two men. They had not hung around to wait for them: as soon as they had thrown their grenades, they had raced towards the rue des Acacias, taking out their Colts as they ran. The first stopped on a level with me and the second with Darbois, who was on the pavement opposite. Then they turned round. There were four of us, marksmen facing the straggling, disorganised group of Germans. After a few seconds I shouted: 'Fire!' Four soldiers fell to the ground. The others dropped to the ground and started trying to aim their rifles. But we were already running. Fifty yards further on, screened by the parked cars, there were two more of Manouchian's men on the look-out, one on either side of the road. I bent down next to the one on the pavement to my side. Now, there were six of us. The soldiers were firing towards us but we were hidden behind the cars. Hounded by the two officers, they came closer. Like in the artillery regiments of a former era, we raised our guns together. When they were thirty yards away, I called: 'Fire!' again. Manouchian's men could shoot. Six soldiers collapsed. We started working our way back as the German soldiers threw themselves to the ground. A hundred yards further back there were two more partisans. The eight-gun salvo was even more murderous. The officers could no longer get their men to stand up. While they ranted and shouted we dispersed into the boulevard des Ternes. There were three cars waiting for us in the avenue Niel. Ten minutes later we were heading out of Paris through the Porte de Champerret, and driving deep into Levallois until we reached a little millstone bungalow. Two men closed the gates behind us. Manouchian was waiting for us, and he greeted each of us by putting his arm around our shoulders. He was smiling from ear to ear, his teeth blindingly white under his black moustache. In his strong eastern accent, he said: 'Fantastic, boys! Not one hitch. We killed at least twenty of them! It's a good tactic, isn't it?'

The following day the Germans took fifty hostages from prisons in Paris, most of them detained communists and foreign refugees. They took them to the Mont-Valérien and shot them. One man refused to have his eyes bound. He turned to face the firing squad and, when the order was given to fire, he cried: 'Long live the German proletariat!', but his words were drowned by the gunfire. An SS officer stormed over to him and, even though he was already dead, fired two shots straight at his neck in fury.

The evening after the operation we had a noisy, well-oiled meal in Manouchian's hideout, and I headed back to the rue de la Pompe on foot just before the black-out. Noor was sitting at the top of the stairs. When I looked up and saw her I hardly recognised her. She had cut her hair and dyed it blonde. It looked scruffy and straggly, and had gone a brassy yellow colour.

'What do you think of my new hairstyle?' she asked.

'It's a disaster! You'll be arrested for an assault on good taste!'

She burst out laughing as she closed the door behind us, then she said: 'How did it go?'

'It went.'

I was pleased that Manouchian's men had been so successful, and I admired their courage, but I felt that there were more honourable exploits than throwing grenades on virtually defenceless squaddies. I knew that the Germans would make cruel reprisals. If the generators of Vichy propaganda knew of my existence they could have put the deaths of 150 hostages on my back in the space of one month and three operations. The record was surely higher. Churchill had said to 'set Europe ablaze with fire and blood'.

That evening we both sat down in the sitting room, Noor with her port and me with my whisky. The only change was that, instead of facing each other, we sat side by side on the sofa, with my arm round her shoulder and her head resting on my chest. I found it difficult to get used to her blonde hair. With her dark skin, she looked like no known specimen of the human race. Perhaps a particular kind of cabaret singer, in an exotic country.

'I don't know what you see in me,' I said all of a sudden, lost in my own bitter thoughts. 'I'm really just a killer. Killing is forbidden in your religion. Even killing an ant.'

'Oh, what a caricature! We do respect animals, it's true. But you're trying to make me seem ridiculous!'

'Not at all. Killing is forbidden, though, isn't it? I've got a lot of respect for that idea. But how do you put up with it? I spend all my time killing people.'

'So long as it's not me who's doing the killing,' she said with affected cynicism.

'Noor, this is important. I want to know what you think. One day you'll end up hating me.'

'The Sufis have known for a long time that the whole world can't be Sufi. They're wiser than you think.'

'But how do they reply to the question that everyone kept asking you during your training in England: how do you not kill in a time of war?'

'For a start, a lot of Sufis have killed. I belong to a particular school, the one founded by my father. He was a *murshid*, you know.'

'Yes, I know.'

'My father spent all his life looking for ways of reconciling Sufism with other religions. On the other hand, most other Sufis right back to the Middle Ages wanted to be exclusively Mussulman. And sometimes they were terribly intolerant. It depended on the political situation. They took part in *jihads*. I don't mean the great *jihad*, the true struggle, the struggle with themselves and the *naf*. I mean holy wars, military conquests.'

'But what would your father have said if he had had to use weapons?'

'My father told us that we should fight the Nazis. I think he would have envisaged the solution that we came up with by ourselves: dangerous jobs but no weapons.'

'It's a bit hypocritical.'

'There's no religion that doesn't have any hypocrisy. The absence of hypocrisy is either saintliness or cynicism. And I've told you that we knew not everyone could be a Sufi. So, the others kill. Not us. Sufism', she said mockingly, 'is for a very small élite.'

'I don't understand anything about this religion of yours.'

'I'll explain. Look, the Pope, for example, invented the concept of a "just war". In some cases, war is justified. If you're fighting absolute evil, you have a right to kill. We're looking for a more difficult response, but not a very different one. Every religion tackles the problems that we're tackling. And very often things aren't really clear cut. There are always obscurities, ambiguities and contradictions in texts. Because God gives men their freedom. They can follow his path or turn away from it. At their own risk. That's why the political regime that corresponds most closely with true religion is democracy. We're free. In fact the worst scourge of any religion is its own clergy. They claim to have come up with the correct interpretation, but they're just hashing over idiotic dogmas, when the texts themselves are always more complicated, more beautiful and more profound than their precepts. The clergy are men, the texts come from God – there's the difference. My father was always looking for the truth in the texts.'

'But you have a form of clergy in Sufism.'

'No, not as such. There are *walis*, *murshids* and sages, but first of all they have to demonstrate, by the way they live their lives, that they are worthy of being teachers. They are recognised within their own community, not named by some higher power like your bishops. Islam is much freer than your Christian religion, on this, anyway. The *walis* show us the way. They teach us spiritual exercises before preaching at us. They don't force anyone into anything, they guide them. We're free to follow or not. Clergy? No thanks!'

She became more animated as she spoke and

her eyes sparkled. The more I watched her, the more I wanted her. 'Tell me, Noor, what does Sufism say about love?'

She wanted to reply seriously to the question. 'Love is inherent in men and women. Even physical love. In the Koran there is an apology for physical love. The Prophet himself had a revelation from the Angel while he was making love to his wife. The Angel didn't mind, he carried on addressing him quite unperturbed. It's all the ulemas, the imams and the doctors of faith who've demonised love. Not God!'

My eyes were filled with desire; she could not help but understand my intentions. 'You're just making fun of me!' she said, starting to drum her fists on my chest. 'You make me talk about religion and all you can think about is sex!'

'Noor,' I said, 'I love you. I'm only thinking about you. Obviously, I'm also thinking about making love to you.'

She punched me all the harder, until she fell into my arms. She wanted me too, and we headed for the bedroom, locked in each other's arms. We got to sleep at dawn.

CHAPTER TWENTY-TWO

'Hide, there are some soldiers!'

Georges, the mechanic, pointed to the trapdoor in the floor of the tender. I lifted the metal plate, and Noor sat down, slipped inside and lay on the board on the left-hand side, which was bolted between the two wheels of the coal wagon, barely three feet above the tracks. I followed her and went to the right-hand board. I heard Georges scattering a few shovelfuls of coal over the trapdoor. The train was drawing into the station at Orléans-les-Aubrais and Georges had made out the reflection on the helmets in the moonlight. They might come to check his papers so we had to disappear into the special hideaway built by the network for difficult journeys. You had to push aside the coal and lift the trapdoor of the tender to find it, or crawl under the coal truck with a torch. The Germans' zeal had not yet extended that far. Huddled into the narrow space hardly big enough to allow us to breathe, we waited motionless for the train to set off again, while the Germans questioned Georges.

Despite these inconveniences, it was a magnificent trip. As a child I had always dreamed of travelling in the engine. At Montparnasse station, we had followed a grumpy railwayman along the rue du Départ, where he took us to a secret door which led straight to the front of the train. We both lay down on the uncomfortable boards while the locomotive hissed out a grey smoke that wrapped itself round us and made us cough. The pistols and the radio lay next to us, towards the front of the tender. Once outside the *boulevards extérieurs*, Georges had opened the trapdoor and helped us up. We stood to the right of the roaring boiler, fascinated by this spectacle that most passengers were forbidden, and juddering with the train through each set of signals. We sped onwards towards the dark point where the gleaming rails met, diving into tunnels and hurtling past convoys heading in the opposite direction with a smack of increased air pressure. Noor had snuggled against my shoulder and was gazing out into the darkness. The noise of the steam meant that we could not talk. We did not need to. I had an idea of what happiness was.

At les Aubrais, Georges had no trouble answering the soldiers' questions. The train was carrying parts for the naval shipyard in Nantes. A look at his papers, a quick conversation, and the whistle blew. There were no more checks after Orléans and Georges brought us back out again. The train went through ghost stations where the occasional sentry woken by the thundering convoy glanced nonchalantly over the wagons as they sped past. We simply had to duck to avoid being seen.

Shortly after Ancenis, Georges saw a signal light above a turn in the tracks. He slowed the train. With the suitcase and the radio in my hands, I jumped down onto the ballast, Noor followed me, and Georges engaged the steam again, waving an expansive goodbye with his other hand. When we climbed out of the ditch we were met by another railwayman, carrying a muted lantern. He led us along the tracks to the far side of a level crossing, where there were two bicycles in a lean-to. It was safest to get to Chaumont at night, and the best means of transport was a bicycle: we would be able to hear cars coming and we would only have to hide in the ditch. A furtive thank you, the squeeze of an arm in the darkness, and we were rolling along in the moonlight towards our destination.

Armed with the Michelin map indicated by Blainville, I had found the straight little beaten-earth path that led off into the woods from the road between Bourgueil and Gizeux. We had left a farm on our right and I had been worried that their dogs might bark, but we were absolutely silent. We had come to a crossroads: to the right another path led to a pond, and to the left it went up between two sloping fields towards a large house with a crenellated tower which stood out as a dark mass against the summer night sky. The parachute drop was to be on the far side, to the north of the house in a huge expanse of orchard deep within the woods. Someone would be waiting for us the next day to take delivery of the weapons in a car. But, in order to have an answer to the question that now obsessed us, we had to be on the spot, watching the parachute drop. Then we would know for sure. So we hid in the undergrowth near Chaumont and slept for a few hours in a thicket amid the rustling of leaves in the gentle night breeze.

The house rose up from the mound about 200 yards away. I could watch it at my leisure through my binoculars. It was a hunting lodge, built in limestone covered in a grey render, with red shutters and a slate roof. On the left there was a barn and behind that there were pens for rearing guinea-fowl and pheasants. On the right there was a farm; I had seen someone leaving earlier, urging on the horse drawing a plough with the ploughshare raised. They had taken the path that led to the pond and had disappeared into the woods. At about ten o'clock an old woman in a smock came out and walked briskly over towards the barn to feed the fowl. At noon another woman wearing a beret and riding culottes came out and waited on the black stone doorstep. She looked along the white sand path that came up the rise towards her. I turned my binoculars to see a man in a blue uniform pushing a bicycle up the slope. It was the postman, and he handed a newspaper wrapped in a strip of paper to the woman, who must have been the mistress of the house, and then he left.

The afternoon went by without any signs of life

round the buildings. The sun beat down on the field of corn in front of us. From time to time a dog would bark behind the house; apart from that all we could hear were the soothing murmurings of the woods. Noor had found some chanterelles on a bed of moss. She picked enough to fill her large handbag. A little way back from the edge of the woods, she had spread her green wire antenna round the branches in a little clearing. The radio case sat at the foot of a pine tree.

We were sitting with our backs against a tree, talking about music, when the dogs suddenly started barking. I rushed to the edge of the woods with my binoculars. To my right, on the track that went up to the house, there were two cars, one behind the other. They were travelling quickly, raising a cloud of white dust with their wheels. The first was a black Citroën, the second a military reconnaissance vehicle, a covered lorry. I trained my binoculars on the house. The woman in culottes was standing in the front doorway but she disappeared. The two cars drew closer. Then I saw two men running away to my left, each carrying a gun and with a haversack over his shoulders. They reappeared in front of the barn and sidled off along a path that I could just make out in the darkness under the trees. The people in the cars would not be able to see them; there were several large lime trees between them and the barn. I had familiarised myself with the site on the map: the two men escaping had taken a woodland path which led back to the Bourgueil road. Unless they had set up an ambush, the Germans would not catch them.

'Two men have run away,' I told Noor, who was trying to understand what was going on.

'Good!'

'But the others are at their mercy.'

The cars stopped by the front door, and two men in suits and four soldiers climbed out. Every one of them had a weapon raised and ready in his hand. The old woman appeared to one side of the house and they pointed their guns at her. She said something to them, and they went into the house. Twenty minutes later they came back out. The two women were weaving round the men in suits, talking and gesticulating. Two soldiers brought out a heavy wooden table and set it on the lawn in front of the house. The two other soldiers came out behind them holding a boy by the arms. He looked about sixteen, with dark hair and a pale face, and was wearing an open-necked shirt. He put up no resistance. Through my binoculars I could see a trickle of blood on his lip.

The two soldiers took off his shirt and lay him face down on the table. While one held him, the other tied his arms and legs to the table legs. The woman in culottes tried to throw herself at the soldiers. One of the two policemen – or so I assumed them to be – took her by the arm and pushed her away. One of the soldiers put his gun under her nose, while the other civilian stepped forward. He had taken a whip, which I had not noticed until then, from his belt. He raised his hand sharply and the whip came crashing down on the boy's naked back. We could hear the cry from where we were.

'They're torturing him,' Noor said. 'We've got to do something!'

'We've got two pistols, and there are six of them, they've got rifles and we'd have to cover at least two hundred yards in the open just to get to them. We'd get ourselves killed for nothing.'

'But we can't just do nothing! They want to know where the other two went. He's just a boy! It must be his father who ran away.'

'No, Noor. We're hidden and we're going to wait. We can't do anything. And that's not what we're here for. We haven't got our answer yet.'

The whip came down regularly on the young victim. Being a little below them, I could not see the result of the blows, but I could easily imagine it. After a while, one of the soldiers went up to the table, untied the ropes that were holding the adolescent, undid his belt and pulled off his trousers and his underpants. Naked and vulnerable he was tied back to the table, on his back this time, facing up towards the sky. The man with the whip went back to work, aiming lower down the body this time. The two women's screams rang out round the woods.

Later two other soldiers untied the ropes. The two women picked the boy up, each putting one of his arms over her shoulders. His naked body appeared: his back was completely red and streams of blood ran down his legs. His head wobbled and lolled; he was not dead. I thought of Christ's body taken down from the cross and carried by two women. When they had disappeared into the house, the man with the whip lashed out at the bonnet of the Citroën. The boy had not spoken. Neither had the women.

It was nightfall, and I was still watching the house. One of the two civilians bent into the reconnaissance vehicle and reappeared with a microphone in his hand. He must have been radioing for reinforcements.

'We must warn London,' said Noor, 'they're going to intercept the parachute drop. We'll have to cancel it!'

'Let's wait a bit. Let's make sure the Germans are here for the parachute drop. It could be a coincidence.'

Yet it was easy for me to deduce what had happened. The Germans had probably been told about the parachute drop, and they had sent a patrol to take up a position at the location in advance. They had found no one except for the two women and the boy. The torture had revealed nothing, and they now needed to rally some troops in case the Resistance were planning to arrive under cover of darkness. But, as I had told Noor, this situation could have arisen by chance. The

Germans were always hunting down members of the Resistance. Perhaps they had come here on a tip-off, without knowing that there was to be a parachute drop that night. Perhaps they were about to leave.

Any uncertainty disappeared an hour later. At about ten o'clock almost a dozen lorries appeared on the track that led to the house. They drove round it, their engines droning loudly. I guessed that the soldiers would surround the orchard to watch the arms drop. I turned to Noor. 'They're waiting for the planes,' I said. 'Now we need to warn London. We're calling it off.'

Noor opened her radio, switched it on and sent the code which announced the beginning of a transmission. I crouched next to her, hiding the radio and its glowing bulbs with my jacket. On a dark night, the tiniest light carries for miles.

'I'm not getting an answer.'

'Try again!'

She transmitted again. Nothing. She repeated the operation five minutes later. Still nothing. 'They must not be receiving it,' she said, 'otherwise they'd reply. They always answer when we call them. We're down in the dip and there's a hill in front of us. The radio waves can't get out!'

'Do you think?'

'I don't know. But it could be that. These machines have a mind of their own.'

We had one hour left. If London heard nothing, the Germans would capture tons of British weapons.

'Let's move. We need to get higher.'

Noor packed away the antenna and closed the case while I hunched under my jacket and checked my compass by the light of a torch. By walking through the woods to the left of the barn, we could get right to the top of the hill and avoid the soldiers who must have been waiting round the large orchard.

We headed off into the woods, guided by the needle of the compass, which I consulted every five minutes. There were great clumps of bracken and brambles. We made slow progress, skirting round them. After half an hour, it felt as if we had hardly gained any height.

'Let's stop and try,' said Noor.

'No, if we can't get hold of them, we won't have time to go anywhere else. We must get higher.'

We carried on, with branches scratching our faces and brambles clinging to our clothes. It was nearly midnight when the ground fell away ahead of us. We had reached the top of the mound, the most favourable spot.

'Quick, Noor, the signal!'

She busied herself with the equipment and three minutes later she was tapping out the signal with the key. I strained my ears. Far away behind us, to the west, I could hear a humming sound, muffled at first but becoming clearer and clearer. 'The planes! Noor! They're coming! They're heading straight into a trap! Quickly!'

'I'm waiting for the acknowledgement.'

A minute went by. My heart was hammering in my chest. It was all my fault. We should have sent the message much earlier. Why wait till the last minute? A criminal lack of foresight!

'There we are,' said Noor, 'they've replied! I'm transmitting.'

The message was brief, it was all over in a minute.

'The planes are coming!' I said. 'Shit, shit, shit! Too late!'

The sound of the engines went over our heads. I could hardly bear it. The parachute drop had happened. A boy tortured, a network torn apart, tons of weapons gift-wrapped for the Gestapo, and it was all my fault! Because of my absurd Sherlock Holmes-style conjecturing. And I did not even have a formal answer to my question. The Germans knew. But who had told them? The mission was turning into a disaster. I could imagine the English operator frantically calling the headquarters having barely had time to decode the message; Buckmaster or Bodington immediately giving the order to contact the planes and call them back. Just as I was cursing my own flippancy, the sound of the engines grew louder again.

'They're coming back!' said Noor.

'Yes!' I cried, with a glimmer of hope in my voice. 'They were taking a look at the site. There's still a minute to get to them. Come on, Buck, hurry up! Call it off, for God's sake!'

I took Noor's hand and we started running towards the orchard, searching the darkness to avoid stumbling over a soldier. The sound of the engines was still getting louder, then suddenly it became quieter. The planes had cut their engines to drop down to the lights sweeping over the site, lights they believed to be friendly. We were getting there just in time to watch the disaster. I could see the shadows of the planes in the sky, far away in the east, having made their descent and heading straight towards us. In thirty seconds' time the parachutes would open out over the orchard like flowers. Then my fears vanished. The engines were roaring again and the planes were banking upwards on full engines, heading towards the stars.

'Hurray!' I said. 'They're turning back. Buck got them. Hurray!'

'Hurray!' said Noor, squeezing my hand very tightly.

The thrum of the engines ebbed away quickly. They were disappearing westwards. This time the Gestapo would not have their present.

A minute later the only sound was the chirping of the crickets. An order in German sliced through the nocturnal murmurings. Torches went on. Other orders were shouted on both sides of the orchard. Several silhouetted figures headed south towards the barely discernible dark outline of the house. We stayed hidden, following the soldiers as they headed back despondently. The back door of the hunting lodge opened, creating a rectangle of light. The helmets gleamed against the darkness. I raised my binoculars: one after the other the soldiers filed heavily into the brightly lit kitchen. Someone in civilian clothes brought up the rear. He stepped into the light. Through my binoculars I could see him from behind, but he was perfectly easy to identify: I recognised his wavy hair. It was Blainville.

CHAPTER TWENTY-THREE

It was time for goodbyes. The day after the cancelled parachute drop we had sent a long message to London with a terrible conclusion: the traitor was Blainville, one of the bravest SOE organisers in France and the man who took responsibility for a large proportion of their communications. Buckmaster's reply had arrived in Paris that same evening: the order to return to England immediately. Buck obviously wanted to unravel the downfall of the Prosper network face to face, and to fine-tune his next response with the two agents best equipped to inform him. That was when Noor changed her role.

'I can't go back,' she said out of the blue. 'The Resistance needs me. I'm the last one. There isn't another radio operator in the whole Paris area.'

I looked at her in amazement, and thought, not for the first time, how reckless she was. 'Look, Noor, I'm not going to leave you all alone in Paris. The network's dead, Noor, your network! It's too dangerous. You won't be any use.'

'Oh yes I will. Now, I'm going to be really useful.

I've thought about it. I know Vienet, and I'll go and see Kerleven. They've got networks that are up and running. One of them's with the Gaullist Resistance and the other with the Communist Resistance. That's quite a lot of people! They must need me. Especially if there's any kind of insurrection. John, I know this as well as you do. I'm the only available radio operator. The only one.'

I stood there, unable to speak. I could hardly question her logic. For an indeterminate period the Aurora set would be the only means by which the Parisian Resistance could contact London. Should we wait for another radio operator to arrive? We would have to wait until the next full moon. And we would have to find some way of travelling which did not involve Blainville's planes. Noor was certainly looking less and less naive to me, and less and less inept. She had followed me to Touraine without a word of complaint, without weakening, and she had kept her cool despite the fear and the lack of sleep. The princess was quick to learn. Quicker than her instructors had thought she was, at any rate.

But this rapid progress chilled my heart. I did not want to abandon her, there were too many risks. The noose was already tightening. The Germans knew her call sign (we knew that Blainville was a traitor and Blainville knew it); the Prosper network was behind bars, its members had been tortured and some were now working for the

Germans. The apartment in the rue de la Pompe could be raided at any moment. She would be extraordinarily lucky to survive.

'I know how you feel, John. I would want to stay with you too.' I had taken her in my arms, and she carried on talking: 'I'm the one doing the reasoning now. There's no other solution. If I went back I'd be handicapping the Resistance. I've looked at it from every angle. There's only one answer. I stay put. Any other decision would be a betrayal. Checkmate, Mr Rational. I'll leave a bit later, that's all. Buckmaster will find someone to replace me. I'm sure he'd be much happier with someone more experienced. At the next full moon, we'll see each other in London.'

'No! It's too dangerous. They'll snap you up in three days.'

'What do you mean they'll snap me up in three days? Why would they? You really think I'm hopeless. I've learned. You learn quickly in a situation like this. For example, I bet you've never even thought of a way of getting out of the back at rue de la Pompe.'

It was true. I had been so involved with my deliberations about Prosper's fate that I had neglected Philby's first piece of advice: a safe escape route wherever you may be.

'Well, I have,' she went on. 'If someone came to the door I'd be able to get away.'

'How?'

'I've got an escape route. I've tested it. You see,

I'm not such a bad spy. You, the great SOE agent, you haven't thought of it. I'll get out of this.'

Her arguments were irrefutable for the very simple reason that she was right. Buckmaster and Section F were dedicated to helping the Resistance. The Resistance needed a means of communication. In the present circumstances, Noor was the only person who could provide one.

The railwayman had given us temporary premises at Montparnasse station, and from there we sent our proposed plan to London. Buckmaster must have been waiting because the reply came just half an hour later. The head of Section F accepted it. He must have hesitated but Noor's argument was irresistible. As a good leader in war, Buckmaster had not dallied for long. If the Aurora radio was useful, let it carry on. And so it was that two days later we stood facing each other outside the door of the apartment in rue de la Pompe, to say goodbye, a goodbye that tore me apart. Two of his men were coming to pick me up in a car, to take me to Normandy, where a Lysander would fly me to Tangmere. I put my arms round Noor. This might be the last time, I thought.

She held me close to her and I barely heard her breathe the words: 'I'm frightened.'

'No, Noor, don't say that. You're killing me. Come on, let's go back together. I'll explain to Buckmaster that it was just too risky. He'll understand. After all, he did give you the order to go back. That was what he said initially. He'll understand. He'd rather have a live agent in England than a dead one in France. Please, Noor!'

'No. I've told you I've thought about it. I've even meditated. I have to stay. It's a question of honour. Of faithfulness. But I am frightened. It's only human . . .'

I ran my hands through her short hair. She turned her face up to mine and kissed me slowly. Then she looked me right in the eye and said the words that crucified me but which I had been waiting to hear for days and days. 'Goodbye, my love.'

She broke away from me gently and backed towards the door on the landing. She pushed it with one hand behind her back, waving to me with the other hand. Then, with a smile, she raised her first and second fingers in a V for victory . . . and she disappeared.

Garry's men were waiting for me at the crossroads in front of Aux Espagnols. I headed for the car and as I passed the police station I caught the eye of the policeman on duty outside. I could see he recognised me. I lifted my arm and saluted him with two fingers against my temple, as I had seen him do. He smiled broadly and returned the salute. I got into the car which set off straight away but then braked suddenly: a young man had just launched across the crossroads without seeing us, he was staring intently down the rue de la Tour. The car stalled, the driver swore and then we set off again. I thought that I recognised the pedestrian, but the driver was talking to me: 'So, when are these landings going to happen, lieutenant?'

'Tomorrow, perhaps. Or in six months.'

'It's about time, we're ready!'

'Do you think so? My network's just been dismantled. We were ready but we aren't now.'

The conversation went on like that until we reached the Saint-Cloud tunnel. It was at Versailles that I suddenly remembered. 'Shit! We've got to go back.'

I remembered everything. The young man crossing the rue de la Pompe, who had forced us to brake, who was looking towards the rue de la Tour, was the one who had followed me all the way to the Lido the day I arrived. He had been wearing a light-coloured suit the first time and today he had a dark overcoat and a hat. That was why I had not registered straight away, but I was sure it was him. I was terrified. It could not be a coincidence. The Gestapo had followed us or they had been tipped off. Either way, they were getting ready to take Noor.

'We must go back,' I said. 'This is life and death.'

'Whatever for?'

I explained the situation.

'It's too late,' said the driver. 'Ten to one they've already gone up. Anyway, there are only three of us. There'll be lots of them, and armed, the place is crawling with police. Impossible.'

'But we've got to do something. I can't leave her to be arrested.'

I tried to think in spite of the panic. Retrace our steps? Garry's friends were right: we would get there too late. They might already have caught her. But what if they had not gone up yet? And what if the young man was just scouting the area and the operation was going to be carried out later? How could I warn Noor? The telephone? The Garrys had no telephone in that apartment. The *concierge*, the neighbours? Impossible. Then someone's face came to me: it was Trochu, the patriotic superintendent.

'I have to make a telephone call. Right now.'

The car forked off at the first crossroads. We were in Versailles. A bus stop, some shops, a bistro. The car came to a stop and I rushed inside. The telephone was free. The directory, the number, the lazy voice of the orderly: 'Sixteenth Arrondissement North Police Station.'

'I'd like to speak to Superintendent Trochu, please.'

'Who shall I say is calling?'

I paused. I did not know what to call myself, but I thought of a way of making it clear. 'It's personal, I'm his friend from Dreux, the one in connection with the railway operation. Tell him that, he'll understand.'

I waited a couple of minutes, then I heard his voice: 'This is Trochu. What's going on?'

Four minutes later Superintendent Trochu was crossing the rue de la Pompe with his hat on his head and his raincoat under his arm, having stolen a glance to his right at the Café Aux Espagnols. The young man in the black overcoat was still there. He was looking up the rue de la Tour with an anxious expression. Trochu slowed down, waited for the man to turn away, and slipped into number 72. In the hallway he did not take the red-carpeted stairs but looked for the other door: every building in the sixteenth arrondissement had service stairs. He climbed up the wooden stairs as quickly as his considerable bulk would allow. On the fourth floor he knocked on the door. No reply. He tried again and pressed his ear up against the door. Through the wood he could hear the parquet floor creaking. He guessed that Noor had come over.

'Mademoiselle Noor! I've been sent by John. I'm Trochu, the policeman from opposite. He's told you about me. Open up!'

There was more creaking, some furtive movements, then the service door opened slightly. Noor's face appeared in the gap.

'You must leave, mademoiselle. They're down in the street. They're going to come up any minute.'

'Are you sure?'

'Your friend called me. I've seen them. But I can't stay. They'll be suspicious if they see me. All I can say is leave. Leave straight away!'

'But . . . wait, I'll be right behind you. I'll just get my things. I'm coming.'

'No. Not this way. This staircase goes down into the entrance hall. We could run right into them.'

Noor bit her lip and then made up her mind.

'Right, I've got another way. Okay, I'm off. You'd better not stay there.'

Just then the front doorbell rang.

'They're here,' said Trochu. 'Go, mademoiselle, quickly! I must go back down. I'll try to avoid them.'

'Yes, go on, go.'

Noor closed the door again and ran to her bedroom. The doorbell rang again. She threw some clothes into a bag and slung it over her shoulders. She closed up the black radio case. Being a conscientious operator she stowed the antenna away carefully in its compartment every time she used it. She could decamp in a matter of seconds. She heard a voice from the far side of the door.

'Open up! Police! We know you're there. You can't get away. Open up!'

Noor put on her coat, took her revolver out from under her mattress and slipped it into her pocket.

'Open up!'

Noor heard something in German which she did not understand. Then suddenly a terrifying thud resounded round the apartment: the policemen were trying to break down the door. With shaking hands Noor went to the wardrobe and took out the curtain pull-cords which she had cut off and knotted together to make a long rope. She tied one end to the handle of the radio case, opened the bedroom window and put the case down on the zinc ledge the far side of the forged-iron guard rail. The front door was still holding up. Noor could hear heavy blows, and angry shouts in German. She calmly closed the bedroom door, took the other end of the rope in her hand and climbed over the guard rail. She stood on the ledge facing towards the building and pulled the two open windows towards her. A few days earlier she had driven two nails halfway up the outside of the upright glazing bar. She took one window in each hand and closed them, slotting them together. At that precise moment, the front door gave way, and Gestapo agents swarmed into the apartment.

Noor turned to face outwards and put her left foot onto the metal catch under the left-hand shutter, the one she had used to deploy her antenna. She gripped hold of the top of the shutter with her left hand, and pivoted round, with just thin air beneath her, so that her right foot reached the catch under the shutter for the neighbouring room. She caught hold of the other shutter and held herself between the two windows, facing the wall, with her feet on the catches and her hands gripping the two shutters, so that she was invisible from inside. There was still the radio case sitting on the zinc ledge. Holding on with her right hand, Noor pulled on the rope which she had wound round her left wrist. The case fell. Noor held it with the rope and let it slide down the side of the building.

A German soldier came into her bedroom. He looked under the bed and in the wardrobe; he glanced out of the window and saw that it looked out onto a dark, narrow, internal courtyard. Noor was just a foot away from him, pressed hard up against the wall, not even breathing. The soldier came back out of the room: 'They're not in there!'

'Well, they're not here then!' said a voice. 'I don't understand it. He told me they would definitely be here. According to him they were trapped in this apartment! Don't understand . . . Search again. They may have a hiding place.'

Noor was having trouble with the weight of the case; the rope was cutting into her wrist. She raised the radio up and put it on the ledge. Then, as she had done several times during her long hours waiting in the apartment, she set about a conversion: she put both feet on the same catch, pivoted round and switched her arms over, spreading her legs again so that she was facing outwards with her limbs stretched out like a victim of crucifixion in Roman times. In front of her, a little to the left, the far side of the shaft where the walls met, there was a ladder of rungs embedded into the wall opposite. It went all the way down to the connecting wall that separated the courtyard from the next-door garden. Noor closed her eyes, waited thirty seconds, opened them again and then threw herself into the air with her arms stretched up. Before she fell, her hands made contact with the rung she had been aiming for. She grabbed hold of it, her feet left the catches and her legs knocked against the rungs built into the wall. She put her feet on one of the rungs, turned round and pulled on the rope. The case toppled and fell, and she held the rope up, steadied it, drew it up and caught hold of the case with one hand before climbing down using her free hand. When she reached the wall she sat astride it and let the rope run through her hands till the radio was on the ground in the neighbouring garden. Then she jumped down into the grass, picked up the case and ran to hide in some shrubs. The German soldier was back in the bedroom and he opened the window. He did not notice the two nails on the outside, and he turned to the man in black behind him and said: 'No, there's no one. You couldn't get out here. It's impossible.'

CHAPTER TWENTY-FOUR

Trochu reassured me. When I rang him back an hour later as we headed for Normandy, fearing the worst and my voice shaking with terror, he said in a comforting, paternal voice: 'She got out. I didn't see her get away, but I know for sure they didn't find a thing.'

'Did they go up to the apartment?'

'Yes, but I got there first. I warned her off. I don't know how she did it but they left without her. She disappeared!'

'Are you sure?'

'Of course I'm sure! She disappeared. I know about these police operations.'

'Oh, fantastic! Thank you, Superintendent, thank you so much. How can I –'

'Oh, leave it. That's the way things are. I don't like the krauts. What matters is that they failed. I don't know how she did it. Amazing woman! She didn't look the sort when I saw her.'

'You're absolutely sure that she got away?'

'Absolutely, I tell you. I watched everything from my office. When I went back down, they were on the other floors. They didn't see me. I went and had a good look. She had them good and proper.'

Buckmaster was all smiles and warm welcome as usual. I had got across the Channel without any trouble, taken to the airfield by Cowburn's and Garry's men. At least the Tinker network was working all right. Before leaving I had had supper in Dreux as a guest of a dental surgeon who was a member of the Resistance. Violette Laszlo was there, still as beautiful and mysterious. I described Noor's situation to them, and she and Cowburn were both concerned.

'A radio operator always needs protection,' Cowburn said. 'We must send her someone.'

'It can be me,' replied Violette. 'I like Noor, I want to see Paris, we'd make a good team.'

Cowburn agreed. He was hardly happy at the thought of being parted from his most exceptional marksman, but he felt that the imperative need for communications overrode that. Paris needed a radio operator. On her own Noor would probably be caught. With Violette she would survive longer. That evening, in a field not far from Dreux, I climbed into the Lysander feeling a little reassured. Three hours later I was in Tangmere and the following day, after half a night's sleep, I was walking into the building on Baker Street, with my planned speech in my head, determined to put Blainville out of action so that he could do no more harm.

Buckmaster greeted me with Bodington sitting to his left as usual, his hands flat on his leather desktop and his head tilted forward slightly as if trying to demonstrate that he meant well. I told him about the disasters that had befallen the Prosper network, the way his friends had been tracked down, Operation Iago, the sabotage in Dreux, and the attack on the lorry in the avenue Mac-Mahon. Buck seemed pleased. Just one agent had caused a lot of damage. Prosper had been taken, but the Germans and the collaborators had suffered. All in all, the mission had had its good results. Then I went back over my deductions in fine detail. He listened attentively. When I had eliminated three suspects – Darbois, Prosper and Vienet – and Blainville was the only one left to consider, Buck objected: 'These are just intellectual machinations. You've no tangible proof of Blainville's guilt. You've done this by a process of elimination, but you don't have anything positive.'

'But I do. I asked him to organise a parachute drop; he was the only person to know about it except for me. The drop was all planned, and then the Germans turned up to receive it. I saw everything. We got there early, on purpose, so that we could catch them out. And catch them out we did. The Germans sent out a patrol on the afternoon of the drop. There was no question about it, they'd been tipped off. By whom? By the only man who knew about the drop – Blainville.'

'It could be a coincidence,' Bodington intervened.

334

'After all, the Germans are hunting down the Resistance everywhere, and it's the same in Touraine as everywhere else. They arrested those people just when the drop was about to happen. Perhaps the boy did talk in the end. A bit, anyway. He might have told them when the drop would take place. So they stayed on to pick up the arms.'

'It's unlikely,' I said.

I realised that Buck and Bodington were playing devil's advocate. I would have done the same. They could not condemn Blainville on the strength of one denunciation based on an abstract process of deduction. Blainville was too useful to them. They trusted him.

'Anyway,' I went on, 'the question is resolved: I saw Blainville that night with the Germans.'

'You saw him?' asked Bodington.

'I saw him. He was there the night of the drop. He was with the Gestapo.'

'But how did you see him, it was the middle of the night?' Bodington did not want to give up. He was beginning to sound like a lawyer.

'I saw him when he went into the house. There was no mistaking. It was him.'

'Why do you say: "There was no mistaking"? Did you not see him clearly?'

'Yes, I did!'

'But how?'

'With my binoculars, from behind, as he went into the kitchen with the soldiers.'

'From behind? Didn't you see his face?'

'No. I was behind him. I couldn't see it. I saw his head, his hair, I recognised the way he walked. It was him. No doubt about it.'

'But you didn't see his face!' cried Bodington.

'No, but I know it was him. It all ties up. He's betraying us. I can understand that you're not sure about this, Buck, but I studied this in situ for days and days. I checked everything, thought through every possibility. The conclusion is terrible but it's right. Blainville's betraying us. I don't know why, I don't know how, but he's betraying us.'

'This is very serious,' said Buckmaster in a peculiarly solemn voice. 'We have to be absolutely sure about this. My dear Sutherland, we're going to undertake an exercise that you're not going to like at all. But we have to, for the sake of the truth and the safety of our agents.'

'An exercise?'

'Yes. Peter,' he said, turning to Bodington, 'on you go!'

Bodington stood up, walked over to the door, opened it and said: 'Your presence is required.'

An athletic young man came into the room, greeted Buckmaster and turned towards me. I recognised his tumbling locks of hair and his blue eyes. It was Blainville.

It took me a while to get over the surprise. Blainville in London! I'd last seen him with the Germans in Chaumont. What was he doing here? Did the

SOE still trust him? I was absolutely sure I was right. I could not understand it.

He did not seem the least bit uncomfortable. He greeted me with a smile.

'I understand your point of view, John. You did your enquiry, you took a lot of risks, you set up the parachute drop. You've made a logical conclusion. In principle I was the only person who knew, but you're wrong.'

I could no longer think.

'I'll explain,' said Buckmaster. 'When you sent us the conclusions of your enquiry three days ago we had a long discussion and we decided to recall Blainville. We had to, he's valuable to us. We could not condemn him on this one denunciation. If he refused to come back that would be an admission of guilt. He came straight away, as soon as he could get into a plane. We interrogated him. His story stood up. That's why we needed a confrontation with you.'

I could feel the anger rising in me. I had put my life at stake, Noor's life and the lives of all sorts of other agents in order to flush out whoever was betraying Prosper. And now my superiors did not believe me. They trusted this traitor standing in front of me, with his honest-looking eye and friendly tone of voice.

'I've given you all the facts. If you don't believe me, good luck to you. Good luck to the SOE!'

'John,' Blainville said gently, 'your reasoning has its weaknesses. You eliminated Darbois and Vienet.

All right. But there's still Prosper. He negotiated with the Germans. He gave away agents and arms caches. What is there to say that he didn't start before that? That he wasn't arrested a week ago or a month ago and sent back out? If that were the case, everything would make sense. You wouldn't need me to be guilty then.'

'I don't believe it,' I said. 'You were the only one to know about the parachute drop. And if Prosper did betray us before he was arrested, I wouldn't be here. I would have been taken straight away.'

'And if I had betrayed,' said Blainville, 'I wouldn't be here. Why risk my life in London, willingly, if I'm working for the Gestapo? And if I'd been the traitor I would have given you away. Why leave you to go free? You're a dangerous agent to the Germans. As a traitor I would have given you away straight away.'

He paused for a moment.

'You don't know where I was hiding,' I said. 'I was in the sixteenth in an apartment you don't know about. And when you did find out about it Aurora was nearly arrested. I imagine you had me followed, or something like that. Then I asked you to arrange the parachute drop and the Germans were there. You were the only one who knew.'

'I wasn't there that day. I asked the Salesman network to arrange it; they've often done them for me in the past. They organised everything, not me. I don't go to all the drops, there are too many of them.'

'But the Germans were there and you were the only person who knew.'

'No, not the only person. The people from Salesman knew too. By definition. They got caught out. That's all.'

That was when I exploded: 'Stop this bloody performance! I saw you. I recognised you, it was you! Don't you understand?'

Blainville was still exasperatingly calm. 'I don't understand how that's possible. I was in Paris that day.'

'No! I'm not mad. I saw you, with the soldiers, behind the house.'

'You must have imagined it. It was dark, you were a long way away, you were convinced it would be me, you wanted to see me. So you saw me. But I'm not the only person with this colour hair.'

'Blainville, this is pointless. I would say that I saw you in a court of law. You were there. And that's all there is to it.'

'I was in Paris!'

'Liar!'

'I was in Paris, you can check.'

Dazed, furious, I turned to look at Buckmaster who was still quite impassive. It was Bodington who gave the final blow: 'He was in Paris that day,' he said wearily. 'I've checked.'

'What?'

'He was in Paris. One of our agents saw him on the Montebello embankment that evening. He's an agent we can trust. You know the letter box,

Sutherland, you've used it. When you were in Touraine, Blainville was in Paris. That's a fact. You made a mistake, Sutherland. No one can blame you for it. You acted in good faith, your work was exemplary. We're pleased with you. You struck some severe blows at the Germans. The SOE can be proud of you. Just, you were wrong about Blainville. We still trust him.'

CHAPTER TWENTY-FIVE

It was midday when I came out of the SOE headquarters, and it took me the whole rest of the day to regain any semblance of calm. I wandered aimlessly through the streets of London, from Baker Street to Piccadilly, along Oxford Street and round Hyde Park. An air-raid warning left me unperturbed as a block of marble, a solitary pedestrian obsessed by his thoughts in a city wearied by war. The sirens drove passers-by down into the shelters. The streets were sad and dark. I did not even deign to look up at the sky. Why should I worry when I had so much to think about? I was carried away by my thoughts. I had to understand. To meet this mental challenge. A challenge to this logical mind which was my only point of reference, my only means of establishing my bearings in the confusion of the war.

I kept going over the events of the last few days. Buckmaster and Bodington had been very pleasant. They said that they held me in high esteem and would send me back out into the field at the first opportunity. But, for now, I was on leave, ordered to rest after a dangerous mission. Whereas Blainville had gone back to France. Bodington had spent two hours trying to persuade me that I was wrong. He had gone back over the details of my enquiry with extraordinary precision. It was in fact true that, if you adhered to formal logic, I could have been wrong. I had investigated as Sherlock Holmes would have done: I had followed each lead and eliminated them one by one. However improbable it might seem, said the detective with the magnifying glass, the last one left must be the right one. And for me the last one left was called Blainville.

Bodington had highlighted the uncertainties of clandestine life, the reckless attitude that Prosper and his men sometimes adopted, and the patient work of the Gestapo. There were ten possible causes for the failure of the parachute drop, for the German reaction in the Foligny business, or at Dreux. The Gestapo had just decapitated the Gaullist Resistance by capturing Jean Moulin in Caluire, along with the main organisers of the 'Army of Shadows'. At the same time it had dismantled the most effective of the SOE's networks, the Prosper network. Their informers were legion, their sources of information countless.

It was all true, but nothing convinced me. But I was the one who saw them, I kept telling myself, I saw Prosper, Vienet, Darbois and Blainville. I was the one who set up the trap of the parachute drop. And I was the one who recognised Blainville with my binoculars. I was the one who trembled with fear for Noor when her hideout – our hideout

– was found, as if by chance, a few hours after I had contact with Blainville. Bodington was using abstract reasoning. He had not lived through all this. But I had.

So my mind started searching for another explanation. I constructed the most whimsical scenarios. 'Blainville is the traitor,' I said out loud as I crossed the Strand, not paying any attention to a bobby blowing his whistle at me. And in that case, I went on, he had duped Bodington. He is under his spell and cannot see the truth staring him in the face. But why, how? How could one of the top men in my organisation, an organisation so well versed in every dirty trick, have the wool pulled over his eyes like that? Unless he hasn't had the wool pulled over his eyes. Unless . . .

I stopped in a pub to try and bring myself back to my senses. I was beginning to ramble. Only one thing mattered to me: what happened to Noor. She was running all the risks. If Blainville really was the traitor, she was heading straight for disaster. He knew our contacts. He would not rest until he had her arrested. She too had lived through what I had lived through. She had a frightening ability to make the right deductions. Blainville would not be able to carry on his work without eliminating her. Death was hovering over Noor. I had to do everything to stop it. I had to hang on to her. At any price.

But, in order to save Noor, I had to unravel this tangle of hypotheses. I was back to square one.

Her life depended on a mental exercise. And so did mine. I was quite sure that, if my deductions were wrong, if my logic were impaired, if my syllogisms failed, Noor would die. I had to find out who was friend and who was foe. Everything was scrambled inside my head. I had glimpses of the chasm that lay ahead of me. I had thought that I was fighting for the clearest, purest cause, for freedom; fighting against tyranny; but now everything was shrouded in darkness. And in the depths of this abyss I could see a dark new world. A world in which every hero was questionable and every ideal somehow obscure. A world in which good and evil were confused. A world in which men strove to find a happiness without a god, without any points of reference or rules. Noor made fun of my logical mind. How right she was! My confrontation with my two senior officers, the men in whom I put all my faith, had knocked me sideways. I had been quite sure of myself as I went to see them, like a child going to his father. They had disclaimed me. A whole universe was collapsing.

I suddenly thought of someone – Philby! My friend from Cambridge was a spy. A real one. He would know. In the labyrinth of intrigues, in the great jungle of different possibilities, he would find the thread. Why did Buckmaster and Bodington believe Blainville when I was convinced he was a traitor? Was there a secret behind all this? Was it naivety or machiavellian strategy? Philby would answer my questions. Sitting with a glass of whisky in front of me on the King's Road, I tried to calculate how he would react. He could not talk, he could not supply me with the tiniest piece of information. But he could set the scene for me, he could widen the circle, generalise, explain a few snippets of this war that I understood less and less clearly. Philby would give me the background, something so important to a journalist, all the distant, useless facts that bad reporters ignore but without which you understand nothing.

Two hours later we were sitting in Indian-style armchairs made of dark wood with deep cushions. On either side of the room, like in a colonial stage setting, there were huge elephant tusks framing the chairs. There were yellowed photographs on the walls of the sitting room, featuring officers on horseback in the blazing, tropical sun, and natives staring nervously at the camera. An ageing waiter popped his head round from time to time to offer us sherry.

During my time in France, Philby had been transferred from Beaulieu to London. The Intelligence Service had given him responsibility for organising surveillance of the Soviet Union's secret service. Stewart Menzies, the head of MI6, who was known at the time as C, was working loyally with our Russian allies. But, like Churchill, who showed him the way in anti-communist attitudes, he knew that sooner or later the USSR would turn against us. We had to be prepared for this change. We had to know what Stalin's spies were concocting. It was ironic that Menzies had chosen Philby for the mission, because what no one – including myself – knew in June of 1943 was that my Cambridge friend was working for the communists.

Philby had been friendly on the telephone. He had quickly grasped that this was a serious situation, and had suggested that we meet at his club.

'My father comes here every day when he's in London,' he told me by way of an explanation.

'What does your father do?'

'He's a spy too,' Philby said, laughing. 'It runs in the family!'

He told me the story of Saint-John Philby, a gentleman from Cambridge with a passion for all things exotic. He had known Lawrence, the man who would come to be known as Lawrence of Arabia, and, like him, he operated in the Arab world. He had connections with the Saoud family and revelled in intrigues about oil and religious issues in Arabia. He had pushed his sense of duty to the point of buying a house in Mecca and marrying a slave girl he had freed. My friend was the child of an earlier union, and he had four half-brothers and half-sisters born to a former slave in Arabia.

'Is he there at the moment?' I asked.

'Yes. He's standing by the Saouds. He doesn't have the same ideas as me. Before the war his leanings were towards the Axis powers. He likes authoritarian regimes. At the moment he's defending our interests in the Middle East. It's very much in our interests – ourselves and the Americans – to keep the Wahhabites in power. They're appalling feudalists but, since Lawrence has been there, they've been our friends. It's a religious dictatorship but they sell us petrol at a good price. To them the ground is sacred, to us it's what's underground. That's the greatness of Allah!'

I smiled and paused for a moment. 'Kim,' I said eventually, 'I'm so disoriented. There's something I'm not getting. I need to understand. There's a woman's life at stake, a woman I care about. Can you help me?'

I had spoken with a gravity which forced him to concentrate. He answered in the same tone. 'I can do anything for you except betray my own duties as an officer, you know that. You must understand.'

'I'm not asking for any secrets. I need an explanation . . . in general terms. I need advice.'

'Okay. Fire away.'

Philby listened without saying a word, with his chin resting on his two hands and his dark eyes focused on me. From time to time he took a sip of sherry without taking his eyes off me.

I told him everything, in fine detail, without missing anything out. Every now and then he nodded his head, or raised an eyebrow but he never interrupted. When I had finished he said simply: 'Are you sure you recognised Blainville the night of the drop?'

'Yes. I'm absolutely certain. But I saw him from behind.'

'But you're sure?'

'Yes.'

'And when you had this conversation with Buckmaster and Bodington, who was leading the discussion, who spoke to you?'

'Umm . . . Bodington. Yes, Bodington. Buck was a sort of arbiter. It was Bodington who contradicted me. And he was the one who tried to convince me I was wrong.'

'Was it Bodington who brought Blainville in?'

'Yes. It was him.'

'So we can deduce that it was him who brought him there.'

'Probably.'

Philby said nothing. I felt that he was hesitating.

'Kim, do you know something?' I asked. 'Something that would shed some light on this?'

He waited before answering. Then he launched himself as if he had reached a decision: 'John, I don't know anything. Each operation is separate, in a vacuum. I take care of the Bolsheviks, not the Nazis. I don't know anything about what we're doing in France. But this whole business seems clear to me.'

'Clear?'

'I'll give you my advice on this problem. I won't give you any information, I don't have any. You're going to learn a state secret, but you've actually already stumbled across it, it's just you don't really realise it. I'm not betraying my own duties by telling you this. Just remember that we never had this conversation. It doesn't exist. It never existed.'

'I don't understand a thing you're saying. But, of course, this conversation doesn't exist.'

'Do you swear to that?'

'I swear to it. Now what is it that's clear?'

He thought for a moment, then leant forwards with a kindly eye as if he were about to explain something that was a little too complicated for me. 'Blainville is very useful to our organisation in France, isn't he?'

'Umm . . . yes . . . unless he's betraying us. Which I believe he is.'

'Yes, he's betraying us. But, at the same time, he's very useful.'

'What do you mean? How can a traitor be useful? He helps our men and then gives them away. How beautifully useful!'

'Yes. He's doing both. And his superiors are covering for him.'

'They're covering for him?'

'They're behind him. You've seen for yourself.'

'They're wrong. They won't admit the betrayal. Blainville's an extraordinary liar.'

'You don't see what I mean. In my opinion it's quite simple: Blainville is a double agent.'

'A double agent? He's working for both sides? He's a traitor then. A double traitor even.'

'No, he's a double agent. That means he's doubly useful. He's actually working for us.'

'But how can he be working for us? He handed a whole family over to the Gestapo and he nearly had tons of arms seized too. That's what I know.'

'That's part of his work for us.'

'How?'

'That's his job. He's a double agent.'

'Do you mean that he's acting with the blessing of our department?'

'Yes, I think so. He's convinced the Gestapo he's working for them, when he's actually still working for us.'

'This is like a book.'

'Yes, just cleverer. It's the truth. I can see that you're not familiar with our traditions.'

'What traditions?'

'Intelligence Service traditions. But you should know. We have the best secret services in the world. *Britannia, rule the waves* . . . But in order to build this empire over the last two centuries, we've had to use more than boats and sailors. We've trained up the best spies there have ever been. The British Empire dominates the world but we're just a little island with quite a small population. It's not just good luck. It's to do with intelligence, in every sense of the word!'

'I know that. But, but . . . what are we doing in France with this double agent?'

'My dear Sutherland,' he said, beginning to sound more and more like a teacher, 'a secret service is there to find out the enemy's intentions, its strengths and its weaknesses. That's the first degree, the elementary art, and that's difficult enough. But there is another register in spying, a higher domain, a domain for the initiated, the secret agents' Olympics, the Holy Grail of espionage. You could trivialise it and call it manipulation, but that's rather a weak word for what it is. We're actually acting directly on Hitler's brain.'

'Directly . . .' I faltered, thinking Philby had lost touch with reality. He was so proud to belong to this grandiose institution, this secret service, that he was attributing supernatural powers to it. For me, a foot soldier and a left-wing journalist, the Intelligence Service had always struck me as the archetypal reactionary institution, where the most twisted minds amused themselves hatching Byzantine intrigues in which to lose themselves while they sipped their sherry in their clubs making jokes about obtuse union leaders and incompetent politicians. When, that is, they weren't conspiring against democracy and the workers' movement.

Philby saw the consternation on my face. 'I can see you think I'm a megalomaniac.'

'No, really . . .'

'You do. Well, I'll give you an example. Blainville. I don't know how he got where he is but I can guess. He's been working in France for two years, hasn't he?'

'Yes, I think so. He's very effective.'

'I would say that he's survived by taking out a kind of insurance.'

'Insurance?'

'Either he's been arrested by the Germans and he offered to work for them, and then told his bosses (or they found out). Or he went to see the Gestapo on orders from his bosses, to establish this situation as a double agent. It's quite clear from your story that he's managed to gain the Nazis' trust without losing the trust of the English. And that he's working for the English. Otherwise, Bodington wouldn't have defended him.'

'That's only a theory.'

'True, but let's say that I'm right. The Germans are convinced they've got an excellent informer, and the proof is that, thanks to him, they're arresting agents, intercepting drops, reading mail, etc. But all this is being done with the full knowledge of Blainville's bosses. Blainville is being operated by remote control in his relationship with the Germans.'

'That's appalling! They're sacrificing agents to make Blainville credible?'

'They sacrifice very few.'

'But that's monstrous whichever way you look at it. They're sending men to the torture chambers and to their deaths in order to plant a spy in the Gestapo.'

'Men or women . . .'

I saw Noor's face in my mind's eye. 'Or women! Their methods are barbaric!'

'Their methods are necessitated by war. Again this is only my opinion, but I think they're mostly sacrificing arms and information. They must be dropping some agents that they think have already been blown anyway. There are losses in every network. Blainville probably just gives a prod here and there. But he must be limiting his information to material things. He must be saying to the Germans: Careful! If the English realise that I'm betraying them, I won't be any use to anyone any more! Don't ask me too much about it. He has to come to terms with his own conscience. What matters is that the Germans believe in him. If they think they've won him over to their cause, then after a year or two, Blainville can become a mortal weapon.'

'How?'

'It's very simple. Let's say Blainville tells them he's heard that the landings in Italy are to be made just south of Rome, or in Sicily. The Germans will believe him because they trust him. They think we're civilised. They think there are things that they would do – and that they do do – but that we would never dare to do. For example, giving a woman up to their torturers in order to reinforce the credibility of a double agent! They've always thought that democrats were wet, over-scrupulous and weak. They think Blainville's telling them the truth because he's made it possible for them to arrest an agent who they've tortured and who's spoken, and because they couldn't conceive that Blainville was acting on orders. And then along comes Blainville telling them where the Italian landings are going to happen! They send their divisions to meet them. And Patton makes his landings somewhere else! We would have a successful operation and would save the lives of our soldiers. The ten agents we sacrificed on the one hand would have saved us thousands of GIs on the other. The human cost is enormous. For whoever picks the short straw, obviously. That's what Blainville and the people like him are for.'

'What do you mean, "the people like him"?'

'Well, just one Blainville isn't enough. What you don't know is that uncle Adolf loves the secret services. Like all dictators. Like all people in power. Winston's an expert. He started right back in the Boer War. As First Lord of the Admiralty he tripled the credibility of the Naval information services. Our dear friend Bonaparte, who actually came very close to beating us, used to read reports from his spies every morning. That was the first thing he did! Before everything else, before the reports from his ministers, before the dispatches from his ambassadors, before the newspapers, the French emperor devoured the reports from spies. He often paid them himself. He would let them in through a little side-door at the Tuileries. He only won at Ulm and at Friedland thanks to this sort of information, and he was defeated at Waterloo because he was ill-informed. His spies had lost the touch – and he lost his empire!'

Philby had a soft spot for history. When we were at Cambridge he was already boring us with his long historical theories.

'You were talking about Hitler . . .'

'Hitler's like Napoleon. Every morning when he gets up he looks at the reports from the Gestapo and the Abwehr. Rudolf Hess told us these little details when he came to England.'

Philby was really warming to his subject now: 'Hitler uses them to plan his strategies, but also to prepare for meetings with his generals. He always knows more about things than they do, which reinforces his authority. So, if Blainville gives the Gestapo a piece of information which has been carefully prepared and gauged by us, it'll be in Hitler's own hands within twenty-four hours. That's why I said we're acting directly on Hitler's brain. It wasn't a metaphor. It's the truth.'

'Does Hitler believe in it?' My innate scepticism about the secret services was resurfacing.

'Yes, when his sources agree, when everything adds up. That's why we have to have several Blainvilles. And plenty of other ruses as well.'

'What sort of ruses?'

'We need to monitor and control as many of the sources of information that reach Hitler as we can. And that presupposes a unified strategy on a global scale. I took the Italian landings as an example. We both know, as many people do, and as Hitler does, that the landings are going to be in France.'

'Quite soon, I gather.'

'Who told you that?'

'Buckmaster and Bodington. Everyone in the

355

SOE knows; that's why we're speeding up the campaign of sabotage.'

'They're not ready then.'

'What do you mean?'

'If the Allies were ready to land they wouldn't go telling the SOE about it. There are too many agents being taken. They're saying it so that some of you give the information away under torture. The Germans will think the landings are imminent. They'll keep more forces in France to the detriment of their front in Russia. Stalin keeps putting pressure on to get on with the landings. Since we can't make the landings straight away, we're pretending we can. It wrong-foots the Germans and keeps Stalin sweet.'

'So they're openly lying to us?'

'Obviously. You're all potential Blainvilles. Anyone who talks under torture is reliable as far as the Germans are concerned because they're giving information they believe to be true.'

I was speechless, but Philby went on: 'There's another tactic. Instead of substantiating a double agent like Blainville we set up an agent who is half-reliable. For example, in a neutral country we choose a local who works in the British Embassy, a Turk, a Moroccan or a Spaniard. He communicates some secondary secrets to the Germans, who have a consulate in the country. He gets paid for it. But, because he needs money, he invents more detail. The Germans realise this and they're about to get rid of him when he gives them another minor piece of information, but something real which is useful to them. So they keep him but they're wary of him. After a while they realise that the man's reliable on a secondary level but that he's fabricating on more important operations. They keep paying him but they weed out what he says. Obviously we oversee every stage. Then one day the chap gives the Germans a really major piece of information like: "The Russians are going to launch a huge attack in the north of the Ukraine on such and such a day at such and such a time"; or: "The Americans will land in France on this day at this time". This time the information is very precise.'

'But . . . that's dangerous!'

'No, it's brilliant. We're giving precise information to the Germans. We're revealing a military secret to them, quite clearly. But it's that very piece of information that they're going to discard. They'll think: "If this agent's telling us that then it must be wrong. So the attack will happen somewhere else at another time." And they withdraw their forces from the area in question. Then the attack does indeed happen at that time and in that place. We warn them and they do the exact opposite of what they should do. We're acting directly on their brains.'

'But after that the agent's cover's blown.'

'Doesn't matter. In the meantime the attack's been successful. You just have to be careful not to waste agents. You have to keep them in stock for when it matters. Then the masks fall. But by then it's too late, the enemy's mystified and defeated. Afterwards you burn the archives.'

'Is that what they do?'

'We're not exactly going to leave that sort of thing for historians and journalists to find out!'

'So they're keeping Blainville in reserve . . . and giving him credibility in the meantime.'

'I think so. And they're setting up the radios game.'

I flinched. The radios . . . Noor's face came back to haunt me.

'Why? Are radio operators mixed up in these operations?'

'Of course they are. The radio is an instantaneous means of communication. Once a set is established, you can use it exactly when you want. You get to Hitler straight away.'

'What do you mean, once a set is established?'

'The Germans have a whole department for eliminating radios.'

'I know, with their detector lorries, etc.'

'When they take an operator, they try to turn the set against us. To use it themselves by making us believe that the operator's carrying on. That way they can infiltrate us.'

I jumped to the obvious conclusion: 'But if we know the set's gone over to them, then we're the ones infiltrating them. We accept their requests for parachute drops. We give arms over to them. We give them carefully selected information until the time comes when we need to give them a decisive piece of false information.'

'You're beginning to grasp the way we work it.'

'But what happens to the radio operator?'

'The radio operator doesn't know a thing. He has to play the game. If he co-operates too much with the Germans, they might become suspicious. They're no more stupid than we are. Before the war they convinced Stalin that half his generals were betraying him. Using similar methods.'

'Did they succeed?'

'Yes. Stalin had all the suspects executed, and they were all innocent. Heroes of the civil war many of them. He decapitated the Red Army on the strength of a fabrication set up by the Nazis.'

'But if radio operators are used in these set-ups then Noor could be too!'

'Very probably. I don't know, but it's highly possible.'

'In that case, she's on a death sentence. Blainville will have her arrested. He's nearly succeeded already.'

'I've no idea. Taking into account what you've told me, I'm hardly optimistic . . . You're very much in love, if I've understood correctly?'

'Yes. You could say so. She's . . . she's just . . .'

'You love her.'

My British reserve made it difficult for me to express the depth of my feelings, but Kim had summarised them well. 'And now,' I said, 'she'll probably die. On the orders of my superiors. How can Buckmaster run Section F knowing that he's sacrificing agents?'

'I don't think he does know.'

'What? How does it work then?'

'It's a perfect secret, and every precaution is taken. Cases are very rare because it takes a great deal of diplomacy. The SOE couldn't set up an army of agents and sacrifice them at the same time. That would be inhuman. It's the Intelligence Service that's at work. We work out which agents are appropriate and we manipulate them, discreetly. I think that Blainville has direct links with our services as well as the SOE.'

'But why's the SOE covering for him?'

'Gubbins, Buckmaster and the others aren't covering for him. It's not them. Do you remember I asked you about Bodington?'

'Yes. He's the one who covered for Blainville.'

'Do you know what Bodington's exact job is?'

'Yes . . . No . . . not exactly. He's the number two . . .'

'He's the number two and, as such, he's responsible for the SOE's relationship . . . with the Intelligence Service!'

'He isn't?'

'Yes, he is. He's a great friend to our services.'

'And Noor's going to die.'

'Unless you save her life.'

I looked at Philby. I was beginning to think he was saying too much. He had forgotten about his emphasis on the need for discretion. With his logical reasonings he had just revealed a vital secret to me. And now he was recommending that I should act alone, without my bosses' blessing. I stared at him intently and said: 'Unless I save her? But there's no way of communicating with her. I can't contact her set and tell her to come straight home. I'm meant to be on leave. Buck's in charge of all communications. I must go back to France. Without Bodington or Blainville knowing.'

Philby said nothing.

'Is there some way I could?'

'There may be . . .'

'Tell me, Kim, why are you telling me all this? We're friends, but you're in this quite deep. I don't want to be a millstone round your neck. You've just done me a huge favour, you've put a tremendous amount of trust in me. I won't betray that trust, but why did you do it?'

Philby gave a slightly embarrassed smile. 'I asked you about this young Noor and you told me that, from now on, she would be working with a partner.'

'Yes, with Violette Laszlo.'

As I said her name I understood Kim's motives. I suddenly remembered a scene from Beaulieu. Of course! Kim and Violette were very close. 'Violette Laszlo,' I said again with a smile, 'a wonderful woman, wouldn't you say?'

'Oh yes, my dear John. You see, you're not the only one who's in love! I know that Violette isn't exactly faithful to me. But that's how she does things. I love her the way she is. She gets all the more out of her life because she's risking it every day. I understand that. When it comes down to it, she's a double agent in love. And I love her doubly for it! But I thought you'd ask me why earlier. You're not a professional yet. Obviously I shouldn't have told you even a fraction of what I've said. If my superiors had heard me, I'd be in front of a firing squad tomorrow. I've taken some risks. I like Noor very much, she was a good pupil. And I love Violette. We're allies. We have a little battle to win within the bigger one. There is a way of getting to France without their knowing you've gone. I can help Noor and Violette and you . . .'

CHAPTER TWENTY-SIX

When Peter got back he was furious. He had taken the stairs four at a time at the avenue Foch to report back on his operation. Ernst Goetz was waiting for him in his little office on the fourth floor decorated with Bavarian engravings, where a ridiculous cuckoo shrilly sounded every hour. He must have had the same sort of thing in his classroom before the war when he had been teaching French to children in Munich. He had hung a portrait of Fouché where everyone could see it. Goetz was passionate about French history and the man he admired most was Napoleon's Minister for Police. Perhaps that was why he had chosen a posting in France, with the police. And perhaps it was also because of this that this man who never set foot outside his office had become one of the most efficient agents in the Paris Gestapo. He was the one who had recruited Pierre de Gensac, a young Resistance worker who had talked before he was even tortured, and had immediately agreed to switch camps. Since then Pierre had been tracking down SOE agents. He only ever read the collaborating newspapers now and he studied the seminal works on national socialism. He had even germanised his name.

'So, Peter, how did it go?'

'They got away. I saw him leaving by car but I was on my own so I couldn't do anything. I thought we'd get the girl. They both went in. I'm sure she was there. When the others arrived we went straight up and broke the door down. She'd disappeared. I can't understand it. We didn't find a thing. She'd gone. And with her radio, too.'

'I've already told you the best thing to do is to wait inside the apartment when you're trying to get someone. You have to find the place first, pick the lock and wait for them there, with someone else waiting on the stairs. If you go and ring on the door like some delivery boy they can escape out of the back. They always have an escape route planned. Well, what a shame. But we'll get her next time. She won't last long. Anyway, the information Blainville gave us was accurate.'

'Yes, absolutely perfect. He's a good agent. He's a bit eccentric, but he's good.'

Peter straightened the crease in his black trousers. He dressed with a studious elegance that Goetz found amusing. Just as the latter's ridiculous cuckoo made Peter smile.

'We've got practically the whole network. The agreement with Prosper was a very good manoeuvre.'

'Yes, but he's stopped talking now. We're going to send him to Germany next week.'

'Well, of course he has! Boemelburg didn't respect any of his side of the agreement. There's absolutely no point in letting people down just so that he can look like a good Nazi. Boemelburg will never grasp that. He thinks that if you're more cruel and devious than the others you can't help but win. It's not a good strategy. You win if you're the cleverest. And that's all there is to it. The Nazis are always lying.'

'Are you not a Nazi then, Goetz?'

'Yes I am. Well, I back my country, and the Reich. I just think they sometimes lack subtlety. By the way, have you heard the latest one about the Minister for Propaganda?'

'Goebbels? No. What are they saying about him now?'

Peter liked Goetz's irreverent jokes. The French professor's intelligence justified his own betrayal. He had not only chosen the stronger party, but also the cleverer one.

'Hitler and Goebbels are dead. When they reach the pearly gates, Saint Peter says: "Right, in here we have paradise, purgatory and hell. But as you are great men, and great Germans, I've decided to give you the choice. Where would you like to go?" and Goebbels says: "To paradise!" But Hitler's more wary and he says: "Show us these places, then we'll choose." Saint Peter shows them paradise. They hear music by Wagner, they see a white cloud, and there are people in white robes sitting on armchairs on the cloud reading Kant and Hegel.

"That's very nice," says Hitler, "but what's purgatory like?" And there they meet Churchill and Roosevelt working in the fields under a blazing hot sun. "All right, all right," says Hitler, "what about hell?" There they see a cave with walls of velvet, carpeted with animal skins, and there are people in leather armchairs drinking schnapps in front of an open fire. There are naked dancing girls undulating backwards and forwards. "Well, there you are," says Hitler, "hell's much better! Just what I've always thought." "Yes, *mein Führer*," says Goebbels, "and you were quite right. We promised people paradise and what we actually gave them was hell.'"

Goetz was laughing before he had even finished the joke. Then he went on: "'Yes," said Hitler. "That's exactly my policy. Come on, let's go!" And they go in. The carpets disappear, the fire burns much more fiercely and the naked dancing girls become devils. They're given chains and prodded with forks. "I don't understand!" says Hitler. "We'd better call Saint Peter back. The place he showed us was completely different." "Yes," Goebbels agrees, and he calls: "Saint Peter! Saint Peter!" Just then they hear the Lord's voice booming: "Propaganda! Propaganda!'"

Goetz roared with laughter at his own joke. Another voice – a booming one, in fact – rang out: 'Goetz, your jokes are all good fun, but I've already told you to shut your door when you're telling them. I don't want the soldiers and the secretaries to hear you.'

'The ones they tell are worse, *Sturmbannführer!*'

Kieffer came into the office. He was a podgy, surly officer with greying hair at his temples, squeezed into an SS uniform which was too small for him. He lived on the fifth floor in an apartment decorated in very bad taste – the carpet was very deep and very purple – and positioned just above the prisoners' cells. He had had Jean Moulin shut up in one of them. It was there too that Pierre Brossolette, another of General de Gaulle's envoys, would climb up onto the roof and throw himself into the street to be sure that he would not talk. The interrogations were carried out at night. They had had to stop torturing members of the Resistance during the day because the secretaries had complained that they could not work with the screaming going on. Kieffer, good bureaucrat that he was, had given in so as to guarantee a high standard of administrative work.

'I gather you didn't get them?'

'No. They disappeared.'

'You see, she's craftier than you thought. She'd planned an escape route. You always have to wait for them inside. To be frank, my dear Peter, I thought she'd give you the slip. They're quite a pair, those two. They nearly found out about Blainville with their parachute drop. He only just got away with it.'

'In the meantime,' said Goetz, 'I've had another idea, *Sturmbannführer*. We need that radio set. At the moment we only have Norman's set.'

367

'That's better than nothing. Getting him to switch was like flipping a coin.'

'Yes, but I'm not sure about him. This business with the double security check is odd.'

'Why?' Kieffer asked.

'Normally, when the second security signal is missed out, London realises that the operator is being manipulated to make their transmissions. London told Norman that he'd forgotten his second signal. That put him completely at our mercy. Either they don't know what on earth they're doing, or they did it on purpose. In that case, they must have wanted Norman to be a traitor. They must have known that we'd caught him. It was their way of suggesting to him that he should betray others. Then they could infiltrate what we're doing.'

'It's very complicated, this idea of yours,' said Kieffer.

'The game is complicated, *Sturmbannführer*!' replied Goetz.

For the last year Goetz had had the upper hand in the *Funkspiel* (the 'radio game'). He was astute and wily, and had become an expert at turning radio operators into Nazi tools. The SOE was playing a sort of game of chess with him. One scheme pitted against another. This time Goetz had spotted London's manoeuvre.

'Yes, we need another radio operator,' said Peter. 'One we can trust.'

'Well, catch this girl, then, instead of complaining!'

'That would be perfect,' said Goetz. 'She's on

her own now. If we get hold of her, London won't necessarily know about it. We can pick up the game again.'

'And what's this idea you were talking about?'

'We could use the North Pole network in Holland. It's completely in our control. I know my colleague in Amsterdam ran a very good *Funkspiel* operation. He's already had hundreds of tons of arms dropped, and we got the lot. Recently he's had a couple of agents sent in and he picked them straight up when they landed. They're Canadian, Pickersgill and MacAlistair. London thinks they've started working, but we've replaced them with two of our men, who are very good and who've been sending convincing reports to London. Thanks to them we've destroyed an entire network in Holland. But we can't use them over there any more. They're likely to be found out. They're going to come to Paris; the Amsterdam Gestapo has agreed to it. Once they're here they can work with the Prosper network, or what's left of it. Then they'll ask to transmit an urgent message. As there's only one SOE radio operator left in Paris, it'll have to be the Aurora set.'

'But how can we introduce them into what's left of the Prosper network? This girl already suspects that Blainville is passing us information, she'll be very wary.'

'We'll find a way of ensuring she isn't wary, *Sturmbannführer* . . .'

★ ★ ★

Noor carried on walking. She was climbing the hill at Suresnes, filled with emotion. Her heavy suitcase was weighing her arm down, but she did not notice it: she was walking up the hill as it had been before the war. Nothing had changed since 1939. The avenue snaked its way up the hillside. She could see all the houses again, all the shops and every stopping place she knew so well that had a lovely view. It was the route she used to take to school. She walked at the same speed as she had then. Instead of the satchel dragging at her shoulder, she had the Mark II radio.

She knew that she was exposing herself to danger. Anyone could recognise her: she was the daughter of the debonair Indian guru who lived at the top of the hill; she had made friends all over the area; she had been idolised by the children of Suresnes for her stories of exotic princes and talking serpents. Someone could stop to talk to her. They could see her from a window and ring the police. But she could think of no other solution.

After her escape she had stayed in the shrubs looking through the leaves up at the windows of the apartment she had just left. She had seen someone open a window, peer down into the courtyard, then close it again. She did not dare step out into the open but a quarter of an hour later she had made up her mind. There was no one in the gardens – they belonged to the Serbian embassy, which was closed – so she jumped over the wall and walked briskly towards the place du Trocadéro.

There she went down into the Métro station and got into the first train she saw without knowing where she was going, to give herself time to think. She had nowhere to hide now, no source of help, no one to turn to for advice. There was still Vienet, whose telephone number she had. But it was too late. Seven o'clock. All the offices would be closed too. Where could she sleep? Outside? Risky. And she could not trust a hotel. Eventually, she thought of Suresnes. It was dangerous, but she would get help. She was alone, they would be looking for her, she was in danger. Going home was a way of finding some form of comfort. An illusory comfort. But it was an illusion she needed.

Halfway up the hillside she rang the doorbell of a pink and white villa which was partly hidden by tall lime trees. A curvaceous woman with curly blonde hair and wearing a taffeta dress answered the door. 'Babuli!' she said. 'How are you? I thought you were in England!'

'I was in England. I came back. Can I come in?'

'But of course! You can't go back home, the Germans have occupied the house.'

'The Germans are occupying Fazal Manzil?'

'Yes, they've been there since 1940. It was the headquarters for God knows which army.'

'That's terrible.'

Lucienne Piat was a friend of Vijay Khan. Noor, whom she called Babuli, used to spend time with her before the war, as all her friends had done. She would have tea, chat, play the piano, tell stories.

Lucienne led her through to the sitting room with its flowery wallpaper and cherrywood furniture, and they sat down on the grey-velvet sofa that Noor had sat on so many times before. She was already feeling stronger. This room felt like a familiar cocoon, a long way away from the terrors of her day.

'Lucienne,' she said, 'I'm working for the English.'

'For the English?'

'Yes, for the English and for the Resistance. There's a radio in this suitcase.'

'A radio?' Lucienne asked, looking at the case as if it were a venomous snake.

'Yes, a radio. I'm a radio operator. I send messages to London for the Resistance.'

'Are you in the Resistance, Babuli? But that's terribly dangerous!'

'Yes, Lucienne, it's dangerous. But that's just the way it is. Vilayat's on a minesweeper. That's dangerous too!'

'But is that what you left France for?'

'Yes, we owed it to our father.'

'I understand. It's very brave of you, though.'

'Lucienne, you have to do me a favour. I don't have anywhere to go. They're looking for me. Could I stay here?'

'Put you up? Well . . . well, yes, of course, Babuli.'

Lucienne had absolutely no desire to take in a radio operator working for the British just a stone's throw from where the Germans were billeted. She felt she had no choice. Lucienne was Roman Catholic and her friend was asking her for asylum.

She had no time to hesitate: Noor was already on her feet and kissing her on both cheeks.

'Thank you, Lucienne, I'm indebted to you.'

Lucienne felt a flicker of doubt. What if they were both arrested? But she answered automatically: 'Don't be silly, it's nothing!'

'Oh but it is something, it's a lot. Lucienne, I need to send a message to London.'

'A message?'

'With my radio. I'll need to spread out the antenna somewhere. You have a garden at the back, don't you?'

'Here? With the radio? But that's dangerous! The Germans are practically next door.'

'That doesn't matter. They need equipment to detect the signal. They won't have it. There's a special unit that deals with it. I'll just have to be quick. They won't have time.'

'They won't have the time to what?'

'They won't have time to get here.'

'To get here? Might they come here?'

'No. I'll be very quick.'

Lucienne was terrorised but she was persuaded by Noor's implacable logic. She gave way. Noor unwound the green wire of the antenna and hung it in the trees round the garden, keeping the window open. She switched on the radio and started transmitting. The silent house was filled with the piercing sound of the Morse.

'Noor, you're making the most terrible noise! They'll hear you!'

'No they won't. They're too far away.'

Lucienne went off to the kitchen to make some tea. Her suffering did not last long. It was a short message. Along with the requisite security checks, Noor sent just two sentences: 'Aurora set still operational. Awaiting orders.'

CHAPTER TWENTY-SEVEN

When we reached the river mouth at Falmouth the sea took hold of the Angèle-Rouge. The white crests of the waves surged towards us as the coast disappeared into the darkness. The wind was blowing towards us from the south-west at more than force 6. We had to head straight into the waves, climbing great walls of black water and then falling down the far side, crowned with foam. The flat bottom smacked down between the waves, making the boat shudder through its hull and up the mast.

Birkin was too tall to stand upright in the pilot's cabin, so his head scraped the ceiling as the waves broke over the foredeck and the seaspray lashed across the portholes like a whip. I gripped hold of the map table, which collapsed as the trawler pitched, scattering naval maps over the floor. The rag that had been stuffed into the speaking tube sprang out and a jet of seawater and rust splattered onto the floor of the cabin. Birkin swore and bent down to pick up the piece of cloth. With the next wave, the compass, the Reed's directory and the parallel rulers were thrown against a wall before they fell into the brownish water. Birkin was just getting down on all fours to gather them up when he was overcome by seasickness. He grabbed hold of the bucket that was rolling on the ground so that he could be sick into it as he knelt in the water that washed backwards and forwards in the cabin. I set the map table back up, picked up the fallen instruments and shut them in the starboard cupboard.

'Thank you,' said Birkin, 'I'm always seasick when we're leaving. It's quite normal. Lord Nelson used to be ill for five days at the beginning of each campaign, so . . .'

The captain stood impassive at the helm, scarcely glancing at us as he concentrated on steering his boat. 'There's a bit of a breeze,' he said, 'you should make some tea.'

We were on a squat trawler about fifty feet long with an upturned nose, a square stern, blue and white planks, a short balsa mast and a narrow cabin with glazed doors. Three hours earlier it had been gently tugging at its moorings in the lapping waters of the river in Falmouth, while sailors loaded it with equipment and jerrycans of fuel. I had been greeted by a tall, thin boy cramped into his tight reefer coat, with a pipe in his mouth and a fisherman's hat crammed down over his head.

'Welcome aboard the HMS *Angèle-Rouge*, the quickest link between England and France!'

David Birkin was the navigator and first mate on the *Angèle-Rouge*, whose real name was MFV (Motor Fishing Vessel) 20023. The SOE had very quickly established that airborne links with occupied France were not enough. They needed backing up with a naval line of communication which would transport mail, arms and agents between the southeast coast of England and Brittany, where there had been several networks operating since 1940. Philby was aware of this. He had got hold of a form from the Intelligence Services' offices and sent a written request for my transfer to France to the office in Palace Street (the City of Westminster department which co-ordinated the SOE's maritime movements on behalf of the Royal Navy). As there was no reason to question the request – why would a soldier mess around asking to be sent to France to risk his life if he had not been given instructions? – Palace Street had found a boat for me, which was leaving from Falmouth. Palace Street would, of course, inform the SOE of my departure, and they would realise that I had left without orders. By then, I would already be on the way to Paris.

The *Angèle-Rouge* was meant to cast off shortly before sunset in order to cross the Channel by night, unseen by German planes. I explained to Birkin that I was also a navigator. He was delighted to have someone to share his anxieties with.

'It's a very straightforward journey,' he said, laughing. 'We have absolutely nothing to navigate by. The Germans have taken away all the buoys and extinguished the lighthouses. We have to go by guesswork, and then at exactly five o'clock we have to hit the Bonaparte beach, which is right at the back of Saint-Brieuc Bay. If I'm one mile out or more than an hour late, we won't make the rendezvous.'

Crouching over in the little cabin, he opened an attaché case bulging with maps, notebooks and well-sharpened pencils. He took out a map of the Channel and spread it out on the wooden desk attached to the right of the helm; then he used a pencil to point to the mouth of the river at Falmouth. 'There. I'll take a compass reading here if there isn't too much mist. Then we have to do all the calculations, bearing in mind the current, how much we're drifting, the wind, our speed, the whole lot, so that we can get to that beach absolutely blind. It's a miracle when it works.'

Birkin had always managed it somehow. Only fog or foul weather stopped him from sticking to his route. He worked for days at a time on his maps, and knew by heart the shape of every last rock in Saint-Brieuc Bay, whatever the height of the tide and the direction he was coming from.

At half past seven, an emaciated sailor, who was also wearing a reefer coat, stepped along the gangway. 'Captain aboard!' cried Birkin and the four sailors stopped what they were doing to salute. The captain of the *Angèle-Rouge* was called Slocum, which delighted me – he shared a name with one of the most important navigators in boating history. At the beginning of the twentieth century a man called Slocum had been the first person to sail solo around the world, aboard the legendary *Spray*. Along with Alain Gerbaud's writings and Adlard Coles's articles, Slocum's account of his trip had pride of place on my bookshelves. The other Slocum, the one who was going to take us to France, was an experienced and laconic officer in the Royal Navy. He was in command of a very special kind of trawler.

The *Angèle-Rouge* had been built close to my home in East Cowes, following Laurent Giles's plans so that it looked like one of the French trawlers that passed back and forth in the waters around Brittany. The trawling net was attached to the stern and on the foredeck a little black whaling boat was held in place with a net – but this boat was hiding a 500 horsepower Hall Scott engine in its hold, which meant it could travel at twenty knots. And in the cupboard in the wardroom there was an Enfield machine gun standing upright between various pistols and grenades. At nine o'clock, as the sun disappeared behind the hills of Cornwall the *Angèle-Rouge* was easing down the river between two green and pleasant hillsides. I thought of Noor, who was now working in mortal danger. If all went well, the following evening I would be in her arms . . . Twenty minutes later the false trawler was pitching through the waves in the Channel.

Looking as white as chalk and with his great bulk bent double, Birkin took his first reading with his hand-held compass, eyeing various points along the coast at length. He was just noting his findings on the map when the nausea gripped him again. This time he hurled himself out of the little cabin and leant over the rails. When he came back to his position his face was streaming with seawater. He shivered as he finished noting our position, then he made some tea on a little stove built into the wall of the cabin.

'We've got 120 miles to travel,' he said. 'At sixteen knots, it'll take seven and a half hours. We'll be there at half past four, an hour before sunrise. That's just right.'

'Why this Bonaparte beach in particular?'

'Bonaparte is a code name. We know it well. It's the only stretch of sand between Saint-Quay and Paimpol. And, anyway, there are very good networks at Saint-Brieuc and Binic. We moor up near the reefs and they come to meet us in a rowing boat. This time we only had equipment to deliver, some weapons and false papers, with some instructions. Then Palace Street told us that we had to take you. Apparently they're having trouble arranging parachute drops in the region. There are very good air defences around Saint-Malo. It's dangerous. It's better to go by sea. In winter we go further, to Benoît or even to southern Brittany, in the Glénan fishing area. The nights are longer, and we have time to get there. In the summer you have to take the shortest route, and the shortest route is to Bonaparte beach.'

'Why don't you go to Normandy? It's closer.'

'No, the area's too well defended. And we have to use fishing areas that are in use. The Germans tolerate trawlers in Brittany, but they've banned them further north. We often stay where we are for a day and set off again the following night. We mingle in with the real fishermen. It's quite funny. Sometimes they realise who we are and they send signals in Morse code with their lamps: 'God save the king' or just the letter V!'

I thought of Noor.

We had trouble keeping our tea in our cups, and we had to yell to make ourselves heard above the sound of the waves and the engine. Slocum had lit his pipe, bending over to shield the flame from his lighter. At sea, the smallest flicker of light can be seen for miles. We were out in the open with no aerial cover. We had to be invisible. To read the maps Birkin used a little lamp that had been painted red and gave off a discreet glow. Towards midnight he showed me the sounder as it dropped rapidly. 'Exactly on time,' he said with obvious satisfaction in his voice. 'My estimate was accurate. We'll be there on time.'

'But how do you know where we are?'

'There's a fault line here, the Hurd Deep, the seabed drops down to more than 200 feet. You can't get that wrong!'

I recognised the sensations I had known as a boy in Cowes when my father took me across the Channel on his little sailing boat, sweeping through the Channel Islands, dotted with reefs, muffled in fog and surrounded by strong, torrenting currents. Now these islands were hostile. Jersey, Guernsey and Alderney were the only areas of British soil occupied by the Nazis.

An hour later Birkin took his large binoculars from the starboard cupboard. The wind had dropped and the sea was becoming calmer, even though the swell still tossed the little trawler about. Birkin scanned the darkness, trying to find the black outline of the coast. But the sky was heavy with clouds. 'That was one of the conditions of the trip, otherwise the German surveillance could have spotted the boat by moonlight – Oh God!' he said suddenly, 'I can see a lighthouse.'

'Well, isn't that a good thing? You can get your bearings.'

'When the lighthouses are working it means there are German convoys working their way up the coast. The rest of the time they're kept dark to make it impossible to navigate.'

'I'm slowing down,' said Slocum. 'Sutherland, take the other pair of binoculars. I want a 360 degree watch.'

We each started scouring one half of the horizon to try and make out the German convoy which should be cutting across our route towards the beach. The trawler carried on climbing up over the swell and falling down into the troughs. I had trouble keeping the horizon in my sights. Half an hour passed as we scanned the black waters, which occasionally twinkled with white when the moon broke through the clouds. I suddenly saw a triangular silhouette a bit darker than the surface of the water. It was coming slowly towards us.

'Ship to starboard!' I cried.

Slocum stopped the engine. Foam is phosphorescent at night: the *Angèle-Rouge* would have revealed its presence by carrying on with this trail of white behind it. I pointed to where I had seen the suspect vessel. Birkin set his binoculars towards it and exclaimed: 'There's another one behind it! And another! It's the convoy! There are at least ten of them!'

Now that we had stopped, the pitching of the trawler was even more unpleasant. It rolled and yawed furiously, throwing us from one side of the cabin to the other. I watched the boats filing through the darkness towards Saint-Malo or Granville, from west to east, going past the reefs in Saint-Brieuc Bay. I suddenly saw one ship that looked lower than the others and stayed close by the one ahead of it. The convoy was beginning to cut across the beam of light from the lighthouse on the coast. For a moment the outline of the ships was carved out by the light of the semaphore. The low-slung boat appeared. I saw a shining metal bridge, the barrel of a massive gun dripping with water and a narrow tower.

'They've got a submarine!' I cried.

'Yes,' said Birkin, 'they're towing a U-boat. Damn it! If only we had a gun we could make a hell of a lot of scrap metal!'

In 1941 and 1942 German submarines came close to conquering England. Invisible and pitiless, they sank more ships than the Allies could build. Then the tide turned. Improvements in the methods of detection and the rapid growth in shipbuilding by the Americans meant that they could meet the challenge. But, to all British sailors, U-boats were like evil predators which should be wiped out without mercy.

'Let's wait for the convoy to pass,' said Slocum. 'They shouldn't be able to see us.'

At that precise moment the sea betrayed us. A much bigger wave lifted the trawler up and it landed on its side. Birkin was thrown onto the map table which collapsed again. His head crashed into the wall in front of him and a harsh light suddenly lit up the cabin: he had smashed the bulb of the red lamp between his forehead and the wall, but he had not actually broken the filament in the bulb.

'God almighty! Switch that thing off straight away!' Slocum yelled.

I took the electric wire in my hand and pulled it violently. It resisted. I tightened my grip around it and it burned me as I shook it frenetically. At last it went out.

'God almighty, almighty God!' Slocum was saying. 'Keep watch again! It'll be a miracle if they haven't seen us.'

I grabbed my binoculars while Birkin got to his feet apologising. It took me a full minute to make out the line of German boats again. As the black outlines reappeared in my sights, the echo of a siren reached us over the noise of the waves. The shadowgraph of the last boat became smaller. It was turning towards us. A large searchlight went on and swept over the sea towards us.

'God almighty!' Slocum cursed. 'They're going to find us! We'll have to move. What the hell!'

I thought of Noor and it hurt me. Slocum had started the boat up again and turned it north-west. It was the only possible manoeuvre. If the Germans inspected a trawler with all its lights out like this they would subject it to a search we could not survive, even if we threw the compromising equipment overboard. Slocum and Birkin did not speak French. And the engines, being so much more powerful than those used by a normal fishing boat, would give us away in an instant. Slocum leant over the intercom: 'All hands on deck, prepare for action!'

One after the other the four sailors came up on deck armed with pistols. The last of them set up the Enfield machine gun on the quarter-deck. But all we had to save us was our speed. German convoys were protected by gunboats, which could pulverise us with one shot. The race was on.

'There will be no surrender,' Slocum warned. 'If they catch up with us, we open fire. They'll return fire and sink us! It's better to die at sea than to be interrogated by the Gestapo!'

Through my binoculars I watched the boat that

had left the convoy to pursue us. The light was still sweeping across the water and it suddenly became much brighter: they had found us. Slocum pushed the engines to their limits. The *Angèle-Rouge* bounced through the waves at twenty knots, raising huge curtains of spray. Behind the gunboat I could see the convoy moving away to the left. It was heading west, probably to have the U-boat repaired in the refitting yard at Saint-Malo. I looked back at our pursuers. The light was still just as bright and just as big. They were not gaining on us; we were not drawing away from them.

Birkin was hunched over the map. I glanced over his shoulder. We were south-west of the Channel Islands. The quickest way back to England was to go along the Minquiers Plateau, an archipelago of reefs and uninhabited islets, before crossing the Channel. More than 100 miles. If the German boat was faster than us, even by just one knot, it would catch up with us.

'Head due north, Captain!' said Birkin. 'We'll go along the Minquiers.'

'I know,' said Slocum.

I picked up my binoculars again and my heart missed a beat. The searchlight looked brighter and bigger through the sights.

'They're coming, Captain. The searchlight's getting bigger.'

'God help us!' said Slocum.

The gunboat was quicker than us: our fate was sealed. In half an hour, perhaps a little more, they would be within range to shoot. We would have to stop and surrender or receive their fire, which would sink us. Only a miracle could save us. An engine breakdown in the German boat, for example . . . We could but dream. I looked back at the map. The scattered rocks of the Minquiers still lay between us and the strait. No hope of shelter there. There was no question of venturing in amongst the reefs, where we could plough straight into a more prominent rock.

I had an idea.

With a torch in my hand I bent wild-eyed over the detail of soundings and rocks surrounded by shallows depicted in dark brown. The map table, like the rest of the cabin, shuddered under the effects of the straining engines.

'Birkin, how much water do we draw?'

He seemed intrigued. 'Just over three feet. It's a flat-bottomed boat.'

'What about him?'

Birkin turned round as if he could gauge the gunboat's draw through the darkness. 'At least six feet, if not ten. It's a narrow boat, it would need a deep keel.'

'Look at this.'

Birkin bent over the map. I had put my index finger on the archipelago of the Minquiers, just to the right of the buoy in the north-west that all boats had to pass on the left. He stood back up, dubious.

'Do you . . . do you think it might work?'

'We'll have to aim to the nearest ten yards. Do you think you could do that?'

'I don't know the Minquiers very well.'

'Yes, but to the right there's this rock here, the Huguenan. It's thirty feet above sea level. It must be pretty easy to spot, don't you think?'

'Probably. We should be able to find it with the binoculars. We'd have to head a bit to the left of it.'

'Yes. What depth of water is there at the moment?'

Birkin opened one of his notebooks. 'An hour and ten minutes before high tide. A fraction over twenty-seven feet,' he said after scribbling a little sum with a pencil.

'The reef rises to twenty-three feet. If we go through there we'll have three feet of water. A bit more . . .'

'Yes, but if we're in the trough of a wave we'll run aground.'

'With a bit of luck we'll get through.'

'They'll go round the buoy whatever happens.'

'We can't be sure of that, they'll be frightened of losing us.'

Slocum had heard everything. He intervened: 'Sutherland's right. It's our only chance. Let's try. Give me my bearing.'

Birkin looked at us both and smiled. 'It's completely mad, but it'll make a good story what-ever happens.' He looked at the map and ran his parallel rulers over it. 'Head for 23,' he said.

'OK,' said Slocum, 'I'll make the turn gently. Check whether they're following.'

I looked through the binoculars again. The light was bigger still. The sea was subsiding and the gunboat was travelling without any trouble, gaining on us with its great white moustache of foam. I felt the trawler turn slowly. The searchlight was still behind us.

'They're following.'

'Perfect,' said Slocum. 'Straight for the Minquiers.'

Ten minutes passed. We were heading right for one of the most infamous areas of water in the northern hemisphere, where countless ships had sunk, their hulls broken by the rocks. The gunboat was now clearly visible through my binoculars. Suddenly there was a flash behind the searchlight.

'They're firing!' I cried.

'Hardly surprising, they're within range,' replied Slocum.

He had only just started speaking when I saw a white geyser a hundred yards away to my left. 'Missed! Too long and too far to the left!'

'They'll soon get it right,' said Slocum, 'I'll have to zig-zag.'

'No, we'll lose our bearing.'

'But otherwise they'll shoot us like rabbits.'

'Well, they'll just have to,' I said. 'We've got to hold out for five minutes.'

'I agree,' said Birkin.

Another flash of light sprang up from the gunboat. This time the shell fell fifty yards to our right.

'We're surrounded,' Slocum said simply.

'I can see the Huguenan!' exclaimed Birkin. 'Left a bit.'

'Left a bit,' Slocum repeated, making the manoeuvre.

A geyser appeared in our wake, to the right-hand side.

'If we hadn't moved he would have had us,' said Slocum.

He zig-zagged slightly and came back to the same bearing. This time the geyser showered us with spray. 'Are they following?' asked the captain.

'Yes. I don't understand,' said Birkin.

'They think we're leading the way. You should always follow another boat through a reef, it's the safest way,' said Slocum with a wicked smile.

'We're passing the Huguenan,' said Birkin.

I saw the great black rock gliding past us, just twenty yards away and I grabbed hold of the table, waiting for the impact. As we drew past it, a rasping sound came up from the hold.

'We're touching,' said Birkin.

'Yes, but we're getting through!' I replied as a smile suddenly spread over my face.

The bottom of the boat had scratched over the reef, but there was enough water. We must have ground up the seaweed but done ourselves no harm. Slocum manoeuvred sharply to the right. He wanted to put the Huguenan between us and the gunboat. A valuable move: another geyser sprayed up ten yards away, exactly where we would have been if he had not turned.

'Missed again!' I said.

Slocum carried on zig-zagging for a minute. I watched the German boat through my binoculars, and I could now see the men working the gun busying round the foredeck. They were aiming at us again. The gunboat was heading at full speed towards the Huguenan. All of a sudden it stopped. The soldiers were thrown forward and overboard. The projector went out. The black outline plunged forwards and sheered sideways. The gunboat had ground straight into the shallows round the Huguenan at full speed. Its draw of six feet of water had proved fatal. Where we had scraped the bottom they had crashed onto the rocks.

'Hurray! Hurray!' Birkin yelled. 'We got them! Sutherland, you're a genius!'

I saw agitated figures silhouetted on the deck of the gunboat. Some were looking for their fellow soldiers who had fallen into the water, others were leaning over the rails to evaluate the damage. The hull must have been shattered by the impact. I saw the boat begin to list. It was sinking rapidly. Only the seabed, which was not far below them, would stop it. In fact, thirty seconds later, the gunboat came to rest just below the surface. Slocum swivelled the helm to the left and turned the *Angèle-Rouge* about. 'We're going to finish the job,' he said.

He opened the cabin door and spoke to the four sailors who listened with beaming faces. 'We're going to finish it off and pick up the crew. If they move a muscle, you shoot.'

An hour later we were speeding happily back to England, and Slocum had taken out his bottle of whisky. After picking up the eight Germans from the gunboat, throwing a handful of grenades at the wreck and watching it burn, we had tied up our prisoners and lined them up, lying side by side in the wardroom. Then the crew had crammed into the cabin, talking loudly and laughing a great deal. Granted, the transport mission had failed. But a poorly camouflaged trawler had sunk a modern gunboat with terrible firepower. Now, that was worth a medal.

Amid the general hilarity, I felt devastated. I was so obsessed with the image of Noor that it obscured my sight. I could not reach her. Once I set foot back in England, I would be found out, arrested and tried for insubordination. I would go to prison and she would die. Slocum saw my grim expression.

'Don't make a face like that, Sutherland! You're the hero! I'm going to brew up a report for you which'll earn you a Victoria Cross. I swear it. And you can get on with your mission in the next few days. We'll get you all the way to the beach this time, don't you worry.'

'No, Captain. The day after tomorrow it'll already be too late. I've got a very precise mission which can't wait. Several of my fellow agents' lives depend on it.'

He looked at me seriously. 'I understand. Listen, I'd really like to help you, but I have to get back. We can't go to the beach now. It'll be light in an hour, and if we're not far enough away we'll be taken.'

'Never mind, Captain. Thanks. I'm very touched.'

Lost in thought, I watched the prow as it plunged up and down through the waves. The water washed over the whaling boat bound to the foredeck, and then streamed back off it. I turned to Slocum: 'Captain, there is something you could do for me.'

'If I can, I will.'

'I'll explain . . .'

CHAPTER TWENTY-EIGHT

It was not long after Noor had escaped from the apartment on the rue de la Pompe and moved in with Lucienne that she met up with Vienet at Le Fouquet and at the Lapérouse, and with Kerleven at Les Négociants on the rue Custine and at Le Balto in Montreuil. They both needed her; they had to pass on military information, arrange more parachute drops, extract pilots whose planes had gone down and receive instructions from London. The Aurora set was working flat out. Noor had not wanted to stay with Lucienne, who panicked every time she made a transmission. In any event, Suresnes was not safe because Noor was so well known there. She had had to leave the hills of her childhood. Vienet had found a room for her on the boulevard Richard-Wallace in Neuilly. It was an austere room on the ground floor of a big white building, where some German officers were also billeted. Kerleven had given Noor the address of a working-class family in Bondy, who lived in a little red-brick bungalow near a small foundry down a quiet road. Noor sent transmissions every day, moving from one address to the other to avoid the German detectors, occasionally going back to Lucienne so that her tracks were thoroughly covered. She left her room early in the morning, took the Métro at Porte Maillot for an interminable trip to Bondy, with her radio case in her hand and her code book in her handbag. She risked her life every time. One day two soldiers asked her to open her bags as she was changing trains at the Gare du Nord. Ashen, she did as she was asked, sure she would be arrested. She told them in a blank, neutral voice that she was carrying photographic material. The two soldiers, who were more interested by her figure than her suitcase and who probably did not want to show their ignorance, let her go. Another time she had to make the transmission from her own room, urged on by Kerleven, who wanted to get a message to London straight away. She started hanging the antenna round the bushes in the garden next to the building.

As she put the green wire through the foliage she heard a voice: 'Can I help you, miss?'

She turned round and felt a tight pain around her heart. It was a Wehrmacht officer she had met before, who lived on the third floor. He was watching her with an amused expression and a smile on his lips.

'Yes,' she said, 'if you don't mind, I need to dry my washing.'

'Hand that to me and I'll stretch the line for you. Shall I knot it to this tree at the end here?'

'That would be perfect!'

'There you are. How odd, to have metal wire for washing.'

'Um . . .'

He winked. 'When you listen to the BBC,' he said with a smile, 'don't put it on too loud. My colleagues might hear you.' And he gave her a little salute and a click of his heels. Noor watched him leave, speechless. He had thought she was setting up an antenna for an ordinary radio, and had decided to turn a blind eye to a lapse like this from a pretty girl. Noor thought that she definitely had luck on her side.

One hot afternoon, she had sat down by the green wooden hut where they hired out miniature sailing boats next to the big pond in the Jardin du Luxembourg. A moment later, two hands had been clamped gently over her eyes. It was Violette Laszlo. She had arranged the rendezvous with her with Garry's help.

'I have come to protect the Aurora radio,' she said. 'Sutherland asked me to. He cares about you, you know! Have you had news of him?'

'No. John's disappeared. I know he's in England, but London isn't telling me anything about him. It's strange.'

'You can't trust men!'

'No! I mean, it's really odd. He was meant to tell London about the Blainville business. Since then, nothing. Blainville's carrying on just the same as before. I'm sure he's a traitor, and London's not doing anything. I can't understand it.'

'Maybe they're not sure.'

'They're wrong. It's a terrible mistake.'

'What does Vienet say about it? Blainville knows him. If he's the traitor he could denounce him any time he wants.'

'London have persuaded him that Blainville's clean.'

'Maybe you're wrong. Once you start suspecting everyone, you can't do anything any more.'

Violette had taken a room with Darbois, who was still living on the rue Joseph-de-Maistre, and the two of them shared the job of protecting Noor. They escorted her on her peregrinations and stayed nearby when she was transmitting, keeping their eyes open and their pistols at the ready. At first Violette would walk thirty yards behind Noor to try and spot potential 'guardian angels' following her, but the two young women ended up travelling together to break up the boredom of the endless Métro journeys.

When the two young women went into Laurent's their conversations stopped. Preceded by a waiter in a white jacket they crossed the hall with their hair awry and a twinkle in their eyes. The drawing room was a large room decorated in Second Empire style with deep carpets and sofas upholstered in green and red velvet. Vienet was waiting for them at a table at the far end of the room, near the window which looked out over the gardens of the Champs-Élysées. 'Young ladies, you look magnificent,' he said. 'Like two amazons back from war.'

'That's about right,' said Violette.

With his thin, well-combed moustache and his perfectly cut Prince of Wales suit, Vienet himself settled Violette and then Noor into their chairs. 'People will think I'm some sort of Don Juan!' he said with a fatuous smile.

'But you are one,' Violette replied.

'Oh, no!' said Vienet. 'My wife's not very keen on it.'

'Aha,' said Violette.

They ordered oysters and three partridges. Vienet was a shooting man, and he launched into an account of a day's shooting in Sologne. Violette parried this with a story of wolf hunting in Hungary, telling it with great gusto as Vienet listened, fascinated. Noor was bored rigid.

'We're not entertaining our friend,' Vienet commented. 'My dear Violette, I will invite you out one evening and we can talk about hunting and shooting without inconveniencing anyone! We could go to the Tour d'Argent. Have you ever had their *canard au sang*?'

'Yes, I used to go there before the war when I came to Paris with my husband. Would we go there with your wife?'

'No . . . she would be away.'

'But how can you know that, we haven't fixed a date?' Violette asked mockingly.

'My wife travels a great deal.'

Noor hid her laughter behind the notebook she had opened during the wolf hunting episode.

'Now what's this notebook for, my dear Noor?' Vienet asked to change the subject.

'It's for my communications with England. I have to note every one. It also has the codes, and the keys for the coding day by day.'

'But why are you wandering about with that on you? It's terribly dangerous!'

'London told me to keep my notebook and to make a note of every message, day by day. So I always keep it on me. They need me to.'

'But why do they need you to? It's a really bad idea.'

'I don't know. It's an order. Anyway, this notebook's not going to get me arrested. Either I'll be taken or I won't.'

'But if you are, they'll have all the codes.'

'Yes, but we have a double security check. If I don't use them, or if I miss one of them, London would know that I was in the hands of the Germans as I made the transmission. They'd cut off the communication and change the codes. There are security arrangements, you know.'

'I don't see why you have to keep all the messages. Who asked you to do that?'

'A high-ranking officer who came to see me before I left Tangmere. I think his name was Bodington.'

'Bodington? Oh, I see. He's the number two. He must know what he's doing. But it still seems odd.'

'This whole job is odd,' said Violette.

'My dear Noor,' said Vienet on a different note, 'we'll be needing you on the ninth of September at Alma. It's not far from here. Would you be able to get there?'

'Of course.'

'The National Committee of the Resistance are having a meeting there, to elect a new chairman. Moulin did an extremely good job. He's dead now, of course, but we must carry on. The General has sent Serreulles as his representative. The different movements and the networks are more or less working as one, but they need a representative, a spokesman. Otherwise the Resistance could fall apart or end up in the hands of the *cocos*.'

'The what?' asked Noor.

'The Communists. Anyway, we'll need you to come to the meeting, to write a report and send it straight to London.'

'I see,' said Noor, 'I'll be there.'

'One last thing,' said Vienet. 'I'd like you to meet two Canadian agents who were parachuted into Holland, but who need to get back to London. In the meantime their reports need sending back. Urgently!'

'Does Blainville know them?' Noor asked.

'Yes, he sent them to me.'

'But what if Blainville's a traitor? We've talked about this, René!'

'If Blainville's a traitor, I should have been arrested!'

'Maybe he's waiting.'

'London has completely cleared him. I do have to trust in something, my dear Noor. Yes, we take risks, but if we didn't, we wouldn't do anything.'

'Right, whatever you say. But I'd like to check with London first, about the two Canadians. Do I have your permission, René?'

'As you wish.'

'What are their names?'

'They're funny, complicated-sounding names to me, but you might find them easier: Pickersgill and MacAlistair.'

CHAPTER TWENTY-NINE

In the glimmer of dawn light the Ecrehous were just a dark patch on the horizon. To keep my bearings I kept an eye on them over my shoulder as I rowed rhythmically over the Channel, which was now calmer. I had hoped to be in Paris within two days but the unfortunate encounter in Saint-Brieuc Bay had lost me a dangerous amount of time. I now had to reach the coast by crossing the German defences in a rowing boat. A ridiculous plan.

Slocum had agreed to my request despite the fact that it was so unrealistic. He felt indebted to me, so he had headed westwards to skirt round Jersey before turning back towards England. When we were three miles from the Ecrehous, a string of tiny islands north-west of Jersey, he had dropped me off alone in the whaler with my pistol, my Sten, my bag and a basket of provisions taken from the reserves on board. For the last hour I had been rowing, helped by the southerly current, as day broke around me. I was going to the aid of my princess, on a rickety little boat travelling at two knots towards an enemy-held coastline, hatching a plan that had every chance of failing.

The Ecrehous, a little scattering of rocks which could be seen from Jersey, lay between the island and the French coast, and were technically under German occupation. But I suspected that there would hardly be a garrison there: why watch over a cluster of rugged rocks boasting no more than a dozen narrow little houses which some of the inhabitants of Jersey used as summer retreats? The sun was rising. I suddenly heard the sound of an aeroplane engine over to the west. The Germans were looking for their gunboat. I slipped straight into the cold water and waited, hiding behind the planking of the whaler, gripping onto a mooring rope. The engine sound grew louder. As it flew overhead I dived underwater and swam round the front of the whaler to the other side, without letting go of the rope. The pilot would see an empty boat adrift. I was hoping I would have reached the shore before a patrol boat came out to check. The plane passed twice, which meant I had to change sides twice, shivering just below the surface. The noise faded. I waited another five minutes, then climbed back into my little boat, dripping with water and shivering with cold. I started to row all the harder.

Thanks to the current I was in the middle of the archipelago an hour later, with the sun rising in the clear sky above the French coast, which I could see in the distance. I looked for an inlet in the steep rocks, and I tied the whaler up in the shade of the morning light. It was black: under the shadow of the rock it would not be visible from the sky.

In the middle of the little island there was a small hamlet of granite houses huddled on a peak overlooking a long stretch of yellow sand. There was not one boat moored in front of the miniature village: there were no inhabitants. I climbed up towards the peak, went up the front steps to the biggest house and broke down the door. It led into a living room with a wooden table and rattan armchairs in front of a clean, tidy fireplace. There was a little kitchen at the back and two tiny bedrooms upstairs. A musty smell hung in the air, and there were patches of damp on the white walls. I pushed one of the armchairs towards the window and sat facing the sea. I had to put up with the delay, my heart aching with anxiety, while Noor still walked through the valley of shadows.

I waited an entire day, surrounded by shrieking seagulls and the lapping waves, watching the rise and fall of the tide and scouring the horizon to the south as I counted the hours. For nothing. That night I slept well in a narrow bed with damp sheets that I had found in a small wardrobe. Finally, the following morning, an hour before high tide, a boat appeared, a local fishing boat which had come to pick up lobster pots. The sun was high in the sky, and the blue sea swayed between the outcrops of reef ringed with foam. From my lookout post I could see the little turquoise-coloured boat with its white wooden cabin as it covered the glassy surface of the sea and picked its way carefully between the rocks. To port it had a large pulley connected to the engine as a driving belt. This was the mechanism used to lift the pots that had been dropped into the inlets. In front of the house I could see little balls of rubber floating on the green water. I knew that they were connected by rope to the steel cages on the seabed some thirty or forty feet below, and that the cages had a funnel-shaped aperture so that the lobsters could not climb back out. My father had brought me here two or three times in his sailing boat during our Anglo-Norman peregrinations. I had watched these Frenchmen who came to collect their lobster pots, sharing the fishing area with the locals from Jersey.

The fisherman anchored his boat just below the house in the middle of the inlet, then he picked up a long gaff and dragged the first buoy towards him. He wound the rope round the pulley and started to raise the pot. Once he had finished I came out of the house quite calmly. His tiny, distant figure froze and I could imagine the astonished expression on his face. I could see him scouring the rocks for signs of a boat. I raised my hand to try to reassure him, then I walked slowly towards the whaler hidden in the shade of a rock. I untied it and started to row out towards him. When I was close enough to hear he cried: 'Stop! Don't come any closer! What do you want?' mixing

English and French in the hopes of making himself understood.

'I'm a fisherman. They left me behind.'

'A fisherman from where?'

I was expecting him to ask me this. I had a one in four chance. If he knew the port I named, then he would see through me. At my feet, at the bottom of the boat, I had hidden my Sten under a rag. The whaler continued to make headway towards the fishing boat. If he was suspicious I had made up my mind to use force.

'From Cateret!'

'What's your name? Whose boat were you on?'

'Capitaine Delassus! On Hénock's boat!'

These were the names of two French families I had met with my father when we called in at Jersey in 1938; we had been moored alongside them in the port at Saint Helier. At least they were local names.

'You mean the Delassus family from Villedieu?'

'Yes,' I ventured.

'What happened?'

'A gambling debt. We played right through the night the other week. One of them was cheating and I gave him away, but they were all in it together. They dumped me here. Now, I've got to get back!'

It was an improbable story. I had not come up with anything better, but the fisherman had been reassured by the name Delassus. He still hesitated.

'I could help you raise your lobster pots,' I said.

'All right then. Come on, get in!'

I threw him a rope which he wound round a steel cleat. I handed him my suitcase and heaved myself on the thwart to jump on board. The whaler started rocking and the rag hiding the Sten slipped off.

'Hey, wait! What's that?'

He looked from my hands to the machine gun. He picked up a big knife that he had left very visibly on the hood of the motor, and he pointed it at me. He took one step to the side, bent over and looked at the Sten.

'That's an English machine gun, there! Just what I thought. You're from England!'

'Yes.'

'Well, why didn't you say so earlier, you cretin?'

Noor and Violette were lying side by side in the double bed nattering to each other like a couple of schoolgirls. They had just come back from Alma, where Noor had taken notes for the report of the national committee meeting and, as soon as the key figures in the Resistance had left, had sent a résumé of the points discussed with the new chairman of the clandestine organisation, Georges Bidault. Violette and Darbois had waited downstairs, one in the entrance hall of the building, the other on the pavement opposite, on the corner of the avenue Marceau, so that they could be sure the meeting was safe. There were other armed agents spread through the neighbouring streets to warn of any intruders. The discussions had been heated and lengthy. The Gaullists wanted to establish the general's authority over the Resistance; they were paving the way for him to take power after the war. De Gaulle particularly needed this as security to give him the upper hand in the fierce battle he was waging with Giraud in Algiers, and to guarantee his domination of Free France. Roosevelt backed Giraud, and Churchill was beginning to find de Gaulle far too rebellious. The Resistance movement valued its independence; the Communists were keen to introduce their own unitarian organisation, the Front National. In the end the more politically minded had grasped what was at stake. If they sided with the General that would mean cutting short Giraud's operation (and they deemed the latter to be too conservative and too close to the Americans) while also limiting the risks of the Communists coming to power after the victory. The text that Noor sent to London was unitarian; there was no room for haggling over the support given to de Gaulle and in exchange he would be reappointed in favour of republican institutions and social reform. Then the two young women had left by Métro, one behind the other, Noor with her radio case, and Violette with her hand over her pistol. Exhausted, they had gone straight to bed side by side on the only bed in the room.

'How do you do division in German?' Noor asked.

'What do you mean, division?' said Violette.

'Division. Making a calculation, dividing something. How do you divide one number by another?'

'But why do you want to know?'

'I've got an idea for tomorrow.'

'Pickersgill and MacAlistair?'

'Yes. They've been sent by Blainville. I don't trust them.'

'What's the connection?'

'I'll explain. How do you do division in German?'

Noor took a page from her notebook and handed it to Violette with a pencil. Even though she did not understand, Violette wrote down a sum.

'Are you sure?'

'Yes. I went to school in Hungary. I know they do it the same way. They put the number they're dividing on the first line and the divider underneath, and they write the answer on the right, above the rest.

'Perfect. The English do it the other way round. That's going to be useful . . .'

The fishing boat was passing the Chausey islands, leaving the little tower at Pignon on its right as it headed for the lighthouse at Roc, where the Germans had built two bunkers, one to the north of the point, the other to the south above the port.

'We're in good time,' said Samoel.

We had spent all day lifting lobster pots in the Ecrehous, then we had gone south to Granville, the home port of Samoel – the fisherman who had a great deal of respect for the Resistance. Like his colleagues, he knew about the SOE boats, but it was understood that no fisherman would ever speak out about their nocturnal trips. Most of them had carried on with their jobs; only those in Sein and Molène had left for England as early as 1940. The rest had told themselves they had to scratch a living together somehow. But their co-operative, unlike many others, was patriotic at heart. Samoel decided to take me to Granville. We still had to bluff our way through German surveillance.

'Evening's falling,' said the fisherman. 'I should be passing the jetty now. Any form of navigation is forbidden at night. But they won't make a fuss about half an hour here or there. When we get there it'll be dark, it'll be easier. Once we're past the bunker, if we get close enough to the coast, we'll be in a blind spot. They won't be able to see either from the jetty or from the bunker. When we get there, you get into your little boat and I'll leave you. Go along the first jetty and go into the old port. The sentry will be watching me. He won't think of looking down round the bottom of the jetty.

'OK. Thanks for everything.'

Samoel handed me a glass of Calvados. 'Here, this isn't the condemned man's last wish – it's just to keep you warm!'

I had put my things back into the whaler, which we had towed behind us. We had run across two German patrol boats, and they had waved to us.

Over three years the occupying forces and the local fishermen had grown accustomed to each other. Nothing ever happened in that part of the Channel, between the Channel Islands and the coast. The heavily armed defences on Jersey and Guernsey were like advanced bastions for the bay of Mont-Saint-Michel. They kept the RAF away. The SOE arranged landings for its agents further west in Brittany, where German vigilance was more relaxed.

The boat drew nearer to Roc, the promontory that pointed westwards and on which the oldest part of the port of Granville had been built, above the bay, which was protected from the north and west winds. We went slowly round the point and kept close to the shore just beneath the lighthouse and the bunker. It was dark now. Samoel had put on his side-lights, which made the whaler behind us invisible.

'Here we are,' he said, leaning backwards, 'they can't see us any more. You've got two minutes, no more!'

'Thanks then, and God keep you,' I said. 'Long live Normandy!'

'That's right. Down with Jersey!' (The fishermen from Normandy and Jersey were constantly fighting over fishing rights. It was thanks to a highly refined sense of their national interests that the people of Normandy had changed enemies, seeing the English as less of a threat than the Germans.)

I jumped into the whaler and Samoel untied the

rope and threw it to me, without slowing his own boat for a moment. I started rowing furiously towards the jetty, which loomed dark above me. With their eyes busy looking at the lights on the fishing boat, the soldiers on sentry duty would have trouble making out the dark outline of the whaler as it sidled towards the coast. I reached the foot of the jetty, where the waves broke over granite rocks, creating sprays of foam. I cut along parallel to the shore, heading for the turrets at the entrance to the bay. The soldiers would have only to lean over and they would see me, but the arrival of the fishing boat should keep them occupied. Five minutes later I was at the mouth of the port, where the tide was beginning to drop. I crossed the red glow thrown by the light to the port side and thirty yards further on, at the end of the other jetty, there was a green light flashing. Samoel had told me there was a set of stone steps which went right down to the water's edge, on the inside of the jetty. I tied the boat up and threw my bag onto the shining steps, which led right up to the top of the wall. I took out my commando knife and a hammer that Samoel had given me. In less than a minute I had broken through the bottom of the boat in two different places. It began to fill with water. I leapt onto the steps and pushed the whaler as far out as I could. It drifted out for about ten yards, slowed by the water streaming into it. A minute later it had sunk. It would be found on the sand at low tide, but by then I would be far away.

I took my bag and climbed carefully up onto the jetty. At the end of the jetty near the light marking the entrance to the bay, there was a soldier looking out to sea. I was fifty yards from him. I headed towards the depths of the port without attracting his attention. When I reached the end of the jetty I could hardly believe what I saw: there below me in the dry dock I recognised an oblong hull with a little turret hidden under a huge tarpaulin so that it could not be seen by reconnaissance planes. It was the U-boat that I had seen being towed two nights previously, before the gunboat started chasing us. A very important discovery. The submarine obviously could not be repaired in Saint-Malo, probably because the shipyards there were overrun with work. It had gone all the way on to Granville, where another team was dealing with it. I walked on briskly while the sentry still had his back to me.

I made my decision quickly. I had disobeyed orders by going to help Noor. A logical move. But I could not leave behind such an important prey for the Navy without trying something. That would have been a betrayal. I had to attack the submarine even if it meant losing two or three days. Noor would run a higher risk of being arrested, but I had no choice. Crouching behind a pile of empty lobster pots, which smelt of dried fish, I constructed my plan.

CHAPTER THIRTY

As Noor walked past she caused conversations to grind to a halt as she so often did. Men turned to watch her and women eyed her with envy or admiration. The terrace of the Café de Flore was full of people but there were no cars on the boulevard. The bell-tower of the church of Saint-Germain-des-Prés stood out clearly against the September sky with its scattering of little clouds. Noor pushed the heavy glazed doors to get inside the café. The two Canadians were waiting for her at the back of the room. Pickersgill was young with very straight blond hair and laughing blue eyes, MacAlistair had a short beard, which balanced out his tendency to premature baldness.

'Hello,' said Noor, 'I'm Aurora.'

The two men stood up and introduced themselves. 'Thank you so much for coming,' said Pickersgill, 'we're stuck in Paris. Without you we can't do anything.'

'Have you been in Holland?'

'Yes, but we can't stay there any longer. We had to leave in a hurry. Our only contact was Blainville. He gave you the message.'

'Is he in Paris?'

'Yes. He's just back from London. He's had new instructions from his superiors. He's stopped all his activities for now. He's in hiding. You can only catch him in the mornings for about an hour a day at the café his wife runs on the rue Saint-André-des-Arts. Prosper's collapse has made him wary.'

'I see he's told you about our problems.'

'The bare essentials. He's not going to be able to get us back to England. We need to go through the Cinema network. Blainville said you had connections there.'

Noor hesitated. 'Yes. I do. But I'll need a bit of time. We'll talk about that another time. But you want to send a message and you no longer have a radio for transmissions, is that right?'

It was Pickersgill, the radio operator, who replied. 'It was taken in Holland. But I managed to disable it before the Gestapo got hold of it.'

A man on his own had just come and sat down on the red-leather seat a couple of tables away. Noor glanced over to him.

'We have to send a message,' Pickersgill went on. 'It's our report on the work we did in Holland, and it's quite long.'

'Do you have the text on you? I could take it with me now, it would be easier.'

'Yes. Here it is.'

MacAlistair produced several sheets of paper.

Noor caught the lone man turning furtively

towards them. She took the pages of paper. 'It's long,' she said. 'I'll have a look at it, I need to know if I'm going to have to make several transmissions. I've got the only radio in Paris and I have a lot of work.'

She started counting the number of characters and the lines, then she did some mental arithmetic. 'At least three hours of transmissions!' she said. 'Couldn't you cut it down?'

She had made a mistake calculating the length of time needed for the transmission. If Pickersgill failed to correct her he was not a radio operator. He did not fall into the trap.

'That's impossible!' Pickersgill said, smiling. 'It couldn't take three hours.'

'Wait, I'll count again.'

Noor opened her notebook and made the calculations again, in writing this time. She closed the notebook once she had finished. 'It is! It's three hours!'

'But there must be a mistake. You can't be that slow.'

Pickersgill was becoming impatient. Noor tore a page out of her notebook and handed him a pencil. 'Count for yourself. I do twenty-four words a minute. You can't go wrong.'

Irritated by the obvious mistake, he took the pencil and set about making the calculation. He multiplied the number of lines by the number of words in each line, then started to divide the total by twenty-four. Noor stared at the piece of paper as he wrote. Instead of writing twenty-four on the same line as the number he was dividing it into, Pickersgill wrote it on the line below.

Noor pushed her chair back and stood up. She thrust her hand into her bag and took out her pistol. 'You're not Canadian! Blainville's trying to get me again. Don't move!'

The customers stared at her. The waiters stopped what they were doing. Pickersgill and MacAlistair sat paralysed on their seats. Noor walked slowly backwards towards the door. The man sitting on the red-leather seat took out a gun. Noor saw him and aimed her pistol at him. 'Put that down!'

The man did as he was told. The two false Canadians stood up, and Noor turned back to aim at them, with her pistol at arm's length. Her hand was shaking. 'Watch out! I'll shoot! Stay where you are!'

Two customers from the terrace had come into the café and were moving closer to her from behind. She became aware of them and turned round. The two men froze, but the Canadians took advantage of the distraction to move forwards. The noose was drawing tighter and the customers watched in silent fascination.

'Give us the pistol, miss,' one of the men said.

'Step back or I'll shoot!'

Her voice sounded less assured. Noor was frightened. She knew she would not shoot. Partly hidden behind one of the pillars in the café, the man from the seat thought she would not see him and he picked up his gun again. A short burst of fire hit him and he slumped onto the table with blood seeping out of him. Several customers screamed, others threw themselves under the tables.

'Come on, Noor, let's get out of here!'

The two young women backed out of the café still aiming their guns into the room. Out on the boulevard a black Citroën was waiting for them. They each climbed in through one of the back doors and the car set off. Three Gestapo officers rushed out and opened fire. In vain: the Citroën had turned down the rue de Rennes and was out of danger.

'You missed her again! This is becoming a habit! And we've got one man dead too,' Goetz thundered in disappointment as he paced up and down his office on the avenue Foch.

'Our men were very well positioned,' said Peter. 'She was surrounded. I was on the terrace with Hans. There were four of us against her. No problem. But she suddenly got up, I don't know why.'

'She got up because she managed to get that cretin to do division,' said Goetz. 'For goodness' sake, it's so elementary! Everyone knows that arithmetic's done differently in different countries! We use that trick the whole time to catch out the English. We ask them to do multiplications or divisions. They don't do them the same way as the French. Neither do we, for that matter. She trapped you. She's very clever and you've underestimated her!'

'Our two agents did manage to trick her, though.'

'Is that what they think? We have to catch her. She's got the last SOE radio set working in the Paris area. If we get hold of it, they won't have anything for weeks. We'll have a good chance of tricking them, because there aren't many people left round her. If we pick her up discreetly, we can use her against Baker Street.'

'I know, *Herr Ober*, I know.'

'And the girl who fired the machine gun! Where did she come from? One of our agents killed and no arrest! Boemelburg's really going to like that! Blainville told us this Aurora was on her own. Oh really! She had a bodyguard and a chauffeur.'

'Yes, and now she won't trust Blainville. He managed to look innocent last time, but now he's suspect again. I think MacAlistair and Pickersgill made another mistake too!'

Goetz stopped for a moment and turned his seething red face and his flashing eyes on Peter. 'What? Another?' he exploded.

'Yes,' said Peter. 'To give their story credibility they mentioned Blainville's café and told her when he was there.'

'But they're mad!'

'No, it made sense. She knows Blainville. By giving her details about him, they could show that they were in the network.'

'But for God's sake! Blainville's our key agent

at the moment. We have to protect him! They gave his whereabouts to a girl who's just killed one of our men, who's seen through Blainville and who's escaped from us twice.'

'She must have known, anyway.'

'What do you know about it! She thought Blainville was in England. Now she knows he's in Paris. That's dangerous, it's dangerous.'

'Blainville doesn't always help us . . .'

'He can't. Kieffer doesn't understand that. Neither do you, Peter. If Blainville told us everything, he'd lose credibility with the English. Then he wouldn't be any use to us at all. He knows a lot, that man, I can tell. He's got the ear of the English high command. He could reveal a really decisive piece of information one day. We must look after him.'

'It's not serious. Blainville just needs to change address.'

Goetz was exasperated. 'He can't, his wife runs the café! And if he moves the English will be suspicious.'

'But what are you so afraid of?'

'That girl, she's what we should be worrying about. She's quite capable of planning to get Blainville. She now knows for sure that he's given her away. She could take him down, or have him taken down. They've just killed one of our agents, Peter, and they've escaped right here in Paris. They're very tricky customers.'

'Yes . . . yes, you're right.'

Goetz had started trying to wind his cuckoo clock. He wound the spring right up then turned round and stood motionless, staring at Peter. 'I've got an idea! This girl knows the time and the place, doesn't she?'

'Yes.'

'We could try to even the scores a bit . . .'

In the little room on the boulevard Richard-Wallace, Noor sat on the worn old sofa facing Violette, who was coolly reapplying her make-up in a mirror speckled with black spots. Noor was fuming as much as Goetz.

'They nearly got us, the bastards! It's Blainville, Blainville again, always Blainville! When's London going to grasp that?'

'They could have got in through someone else,' said Violette. 'The Gestapo have clearly infiltrated the whole Prosper network.'

'No, that's wrong, Violette! Vienet told me about two Canadians who'd been sent by Blainville. And those two Canadians were from the Gestapo. I trust Vienet completely. I know he's safe. It's Blainville. We've got to stop him doing any more harm. It's too dangerous working in these conditions.'

'Well, we got one. There's always that.'

'That's true. But why did you shoot?'

'He picked up his gun. I wasn't going to miss him. Noor, your pacifism will be the death of you.'

'I'm becoming less of a pacifist by the day, you

know . . . Violette, I do have one good piece of information.'

'What's that?'

'Blainville's in his café every morning at about nine o'clock.'

'He has a café?'

'Yes. He bought it with his wife. It's a cover that the SOE paid for him. John told me everything. It's on the corner of the rue Saint-André-des-Arts and the rue Gît-le-Coeur.'

'So?'

'So we can take him down.'

'Kill him? Noor, you really are learning!'

'He's a pest. We'd be saving a lot of lives.'

'I can't disagree with that, and I know that killing traitors is a basic rule. But we must warn London.'

'They'll only tell us that we can trust Blainville.'

'We can't kill an SOE agent without specific orders.'

'We've got proof that he's a traitor. What more do we need?'

'Orders.'

'We'd just lose time. He'll disappear.'

'No. We can talk to London and track Blainville down at the same time. Then we'll see where we stand.'

'Violette, it's him, he's the traitor. He's got to be liquidated. John taught me not to beat about the bush.'

'If he's a traitor, I'll take him out myself.'

'Let's start straight away,' said Noor getting to her feet.

'We'll have to be careful. He'll be very cautious. We'll have to find where he is without being seen.'

'I can take care of that. I know Blainville. After that, I'm counting on you.'

CHAPTER THIRTY-ONE

I pulled the soldier from behind with my hand over his mouth, then I drove my dagger down into him. The blade went in right up to the hilt. I pulled it back out but kept my hand in place. He did not cry out. The steel had cut right through his torso; I knew it had perforated an artery, perhaps even his heart. Blood was flooding into his lungs and no longer getting to his brain. He was losing consciousness. He fell slowly. I held him up by passing my right hand under his arm, with my left hand still over his mouth, and I lay him quietly down on the ground. He would be dead in twenty seconds.

I had crawled through the grass a few inches at a time for ten minutes in order to get close to him without making any sound. He was nonchalantly looking out over the sea some sixty feet below him. He was on guard duty on the southern point of Roc, in front of the bunker that the Germans had built beneath the lighthouse. He did not turn round as I moved forwards, if he had he would have seen me by moonlight. I flattened myself against the ground in the darkness with my commando dagger in its sheath attached to my thigh. I had rehearsed this exercise a hundred times in training. He was dead without even knowing how or why.

I pointed my torch behind me and made one quick flash of light. Four black silhouettes emerged from the slope and hurried into the bunker. I heard the dull crump of the Welrod silencers. The two soldiers inside must have been sleeping. They too had died without a sound. One of Cowburn's men dragged the sentry's body into the bunker, and he started to undress him to take over from him. At the bottom of the slope we could see the calm water reflecting the moonlight. It was high tide and the sea had filled the first dock. The other one, on the far side over by the town, had been closed off with a lock. The dry dock had been carved out of the rock below us, at the foot of the jetty that I had rowed along two nights previously. Trawlers that needed repairing came in at high tide, then keeled over as the water ebbed back. At low tide the dock was like an oval amphitheatre with its rows of little recesses carved out of the rock so that men could work on the underside of the hull. The U-boat had replaced the usual trawlers. There it was, just below us, hidden under a big dark tarpaulin.

There was one guard left to neutralise, then we had the barbed-wire fence to negotiate. We had taken possession of the bunker to the north, on the far side of the point, near the casino. We had left behind two stand-in guards, who spoke German. The SOE had found out from the Resistance the work schedules (which were more or less the same all along the coast) and the surveillance procedures used by the Germans on the Atlantic wall, and they had passed them on to Cowburn months before. Thanks to the men who had taken the places of the soldiers we had killed, we would have an hour or two to play with, time enough to work on the U-boat.

I had got back in touch with Cowburn through Garry's letter box in Dreux. I had told him about the submarine which was being repaired and we had decided on a plan of attack. The port of Granville was guarded on two sides. We could not get through the town because it was too well defended, but by coming round the point at Roc, near the casino to the north, we could get to the port by going under the lighthouse as if coming from the sea. There were two bunkers with cannons pointing out to sea. If we could neutralise them we could get through the defences. The Germans would not be expecting to be attacked from there. Granville was deep in the bay of Mont-Saint-Michel. In order to reach it, a hostile flotilla would have to come through the Channel Islands, whose huge cannons could sink any ship. The bunkers at Granville were there only as a precaution.

While Cowburn and Garry made their way towards the last guard on the quay under Roc, I lay down in the grass on the parapet halfway up the slope. I took out my binoculars and lay my Sten down in front of me. I had to stay as a cover in case a patrol came out from the town. If there were any sort of problem I had to call Cowburn on the walkie-talkie. I started sweeping backwards and forwards over the port by the light of the moon, which was reflected in the water. In the wet dock there were several cargo boats and trawlers moored side by side in front of the dark hangar used for auctioning fish. Above the dock I could see another feebly lit sentry post surrounded by chicanes and barbed wire to stop intruders getting to the town. Nothing moved.

I looked back towards the port, which was still dark and deserted, then to the sentry post. I froze. Something had caught my eye in the red glow of the beacon at the mouth of the port. I focused the binoculars on the surface of the water, down below the jetty. Intrigued, and then fascinated, I saw a small wake moving into the first dock. A succession of bubbles had broken along the surface. This tell-tale wake was produced by scuba-diving cylinders: there were a number of divers under-water in the port.

'Cowburn,' I said into the walkie-talkie, 'there's a problem.'

'What is it?'

'You'll have to come and see.'

'What are you on about, Sutherland?'

'There's something going on in the port, and it changes everything.'

'But what is it?'

'Come. You'll have to come.'

Cowburn was back within five minutes, followed by Garry and the third saboteur. They lay down in the grass a little way away and looked at the sentry. I handed the binoculars to Cowburn. 'There, in the middle of the port,' I said, pointing.

He focused the binoculars on the calm surface of the water.

'What is it?'

'Divers. They're coming over to the U-boat.'

'What are they doing here?'

'The same as us, I should think. Birkin and Slocum must have sent a report, they've identified the U-boat from the air, and they've decided to blow it up. It's a good opportunity. They'll do anything to destroy a U-boat. They had the same idea as us and they must have sent a submarine, which is probably waiting a few miles away. The divers move about on those underwater propeller-driven contraptions, like giant torpedoes. There must be four of them, two going towards the U-boat and two waiting outside on the torpedoes.

Through my sights I saw a shiny black head break the surface to get its bearings. I could imagine the diver assessing his position using the phosphorescent compass on his wrist. He dived back down. He would now be using his compass to navigate. The trail of bubbles was heading straight for the submarine.

'They could have told us!' said Cowburn.

'We didn't tell them.'

'What should we do?'

'Nothing, I would think. We can't contact them, and they're getting to the U-boat. Look.'

The trail of bubbles had disappeared under the tarpaulin hiding the submarine. The two divers must have been fixing time-delayed mines onto the hull.

'But this is ridiculous!' said Cowburn. 'We're risking our lives to sabotage this submarine, and they're going to blow it up before we get there!'

'Let's wait and see.'

Five minutes later the bubbles reappeared. The two divers were heading back towards the mouth of the port. I watched the sentry through my binoculars.

The soldier was no longer looking out to sea. He was leaning his elbows on the iron guard rail facing towards us on the top of the jetty, and he was looking towards the port. His silhouette was clearly defined against the glittering waves.

'It's dangerous! He could see the air bubbles.'

'Garry!' said Cowburn. 'Get your rifle. The guard, over there, on the jetty.'

Garry picked up his rifle, shouldered it and aimed. 'I've got him in my sights.'

'Wait. On my order. He might not see anything. If we have to shoot, we'll pull out straight away at the run.' Cowburn turned to Garry and added: 'You'll have to kill him. If you miss him he'll tell the others. They'll search the bay, and they'll get the divers.'

Then Cowburn took off his rucksack, put it in front of him and took out three grenades. Through the binoculars, the guard looked motionless, still leaning against the railings. The trail of bubbles was coming over towards him. It would have to go through the light from the beacon to get out to sea. The soldier stood up and leant over towards the black water. He stood still for a moment and then took a step to the right, and a second. He had seen the trail in the light. He was moving slowly to follow it.

'He's seen him,' I said. 'He's going to raise the alarm.'

'Fire!' said Cowburn.

Garry fired. Through the binoculars I saw the soldier tossed backwards onto the far railing. He was about to fall to the ground when Garry fired again. His head was thrown backwards. His body tipped over and he disappeared on the other side of the jetty. He must have fallen in only yards from the divers.

The shots had rung out round the port. The door of the guardroom above us opened and a soldier appeared in the rectangle of light. He turned towards the top of the point where the shots had come from. Cowburn killed him with three shots of his pistol. Then he pulled the pins out of his grenades and threw them through the doorway one by one. The whole room collapsed in the explosions and started to burn. Garry had turned the sights of his gun onto the other guardroom, near the town. A soldier came out. He fell, struck down by Garry. The other guards stayed inside. They must have been telephoning for help.

'Let's get out!' cried Cowburn.

We followed each other in single file along the path that wound round Roc. As we reached the bunker the telephone rang. Cowburn's man who had taken over from the sentry went into the bunker and picked it up.

'*Ja, ja,*' he said, '*ich habe sie gesehen. Nein, Oberleutnant, sie will nicht gehen!*'

The fake soldier came out with a broad smile on his face. 'They think the bunker's still in their hands. They've given me orders to watch the pathway to the port and stop the commandos from getting away.'

'Perfect. Come on,' said Cowburn. 'Quickly!'

Five minutes later we were on the other side of the point, under the casino, which loomed dark above us. The other stand-in sentry had received the same telephone call and he joined us. There was a little path that led to the town. The Germans thought that the two bunkers on the point were blocking the way to the commandos. Cowburn's ruse had worked. In three minutes' time we would be scattered through the streets of Granville, heading for houses we could hide in. As we came to the end of the path, near the Plat-Gousset jetty, there was a huge explosion.

'That's it!' I said. 'The U-boat's gone up. Well played! They only used a short time delay.'

'I can't believe it!' said Cowburn. 'I can't believe it!'

'The Germans won't understand a thing. The barbed wire hasn't been cut, and they won't know how we got to the submarine. And, because Garry's such a good shot, they'll never know about the divers! It's going to drive them mad.'

Cowburn, the man who never smiled, started to laugh.

'And the divers are going to spend the rest of their lives wondering why a soldier jumped into the water in front of them. I hope he didn't fall on top of them. What a stroke of luck! I can't believe it!'

'Don't say that,' I replied. 'The success of this operation hinged on the perfect co-ordination between the two teams. That's what we'll tell the historians.'

CHAPTER THIRTY-TWO

Goetz was winding up his cuckoo clock again as he listened to Peter. The young man could see the former French teacher's broad back and his head nodding after every sentence.

'Blainville has breakfast in his café in the mornings. The place is called Le Latin. His wife serves him. I don't know if he always does but he was there yesterday. He obviously sleeps there. He sits near a window and reads the paper while he has his coffee and butters his bread. He's very vulnerable there.'

'We'd better not say anything to him,' Goetz replied. 'No point in making things any more complicated. If he knows he's in danger, he might hide and we'd be in deep water. Same story with the others. It's the girl we're interested in, Peter. She's our first priority. We must get her radio. This time, no false moves. We find her apartment and, when she goes out, we go in and wait. I want to be absolutely sure of success. No shooting in the street or escaping out of the back.'

Goetz had finished winding his clock. He made

it cuckoo by turning the hands round to the correct time. The mechanical bird made its shrill little noise. He sat back down at his desk and looked at Peter, who was picking a speck of dust from his trouser leg. 'Did you see anything suspicious this morning?'

'No. No one stopped. There were a few passers-by but none of them so much as glanced at the café. One young man, at a pinch, who looked inside as he walked past very quickly. There's no one there in the mornings. And there aren't any customers either.'

'So they haven't carried out their reconnaissance yet. What's one way of protecting Blainville?'

'To watch him. But I don't know how we can do that without him knowing. We'd have to stay inside the café.'

'If he knows, we'd lose our bait.'

'That's true. But it's very complicated. The rue Gît-le-Coeur runs off the rue Saint-André-des-Arts. They're both small streets and there's no one in them in the morning. If someone stood about in a doorway or outside the bookshop next door – which is called the Chevreuil or something like that – they'd be spotted straight away.'

'They're going to have the same problem. They'll have a look down the street and decide it's going to be impossible.'

'Can't be sure of that. They're going to want to get rid of the traitor. The SOE's instructions are very clear. You execute traitors as soon as they're found, no trial, no hesitation. All things being equal they'll try and kill him. And as they know he's in his café at nine o'clock, that's when they'll try it. But they can't just come along with a pistol and shoot him. It's too risky. They'd have to check first that there wasn't a trap, and they'd have to plan an escape route.'

'I can't see how they're going to do it,' said Peter, spreading his arms.

'They could take up a position in the staircase of the building opposite the café.'

'No, I've checked. There are three buildings that overlook the café. One of them's closed. It doesn't have a door. And the staircases in the other two don't go down onto the street. They'd have to get into one of the apartments, which presupposes having an accomplice on the premises. Impossible.'

'Did you think about the hotel?'

'The Hôtel Eugénie? Of course. But from the inside you can't see the café. I've checked that too.'

'No, the other hotel.'

'Which other hotel? There isn't another one near the café.'

Goetz looked at Peter triumphantly, took out a rolled-up piece of paper and started to unroll it towards him. 'While you were doing all the work on foot, I was doing the work in my head. I asked the town hall for plans of the area. This shows the area round the intersection between the rue Gît-le-Coeur and the rue Saint-André-des-Arts.

Peter walked round the desk to look at the plans.

'Ha, ha,' said the German. 'You see this building,' and he pointed to a building a little to the left of Blainville's café. 'It's L-shaped. It's got the rue Saint-André-des-Arts to the back of it, but at the front it's on the place Saint-André-des-Arts, just outside the Métro station. It's a hotel called the Gentilhommière.'

'Do they have rooms at the back?'

Goetz turned to Peter, his eyes twinkling. 'Yes.'

'That's very clever. But they may be taken.'

'I've rung. They're available . . .'

'They know that we know,' said Darbois. 'They'll probably have the café watched. When we get there they'll jump straight out on us. I went past it this morning. Blainville was sitting at a table. He didn't see me. But it's on two very small roads and they're practically deserted in the mornings. There was one suspicious chap, dressed like Beau Brummell, walking past slowly, looking at all the buildings. He saw me. If they put two or three men in the area, they'd be sure to catch us.'

'We'll have to do a reccy,' said Violette. 'We'll have to get him from somewhere we're sure we're safe, with an escape route at the back.'

The three of them were sitting in the red-leatherette armchairs in Darbois's apartment on the rue Joseph-de-Maistre. He had poured them each a glass of cognac.

436

'Derek is quite sure that the place is deserted,' said Noor. 'We'd be spotted straight away.'

'We'll have to find a way of getting near to the café discreetly,' replied Violette. 'Derek was seen, he can't go back today. I'll go this afternoon. It must get busier.'

'There's no guarantee of that,' said Noor. 'Be careful, Violette. They know you now.'

'I'll take a *vélo-taxi*. Once you're inside it, no one can really see you. And I've got an idea. Do you have a camera, Derek?'

The train from Granville to Paris travelled slowly through the Normandy countryside. The hills gleamed in the sunlight and the valleys were beginning to emerge from the shadows. Mist hung over the patchwork of farmland. Tired from the night operation, I drifted in and out of sleep, thinking of Noor. I had taken the first train the very next day after the attack on the submarine. Cowburn had leant me a suit and a tie, and given me news from Paris. He had received an encoded letter from Violette. The two young women were still free, active and useful. Noor was alive. The Germans had not arrested her. Not yet. I was a typewriter salesman again now. Two soldiers had checked my papers before I stepped into the train. Everything was in order.

My plan was quite clear. I had talked to Cowburn about it – I trusted him – and he had approved it. Noor was running too many risks in France. If we were not to sacrifice the operator herself, we had to stop the activities of the Aurora radio. The SOE could send someone else. Blainville at large represented a mortal threat. As soon as I arrived at the Gare Montparnasse, I would go to Darbois and he would tell me where to find Noor. We would leave for Normandy as soon as possible, and there Cowburn would arrange a plane for us. I would explain myself as best I could to Buckmaster and Bodington. I looked at my watch. It was twelve minutes past nine. In three hours Noor would be saved.

At a quarter past nine that same morning, Noor came out of the Saint-Michel Métro station on the place Saint-André-des-Arts. The previous day Violette had returned from her expedition in triumph. She had travelled the length of the rue Saint-André-des-Arts, hidden in a *vélo-taxi*, taking masses of photographs through the little windows in the hood. Darbois had developed the photographs in the bathroom with equipment from the SOE. Noor had found the solution. Through the windows of a building a little to the left of the café and on the other side of the street, the blinds could be seen half lowered. In the photographs the faded inscription on them was clear: 'La Gentilhommière'. It was the hotel whose entrance was on the place Saint-André-des-Arts, and which backed onto the street opposite Blainville's café.

'I'll go there tomorrow morning,' Noor had said. 'It's my turn.'

'You'll have to see if there's a line of fire,' said Violette.

'I'll take a room at the back,' Noor replied. 'If I've got this right the main entrance to the hotel is just by the Métro station. If they're watching the café they'll be on the rue Saint-André-des-Arts and not on the *place*. It's good and safe. I'll take a picture. You'll be able to check the sight-lines for yourself, Violette.'

At half past nine, Noor went into the hotel. She asked for a room at the back. She was given room 27, on the second floor. She went up a narrow staircase with irregular treads. It was in one of the oldest parts of Paris; the walls were made of old stone and the stairs were of dark, well-worn wood. Noor went into the little room with its iron bedstead and a mirror on the front of the wardrobe. There were beams on the ceiling, and there was a small ceramic basin by the door. Noor went over to the window, lowered the blind with the words 'La Gentilhommière' on it, and looked down into the street by drawing it aside. She could look straight down onto the café. She could see Blainville sitting at his table, leaning over his newspaper. She took several photographs. Then she waited. At ten o'clock, Blainville got up and disappeared towards the back of the café. Noor took some more photographs to left and right in case she caught anyone keeping an eye out. No one. From this window

Violette would have no trouble aiming at Blainville. Then she would have to go down two floors, run from the hotel foyer into the Métro station and leap onto the first train. By the time the police arrived she would be long gone. Darbois could cover for her, waiting down in the foyer to cope with any unforeseen interruptions. Blainville's fate was sealed.

Noor put her camera in her handbag, opened the wardrobe and hung up a few clothes that she had brought in a suitcase, and then left the room. She looked round carefully as she went back down the stairs. The hotel was deserted. No one would get in their way. She did not stop on the first-floor landing; a quick glance round was enough. She left her key with the *concierge*. Once out on the square she hunched her head down between her shoulders and covered the few yards before disappearing into the Métro entrance. She looked at her watch. Ten past ten. She hardly had time to go home and change before her meeting with Vienet and the others. As she was short of time and felt reassured by the set-up, she had not noticed that the door to room number 17, the room on the first floor just below hers, was ajar.

CHAPTER THIRTY-THREE

It was eleven o'clock when the train from Granville drew puffing and screeching into the station. I jumped down onto the platform and ran towards the exit, where there was a queue of gas-driven taxis waiting on the rue de l'Arrivée. Half an hour later I was climbing the stairs in the decrepit building on the rue Joseph-de-Maistre. Darbois had just got up, probably exhausted after a night of licentious activity.

'Arthur, you're back! I'm so glad to see you again. I thought you'd been withdrawn to London. They've sent you back quickly!'

'Yes, well, no, not exactly . . . Where's Noor?'

'Where? I don't know. But I'm seeing her at lunchtime. We're working on the Blainville case.'

'Blainville's a dangerous character.'

'Yes, I know, he's a traitor.'

'A traitor. I'm not so sure.'

'You're not sure? But, I can tell you, we're sure. He nearly had Noor taken. We only just got away. We've decided to execute him.'

'He nearly . . . already? Derek, I'll have to explain to you. Have you arranged to meet Noor?'

'Yes. Her, Vienet and Violette. We've got a plan. We're meeting to finalise things.'

'Where and when?'

'At the Hôtel Régina at one o'clock. It's on the corner of the rue de Rivoli and the rue des Pyramides, opposite the statue of Joan of Arc. It's the only hotel in the street that hasn't been requisitioned by the Germans. Vienet likes that sort of place. He knows the *patron*; he would warn him if there was any danger. It's safe.'

I looked at my watch. It was a quarter to twelve.

'We'll leave in half an hour. Sit down,' said Darbois.

The hotel was built in stone and it had tall windows with intricate wrought-iron balconies. The back of the building looked over the Tuileries gardens near the Pavillon Colbert, the only vestige of the former kings' palace which was burned during the time of the Commune. The front overlooked the golden statue of Joan of Arc pointing her flag up the rue de Rivoli, in the middle of the little square where the rue des Pyramides started. As we came out of the Tuileries Métro station, alongside the gardens, we could see the big red flags with their swastikas flying to our left by the place de la Concorde. This part of Paris was all hotels, wealthy tourists, the head offices of banks and luxury boutiques. The Germans had settled here in 1940. Vienet felt that it was easier to hide in all this wealth and amongst the Nazis themselves. He would not have liked it if the Resistance had forced him to live meagrely. He was quite prepared to sacrifice life itself . . . but not his way of life.

The entrance of the Hôtel Régina was set back in half-shadow under a series of arches. At ten past one I pushed through the revolving door with its big brass handles, with Darbois close behind. I was greeted by a bellboy in a red uniform as I stepped into the foyer of carved marble and wood, with two crystal chandeliers.

The restaurant to our right was full of people carrying on their quiet conversations. Not a single German. Vienet was sitting at a table at the back of the room, with Violette. Noor had seen me coming along the rue de Rivoli. My heart missed a beat when I saw her again after dreaming of her so much; she was even more beautiful than I had remembered. She had got up to come and greet us, her face alight with laughter and her eyes sparkling. She was wearing a blue blazer with wide lapels, a short pleated skirt and short white socks which brought out the golden glow of her long legs. There, in the middle of the restaurant, she fell into my arms.

'My love, you're here . . .'

She brushed her lips over mine, then rested her cheek on my chest, squeezing me with both her arms round my back. We stood there in each other's arms, quite motionless as the other customers watched, amused and in sudden silence. After about thirty seconds, Darbois, who was fidgeting from one foot to the other, looking at the carpet, gave a discreet little cough. 'Perhaps we should sit down.'

Noor did not move. I could smell her perfume all around me. She pressed herself against me without a word. I pushed her back gently and put one arm round her waist. She looked ahead with a serious expression on her face, but I could feel her shivering. She touched my arm with one hand, and squeezed it tightly. Vienet and Violette were laughing out loud. Vienet stood up and pulled back Noor's chair. 'Such passion!' he said, still laughing.

He was wearing a white double-breasted suit with a red carnation in the button-hole, and was carrying a cigarette-holder.

'How are you, John, did you have a good journey?' asked Violette.

'Eventful. I came by sea. But I like sailing . . . Your friend Cowburn took care of me in Normandy. He's still just as good.'

'He's a real fighter,' she said.

'No more or less than you are,' said Vienet, looking her in the eye. 'Our amazon,' he muttered, taking her hand and bringing it up to his mouth as he leant forward.

'My dear René, please stop making these overtures. You know that I have a boyfriend.'

'This is war, my dear, life is shorter. A woman like you can't live like a nun.'

'Enough!' said Violette with mock fury. 'You're becoming tiresome!'

'John's got something important to tell us,' Darbois interrupted.

'Let's order,' said Vienet, 'then it'll be easier to talk. First, some champagne for the lovers!'

With a glass of champagne in my hand I told them about my time in London. Instead of telling them about the confidential conversation with Philby, I presented it as if I myself had done the reasoning that led to such a paradoxical conclusion: Blainville was a traitor, but a useful traitor working for the Intelligence Service.

'That's so twisted!' said Violette. 'Blainville lets them capture our materials and our agents so that he looks good with the Gestapo. It's monstrous.'

'It does happen,' said Vienet. 'If the Germans trust him, London can use him to infiltrate them. That's the game.'

'Well, it's a barbaric game,' said Noor.

'We have a barbaric enemy,' said Vienet. 'If we respected the rules of a civilised society, we'd die.'

'If we're barbaric too, what's the point of fighting?'

'We don't have the same goals, my dear Noor. That's the difference.'

'We have the same means.'

'Sometimes.'

'But', said Darbois, as if emerging from a dream, 'we mustn't kill Blainville then.'

The waiter came over to take our order. Without hesitating, Vienet took it upon himself to order oysters, game and a Nuits-Saint-Georges 1932. 'There are some good things about the black market,' he said, closing the menu while Violette watched him disapprovingly.

'Derek has got it,' I said. 'We mustn't go ahead and execute Blainville. If my deductions are right, then we'd be risking court martial for stupidity or insubordination. I think that Blainville is Bodington's man. It seems incredible, but there you are.'

'He's a bastard through and through,' said Violette.

'A useful bastard, though,' I said, 'there is such a thing.'

'But look,' she retorted, 'he's trying to get rid of us every way he can. We're not going to let ourselves be arrested to facilitate this Bodington's twisted strategies. I'm sure Buckmaster doesn't know about this. They're sick, these people at the Intelligence Service.'

'People who keep their hands clean lose the dirty wars,' I went on. 'But you're right on one point: we must stop any form of contact with Blainville. I've thought about it. René you're in the most danger: he knows you.'

'He doesn't know my real name. And he's probably decided not to give me away, otherwise it would already have happened. What you've explained is very clear, John. He's not telling the Germans everything. He's only doing the bare minimum to look credible to them. I'll be careful.'

'Derek and Violette are vulnerable. I think it would be safer for them to go back to Normandy with Cowburn.'

'I could hide Violette,' Vienet suggested.

'You're very kind,' said Violette, laughing. 'But why not Derek? Anyway, my place is with Noor. We have to protect radio operators.'

'That would be pointless,' I said. 'Noor's leaving with me tomorrow morning. We're going back to England.'

'What?' said Noor. 'But why? They need me in Paris.'

'It's too dangerous now, Noor. They know you, they're frantically looking for that radio and Blainville's helping them. They've nearly caught you twice. The SOE will send someone else very quickly. You need to stop for a bit. No one could possibly hold that against you.'

'But I came here to work. I can't just leave after three months when there isn't another radio in the Paris area.'

'There will be another. I'll talk to Buck about it. He'll understand.'

'He's right,' said Vienet. 'You must get back to England,' and he looked her right in the eye. 'You've done far more than you should have done. You'll get the *Croix de guerre*, Noor. If you stay on, you won't gain anything and neither will we. Unless you're determined to be decorated posthumously.'

Violette took Noor's hand and nodded her agreement. Noor sat back against the back of her chair and dropped her shoulders in acquiescence.

'A bit of Nuits-Saint-Georges to celebrate your going home,' said Vienet, picking up the bottle and smiling at Noor. 'Another one the Germans won't get.'

The meal ended happily amid general laughter. Reassured by Vienet and his agreement with the hotel's *patron*, we were able to relax in this unexpected haven. Vienet carried on with his concerted effort to woo Violette, putting his every ounce of wit into it. 'You push them back,' he said suddenly, looking at her with his head on one side.

'What?' said Violette.

'You push them back.'

'What do you mean, I push them back, what does that mean? I don't push anything back. I'm not pushing back.'

'But you do, you push them back.'

'What on earth do you mean?'

'The limits of beauty and charm, you push back the limits!'

As we all laughed, he tried to guess who Violette's English boyfriend might be: Buckmaster, Bodington, Montgomery, Mountbatten – he tried them all. Vienet dreamed up a complicated romance for Violette with each of them. The laughter grew louder. Noor cried, she was laughing so much. She leant against me in her abandon, with her hand on my arm. I could feel her knee brushing against mine under the table.

'I know,' said Vienet, 'it's Churchill! That's why they sent you to France. The idyll is an embarrassment to the government. You had to be separated. For reasons of state! Forget it Violette, it's doomed to failure. Clementine wouldn't put up with it, anyway.'

With the help of the Nuits-Saint-Georges he went on: 'Winston's jealous. And that's the nub. There are too many people after you, Violette, and he can't bear it. MI5 must have got involved. Then MI9 and the SOE, all of them. National security. Just the other night we heard him in his bunker saying' – and here he started to imitate Winston Churchill – 'Never in the field of human conflict have so many men wanted so much from just one woman.'

We laughed all the louder. He carried on in the Prime Minister's slightly nasal voice: 'And it is I who achieved it. Twice in one night. It was my finest hour!'

At four o'clock, more than a little tipsy and with our ribs hurting from so much laughing, we had to go our separate ways. In the foyer I told the others: 'I need to have a word with Noor.'

'Message received and understood,' said Vienet. 'I'll come back later with the mail for England. I'd rather give it to you than to Blainville. Will you be here?'

'Yes. I'll be waiting for you.'

Darbois and Violette said their goodbyes and wished us a good trip back. Then the three of them stepped into the revolving door. Through the glass I saw Vienet take Violette's arm. She let him, but she also took Darbois's arm, and the three of them set off arm in arm along the Tuileries gardens. We stood in the hall watching their outlines growing smaller down the rue de Rivoli. It was probably the best afternoon I had spent since the beginning of the war. The fear had evaporated for three hours. Seeing them disappear into the hostile city, I felt it come back again.

'Noor, we're leaving at seven o'clock tomorrow morning on the train to Dreux. We've got some time.'

'Some time?'

'Yes, some time to ourselves.'

She looked up at me with a smile and a twinkle in her eye. 'Some time to ourselves . . .'

Two minutes later we were walking into the hotel's royal suite, which was draped with velvet and tapestries, with tall windows looking out over the Tuileries gardens. Noor ran over to the balcony and opened the windows while I tipped the bellboy.

'I can see Suresnes!' she exclaimed happily. 'With a pair of binoculars I could see Fazal Manzil!'

I went over to her and put my arm over her shoulder. She leant against me and pointed over towards the west. The suite was on the top floor of the hotel. In front of us the greenery of the Tuileries gardens ran along the Seine, where each stone bridge glowed golden in the sunlight. To our left the dome of the Institut de France gleamed in the light; and to our right the Eiffel Tower stood out black against the blue sky. On the horizon we could see the shadow of the hills at Saint-Cloud and at Suresnes.

'This was the capital of the world,' I said, 'and now it's a prison.'

'Well, it's a beautiful prison. And the French will escape. I'm sure we're going to win now.'

'What makes you say that?'

'What you told us. If we're capable of that sort of ruse, then we can't lose. I was naive. With the Gestapo you have to use every way you can. It's our duty. Bodington's right. We'll talk to them about it. In London.'

She looked dreamily into the far distance. I realised that as we looked towards Suresnes and the Bois de Boulogne we were also looking towards England.

'John,' she said after a moment, 'I'm so happy.'

I turned her towards me. Standing with the light behind her I could only make out the shine in her dark, dark eyes. She kissed me, pressing herself against me, and I took her in my arms.

Moments later we were lying down on the huge bed. We had plenty of time. Noor undressed me slowly.

At six o'clock the telephone rang. It was Vienet, who had come back with the mail. Noor jumped out of bed, naked and light on her feet, with her black hair swishing over her brown back.

'I'll get my things while you're talking to Vienet,' she said as she got dressed. 'I'll only be an hour.'

'Don't you want me to come with you? It might be dangerous.'

451

'No,' she said, 'you must have things to talk about. Anyway, I have an agreement with the *concierge*. She tells me if anything different has happened. I have to pick up my notebooks and my codes. I'll leave the radio there. My successor can use it. I'll be back in an hour.'

'All right. Tonight we'll have supper in the Latin Quarter. I'll see you later, my love.'

'I love you,' she said, closing the padded door.

'German police. Don't move!'

The *concierge* had left a little board in the window of her *loge*, as she sometimes did. Noor had not seen anything suspect about it. But when she opened the door to her room, Peter grabbed her by the wrists.

'You bastard!' she started to scream.

She tried kicking him but he dodged. She leant over and bit his hand deeply. The pain grew, he could not pull away. He let go of her other wrist and with his left hand he got hold of his pistol from his belt. He thrust it into Noor's mouth. 'I'll shoot!'

She held firm so he aimed the pistol lower down. 'I'll start with your knee.'

Noor could tell that he was about to pull the trigger. She let go of him and he threw her down onto the sofa next to the bed. 'Help, help!' she screamed. 'The Gestapo!'

He realised that she wanted to alert the whole neighbourhood and he stormed over to her. She tried to trip him by grabbing hold of his clothes but he tore himself free. She cried out again. He backed over to the door and pointed his gun at her. She looked at him with a wild glint in her eye, crouching on the sofa, gripping the fabric in her hands, ready to leap at him. He would not kill her. He would not overpower her. And he certainly would not take her with him. They stayed staring at each other for two whole minutes.

'Bastard,' she said, 'you got me when I was just about to leave.' Her natural candour was back.

'You shouldn't have gone to the Gentilhommière! We knew you'd try to kill Blainville. Once you left room 27, all he had to do was follow you.'

He suddenly saw the black Bakelite telephone next to the bed. He stepped slowly towards it, still watching Noor. He picked up the handset and, with the same hand, dialled a number. 'It's Peter, let me speak to Goetz.' He waited with a mocking smile on his face. 'Yes. I've got her.' Then he paused to listen. 'Yes, and the notebooks . . . No. I'm on my own. Send two men. She's dangerous.'

Noor threw herself back on the sofa, bit her lip and burst into tears.

CHAPTER THIRTY-FOUR

The car stopped under the porch of number 84. It was a six-storey building which dominated the avenue Foch and the Porte Dauphine. Noor was on the rear seat squeezed between two military policemen in grey suits; she had seen the trees of the Bois de Boulogne skimming past through the window. Beyond them lay Suresnes and Fazal Manzil. As they came out in front of the Porte Dauphine she had caught sight of the Arc de Triomphe at the top of the avenue. She knew that on the other side of the hill at the Étoile, down at the bottom of the Champs-Élysées, I was waiting for her happily in that big bedroom gilded by the sinking sun. She bit her lip again.

'The end of the line,' said Peter. 'No more fun now.'

Noor walked into the Gestapo headquarters like a film star. The guards on duty stared at her, the officers looked up, the secretaries came out to the doorways of their offices. Still led by Peter, she climbed up the stone staircase. Goetz had come out of his office. He raised his arms and smiled. 'Mademoiselle Aurora! At last! We haven't stopped thinking about you for weeks. I'm so glad you're here.'

He was like an old uncle happy to see his niece. Noor eyed him coldly. 'I'm so sorry,' he went on, 'but that's how the game goes. You can't always win. Your network had had it, anyway. Informers, all of them.'

'I know, there's a traitor,' said Noor between her teeth, 'a little goes a long way.'

'A traitor? No, *several* traitors, all sorts of traitors! They're almost all traitors.'

He's still trying to protect Blainville, thought Noor. Suddenly, at the end of the corridor, she could see a pair of gleaming black boots coming down the stairs. Kieffer appeared, squeezed into his tight uniform. He too smiled in that amicable way as he came over towards her. 'She's quite charming!' he said greedily. 'My dear Aurora, you've given us a lot of trouble. Congratulations! But now it's over. They've dropped you. Your superiors sent you straight into a trap, I think you see that now. You're going to have to help us . . . Would you like a sweet?'

Kieffer liked to visit his prisoners with a little bag of sweets which he had brought in for him from the officers' mess set up in one of the buildings near the Porte Dauphine.

'Help you? I imagine you're joking, corporal!' His brow creased when he heard the incorrect rank. 'You're a bastard, and everyone else here is. You've already lost the war, and you know it. Help

455

you? You're already condemned, my poor friend.'

Noor flung the bag aside with the back of her hand, and the sweets scattered across the floor. Kieffer blenched.

'You're the one who's condemned! Go on! Take her away!'

The two policemen picked her up under the arms and dragged her over to the stairs. They passed a soldier who had come out into the corridor to have a look at the prisoner. Behind him there was a long room with walls covered in shelving. Noor could see that it was a library. Glancing over the shoulder of the *Feldwebel*, she suddenly saw a tall man with a protruding chin; he was holding a book in his hand and watching her with undisguised curiosity. It was John Starr. She then remembered Arisaig and Beaulieu and the sarcastic painter who used to make the whole intake laugh. She smiled. Starr winked at her and, as the soldier looked back at him, he opened the book and buried himself in it.

When she had disappeared and while two soldiers picked up the sweets, Kieffer turned to Goetz. 'What a temper!'

'She called you "corporal",' said Goetz with a smile. 'Don't take it too badly. That was the Führer's rank during the last war.'

'Very funny, Goetz!'

'She won't have so much fun tomorrow, *Sturmbannführer*,' said Goetz, correcting the error.

★　★　★

Up under the roof on the sixth floor, Noor walked past a bathroom with a half-open door, then a small room where a *Feldwebel* was sitting, busy reading a colour review called Signal with a picture on the front cover of a soldier in the Waffen SS gazing towards the horizon. The two policemen made her turn right down a corridor with a sloping ceiling. On either side there were doors in unfinished wood, locked with large padlocks. The *Feldwebel* had followed them with a bunch of keys in his hand. He passed them and opened the middle door on the left. Noor was pushed into a windowless room. The door closed behind her with a clanking of metal.

It was a former maid's room which had been made smaller with an extra partition wall. In the right-hand corner of the cell there was an iron bed with an old mattress covered in brown ticking. Apart from a chair in the other corner, there was no other furniture. When she looked up Noor saw a skylight at the far end of a sort of chimney, the bottom end of which had been blocked off by horizontal bars, despite the height of the ceiling. The light of the setting sun slanted through the window, throwing the shadow of the bars across the floorboards. Noor sat down on the bed, devastated.

She lay there prostrate for a quarter of an hour with her hands flat on the mattress. Then she got up, went over to the door and drummed on the wooden boards. A minute later she heard the soldier's heavy footsteps.

'*Was ist das?* What is it? Calm down! They'll come and get you.'

'I need to use the bathroom.'

'You can go later. There's a timetable for that.'

'No! I want to go right away. I can't wait. You couldn't stop me doing that.'

There was a pause, then the soldier made up his mind. He went back to the guardroom and came back with the keys. 'All right, then, go on. But I'll follow you.'

She walked ahead of him, turned left and went into the bathroom that she had seen when she arrived. She was about to shut the door behind her when the soldier held it back with his hand.

'You mustn't shut the door.'

'What?'

'The door has to stay open. Those are my instructions.'

'Open? But that's indecent. I'm not having you watching me. I'm not an animal.'

'I won't watch, but the door stays open. Those are my orders.'

'You really are barbaric!' she started screaming. 'Either that or you're all depraved!'

The soldier stared at her wearily although he did not fully understand. 'Come on, *Fräulein*, don't make any trouble.'

'I'm not getting undressed in front of you, you pig!'

'It's all right, soldier! Let her shut the door. It doesn't matter.'

Goetz had come up, drawn by the noise. He watched the scene indulgently. The soldier looked disillusioned and stepped back, and Noor turned the lock.

She glanced round the bathroom: a shower to one side, a stoneware basin in the middle with a cast-iron waste pipe underneath it which disappeared through a grating, and on the other side the lavatory pan with a wooden seat. The room was lit by a frosted-glass window above the basin. She went over to it, turned the handle and opened it. There was a deep, dark internal courtyard, its walls darkened by smoke and interrupted at intervals by rectangular windows. Noor leant forward and saw that on each floor there was a little ledge of grey cement. Opposite her, on the far side of the courtyard, there was an open window. She made up her mind straight away. She closed her eyes, concentrated for a moment and then climbed onto the wooden lavatory seat, caught hold of the window frame with both her hands and pointed one leg through the open window. She turned back towards the room and put the other leg outside. Then she slid down the wall and the tips of her toes came to rest on the cement ledge. With one hand on the wooden window sill, she gripped hold of the next window with the other. She slid her right foot along, then her left, and she started to work her way round the courtyard from one window to the next, clinging to the brick walls, six floors up.

Five minutes later she reached the open window on the far side of the courtyard. She was about to balance herself before climbing inside, when someone grabbed her by the arm. She heard Goetz's mocking voice: 'Be careful, Aurora, you could fall. I knew you would try. Come in slowly, I'll help you.'

An hour, Noor had said. Why did I let her go on her own? She seemed so sure of herself, so calm. At half past seven I asked the hotel switchboard to dial her number. A man's voice answered. 'Aurora? No, she isn't here.'

'When's she coming? It's Jules.'

'Jules? Yes, she'll be back in an hour.'

'Okay. I'll call back.'

Obviously, Noor did not know anyone called Jules. The man had replied without knowing the facts. I hung up slowly and dropped down onto the bed. It was a military policeman who had answered. Noor had been arrested. A whole world was falling apart. I sat motionless, gazing at the window. Two hours earlier I had seen her silhouetted against that sky. Now, she was in hell. But how could I have let her go? She had disappeared when I had only just found her again. And it was my fault! My fault! I felt tears rising in my eyes.

I went back to see Vienet. He was waiting for me in the foyer, deep in a club chair.

'Noor's been taken,' I said.

'No. Where?'

'She went back to her room to pick up her note-books and things. She hasn't come back. I rang and a man answered. She and Violette are the only people who knew about that apartment. He must have been a policeman.'

'God, that's terrible!' said Vienet. He looked as if he were grief-stricken but after a moment he collected himself. 'We must leave the hotel immediately,' he said. 'Hand in your key. I'm taking you with me.'

'Noor won't talk.'

'You can't know that.'

'She won't talk.'

'Don't let's argue. This is the procedure. When an agent's arrested, the others have to change address.'

In the car he thought out loud: 'The first thing we must do is let Derek and Violette know. We'll go there straight away. Then we'll try to find out where they've taken her. We'll see what we can do.'

I sat mutely beside him, staring ahead but hardly even seeing the road as I went over and over my catastrophic mistake.

'What about you?' I asked ten minutes later.

'I'm going to lie low. I've got a bolt-hole in Pigalle and I'll tell the people I work with that I'm taking a few days off. If the Gestapo don't come, then Noor hasn't spoken, and I'll be able to start my professional activities again. We have to apply the rules. We take enough risks as it is.'

On the rue Joseph-de-Maistre news of the disaster

461

drained the colour from Darbois's and Violette's faces. They packed their bags in silence. They had a back-up apartment that Darbois had rented in La Chapelle when he very first arrived.

'We've got to get her out of there,' said Violette. 'We have to find a way.'

'Of course,' said Vienet, 'it's so simple. Right in the middle of Paris, at the police headquarters, in amongst the German army. No problem.'

'René, you know the Germans,' said Violette, grabbing his arm, 'you've got men. We could try to do something.'

'We don't even know where she is. Hurry up, for God's sake, the Gestapo could get here any minute. Take the Métro. John and I are going to try and find out where they've taken her.'

Vienet drove round the outer ring road until the Porte de Clignancourt and then went back out onto it at the Porte Maillot. He went through the Bois de Boulogne and turned down the boulevard Richard-Wallace. There was no one outside Noor's front door, but Vienet pointed out a man to me on the corner of the next street; he was wearing a raincoat and leaning up against a garden fence, reading a newspaper. 'They're here.'

We went back to the Porte Maillot. Vienet stopped outside a café. 'Ring and say you'll be over in ten minutes to deliver a letter.'

The voice on the other end told me that Aurora was running late. I suggested coming over anyway. 'I'll be here,' he said.

462

I came out of the café and got back into the car, and Vienet headed back down the boulevard Richard-Wallace. The man in the raincoat had disappeared.

'He's gone up. They're going to wait for you inside, one in the apartment, the other one hiding somewhere on the stairs or on another landing.' Vienet parked his car a little further along. 'We can hide here. They'll hang about waiting for you and when you don't come they'll realise that we've sniffed out their trap. They'll give up and go back to base.'

I admired Vienet's shrewdness and his cool head. An hour later the two policeman did, indeed, come out of the building, turn left past us and get into a green Renault. Vienet started his car as they walked past, as if he had just got into the car. He set off after them, following from a safe distance.

'It's a bit risky,' he said, 'but they won't think we're mad enough to follow them. Anyway, I shouldn't think they're going far. The avenue Foch or the rue Lauriston. It's in the sixteenth arrondissement, not far from here.'

At the Porte Dauphine the Renault turned down the service road on the avenue Foch and stopped outside number 84.

'There!' said Vienet, who had stopped on the square. 'Now we know. The Gestapo controls the whole of the bottom end of the avenue. Boemelburg's there, and Kieffer and Schmidt, all the big names! They take care of Resistance

463

workers, Communists, Jews, radio operators . . . Kieffer lives here and Boemelburg lives in Neuilly. They must have shut her up in there, up under the roof. I think I've already told you this is where they held Moulin before they transferred him to Boemelburg's villa. We set up an escape plan, but they moved him too soon. They used to take prisoners to Fresnes, but they could talk to other people they were holding and get messages out. So now they put them here, in the maids' rooms – well, the more important ones, anyway. They guard them themselves and it means they've got them close at hand for interrogations. My dear John, we do have one hope. One glimmer of hope.'

CHAPTER THIRTY-FIVE

Noor looked at them sullenly.

'You'll have to tell us everything,' Goetz said again. 'Your friends have already spoken. If you don't say anything, we'll just lose time and we'll be forced to use other methods.'

The tick-tock of the cuckoo clock was clearly audible. Peter was sitting on the desk, to the right of Goetz, who was facing Noor. She was sitting awkwardly on a wooden chair.

'I won't say anything.'

'I know, those are your instructions from your organisation. You have to remain silent for forty-eight hours. But it won't do any good. We know almost everything about Prosper. You know that. So you're going to tell us everything, and we can fill in our forms.'

'If you know everything, you don't need me. And if you're interrogating me, it must mean you don't know everything.'

'She's beginning to annoy me,' said Peter, adjusting his shirt collar. 'My dear Goetz, we're going to have to change tactics. We're not going to spend all day like this.'

'Wait, Peter. I'm sure she's going to be sensible about this.'

He opened the drawer in his desk and took out a file, which he put down in front of Noor, turning it round so that she could read it. Noor looked at the pages as Goetz turned them over like a sales rep going through a catalogue. On the first page there was a heading in heavy print: 'Special Operations Executive', with a sub-heading in German which Noor did not understand. Overleaf there were the addresses of the headquarters in London and the names of the training camps. The third page featured a flow-diagram of the organisation, with the names Dalton, Gubbins, Buckmaster, Bodington and a dozen or so others. Then there was a long block of text in German. On the tenth page Goetz stopped leafing through: it showed a map of France with the names of the SOE networks: 'Salesman, Tailor, Butcher . . .', most of them, like these, were the names of professions. Noor concentrated on it. The word 'Prosper' was written next to Paris, but to the left, over Normandy, the Cinema network did not feature. She thought to herself that this Cowburn I had told her so much about certainly was very good at what he did.

'Very impressive, Doctor Goetz. But you're missing some.'

Goetz scowled and Peter stiffened.

'Well, you're going to help us, Aurora.'

'Never. I'm not an informer. I won't say anything.

Nothing. All these networks you've got, they're just the beginning. When you capture an agent, we send another five. And that's excluding the French. The old Maréchal betrayed them. They know that now. They're not going to leave you in peace.'

Noor remembered Blainville's lessons on policies, and she went on: 'Have you worked out how many German soldiers we can kill with these networks? You should do the sums.'

Furious, Peter jumped to his feet. 'The stupid bitch is insulting us!'

'And you, you little good-for-nothing,' said Noor, 'you're French, aren't you? Do you know what'll happen to you when our armies come to France? You know, don't you, you'll be shot.'

'That's enough,' Peter bellowed, 'you will be quiet!'

'I thought you wanted me to talk.'

Peter went over to her and slapped her with all his might. She almost fell. He slapped her again with the back of his hand, and then again. 'You're going to find out exactly what the Gestapo is all about. You've had it! This little game won't last long. Now we're getting to the serious bit.'

He struck her again, so hard this time that she collapsed onto the floor. He kicked her repeatedly as she curled up on herself, putting her hands over her head for protection.

'That's enough, Peter,' said Goetz after a couple of minutes. 'She understands. We'll start again tomorrow when she's had time to think.'

He stood up and called the guard. 'Take her away!'

The soldier bent over and took Noor by the arm to pick her up. Her lips were bleeding and a red bruise was beginning to appear round her right eye. Peter slapped her again as the soldier dragged her into the corridor.

Noor woke with a start. A long wail had broken the silence of the night. The wail of a man pushed beyond his every limit, a man expressing his appalling suffering, in a hoarse but powerful voice wrenched from the depths of his chest. The cry subsided into sobs. It was followed by a moan, which was suddenly overlaid by other people shouting. Then the wail came again, louder than the first. Through the floorboards Noor could make out footsteps and questions she couldn't quite hear, as well as cries of pain and the bestial wails which recurred from time to time.

She could see the moonlight through the skylight. After her interrogation she had sat down on her bed, feeling the wounds on her face where Peter had slapped her, and the deep bruising along her ribs where he had kicked her. Her anger and her hatred had kept her going. When night fell, the fear had risen up in her stomach once more. She had cried, unable to stop herself. As she ate her supper – a mess tin with a sausage and some mashed potato in it – she had seen a hint of compassion on the face of the soldier who had handed her the meal. This little sign of humanity had frightened her all the more. She finally fell asleep, exhausted, long after the sun had set. Now, she stretched out her arm and her watch caught the beam of moonlight coming down from the window. Two o'clock in the morning. The wailing started again. A cold sweat broke out on her forehead. Tomorrow, she thought, it will be my turn.

At the same time, Goetz and Peter were leaning on the bar at One Two Two. Two or three times a week they would go together to 122, rue de Provence, the most famous brothel in Paris. In amongst the velvet and the gold of this establishment the prettiest prostitutes in the capital drank with Wehrmacht officers, the top brass of the collaboration and the bigwigs in the black market. By offering a tidy sum, they could go up to one of the special salons on the floor above with one of these beauties. There was something of the colonial exhibition about the One Two Two: after the Egyptian salon, with its statues in profile, its stuffed snakes and its views of the pyramids, there was the African salon with its Negro women in loincloths, and its leopardskins at the foot of the bed; after that there was the Louis XV salon, with its silk-curtained boudoir and its Watteau reproductions.

'Peter,' said Goetz, 'you're a good agent, but you don't use your head enough.'

'We can't let that girl insult us,' said Peter,

knocking back his third whisky and eyeing a sylph-like creature in a minimal dress. She smiled at him and he went on: 'We're the German army, after all!'

'You're right and you were right to react, but she needs handling differently. She's mad, she's an idealist. You saw that. She'd let herself be chopped up into little pieces.'

'I'd be happy to direct the interrogation.'

'I can assure you that it wouldn't be any use.'

'What do you mean it wouldn't be any use? She said herself that we're missing some networks. We've got to make her spit out what she knows.'

'She doesn't know much more than we do. What we're interested in is the radio.'

'But we've already got it . . . Not how to use it . . .'

'All dealt with, my dear,' said Goetz with a triumphant smile. 'After the interrogation I looked through the notebooks that you so cleverly took. It took me four hours. I've got everything. The code, the keys, and even the security checks. She's written it all down, it's incredible! All her messages are there, written out properly and in code! The first check is shown and as for the second, well, I've worked out how it's done. They make an obvious spelling mistake in the first word of the first message, in the second word in the second message, and so on, then they start again. If they send a message without spelling mistakes, it means they're under our control. It's so simple. This evening the Aurora set will be operational again. I think we're on the right tracks.'

'But the others will tell London that we've got her.'

'Not necessarily. They don't have a radio any more. She was the last one in the Paris area. They haven't got any means of communication.'

'They'll find a way.'

The sylph had come over and sat down on the stool next to them. Peter smiled at her as he listened to Goetz.

'I'm not sure,' Goetz said. 'Their instructions are to disappear into thin air when one of them's arrested. They'll go to ground. If they try to get in touch with London Blainville will know about it. He'll let us know.'

'And if they use another contact?'

'They usually escape through Spain, which takes time. We've probably got a few weeks to play with.'

'In that case why do we need to interrogate her?'

Peter had put his arm round the girl's waist and they both stood up.

'I'm very wary of the English. They're gradually getting used to our little games. If they're on their guard, they might ask for some personal detail. We've got to be able to reply as if we were Aurora herself.'

'If she refuses to speak, no softening . . .'

'No, no softening. We'll carry on tomorrow. But I'll work on her myself. If that doesn't work, you can take over.'

★ ★ ★

471

At ten past three Noor heard slow footsteps in the corridor and something being dragged along the floorboards.

'*Ach*, he's heavy!' said a voice.

'Let's chuck him on the bed and get to bed ourselves,' came the reply with a strong Midi accent.

The lock of the neighbouring cell clanged, the door creaked and Noor heard the thud of a body on the bedsprings, on the far side of the partition wall. The door was closed, the lock clanged again and the footsteps receded into the stairwell.

Everything was quiet for a quarter of an hour. Noor could not get back to sleep. She kept trying to imagine the state of the man lying just a couple of yards from her on an iron bed like her own. She trembled as she strained her ears. She thought she could hear a slight moaning. Then the bed springs creaked. The prisoner was moving. She sat up on her bed. Another moan. She got up and went and crouched down on the floor on the other side of her cell, with her ear up against the parti-tion. Now she could hear the springs being crushed and released as the man moved his body, and she could hear the regular whistle of his breathing. He must be only ten inches from her. She took off her watch and held the face between her thumb and forefinger. She tapped on the thin wood to spell out three characters in Morse code: 'OK?' Still nothing. She was about to repeat the message when the little thuds came back, even quieter than her own. He must have been knocking on the wall with his finger. She understood the reply and she felt a thrill of joy: 'OK'.

Now the conversation could start. Her neighbour tapped more slowly than her, but she listened to the halting little sounds as if they were words of hope.

'I am Aurora, hello.'

'Hello, Aurora.'

'How are you?'

'Not bad.'

'In pain?'

'Less now.'

'Injured?'

'They tore off four nails.'

Noor shuddered with horror. The prisoner went on: 'I said nothing.'

'I knew.'

'Have they beaten you?'

'Not yet.'

'Which network are you from?'

Noor wondered whether this was a set-up to get her to talk. But she had initiated it. She decided to be cautious.

'SOE,' she replied, feeling that this did not commit her to much.

'SOE?'

'An English network. And you?'

'ORA. Army Resistance Organisation.'

'Do you have a name?'

'Faye.'

'Are you tired?'

'I've had a long evening. Aurora?'

'Yes.'

'Are you pretty?'

She smiled to herself in the dark. 'Are you French?'

'You don't miss much. Goodnight.'

Culioli lived at the top of the rue Lepic, on the slopes leading up to Montmartre. When he was not shooting at Germans, he carried on with his rather special version of being a businessman. He got up late and went down onto the place Pigalle at about midday. He had lunch in the café owned by his friend Pierre Poggioli, just to the right of the statue, opposite the Moulin Rouge. In the afternoon he played cards in the rue de Châteaudun or the rue Richer. At about six o'clock he went back up the rue des Martyrs to check that the girls were all in position, leaning in doorways, showing lots of cleavage and with shiny little skirts tight over their buttocks. Then he did the rounds of the bars and of the little hotels where they took their customers, taking his percentage straight from the tills.

He had abandoned his business for the last two days. Vienet and a great beanpole of a friend of his – with whom he had put together the Foligny job – were living with him. That morning we were all having a council of war. We sat in deep armchairs and velvet-covered sofas while Suzy, Culioli's 'regular', moved between us in her silk negligee and her mules, pouring the coffee. Darbois and Violette had arrived together. They dunked their croissants in their cups of coffee while 'Paul' and 'Dominique', Culioli's two friends, poured themselves a glass of pastis each at the little mahogany bar.

'Violette,' said Vienet, 'you could come and live here. My friend Culioli suggested it. There are ten rooms at the back. You'd have the most lovely room looking out over Sacré-Coeur.'

'René,' said Violette, 'let's get back to business.'

'All right. I'll see this girl tomorrow,' he said, resuming the conversation. 'She works on the third floor on the avenue Foch. She mentioned an Englishman who's been a prisoner there for weeks. One John Starr. Does his name mean anything to you?'

'Starr? Yes!' I said. 'He's one of ours! I was even his instructor. He's very shrewd.'

'The problem is, I don't know whether we can trust him. From what she tells me he's very pally with the Germans and they've given him privileges. During the day he's in the library or one of the offices. Apparently he can draw.'

'He's a painter in civilian life,' Violette confirmed. 'He's good at it. He has exhibitions in England.'

'Well, now he's having exhibitions for the Gestapo,' said Vienet. 'He does their portraits and he makes maps and flow-diagrams for them. Kieffer likes him very much.'

'He must have gone to considerable lengths to be granted so much freedom,' I ventured.

'Perhaps,' said Vienet. 'In any event, we don't have any choice. Given the layout of the place, we cannot, under any circumstances, get into the building. There are soldiers everywhere. They'll have to escape on their own. Along the rooftops. From what I understand, it's not impossible. Their cells are under the eaves, and there are skylights. We could pick them up once they get down so long as they can get down to street level at the back. When we looked into the problem for Moulin that was the only solution. Obviously we'll need Starr's co-operation. If he's with the Germans there isn't a hope.'

'Let's try,' I said. 'What other solution is there?'

'There isn't. The girl can get a message to him tomorrow. We'll soon see . . .'

CHAPTER THIRTY-SIX

Noor had gone into Goetz's office looking pale and bedraggled. She had managed to get to sleep at about six o'clock. She had woken in a sweat at the point when, in her dream, they were about to rip her nipples off. The German looked at her. He could see that the session inflicted on Faye had not been lost on her. He admired her face and her figure as she sat down. 'Good morning, Nora Wilson!'

She looked up, surprised.

'Ah yes! I know your real name. You're in the RAF, you were a radio operator. You see, you can't hide anything from Uncle Goetz.'

She said nothing.

'Did you hear what happened in the night? That's what you'll get if we can't reach some understanding, you and I. I don't like those methods, but . . .'

'But you use them.'

'If I don't have any choice. We do have to protect our own soldiers. People like you are quite without pity. You operate without a uniform, and outside any system of law. You kill, you sabotage, you massacre. And then you're surprised when the SD reacts.'

He used the initial SD and not the name Gestapo, because this was the official name of the German police, *Sicherheitsdienst*, which meant security service.

'Are you saying you respect some sort of law?'

'When it's a proper war in uniform, yes. But with your dirty war, that's impossible. You use terrorism, which is exactly the opposite of the rules of war.'

Again, she gave no reply.

'I don't understand you, Nora. You're pretty, cultivated, idealistic. What are you doing with these low-lifes?'

'They're not low-lifes, they're fighters. And they will be victorious.'

'At the moment we're winning. I'm sitting at the desk and you're on the other side. When it's the other way round we'll see.'

'It won't be long.'

'Perhaps. But in the meantime the Reich has control of all of Europe. The Russians are in the Ukraine and the Americans are in North Africa. We've got quite a lot of leeway! You've allied your-selves with the Bolsheviks, who are complete savages. The Wehrmacht will win. We're defending Western civilisation. All of Europe is behind us. If the communists won, everything would be destroyed: culture, learning, art, religion. Do you believe in God, Nora?'

'Yes.'

Noor had given an answer. She bit her lip. She was gripped by her fear of torture. She told herself it was all right to answer harmless questions. The time for blows might be delayed a little longer. Her brain kept saying: 'Be careful!', but her tired body was frightened of the pain. Conversation gave her a feeling of respite, almost of safety.

'If you believe in God, you can't approve of the Bolsheviks. They don't have a God.'

'They have every right –'

'What do you mean, they have every right? There is no society without God. Without religion, society falls apart. Men without faith are just animals.'

Noor remembered her father's teachings. 'The Nazis are pagans. They love the gods of the forests and the mountains. They're right back there with the Vikings. They light fires in the fields, and stand round them in circles and they think that's a form of worship. Nazism worships power. Listen to Wagner. Siegfried is a barbaric idiot. He has a sword and plenty of power. That's not a religion!'

'You seem very interested in music, Nora. In that case, you must know that Wagner wrote Christian operas. And the Führer defends Roman Catholicism.'

'He sends priests to prison.'

'When they conspire against him.'

'But religion is tolerance.'

'Tolerance? That sort of idea belongs to the weak, and the democrats. It belongs to the Jews.'

Noor had forgotten about torture, and Goetz also seemed to be enjoying their discussion. He had taken out a notebook and was making notes of what Noor said.

'Doctor Goetz, you don't know anything about it. All religions are tolerant, if you go by the teachings of their prophets, in other words the teachings of God.'

'What is your religion, Nora? You seem very knowledgeable.'

'Every religion.'

'What do you mean?'

'I won't say more than that. But all the religions are alike if you look at them carefully. There is only one God. He spoke through several prophets – Jesus, Buddha, Mohammed. What matters is having access to direct knowledge of him!'

His wrist scurried across the page as he wrote while she was talking. He looked up. 'But you're a mystic, Nora. How interesting! I like those Eastern religions. You must be Indian or something like that. Do you know where the swastika comes from, Nora? From ancient Indian faiths. The Führer has the greatest respect for Aryan religions. What you haven't grasped is that the Third Reich is bringing in the dawn of a new era. A sort of Renaissance. We'll have got rid of the Jews, the Bolsheviks, the democrats and their materialistic world. You're a mystic, Nora, and yet you're defending these materialists. You're defending the Jews and money. How strange!'

'I'm defending freedom of choice. Each man has to find his path himself. You want to do all the thinking for them. You want to snuff out their own ability to think.'

'We want to found a new civilisation, Nora, and that's worth a few sacrifices, surely. Beware to anyone who stands in our way.'

'All you can think about is killing!'

'That's enough, now!' he barked.

Noor felt the fear lurking again. She started to tremble. Goetz realised this and softened again.

'Look, I'm going to prove to you that we're not what you say we are. You can go back to your cell. The interrogation is over for today.'

She looked at him in astonishment.

'It's over. You see, I didn't lay a finger on you. You can ask for some paper for writing, if you like. The intellectuals always do. You can also go to the library on the third floor. There are books by Hugo and Dumas. They'll keep you occupied. Guard!'

Noor left and Peter came into the office. 'Did she talk?'

'She started to. I'm getting there . . . I'm getting there . . .'

When the young woman put the little piece of paper on his desk, Starr looked up. She stared at him intently and breathed the word 'Byron!' to him. He took the piece of paper and instinctively put it straight into his pocket. She turned away and carried on running the carpet-sweeper over the guardroom. The soldier, who was lying back in his chair with his feet up on his desk, had not seen a thing. Starr dipped his paintbrush into the glass of coloured water. When the girl left the room with her carpet-sweeper in one hand and her pail of water in the other, and with her little blue apron tied round her waist with string, she did not so much as glance at him. He carried on concentrating on the pastoral scene that he had started for Kieffer, who wanted to give his wife an original painting when he was next on leave.

While the soldier avidly read his review, Starr took out the piece of paper and unfolded it. A sequence of unconnected letters had been written in a series of lines in columns, forming incomprehensible squares. Starr recognised the double transposition system he had been taught at Beaulieu, and he realised that the word 'Byron' was the key word, with which he would be able to decipher the message. He asked to go back to his cell.

That afternoon Starr went back to the library to finish his landscape. He stayed there for two hours. As the sun began to set he closed his box of watercolours and picked it up with the three paintbrushes clasped between his hand and the box. He got up, but before leaving the room he went over to the shelves, looking for a book. He took Émile Zola's *Le Rêve*, the only novel by that author that had not been blacklisted by the Vichy government. Then he followed the soldier who was taking him back to his cell. In order to close the library door behind him he had to clamp the box of paints and the brushes under his arm.

Up on the sixth floor he had the end cell, slightly apart from the other prisoners. To get to it, you had to carry straight on past the guard's room instead of turning right. As he reached the end of the corridor in which Noor and Faye had their cells, he dropped the little box and the paintbrushes. He swore. And before the guard had time to turn round, he gave one of the paintbrushes a little kick over towards Noor's door.

'Shit,' he said, 'I'm so sorry.'

He walked down the corridor to get it while the soldier obligingly bent to pick up the box, which had scattered several of its little blocks of colour. Starr knelt down on the ground to pick up the paintbrush and quickly took a piece of paper from his pocket and slipped it under the door. The soldier did not notice. Starr came back over to him, took the box he handed to him and headed towards his cell.

'Thank you, that's very kind. I'm sorry . . .'

Noor had heard the box of paints falling to the ground. When she saw the piece of paper she understood straight away. She picked it up, unfolded it and read these simple words: 'You are not alone. I'm watching out for you. So are your friends. Go to the bathroom, under the grating by the basin. Starr.' She put the paper in her mouth and swallowed it.

At seven o'clock she knocked on her door and the guard accompanied her to the bathroom. He let her shut the door but not lock it. She turned on the tap and then knelt in front of the metal grating, lifted it off and put her hand inside. There was a damp little cavity which widened out. By feeling around inside she found a piece of rolled-up paper which had been tucked out of sight in the bend. A few minutes later she was back in her cell reading Starr's message with a thumping heart: 'My dear Nora, I was so happy to see you again. Don't feel too alone. I've been contacted by your friends and they're going to help you. I've had two months to think about this. If we can pull the bars loose we can get out onto the roof. They'll be waiting for us below, in the blind alley at the back. I'll give you more details in another message in the same place. Give me a reply using the same method. Have strength and hope.'

That night Faye was tortured again. Noor waited until he came back, and at two o'clock she heard his news. This time they had driven pins into his chest, and they had broken two of his fingers by bending them back slowly. He had resisted again. He lay groaning on his iron bed. At half past two their conversation was interrupted by an air raid. They could hear aeroplanes away in the west, and the intermittent anti-aircraft fire. Searchlights swept across the sky, and their harsh light reflected through the skylights. Acting on orders, the guard got up and, in his pyjamas, did the rounds of the cells, opening them one at a time. As he was not allowed to switch the lights on, he inspected the cells by torch light. Noor got back into bed and waited for the end of the air raid. When everything was quiet again she told Faye about Starr's message.

'It's going well, Peter. She's beginning to trust me.'

'But she hasn't said anything about her operations, or the network.'

'Couldn't matter less. We knew everything already. She's telling me the bits I didn't know: her background, her culture. I'm getting to know her. If the English try to trap me, I'll be able to answer.'

'Have they tried?'

'No. For now they're swallowing every message, hook, line and sinker. They think the Prosper network is being put together again. Next week I'll arrange my first parachute drop. I was even congratulated by Buckmaster, and he's told me to be careful. He said: "Be cautious, Aurora. Keep a gun with you when making transmissions." You see, Peter, I know why he's saying that: the girl's a mystic, she must be a Hindu or something like that. And those people can't bear violence. That's why Buckmaster keeps giving that sort of advice. And I replied: "You know my convictions. God is with me."'

Goetz laughed out loud and Peter watched him open-mouthed, not fully understanding him.

Noor had long conversations with Goetz, who became a little more familiar and personal every day. Noor saw something close to admiration or even tenderness in the way he looked at her. Without ever talking about her family, she ended up confiding in him, although she did change the places and some of the circumstances of her childhood. He discovered that she played the piano and the harp, that she wrote children's stories and that she far surpassed him in theology. Oddly, he continued to make notes of everything she told him.

After two days Faye started to talk. He had respected the required delay. He told Noor that he was giving them information they already had or which was not really important. So that he could sleep in peace, Kieffer had satisfied himself with these results and had asked for the torture sessions to be stopped. Starr painted all the more enthusiastically. As well as his landscapes, he had been drawing caricatures of the key officers at number 84. He showed them to the soldiers and the secretaries, who choked with laughter. He had proved to be a jack of all trades and he repaired machines that employees brought him from all over the building: lamps, staplers, typewriters. They would lend him a tool kit, which he gave back as soon as he had finished each job.

One day when he had repaired a large alarm clock, he closed up the back of the clock, screwed it into place and, instead of putting the screwdriver back into its compartment, checked whether the guard was watching and hid it by the fireplace, behind the sheet of steel that hung down between the hearth and the rest of the room. If anyone noticed that it was missing, he would not have it on him. He gave the tool kit back and went back there that afternoon to paint.

That evening Noor found the tool under the basin with the message: 'Use this to remove the bars. Just dig straight into the cement that holds them in place. It's a question of time. When you've finished I'll get the screwdriver to Faye. Explain to him. My bars are built into a wooden frame. I can undo them in an hour the day we leave. Keep the screwdriver well hidden. Strength and hope!'

Noor looked at the screwdriver, and then up at the bars. They were too high off the ground. She climbed up on her chair but she still could not touch them, even on tip-toe. She thought. There was only one solution. She took the mattress and the blankets off the bed, moved the bed infinitely carefully and managed to tip it up silently so that it was leaning vertically against the wall. She put the chair next to it, climbed onto it and put one foot up on the head of the bed. She ended up teetering on the top of the iron frame. She grabbed hold of the bars with one hand, and knew that she would be able to dig round the ends of the bars with her free hand. She climbed back down to get the screwdriver. Just as she was scraping at the cement round the first bar, the bed started to slip down the wall and crashed to the floor with a hellish noise. Noor was left hanging by one hand from the bar, three feet above the bed. Terrified, she hung there paralysed, waiting for the door to open, not knowing how she would explain her peculiar situation.

The key turned in the lock and the door opened. The guard stared at her in astonishment. Noor looked miserable. She had taken her belt out of her dress and was holding it in one hand. The guard interpreted what he saw.

'*Fräulein*, what are you doing? You mustn't. If you help them, they won't hurt you. You mustn't kill yourself! If you speak, you'll live.'

He tore her belt from her hand as she burst into tears.

'Anyway,' he added, 'it's too high up. Come on, calm down! I'll talk to Doctor Goetz about this tomorrow morning. You go to bed and get some sleep.'

Vienet had spread the plan out in front of him. Suzy was wearing a bright pink clingy skirt and coming round to serve gin and tonic, and whisky. She kept flashing smiles at me, under the darkly watchful eye of Culioli, who was beginning to find that the head of his network was outstaying his welcome in his house.

'Here's the avenue Foch, and this is the building where they're being held. They've started to loosen the bars. They'll get out onto the roof here, and they'll walk parallel to the avenue towards the buildings round the blind alley. Here there's a rather tricky bit, but if they jump they can get onto this building here and climb down the staircase inside. Then they'll come out in the alley here.'

'Where are the guards?' said Violette.

'Here, here and here. There are two at the entrance to the blind alley and there's a sentry post at the corner of the Porte Dauphine. As soon as we see them coming out of the building at the end of the alley, we have to neutralise the guards. They run over to us and we decamp. There are three of them. We'll need two cars to get them away, and two cars to cover.'

'We hid there all of yesterday evening and all day today. The place is crawling with guards and policemen. But there are only two guards at the entrance of the alley. The others are on the corner of the avenue. They chat to each other and they don't always watch what's going on behind them. If we're quick and quiet, we've got a chance . . .'

CHAPTER THIRTY-SEVEN

'I don't understand why they're not torturing me.'

'They don't torture everyone.'

'But they want things from me. I'm a radio operator.'

'They know enough already.'

'Maybe. But why are they keeping me here?'

In the quiet of the night, Noor was sitting on the floorboards of her cell with her ear up against the wall, conversing with Faye in Morse code. Their conversations had taken an amicable, amusing and personal turn. In the daytime they were more abrupt and objective. In the dark Noor was reminded of her childhood, when she and her brother had chatted into the night in the big bedroom at Fazal Manzil. Despite their slow means of communication, Noor enjoyed Faye's company, even though she had never seen him. He was sharp, very clever and rather paternal. Suddenly the air-raid sirens wailed. She had to go back to bed, wait for the soldier to come by with his torch, and then wait for the end of the air raid. She went back over to the partition.

'Have you moved the bed?' asked Faye.

'Yes. It's at the end opposite the door.'

'Did they complain?'

'No. They thought it odd, but I am odd anyway.'

'Yes, I thought so too.'

She had moved her bed the day before. The soldier had asked her why and she had explained that her life was so monotonous that she felt like moving the furniture. When Goetz was called up to help, he had smiled indulgently at Noor and shrugged his shoulders. The bed stayed in its new position.

'We'll be ready in a week at the most. The bars aren't well set.'

'I'll meet you on the roof.'

'And I'll be able to check whether you're pretty.'

'What about you? Are you good-looking?'

'Very.'

'We'll see.'

Two days later Noor moved her bed so that it was up against the partition between her cell and Faye's. The soldier said nothing. Two days later she put the bed in the middle of the room with the chair next to it. She waited until the evening. The soldier who handed her her mess tin did not even notice the new arrangement. She waited for an hour, then she picked up the chair and put it on the bed. She climbed up onto the bed and onto the chair which tipped slightly on the springs. She raised her arm and gripped hold of one of the bars to balance herself. Then she took the screwdriver out of her belt and started digging round the first bar. If she heard the soldier walking along the corridor for a surprise inspection she would just have time to get down, put the chair back in its place and lie down. She had done it three times already, digging away and listening out intently.

'You can't found a whole civilisation on its individuals,' said Goetz. 'They're all so different. Too many of them are mediocre. Great things are done by great men. And a race that produces great men is a superior race.'

'To God a man is a man,' Noor replied. 'God made man in his image.'

'Well, when he looks at a Jew he must have trouble recognising himself!' Goetz said, laughing.

'The Jews again! You're obsessed with them.'

Goetz spoke to Noor every day, often about religion and politics. Each time he steered the conversation towards the prisoner's private life, her feelings, family and childhood. Noor resisted. But she eventually took some pleasure in this exchange of ideas with the former professor. She was always incisive and focused, never giving way to him in their intellectual jousting. She remembered her philosophy lessons and her debates with her brother. Goetz inspired a fundamental disgust in her but it was mingled with an involuntary gratitude for sparing her from torture. A complicity developed between the captor and his victim, and

Noor felt ashamed of it. At heart, she sometimes admitted to herself, she just wanted to avoid insults and pain.

'No, no!' he went on. 'The Jews have a weak religion and because of that they corrupt everything. Anti-Semites think the Jews are evil, grasping and cunning. They hate them for these faults, but that's not the question. The Jews are dangerous because their religion favours the weak. What any group needs, what our race needs, is a strong religion, one which can do great things. The works of the group as a whole are all that count. The individual shouldn't matter. We are nothing. The group is everything!'

'But democracies have achieved great things: industry, schooling for every child, modern art, America – they're all inventions of democratic civilisations.'

'No, they're not! They were achieved by great men! You make me laugh with your democracy. One man, one vote. As if one man was worth the same as another. It's laughable. If the majority agree on a lie, does it become the truth? Is that what your father taught you?'

'I won't tell you anything about him.'

'You had a very good education, Nora. I would like to have met your family.'

'They wouldn't want to know you, Doctor Goetz.'

'And your mother,' he said, not picking up on the insult, 'where is she?'

'She's in England. If you want to see her you'll

have to get there with the Wehrmacht. I'm afraid you'll have to remain strangers.'

Goetz listened attentively, and Noor realised that he had managed to take her somewhere she did not want to go. She closed up like a book.

'What a shame,' he said. 'Perhaps after the war . . . In any event, your theories about democracy don't hold any water. You believe in God. Democracy believes in nothing. It has no truth, no ideals, no passion. It puts the true and the false on the same plane.'

'The truth always works its way out. All you have to do is turn to God.'

'And what if there is no God?'

'God isn't only in religion. He's in life, and nature, in the love people feel for each other. Once you've acknowledged that, God's presence is self-evident. You can come to know him. You just have to open your heart.'

'But most people only think about themselves, not about God. They need a leader. Religion's there to help the leader. It's the leader who shows the people their own greatness. Freedom is decadence.'

'Men are weak,' replied Noor, 'they committed the original sin. But they can atone for that, that's the whole meaning of religion. Everyone has a chance. It's just arithmetic, Doctor Goetz. God also talks through mathematics. Haven't you ever wondered why nature can be explained by equations and calculations? You see, there's a connection between the laws that govern our minds and the laws of the physical world. God created them both. They're the same laws. The greater advances we make in science, the closer we come to understanding God's intentions. In mathematics there are some operations that are reversible and others that aren't. You can do an addition or a multiplication either way round. Two plus three or three plus two is the same thing. But two minus three or three minus two is not the same. A good civilisation is one where the operations are reversible. I help my neighbour, he helps me. He is free and so am I. Everything is reversible and reciprocal like additions and multiplications. That way everyone wins. In your arithmetic there are only subtractions and divisions. All you can think about is overcoming, mastering. When it comes down to it, all you can think about is killing.'

'Don't start that, Noor. You don't appreciate your privileges. In this place, I'm the one defending you.'

'But why are you, Doctor Goetz? Why do we have these discussions?'

He looked slightly embarrassed. 'Umm . . . I have to write a report. About the enemy. I work for the police. They want to understand the enemy. So, I study them.'

Noor did not believe a single word Goetz had just said.

They had to solve the problem of the bread dough. The holes that Noor was making in the cement could be seen from below. If the guard looked up he would realise they were making a bid to escape. Noor questioned her two accomplices. Faye suggested filling the gaps with bread. Noor ate only the crusts, and kneaded up the white dough but it was a lighter colour than the cement. Starr found the solution. He tinted balls of dough with his watercolours and left them under the basin for her. Noor tamped them into the holes and her excavations became less obvious.

A long discussion about covers went on for three days. They needed ropes in case they had to climb down the face of the building. They could not picture the journey from their cells to the building which went down to the back alley. The Germans had not given them sheets, just blankets, which, once folded, would be too thick to knot together. They would have to be torn up, but that would be a long and difficult job, and if it were done in advance it would give away the whole project. Starr eventually overcame the problem. He got hold of a knife and decided the blankets could be cut up once they were on the roof.

The following morning Starr came across the girl doing the cleaning on the stairs. Without even looking at her he handed her a screwed-up ball of paper, which she took from him without slowing in her work. When Vienet opened it out it read: 'Are ready for tomorrow evening.'

That same evening at the One Two Two Goetz was exultant.

'I'm finding out more and more about her! A lot of my attempts fail, but I've got a lot of information. I know about her family, her father's dead or has gone away, either way she hasn't seen him for a long time. I know how she was brought up, that she plays the piano and the harp.'

'What use is that?' asked Peter, who was onto his fourth glass of cognac and was eyeing a green-eyed brunette with a sharp fringe and a long cigarette-holder. 'All that's happened is you've taken a fancy to her, and she's twisting you round her little finger.'

'Not at all! She's fascinating but I'm too old for all that.'

'What do you mean too old? Are you acting like a father to her, then? I can see you're protecting her.'

'You've had too much cognac, Peter. You're not using your head properly again. We're making better progress than we have for a long time. I'll give you an example. Yesterday, the English sent news of her mother. They said: "Your mother's well; her health is improving." That was a trap.'

'In what way?'

'Well, not a trap, but a difficulty. I don't think the English intended it as a trap. They're confident, they think Aurora is still active. If I hadn't known that with the SOE family information only ever goes one way – from the parent to the agent and never the other (Norman, Prosper's radio operator, told me that) – I might have said something like: 'Give her my love.' And we would have had it. They would have known straight away that it wasn't Aurora transmitting, that we had control of the radio. Aurora would never have replied like that. She knows perfectly well that her mother doesn't know anything about her SOE activities and that the SOE doesn't tell her anything. Buckmaster finds out about agents' families and gives the agents news himself to keep up their morale. But nothing goes back. With the simple words 'Give her my love' the Aurora set would have been out in the open. You have to know everything, Peter, everything. If they ever say: "Your father's well," then I'll know it's a trap, because the father's disappeared. From time to time they make personal references; it's like a third security check.'

'I don't know the half of it . . .'

'Don't worry about it. We're winning this one. This girl is like gold dust, Peter. We're onto something really good. You'll see, in a few more weeks the Aurora set will be our greatest success story.'

The following afternoon Culioli parked a beige Citroën to the south of the Porte Dauphine, opposite the Villa Fouché. He got out of the car, pretended to lock the door and walked away. We had done it twice already. The two soldiers on duty at the entrance to the blind alley watched him without showing any interest. Culioli had a doctor's *Ausweis* in case the soldiers came over to check, but we had made an important discovery: the cars parked near the Gestapo headquarters were neither checked nor searched. The Germans were very sure of themselves here in the heart of Paris.

An hour later I came out of the Porte Dauphine Métro station with my arm round Violette's shoulder. There was a small park near the blind alley, to the right at the end of the avenue. We went and sat down on a bench, kissing, and then we started to chat with her head resting on my shoulder. A little lorry with a tarpaulin over the back came and parked some fifteen yards behind the Citroën. Vienet appeared, dressed as a chauffeur, and walked off. We watched the comings and goings round the Gestapo building. A few cars came and went. At seven o'clock various employees and secretaries left the office. Only the duty soldiers were left outside, two on each door. On the other side of the square there was a large guardroom, and through its windows we saw silhouettes in uniform hats picked out by the electric light.

At five past eight, when it was dark, we went over to the two vehicles. Two minutes later a motorbike with a side-car swept onto the square and knocked into a lorry. As one, the soldiers turned to look over to the accident. At that exact moment I hopped into the driver's side of the Citroën and Darbois, who had slowly made his way over from tree to tree, slipped into the back, while Violette and Culioli climbed into the little lorry. The three accomplices on the square exchanged copious insults, keeping the soldiers' attention. Eventually, an officer came out of number 86 and told them to move on. The soldiers pushed the damaged side-car onto the pavement and the lorry set off once the two men in it had given their address to the furious motorcyclist.

I lay on the floor of the Citroën with my head under the steering wheel. I found the gun and silencer that Vienet had hidden in the glove compartment. Darbois was lying in the back of the car and had taken his gun from a pocket of fabric stitched to the back of the passenger seat. I knew that inside the lorry Violette would have unscrewed a metal panel from the floor and taken out a rifle with telescopic sights and a machine gun. The soldiers guarding the alley were ten yards from us. The others, on the corner of the avenue Foch, were looking over towards the Porte Dauphine. The waiting began.

CHAPTER THIRTY-EIGHT

When Starr opened the skylight and stepped out onto the roof a light wind stroked his face. It was a mild October night. To the right he could see the trees of the Bois de Boulogne. The smell of yellowing autumn leaves swept over him. To the left the imposing bulk of the Arc de Triomphe glowed white in the moonlight at the top of the avenue. He took off his shoes, tied the laces together and slung his shoes round his neck. In his stockinged feet he slunk over the zinc rooftop towards the other skylights.

It had taken him only ten minutes to loosen the wooden frame holding the bars in his cell. The Germans did not believe that escape was possible in this part of Paris, where they owned so many of the buildings. Starr was a tall man. When he had put his bed vertically against the wall he could then pull himself inside the shaft. He just had to stretch out his arm to open the skylight, catch hold of the edge and heave himself along the shaft. He had put his elbows down onto the zinc and swung himself quietly out onto the roof.

He listened out, but all he could hear was the rustling of the leaves. He reached the first skylight and opened it. Below him he could see Faye's upturned face. He signalled to him to climb up. As planned, Faye had loosened two bars and left the third one in position as a rung. Starr saw his fists closing round the steel bar and Faye's head coming up towards him. There was a scraping sound and a muffled curse, and Faye's head went back down again.

'Shit,' he said, looking up at Starr. 'They've broken two of my fingers on my right hand.'

The shaft was longer than the one in Starr's cell. Faye could not catch hold of the edge of the roof. He had to gather himself on the bar, as if he were on a trapeze, and then thrust forwards with his legs to help heave himself up. He was handicapped by his injury. Starr leant down and held out his arm to him.

'Try again!' he said, 'and take my hand.'

Faye bunched himself down again. Starr saw his head appearing rapidly as he launched himself forwards, and he felt a hand gripping onto his. Faye's fifteen stone weighed down on his arm. He held himself on his elbow, took a deep breath and managed to lift the prisoner up gradually. Faye was able to grip hold of the edge and Starr then pulled him out by holding him under the armpits.

'I'm so sorry,' whispered Faye. 'They've ruined my hand. Thanks!'

'Let's go and get the girl.'

Noor could hear furtive sounds up above her. Her skylight opened onto the starlit night, and a shadow appeared in the opening. She too had put her bed in the vertical position. She hung on the remaining bar with both hands and when she was halfway into the shaft Starr held out his hand to her. She took his hand and let him pull her up, helping herself slide out by pushing off the steel bar with her feet.

'Now that was easier!' said Starr. 'You haven't been tortured have you.'

'No. They left me alone.'

'Well, you are a radio operator.'

Faye was untying his shoe laces slowly, hampered by his damaged hand. Noor sat down and did the same. 'I knew it!' said Faye. 'You are pretty!'

She wasn't listening, she was intrigued by what Starr had said. 'Why?' she asked. 'Don't they torture radio operators?'

'Not when they've got their notebooks. They got yours, didn't they?'

'Ahh . . . yes.'

'Could you not destroy them?'

'Bodington told me to keep them.'

'Bodington? That's strange . . . That's against all the guidelines.'

'I'm ready,' said Faye.

'Let's go then,' said Starr. 'We have to walk at right angles to the avenue. The alley's over there.'

With their shoes swinging round their necks, they moved over the gently sloping zinc in their socks.

Down below them to the right there was another roof at right angles to them. Starr and Faye reached it first and turned round. To their astonishment they saw that Noor had stopped on top of the gabled roof. Her silhouette stood out dark against the sky, like a statue on a monument. She stood motionless with her head lowered, thinking. Starr came back towards her and as soon as he was close enough he hissed to her: 'What on earth are you doing, Nora?'

'Why did Bodington ask me to do that?' she said as if she were talking to herself.

'What do I know? Who cares? This isn't the time.'

'No, but we should care,' she said, 'there must be a reason, and I think I understand.'

'Nora, that's enough, you can talk about this in London. For now, come on!' He took her hand and she followed him listlessly.

At the back of the roof of number 84, on the left-hand side, they found some metal rungs that connected them to the next building. They put their shoes back on. While Noor tied her laces Starr could hear her muttering to herself.

'That changes everything,' she kept saying.

They climbed down one after the other.

The raid started as they reached the middle of the second roof. First there were the planes in the distance, then a warning alarm nearby and finally a cacophony of sirens and a whole forest of search-lights aimed up at the sky.

'Oh no!' Starr said out loud in the midst of all the din. 'An air raid! They're bombing Asnières and Suresnes again. The guard will inspect our cells. They'll know we've gone in about two minutes.'

'Let's hurry up,' said Faye.

He walked briskly along to the edge of the roof, where there was a drop of a few yards down to a flat terrace of cement, which abutted onto the back of another building.

'Let's jump,' said Starr. 'You go first, Nora.'

'They're going to catch us,' she said. 'As soon as they see that we've gone, the whole area's going to clamp down.'

'Now, don't start again, Nora. We'll see what happens. We'll try our luck. Jump! That's an order.'

'Jump, for God's sake!' said Faye. 'You've got to trust us.'

'It's not you I'm worried about,' said Noor just as she launched herself into the dark.

She landed blindly on the rough surface. Starr landed lithely beside her, and they hurried to the other end of the terrace.

They were about to reach it when a more strident siren rang out. Thirty seconds later the beam of one of the searchlights was lowered and ran along the rooftops.

'The guard's sounded the alarm,' said Starr. 'They're looking for us.'

'It won't work,' said Noor. 'Forget it, let's give up.'

'Stop being such a defeatist, young woman,' said Faye, 'we're carrying on.'

'Watch out!' said Starr. 'Searchlight!'

They flattened themselves on the ground and the beam swept over them without stopping. Starr stood back up.

'They missed us, let's go!'

They ran over to the building at the end of the terrace as the searchlight carried on beyond them.

'It won't work!' said Darbois when he heard the air-raid signal.

'We can't be sure,' I replied, still lying under the steering wheel of the Citroën. 'If they're busy thinking about the air raid they won't be so vigilant.'

We didn't know at exactly what time the three prisoners would try to escape. It did not matter much. It had been agreed that they should get to the building at the end of the blind alley, come out onto the pavement and wave a white rag. From midnight Darbois and I had to watch the entrance, which we could see by glancing cautiously out of the car windows. We took turns risking a glance out every thirty seconds. Thanks to the air raid, the soldiers were now looking up at the sky.

'I can't see anything for now,' I said. 'The guards have got something else to worry about. They've still got a chance.'

The searchlight swept back the other way. The three escapees flattened themselves against the cement again and stood back up when it was dark again. They reached the edge of the terrace. There was a six-foot gap to the back of the adjacent building, which had a metal staircase running down the wall. They leant over the dark abyss like climbers on the edge of a crevasse.

'No choice,' said Starr. 'We jump and we catch hold of the rail. I'm going, then I'll hold out my hand for you.'

He took three strides to gather speed and then jumped, throwing himself at the metal staircase and gripping hold of the rail with both hands. He twisted round and put his heel onto the rail but as he jumped over he slipped and fell onto the narrow ledge. He swore, got back to his feet and climbed back over the rail, grabbing hold of it with one hand and reaching the other one over the gap.

Noor jumped and ended up hanging by one arm with her legs swinging over the courtyard far below. She hung there for several long seconds. Then she grabbed hold of the metal tread beneath Starr and dropped down onto the landing below.

Faye had taken four steps back and now hesitated before launching himself. And it was as he stood there that the searchlight picked him up. As the white light flooded over him, he bellowed in frustration and anger.

'Never mind! Just go!' cried Starr.

Faye ran towards the gap, threw himself forward and landed in Starr's arms. He hung on to his neck and managed to grab hold of the rail with his good hand. Moments later they were climbing down the metal staircase followed by the search-light.

'They know where we are,' said Starr. 'If this building backs onto the alley we still have a chance. Otherwise . . .'

On the ground floor they broke a pane of glass in a door and let themselves into a kitchen. Starr ran over to the door, down the corridor, through two rooms lit by moonlight and into a dark sitting room. He felt along the walls for a light-switch. A glass chandelier filled the room with light. There were large armchairs, a sofa and a coffee table, all covered in dust sheets. Starr saw that the white metal shutters at the windows were all closed. He hurried over to the one on the far left-hand side, grabbed the handle and pulled it back so that he could open the shutter wide. He leaned out: it was the blind alley and it was empty. There was a guard with his back to him at the end of each pavement. Noor and Faye came to join him. 'There are keys in the doors,' he said. 'Lock all the doors behind us!'

Then he climbed out of the window, slipped down onto the pavement and started waving his handkerchief above his head.

It was Darbois who saw the signal. 'They're there!' he said.

'Are you sure?'

'Yes. I'm certain.'

'Right. Ready?' I asked.

'On three!' he replied.

'One . . . two . . . three!'

We simultaneously opened the doors of the car. The guards saw us too late. The Welrod silencers made their dull crump, and the two Germans fell to the ground. A quick glance to left and right. The soldier on duty on the corner of the avenue Foch was watching the air raid. He had not seen a thing. Followed closely by Darbois, I leapt over to where the two men had fallen. The first was dead and the other was writhing on the ground with his hands on his stomach. I loaded my Welrod and aimed it just below his hat, between the eyes. His body twitched and then fell still.

At the far end of the alley, Starr had watched the operation, and he turned to the other two. 'Right, let's go!'

He ran over towards me. I saw Faye climb through the window. Starr passed me and Darbois waved him over to the Citroën. He threw himself at it. Faye reached me.

'Go on!' I said. 'Where's Noor?'

'She's with us, she's coming!' he said, hurtling towards the car.

The soldier on the corner of the avenue Foch had still not noticed anything. I turned back towards the end of the blind alley, hoping to see Noor coming out now.

'What the bloody hell's she up to?' Darbois muttered next to me.

'I don't know.'

'We can't stay here!'

'I'll go and see. Wait for me.'

Furious and confused, I rushed to the end of the alley where Starr and Faye had appeared.

I quickly found the open window and jumped inside. There in the middle of the salon, Noor was sitting on the sofa with her head in her hands.

'What are you doing, Noor?' I asked.

She looked up and saw me. 'My love!' she said and ran towards me. 'My love, you came!'

She fell into my arms, held me to her and kissed me.

'Noor, we must go, quickly!' I said, pulling myself away.

She stopped trying to kiss me, stepped back and looked me right in the eye. 'No,' she said. 'I mustn't. You go! The others are safe. I'm staying.'

'Staying? You're mad? You're staying? But that's ridiculous!'

I had an uneasy premonition. Against my better judgement I instinctively asked the question that was to haunt me: 'Why?'

'They haven't tortured me, you know,' she said. 'You mustn't worry. I've worked it all out. Bodington is a real master. He deliberately told me to keep the codes. Now the Germans think the Aurora set is safe for them to use, and it's going to cost them very dear! I have to stay otherwise Bodington's whole plan will fall through.'

I could not believe it. Despite the danger, my mind was whirring. Noor had worked out for herself the set-up that I would not have grasped without Philby's help. She was just a pawn in a game that was far bigger than us. And she knew it. The Germans believed in the Aurora set. We could infiltrate them. We should not disabuse them.

'No, Noor, you mustn't! It's such a twisted campaign. You're not expected to know about all that. Come on! They're hardly going to hold it against you! You've already done more than was expected of you. Come on! We've got our lives to live.'

She looked me squarely in the eye, and I could feel her body against me. 'It's too late, John.'

'They're coming, Noor. Let's go!'

'No! If I go with you that would be a betrayal. I have to do my duty. I know that. The Aurora radio is a weapon. I have no right to destroy it. I love you, my darling! Don't worry about me. I'm the Aurora radio. The Allies need me. Oh, my love. We'll find each other after the war.'

I could hear noises along the corridors. Someone said something in German. The patrol was on its way. They were knocking down a door. That was when Darbois jumped in through the window. 'What are you doing? Come on! You're mad! You can do your canoodling later!'

The shots rang out as he said it.

From the lorry, Violette and Culioli had seen us kill the guards and head over towards the Villa Fouché. Then the searchlights had started working up and down the streets. There were soldiers running in every direction on the avenue Foch. Violette had realised that the soldiers were now looking for the escaped prisoners. She had lifted up the tarpaulin and watched through her sights as the guardroom suddenly became a hive of activity, having probably been warned by the staff at number 84. The first soldier who stepped out on the far side of the Porte Dauphine took a bullet in the forehead. The second was thrown to the ground, hit in the chest. The others flattened themselves on the ground, sheltering behind the walls.

A squad appeared at the corner of the avenue Foch, urged on by their officer. With just two bursts of fire Culioli had all of them on the ground. Then he sat at the steering wheel of the lorry, started it up and turned to Violette, grunting: 'Right, we've got one minute left, and no more! We're pulling out, the others can follow.'

Darbois looked at us as we stood undecided in each other's arms. He made a decision. 'She doesn't want to come, John. Leave her! Let's go!'

I held Noor tightly. Darbois grabbed one of my arms and tried to pull me away. She pulled free and stepped back. She had tears running down her cheeks.

'Noor, I'll stay with you. What the hell!'

Darbois looked at us in amazement, astonished by what he saw as our madness. He looked from one to the other and suddenly said resolutely: 'She can do what she likes, John, but you have to come with me.'

'I'm staying!'

His fist caught me right in the jaw. I nearly fell. Darbois took hold of my arm and dragged me away. As if through a haze I heard the gunshots to one side of me, and the sound of doors being hammered down to the other. Darbois hauled me over to the window and got me out onto the street. A terrible pain wracked my chest. I turned round and saw the sitting room door giving way and Noor standing alone in the middle of the room by the light of the glass chandelier. She had raised her hand. Her eyes stared right at me. Her first and second fingers pointed upwards. She stood there, smiling in the midst of her tears, waving V for victory.

EPILOGUE

Until the end of the war I was haunted by that image of Noor. My heart ached for her but no one mentioned her any more. The SOE did not know what had happened to her. And her brother, Vilayat, knew nothing either. I had spoken to him in London after the Germans surrendered. I continued to ring him from time to time. Noor never reappeared. Her family mourned her. We all assumed that she had been killed. She was posthumously awarded the Victoria Cross, and her name was engraved on a little monument out in the country near the manor at Beaulieu, where we had had our lessons with Philby. Then one day in 1946 Vilayat said: 'Come. The SOE have written to me.' And in the large drawing room at Fazal Manzil which overlooked Paris, sitting in the sinking afternoon sun, he told me what had happened.

The patrol had taken her back to number 84, handcuffed and shaking with fear. Kieffer was in a towering rage. When he saw her he told the soldiers to put her up against a wall. 'Line up,' he cried.

They did not understand him. 'Line up, that's an order! On my command, fire!'

The five soldiers had slowly formed a line in deathly silence. Goetz and Peter stood behind Kieffer, speechless. Noor faced them defiantly.

'Aim!' said Kieffer.

Just then a guard who had searched through the cells arrived. He handed Kieffer a wodge of pieces of paper with pictures on them. It was the caricatures that Starr had done of the officers and employees at number 84. Kieffer looked through all of them. Within a minute his anger had abated. A smile appeared round the corners of his mouth. When he saw the picture of himself he laughed out loud. 'Right,' he said, looking up. 'Take her back to her cell. I'll think about what we'll do with her in the morning.'

Noor stayed at number 84 for another five weeks, and she continued to be interviewed by Goetz, who noticed, to his surprise, that she co-operated more readily. He put this change down to despondency after her failed bid to escape. Then he no longer needed Noor. Kieffer signed a transfer order for her, and she left for Germany in a convoy of women. She was imprisoned at Pforzheim. One day the order came and she and three deported members of the Resistance were sent by train to Dachau. She was chained in a cell by her wrists and ankles. At dawn an SS officer opened the door, untied her chains and asked her to step out. She was in a small courtyard surrounded by military buildings. She saw another young woman whose dress was torn and whose face was swollen with bruises. The SS officer told them to kneel side by side. The young woman started to cry. Noor took her hand. The scene was lit by pale sunlight. The mud felt cold against their knees. Noor jumped involuntarily as the first shot was fired. Blood sprang up from the young woman next to her, and she fell forwards. Then Noor straightened herself, bit her lip and cried out loudly: 'Long live freedom!' Her words were interrupted by the second shot, and she fell to the ground with a bullet in the nape of her neck.

When he had finished speaking Vilayat stood up. So did I. He came over to me and took me by the shoulders. There in the encroaching shadows in the drawing room at Fazal Manzil, there was nothing to be heard but the sound of two men weeping.

I went back to London, devastated. I went to see Philby, who invited me to his club, where he sat with a glass of sherry in his hand. He too had heard of the horrors of Violette Laszlo's fate. She had been arrested shortly after the escape from the avenue Foch. She had killed three military policemen before they managed to capture her. They had tortured her for three successive nights. By the time she was shot her beautiful, smooth face was nothing but a mangled, bloody mass.

Sitting in the Colonial Club room we remembered all the heroes of the Prosper escapades.

516

Prosper had been shot, as had Norman and Andrée Borrel.

Professor Adamowski came home from deportation very weak, and died a few months after the Liberation.

Manouchian had been caught and also shot with his whole group. The French Parti Communiste were suspected of having helped with his arrest.

Kerleven, on the other hand, had become a leading figure in the party.

Darbois had survived, having achieved one of the most glorious careers of the SOE. He lived in London with two cats. We saw each other regularly.

Vienet had continued to inflict damage on the Germans. He participated first hand in the liberation of Paris. Then – still his amusing, elegant self – he had slipped happily into civilian life. He ran his own business, was seen in all the best company in Paris and collected mistresses.

Finally, Blainville had carried on his activities for six months and had then come back to London. Towards the end of 1945 several members of the Resistance lodged complaints against him for betrayal. He went back to France still with his permanent smile on his face. He was locked up at Fresnes and faced the judges. The accusations carried insurmountable proof that he had betrayed others, but some of the more prominent figures for whom he had made clandestine travel arrangements – notably Félix Gouin, who was then high up in the government, and François Mitterand, who had just been elected to the Assemblée Nationale – gave testimony in his favour. Blainville maintained that he had been working for the Intelligence Service. I was in Paris at the time but I was not called as a witness. On the second day the court convened in camera to hear the testimony of a British witness. The man had been given permission by his superiors to explain that Blainville had been acting on orders and had been eminently useful to the Allies, although his services were covered by the Official Secrets Act. Blainville was acquitted.

The following day in *France-Soir* I read the name of the English witness, discovered by a journalist thanks to an indiscretion: Nick Bodington.

'What a business!' said Philby. 'What a business! But, my dear John, I know even more than you do.'

'What do you mean?'

'I've just been looking at the Prosper file, which C lent me for personal reasons. I wanted to know about Violette. Do you know, my dear chap, if our involvement with those two girls hadn't caused us so much pain we would derive tremendous satisfaction from that file. Especially you. Your lady-love played a very important role, dear boy, very important.'

Philby told me the end of Noor's story, a story that no one really knows. The Aurora radio continued to be in use for another six months. Goetz was too proud of his own machinations to grasp the fact that the English had sniffed him out. They even treated themselves to setting traps for him by asking for details about Noor, details which he furnished with a feeling of triumph. He organised twelve parachute drops, which the Germans intercepted. He succeeded in arresting three further agents (who had been sacrificed by London). He dismantled an entire network. And on 22 April 1944 he thought he had reached the pinnacle of success. In a short, routine message London had asked Noor to give the following order to the SOE networks in the Paris area: 'Deploy the arms cache in Sologne in the north and the Pas-de-Calais. Reinforce networks in Amiens, Arras and Lille.' Intoxicated with his success, Goetz immediately sent a report to the OKW, the Führer's headquarters. The following morning Hitler greedily devoured Goetz's report, which had been countersigned by Kieffer and Kaltenbrunner.

A week earlier he had assembled his generals round a map of France and had pointed to the straight coast of Normandy, to the north of Caen. 'Gentlemen,' he had announced, 'that's where I would make a landing if I were Eisenhower!'

But the following morning he had told himself that he was not Eisenhower. Several elements in that morning's reports led him to believe that the Allies would after all choose the simplest solution: to make their landing in the Pas-de-Calais, at the narrowest point in the Channel, a few days' march from the industrial heart of Germany. Patton had been appointed Commander-in-Chief of the huge army stationed in Kent, just opposite Dieppe and Dunkerque. The bombing raids on that part of the coast were twice as intensive as those on Normandy. Goetz's report served to confirm these beginnings of a certainty. The Resistance wants to reinforce itself in the north, Goetz and Kieffer said in the message taken from the intercepted Aurora radio, to hit the German defences deployed along that coast in the back. The following morning, by coincidence, Blainville confided something to Kieffer. According to this double agent, whom the Gestapo believed they controlled, persistent rumours within the SOE put the forthcoming landings in the Pas-de-Calais.

In Hitler's eyes, everything seemed to be converging. If there were any landings in Normandy they would be a decoy to draw away the armoured divisions defending the key passage round Lille and Dunkerque. The real landings would take place in the north. Hitler decided to act accordingly.

'Along with a few others like it,' concluded Philby, raising his glass, 'the Aurora radio made sure we won the war. Not bad for an Indian musician.'

A year later, on 24 October 1947, I walked alone through a field of grass still lushly green despite the autumn, a mile or more from the river at Beaulieu, the military base that had now been handed back to sailing and angling. In the middle of the field there was a little stone basilica and inside it a marble slab with a hundred or so names engraved on it. I had a wreath in my hand. I went up to the plaque and, as I had done the year before, looked down the first column of names. I stopped in the middle. There she was, *'Noor Vijay Khan, agent of the Special Operations Service, killed in the field, Victoria Cross'*. I stood lost in thought for a moment, then I put my wreath down at the foot of the marble plaque. I noticed that someone had put another wreath there. It had a strip of ribbon across the middle of it with the words: *'For Noor, the princess who will not be forgotten'*. I turned round. That was when I saw them.

On the far side of the basilica, hidden until now by a section of wall, there were two men watching me, unsure how to react: Bodington and Blainville. I watched them for several long seconds. They stood motionless and silent. I went over to them quite calmly and without hatred. They smiled gently and stood on either side of me. A tear ran down my cheek.

Blainville looked at me, still not sure of himself. 'It was a dirty war, Sutherland, a dirty war.'

Bodington put an arm on my shoulder. 'Sutherland, she was the sweetest, gentlest fighter I ever knew.'